CAGED

SINS OF THE SIGMA

BOOK 1

A DARK SECRET SOCIETY
REVENGE ROMANCE

SUMMER ROBERT

CONTENT WARNING: *Caged* and the *Sins of the Sigma* series in general contains some themes that may be distressing to readers, including narcissism, references to Narcissistic Personality Disorder (NPD), memories of neglect and abuse from a narcissistic parent, Borderline Personality Disorder (BPD), references to attempted suicide, gaslighting, obsession with and desire to possess another human, holding another human captive, withholding of food, stalking, drug and alcohol use, death and dismemberment, emotional and physical abuse and torture, particularly torture used as a means to extract information.

Most importantly, as someone who has had personal, childhood experiences with NPD and BPD, please heed the following content warning: *If you have been in a relationship with a narcissist, have a close family member, including a parent(s) who is a narcissist, or have difficulty reading about narcissistic behavior, please consider your mental health before reading this series.* Although there are moments of redemption and scenes of triumph throughout this series, it does not come full circle for the heroine Monroe until the last book. Writing this series was both cathartic, heartbreaking, and redeeming, and my wish for anyone reading this series is to feel the same.

SEXUAL CONTENT: This book and series also contain detailed and explicit two-person and group sex scenes that include elements of degradation, choking and breath play, bondage, captive prisoner role play, pain play, primal play, and other BDSM elements.

AUTHOR'S NOTE: If you feel inclined, I welcome you to read the short note at the end of this book for additional context on my own experiences with mental health, childhood trauma and my journey toward healing.

BLURB: CAGED

CAGED

Book 1 of the Sins of the Sigma Series

Repeat after me: *I swear my soul to Sigma; the spilling of Sigma's secrets is punishable by death; a death which I will gladly accept should I prove disloyal.*

How much would you sacrifice in the name of family? What sins would you commit for the promise of wealth and power?

Kieren Hunt made a deal. Resurrect his fraternity's secret traditions, and the most powerful Sigma alumnus will save his family from ruin. As the incoming chapter president, it was an easy deal to make because Kieren Hunt knows he is ruthless. He was always meant to play God, and once he wins back his prized obsession, Monroe Campbell, they'll be none the wiser.

But the thing about secrets is, just like blood, they tend to get spilled.

Kieren's deal has a problem and her name is Monroe. He never thought Sigma would come for her nor did he ever think his perfect pet would try to run. Sigma can have his soul, but Monroe? She was never part of the deal, and if he must cage his trophy to keep her, so be it.

Monroe would be his until the bitter end, if only she didn't escape.

She's coming for you Kieren, because this puppy bites back.

SINS OF THE SIGMA SERIES OVERVIEW

Important Information About the Series:

Sins of the Sigma is a dark and suspenseful secret society romance series with elements of mystery, revenge, betrayal, power, greed, carnal desires, obsession, and love. This four-book series and prequel novella follow a fluid group of villains, vigilantes, and antiheroes on their quest for greatness, legacy, understanding, and justice.

Throughout the series, enemies will become lovers, lovers will become enemies, past lovers will get a second chance, and above all else, blood will be spilled. What starts as the resurrection of Sigma fraternity's secret tradition at Dornell University unfolds into a sinister web of boundless greed and unchecked fanaticism that doesn't come full circle until the last book.

Great power demands sacrifice, after all. You must give in order to get.

The following is helpful to know when reading the series:

CAGED (Book 1) and *COLLARED* (Book 2) follow the same set of characters and take place during the same time period at college. Books 1 and 2 are not a duet in the traditional sense but can be considered a 'cluster'.

CARVED (Book 3) and *CROSSED* (Book 4) follow new characters (although some may be familiar but just look a little different) and take place in the near future after the conclusion of Book 2. As is the case for the first two books, the last two books are not a traditional duet but can be considered a 'cluster'.

Each book has a different Main Male Character, although many characters crossover into multiple books throughout the series. Books 2, 3, and 4 do end with a happily ever after.

Note: Other than the prequel, the series is meant to be read in order.

———

Tentative Release Dates:

CAGED
A Dark Secret Society Revenge Romance
(Book #1, November 2025)

CLAIMED
A Dark College Romance Novella
(Prequel, Expected Release Early Q1 2026)

COLLARED
A Dark Secret Society Second Chance Romance
(Book #2, Expected Release H1 2026)

CARVED

A Dark Secret Society Workplace Romance
(Book #3, Expected Release H2 2026)

CROSSED
A Dark Secret Society, Enemies to Lovers, Second Chance
Romance
(Book #4, Expected Release H1 2027)

ALSO BY SUMMER ROBERT

The Good Hurt Series

Good Hurt

(Book #1, a Dark College Romance)

Splinter

(Book #2, a Dark College Romance)

Salvation

(Book #3, a Dark College Romance)

This series is dedicated to those who rise alone in the dark, who face the villain with fire in their eyes, smile like an unhinged psychopath, and bring the monsters to their motherfucking knees.

PROLOGUE
KIEREN

Fifteen Months Prior to Present Day
Summer Between Sophomore and Junior Year of College,
Connecticut

No one gives a fuck if this man survives, so why am I sitting here, waiting for this pathetic coward to wake up?

Who am I kidding? I know why.

I want this fucker to explain himself.

What sins have you committed this time, Father? Did you embezzle away my inheritance as I always suspected you would? Did another one of your investment schemes go belly-up?

Hunt Wealth Management is supposed to be my legacy. My grandfather founded the company and grew it to become one of the most prestigious and trusted asset management firms, sought after by the world's wealthiest families. Old money billionaires. Quiet money. Ultra-high-net-worth families who have birthed generations of aristocrats, royals, oil tycoons, railroad and shipping barons who struck it rich during the Industrial Revolution, and of course, the upper echelon of the Sigma brotherhood. Is Sigma a good ole boys club? Sure. But everyone knows the world runs on the unchecked greed of entitled nepo babies, and if you're one of the fortunate few, you're simply playing your part.

My grandfather was not one of the fortunate few. He clawed and scraped and sacrificed his way to the inner circles of Sigma elites. He gave them everything, traded his soul for sovereignty, and then turned the hard-earned fruits of his labor over to my weak excuse of a father who squandered my grandfather's selflessness on country club memberships, flights on private jets and a grotesque mansion in Connecticut with round-the-clock staff serving a total of three people. Two, really. My mother and me, since my father was hardly home during my childhood, too busy with whatever *urgent business* he had to conduct on private islands in the Caribbean.

If my father thinks his infidelity has gone unnoticed, he'd be mistaken, but I don't think he gives a fuck, and truthfully, I don't think my mother does either. She's content to look the other way so long as the credit cards my father provides keep swiping. Plastic surgeons, filler, and Botox are expensive, after all.

While my adolescence certainly reaped the benefits of my parent's social climbing gluttony, it seems as of late that the legacy I stand to inherit is fucked. The continuous need to refill the Hunt family coffers has made my father reckless. He forgets I've worked at Hunt Wealth Management for the past two summers, once I was finally deemed mature enough to be let behind the curtain.

How is it, dear father, that Hunt Wealth Management has

some of the highest returns on Wall Street, repeatedly outranking the likes of Blackrock and Goldman Sachs? Would it be the questionable investments made with strange overseas ventures that always seem to deliver a very specific return, almost as if it were *guaranteed?* Miraculous, really. Earning a consistent fee for managing your clients' money certainly does help to maintain your garish lifestyle, doesn't it? Last I checked, HWM had three billion dollars in assets under management, and when you factor in an average annual fee of one percent, it pencils out to quite a comfortable living. Frankly, I'm surprised the SEC or FINRA hasn't come knocking, but everyone has a price.

If my grandfather wasn't rapidly deteriorating from dementia, he'd be disgusted. I think he knew the type of imbecile my father would become, which is why he stashed a sizable portion of his wealth in a trust fund with me as the sole beneficiary. The only obstacles standing in my way of accessing said trust fund are that I must attend Dornell University, become a member of Sigma fraternity, and graduate to my father's satisfaction, whatever the fuck that means. I've never spoken to my father about his definition of *satisfactory*, but I'm sure the conniving motherfucker will find a way to hold this over my head as leverage to siphon off a portion of my inheritance for himself.

My father and his schemes. I expected in time he would trip over his own two feet, falling victim to his stupidity and avarice, but I hadn't predicted it would be this soon. A heads-up would have been appreciated, as I'm sure I'll have to clean up whatever pile of shit he's so graciously left me.

I pick at my jeans, waiting as I have done for the past two weeks, monitoring the rise and fall of my father's chest. The nurses claimed he was lucid this morning while they changed his bedding, but I'm not surprised he decided to return to his catatonic state the moment I entered the room. The fucker probably heard my footsteps approaching from down the hall and decided now was the time to become the world's worst actor.

I lift my head, zoning out as I focus on the navy and cream-colored French toile wallpaper, hideous in its cliché predictability. New money masquerading as old money. Of course, the decorator my mom hired would have selected this pattern to fit the persona. Scenes of lovers dancing, picnicking, tending to lambs and other subservient farm animals spread across the wall remind me of Monroe. I believe we're approaching the two-month anniversary of her telling me to go fuck myself, although admittedly, between my own hospital stay and recovery, I've lost track. She's as much to blame as I am, perhaps more. She fed the flames of my demons, wanting what only I could give her, until one day, she conveniently decided I was too much. Then she left.

She fucking left me, and if I ever make my way back to her, I will make her pay. You don't get to take and take and take, to standby while I become a shell of myself, then abandon me like garbage once you've had your fill. You swallow the bad with the good. That's real love. She used me, used my name, my clout. Everything she is, the person she has become, is thanks to me.

The dichotomy of her existence claws at my mind, yet the absence of her is suffocating. I want to keep her in a cage for the rest of eternity. I want to bind her to me, tie her down with chains, drain every last drop of essence from her body. Our link may be temporarily severed, but once I get my mind right, I'll make my grand return, and never let her leave me again.

Blinking away my reverie, I huff a sigh of frustration at my vegetated sperm donor who continues to feign incapacitation. Part of me wants to rip out the designer pillow positioned under his fragile head and smother him. How easy it would be to end his bullshit reign. Right here. Right now.

A knowing grin spreads across my face.

No, I'll deal him a gift far worse than death.

I rise from the padded armchair and stride to his bedside, pulling back the navy duvet cover, no doubt intentionally picked to complement the repulsive wallpaper. His hand is speckled with sun spots and patches of chapped skin from age. A bulbous, black and gold ring adorned with the Sigma emblem encircles his pinky finger. My grandfather's ring, passed down to my father when he was initiated into Sigma. A ring which now rightfully belongs to me. If he were a selfless man, a caring father, he would have given me this ring my freshman year when I pledged the fraternity. Of course, he didn't.

"Not until I earned it, isn't that what you said, Father?" I ask aloud to the quiet room. "Well, I'd say at this point, I've fucking earned it."

I've bled Sigma black and gold for the last two years, willingly destroyed myself in the process. In seven months, I will take over as president of the oldest fraternity in the nation, and not just any Sigma chapter, the Founding Chapter. This ring, and the legacy it bears, are mine.

I work the oversized ring from his finger, his crepey skin bunching around the joints as I jiggle it off. His eyes flare open like a resurrected dead man, just as I fucking expected, the instant I've slipped the piece free.

"Father. Welcome back to the land of the living," I smirk as I slide the cool metal down the length of my own pinky finger, admiring how perfectly it fits.

He furrows his brows, craning his neck to see his hand, his bare hand, and I grin at his malice-ridden face.

"Mine now, don't you think?" I state in conquest.

His head settles back against the pillow in defeat as he blinks his eyes, realizing he's been duped into waking up from his supposed *coma.*

"Kieren," he says in acknowledgement.

"Father," I say back.

I saunter back to my chair, crossing my legs like a therapist ready to conduct a session with my most detested patient. "Explain."

The old man says nothing.

"Father," I growl in frustration, "explain why Mom found you unresponsive on the floor of your office three weeks ago. What did you do?"

He shifts uncomfortably as I pin him with my glare.

"Speak, Father. This is my fucking company too. What happened?"

I watch his throat strain to swallow.

"The Southeast Asia strategy didn't perform as expected," he croaks. His voice is hoarse from weeks of disuse. I could offer him water, but I won't, he doesn't deserve it. "And it was a large part of our investment portfolio."

"How large?" I press.

"Half."

I jerk my head, certain I misheard. "Half?! And the money is..." I let my question trail off because I want to hear the fucker say it out loud.

"Gone," he states, confirming my suspicion.

My fingers flex and relax, over and over. Rage boils under my skin.

"Gone?" I sneer, pure wrath flooding my nervous system.

"Gone?!" I scream. "And just how the fuck do you plan to get back one and half billion dollars? It's impossible! If any of our clients get wind of this and want to pull their money...

We'll have to declare bankruptcy. Our family's name, *my name*, will be ruined."

My thoughts spiral as I scramble to think of solutions. "Stop taking a management fee. Sell the house. Blame the downgrade on empty-nester syndrome now that I'm gone."

"No," he garbles. "We aren't going to do anything rash that will draw attention."

"Rash? You don't consider trying to take your own life *rash?* You were going to take the easy way out and let me deal with the fallout. You couldn't even kill yourself properly!"

"*Fucking pathetic,*" I mumble. "What's your plan now, Father, since plan A clearly failed?"

"An opportunity has presented itself," he says.

"Oh, is that right?" I laugh. "Let me guess, another one of your Ponzi schemes? We can't get that amount of money back. You do understand that, right? We'd have to invest all the remaining funds, and even then, we would need to find investments that have the potential to return over one hundred percent to earn back the money lost and the gains you've reported *in writing* to all of our clients. Investments like this don't exist unless there is serious risk involved, or you're part of the fucking mob."

I scoff, realizing his intentions. "I always knew you'd turn out to be criminal, dragging our family name down with you."

"I'm not talking about the fucking mob," he sneers, spittle spraying from his pale, cracked lips. "Get me a pen and paper," he demands.

"Why? You plan to scribble out this ingenious plan of yours like a fucking toddler?"

"Watch. Your. Tone. If I wasn't bedridden, boy, you'd be black and blue."

It's not the first time my old man has threatened me physically, and both of us know how such a threat would end. Part of me wishes he would finally find the balls and try. The urge to strangle him grows overwhelming, but if I kill him, our family would have to declare bankruptcy. We'd never recover. *I'd never recover.* The stench of scandal would plague me and whatever offspring I decide to have for centuries, and I simply don't have that kind of time or patience.

Begrudgingly, I appease the bastard, finding a basic ball-point pen and small notepad on his bedside table. The notepad fittingly has the letters "H – W – M" for Hunt Wealth Management printed in embossed, gold cursive on the top of each note.

I hold the two items in front of his face, and my father has the audacity to pretend that lifting his arms to take them is a strain. He writes a barely legible email address, his hand-writing taking up the entire expanse of the paper: *X@sigma.me.*

"What is this?" I ridicule.

"The email address for X."

"*X?*" I ask with mocking indignation. "As in, the letter of the alphabet?" I wonder just how many braincells my father forfeited in his poor attempt to take his own worthless life.

"I'm surprised you don't know, but then again, you've always been a disrespectful brat. Your mother and I have been too soft on you."

"Well, that's absolute bullshit, Father, but cut to the chase."

"X is one of the most powerful Sigma alumnus."

"Okay, and who is he?" I ask.

"No one knows. He could be the president of the United States or our next door neighbor. He protects his anonymity at all costs. Every Sigma worth their salt knows of him."

I flinch at the intended dig, unable to ignore the weight of the notepad in my hand.

"And why is it that I need to email him?" I push, struggling to douse my temper.

"Because he will take care of our issue."

"You mean *your* issue?" I grind out.

My father glares at me through narrowed eyes, before closing them again.

"Fine. I'll email him," I relent in frustration, sick of this game. "But why would he help us?"

"Sigma protects their own," my father answers cryptically, eyes still closed. My fingers curl into a fist, begging to slam into his unguarded, smug face.

"This isn't just some simple favor," I remind him. "No sane person would offer to help cover up a scandal of this magnitude."

"There are many things you've yet to understand, Kieren. Ways in which the world works. Underlying motivations."

Ah, yes. My father's favorite way to chastise me, to treat me like a fucking clueless child, but he forgets the type of man I have become. *Don't provoke the bear, Father.* I just might bite.

"And what, pray tell, motivates our dear friend X?" I hum. "Does he want control of our company? My first born? A kidney?"

"I've already been in contact with him. He knows about you, and your unique position. He's intrigued, but said he needs to be convinced you have what it takes to give him what he wants."

"Stop speaking in riddles, Father," I say through clenched teeth. "What the fuck does he want?"

My father cracks one eye open in my direction, holding my stare.

"Blood."

1

MONROE

Five Months Prior to Present Day,
April of Junior Year,
Sigma

Five steps separate me from freedom.

Then I hear him.

The sound of a deranged man screaming my name echoes in the night. I wasn't able to shut the window. I barely got my legs over the rusted metal bars of the fire escape, which for some incomprehensible reason was not built directly under the fucking window.

My legs are cumbersome as I try to run. I plead with my body, begging it to move faster. Days of confinement have robbed me of my agility. Days without food have stolen my strength. The pitch-black night impairs my vision, and I don't know where the woods end and the drop begins.

Male voices descend around me, shouting, barking orders

to search the perimeter of Sigma fraternity. Flashlight beams roam in my periphery. I'm moving slower than I think if they're already upon me.

Distracted by the growing roar of water in the gorge below, the tip of my sneaker connects with a raised tree root, hurling me forward. Twigs and small stones spear the flesh of my palms. A piercing pain in my kneecap rips through my resolve to keep running. They'll find me now; it's only a matter of minutes.

I push myself onto all fours and manage a haggard, defeated crawl to what I believe is the edge. Two are already missing, and I'm next.

May twelfth.

My death day.

But I'll be damned if I let him spill my blood.

I've survived this hellscape of a life for twenty-one fucking years, and the only one who gets to spill my blood is me.

Shouting male voices must be no more than fifty feet away. I swing my legs over the cliff ledge, thick with fallen leaves from past seasons. Slender tree stems jut out from the craggy rock. If it were daylight, I suspect I would see an inkling of baby leaves sprouting to life in the mist.

If it were daylight, I would lose my courage.

A memory of my childhood self jumping from a high diving board chooses this moment to resurface. Another scene redacted by my brain to protect me from my painful past is set free, and at the most curious of times. I take this as a sign of encouragement.

You're right, I think. I'm out of time and out of options. Drawing in a breath I know will be my last, I decide it's time, for once, to make myself proud.

And I jump.

2

GABI

Present Day,
Beginning of Senior Year,
Dornell University

This is wrong.

Everything about this is horribly fucking wrong.

I can still smell the remnants of her favorite perfume – Queens and Monsters from the brand Henry Rose – like she spritzed it mere hours ago before heading to campus. The half-used bottle sits on her cluttered dresser, and I swear my poor heart is convinced she might come back at any moment. My lower lip quivers as I slowly scan her bedroom, untouched from the last time she was here, as if it were frozen in time and converted into a mausoleum the day she disappeared. Textbooks are stacked haphazardly on the floor, school papers litter her desk, and worn clothes are tossed in a heap atop the chair in the corner.

We would have called the police if she hadn't texted us from an unknown number at the beginning of June, telling us that she was fine but not coming back and told us not to come looking. We all immediately called the number after receiving the text, but received the standard operator message stating the number we dialed was no longer in service.

Monroe.

What the fuck did he do to you, Monroe?

I slump onto her unmade bed, unable to stop the torrent of tears. This was supposed to be our year. After Viv, Ele, and I returned from studying abroad, the four of us were going to take our senior year by storm, partying like the most feral and unhinged motherfuckers this campus has ever seen. We were supposed to go out with a bang.

Instead, my best friend in the entire fucking world is gone and I'm supposed to go about my day-to-day like she didn't vanish into thin air. Not gone, *missing*, I correct myself. I'm not supposed to say *'gone'* because that word makes it seem like she's never coming back, and that's simply not a reality I can accept.

I *will* get to the bottom of this, and I *will* find her because I know deep in my soul that she's not fine.

Nothing about this is fine.

"Gabi?"

Vivienne stands in the doorway of Monroe's room, her straight black hair freshly cropped into a blunt, shoulder-length bob for the new school year. She looks at me with sorrow-filled eyes because none of us know what to do.

"Hey, Viv," I sniff and wipe at my nose. "When did you get in?"

"A few hours ago, actually. My mom insisted on driving me, so I took advantage of the parental credit card and asked her to take me to the market. Our fridge is stocked, at least," she offers with a timid grin.

"Thank God for that," I sigh. "Has Ele arrived yet?"

"She texted me about an hour ago, saying she was almost to campus."

I nod. "I'm glad one of us will have a car," I say. "Monroe would have had one too, if she were here – that silver jalopy she inherited from her grandmother – but..."

I can't finish the sentence, folding in on myself.

"Come on, let's get out of her room," Viv coaxes as I fight back a complete breakdown.

"It's not right, Viv. It's not right," I stammer.

"I know, but Monroe must have had her reasons. She'll resurface at some point, Gabi. She wouldn't just leave you."

I want so desperately for Vivienne's words to be true. Other than that single text back in June, no one has seen or heard from Monroe. I have no idea if she's still a student at Dornell, or if she managed to complete her classes and exams. Did she fail out? Communication from her became increasingly scant, and by the end of last semester, her presence was a ghost in our group chat.

At first, I chalked it up to her busy schedule and obligations as sorority president, but when weeks passed without a message from her, I could sense that something was off.

Vivienne guides me out into the living room area of our apartment, her delicate hand pressed to the small of my back. We walk over to the window, which has been slid fully open to let in any trace of breeze. Upstate New York is notoriously humid at the beginning of September, the lingering summer weather biding its time until it is replaced by the lashing winds of winter. In a few months, Dornell will be blanketed in newly fallen snow, and this blissful heat, sticky and draining as it is, will feel like a distant fever dream.

We each perch a hip against the ledge to study the commotion below. We'd strategically picked this apartment for its central location smack in the middle of College Avenue and directly across from Tommy O's, the shitty dive bar that was and still is the epicenter of nightlife for upperclassmen. The way we squealed with manic exhilaration the day the landlord handed us the keys is cemented in my memory. The people-watching is unmatched. We moved in at the beginning of our junior year, thinking we had won the lottery.

I tear up as I remember the four of us seated along these same windows that semester, two at one, two at the other, watching like vultures as our fellow students queued outside Tommy O's, hopeful and desperate to be let inside. Our running commentary was judgmental and merciless. We were such assholes. Not about the women, but we couldn't help but roast all the dickhead frat guys who would saunter up and expect to be let right in as if they were royalty.

At the beginning of that semester, all of us were underage, so we would wait until one of our guy friends took over as bouncer and then dash across the street. He would pretend to check our IDs, a performative show for the boss, then shoo us inside. Once the rank smell of stale beer and bad decisions grew strong enough to singe our nose hairs, we knew we were in the clear.

Vivienne roots around the bag slung over her shoulder and pulls out a box of Parliaments.

"I thought you quit?" I frown.

"I did," she answers as a cigarette dangles between her teeth. She lights it, taking a long drag, then blows a plume of smoke out the window. I wave it away from my face, disapprovingly. "I'd like to see you try to survive investment banking at Morgan Stanley, Gabi. You'd become a smoker, too."

"Doubtful. My dad used to smoke," I say with a shake of

my head. "It drove my mom crazy. They would fight about it constantly."

"Yeah, well, it's gross. I know," Vivienne agrees. "But whatever."

"What does Sophie think about it?"

"We broke up," Vivienne says with another blow of smoke.

"Oh. I'm sorry," I stutter, stumbling over my condolences. This explains the smoking. I can see the underlying hurt in her eyes, so I don't pry any further.

Vivienne shrugs, and neither of us can find the right words to say, so we sit silently and watch the scene unfold below.

The sound of our front door swinging violently open catches us off guard.

"Some help here!" Eleanor groans as she struggles to shove an oversized suitcase across the entryway threshold and into our apartment. Springing to our feet, we run to help her.

"I've got more downstairs," she explains, sprinting back down the two flights of stairs. I follow her as Vivienne pushes the massive suitcase across the linoleum floor.

Ele and I race to unload her double-parked car. I grab as many bags as I can carry and dump them right inside the building door, then run back for more. After several rounds of this frenzied dance, we've successfully unloaded her car, and Ele drives off to find street parking. The downside of this place is that there's no designated parking for building tenants. Monroe was always good about moving her car to avoid getting tickets, but I'm convinced Ele got enough tickets last year to keep the local police force funded for decades.

"Damn, she has a lot of stuff," I say aloud, sighing as I load myself up with more duffle bags than I can realistically carry. The trudge upstairs feels like I'm training for combat, and I cling to the railing to prevent myself from falling backward. By the time I reach the second floor and door of our apartment, I'm profusely sweating and ready to collapse.

"Jesus fucking Christ," I complain, dropping to my knees as Vivienne rushes to help remove the bags.

"How much more is there?" Viv asks.

"Too much," I groan. Viv scoffs and heads downstairs.

I decide to take a well-deserved break and begin inspecting the contents of Viv's grocery haul when Ele bursts through the door.

"There is no parking anywhere in this bitch," Ele shouts. "Oh, you guys brought my stuff upstairs!" she exclaims.

"Yeah, you're fucking welcome," I say playfully. Settling on a bottle of cheap rosé and a block of cheddar cheese, I close the refrigerator door with my hip and grab an unopened box of crackers from the cabinet.

"Are we having a girl dinner?" Ele asks gleefully.

"Unless you have a better idea," I say.

"Listen, returning to our staple diet of cheese and crackers is fine with me. I definitely overindulged at Google this summer. Having unlimited access to fully stocked micro kitchens and dining halls serving any food you can imagine is dangerous."

"Sounds amazing," I say, sighing wistfully. "My internship at NBCUniversal did not come with such perks."

"But you liked it, right?" Ele asks, slicing off a piece of cheese.

"Loved it," I say. "I definitely want to find a job doing sales partnerships when I graduate. Hopefully, a position opens up at NBCUniversal, because the team is amazing, but it's not a guarantee."

"Viv, how was Morgan Stanley?" Ele asks.

"Not the best," she responds, assembling a cracker and cheese sandwich stack.

I give Ele a subtle shake of my head, hoping she'll get the hint.

But, of course, she doesn't. "What?" Ele asks me. "Is it about Monroe?"

"She's probably referring to my breakup with Sophie," Viv says, unamused. "Which, by the way, I'm fine. Yeah, it sucks. I really liked her, but I'll live."

"I'm sorry," Ele offers. "That does suck."

We crunch uncomfortably on our cheese and crackers until Ele breaks the tension.

"Has anyone heard from Monroe?" she asks hesitantly.

Both Vivienne and I shake our heads.

"God, this is so fucked. You two heard the rumors, right?"

My head snaps up. "No! What rumors?"

"Should I light a cigarette for this?" Viv asks.

Ele scrunches her face. "You're smoking again?"

"I don't need your judgment," Viv huffs, pulling another cigarette from her bag.

"At least go over to the window," I point.

Viv flips her arms in resignation and waits to light her cigarette until she's leaning halfway outside.

"What rumors?" I ask again.

"That it was Kieren," Ele says.

"Of course it was Kieren," I say, my face contorting into a disgusted grimace.

"He's still here, right?" Vivienne asks from the window.

"You mean here as in not back in rehab or some mental institution where he fucking belongs?" I quip. "As far as I know."

"Dude, what happened here last semester?" Ele asks rhetorically. "My parents bought me ten things of pepper spray and four tasers. They're in one of those bags," she says, motioning to her luggage sitting right inside the door. "I almost thought they wouldn't let me come back."

"They're claiming they were suicides," Viv adds.

"Who's *'they'*?" I ask.

"The police."

"The police don't know shit," I grumble. "Weren't those two girls in sororities?" I ask.

"Both Tri Delt," Ele comments. "One was a freshman, the other a sophomore, I think."

"I know suicides happen here because Dornell is a fucking pressure cooker, but I refuse to believe that's what happened to those two missing girls."

"You never know what someone is going through," Viv states.

"I know, but I just have this sickening feeling that whatever is going on with Monroe is somehow connected to these missing girls."

"Listen, the world is fucked," Ele states. "I saw my sorority Little a few weeks ago in Manhattan for coffee, and she said people are scared to be out alone at night. Like maybe this could be some serial killer."

"I'm the worst big sister," I lament, rubbing my forehead. "I haven't spoken to my Little since before I went abroad."

"What about Monroe's Little, Kasey?" Viv asks. "Maybe the three of us should adopt her."

It's not a bad idea, I think, making a mental note to reach out to Kasey so she doesn't feel abandoned. It's important for younger sorority members to have a Big Sister, someone they can lean on and ask for advice. The situation with Kasey is unique because she's technically Monroe's Grand-Little, but Monroe's Little transferred to UCLA at the end of her sophomore year, leaving Kasey without a Big. Sorority lineages can be unnecessarily complicated, but suffice to say Kasey, now a sophomore and living in the sorority house, is adrift and in need of mentors.

"When did Jace get a motorcycle?" Viv sneers from the window. I spring to my feet with more eagerness and curiosity than I'd like to admit.

I peer over her shoulder, studying the crowd now formed outside Tommy O's. Ele joins our cluster, wedging herself into the triangle of space between our shoulders.

"Isn't it too early for the bars?" Ele comments.

"I guess people are getting a head start," Viv responds. "Senior year and all," she says, blowing out a puff of smoke.

The distinctive tattoos covering both arms are unmistakable. For whatever reason, I've never met another Ivy League boy with as many tattoos as Jace. Kieren has them, although Monroe said his tattoos are mostly on his chest and back, places where clothing can keep them hidden from Kieren's grandfather, who apparently disapproves. Jace just does not give a fuck. He once told me they were an act of defiance against his parents for making it clear that Jace's brother, Reid, was the golden child and Jace was the unplanned fuck up. He decided to lean wholeheartedly into his role as the black sheep of his family, much to his parents' displeasure and his sickened delight.

Jace straddles the seat of a motorcycle wearing a tight black T-shirt and jeans. The small crowd outside Tommy O's has all turned to stare as he removes his helmet.

"So, he became a walking thirst-trap," Ele jeers.

"Such a fucking cliché," I say through clenched teeth.

"You two still hate each other, right?" Viv asks.

"With every bone in my body," I retort. Viv and Ele know I dated Jace our freshman year, and that our relationship ended badly. Well, badly is an understatement. Viv, Ele and I didn't become close until we lived together in the sorority house our sophomore year, but at that point, all I wanted to do was forget. Only Monroe knows what really happened because she was there, holding my hand, when I shattered into pieces.

Judging by Jace's continued wrath for me over the past two years, he never learned the truth either, which is fine by me. It's better that our hate remains mutual. In some ways, it makes it easier.

Jace saunters up to the front of the line, cradling his helmet under one arm, and gives the bouncer some obnoxious bro handshake.

It happens in an instant, but I see it – we all see it.

His eyes flick up to the windowsill where the three of us stand gawking, his stoic expression unreadable, and then, without any acknowledgement whatsoever, he turns to disappear inside.

"Gabi," Ele pokes a finger into my side.

"What?" I snap, turning my head.

She gives me a knowing look.

"You stopped breathing."

———

"Goddammit, I fucking hate this!" I yell, flinging my eyeliner pencil into the sink hard enough to leave black smudges on the porcelain.

"What's wrong?" Ele shouts from her adjacent bedroom.

I white-knuckle the edges of the countertop as I fight back tears. When I don't answer, Ele snakes her head around the doorframe to check on me.

"Shit, Gabi," she soothes. "Hey, we don't have to go out."

"No, we do. It's the first night of our senior year, and... she would want us to go out... if she were here." I clench my jaw in anguish as tears streak down my cheeks, and my shoulders shake.

"Ele's right," Vivienne says, joining my meltdown. "We don't need to go out."

"Yes, we do," I growl, pounding my fist against the sink.

"Okay, well, we don't need to go to Tommy O's. We can go to The Woods or Gino's."

"That's ridiculous," I say, swiping at my mascara-stained cheeks. "No one goes there."

"Everyone goes there," Ele corrects me. "It's just our circle of friends who only go to Tommy O's."

"Because we're the cool kids!" Viv says in a sing-song voice.

"Not helping," Ele scolds.

"I don't think I can face him," I admit.

"Who? Jace?" Viv asks.

"Any of them," I say. If Jace is there, Kieren must be as well, and I don't know if I'll be able to contain my hatred for that piece of shit. He was the worst thing to ever happen to Monroe. I know he had something to do with her disappearance, and once I get a few drinks in my system, I won't be able to stop myself from confronting him.

"Fuck, I look like shit," I say, eyeing myself in the mirror.

"No. No, no, no, see, this is fixable," Ele says, spinning me around. "Here, sit down, Viv will make you a fresh drink, and I'll finish your makeup."

I huff, blowing a strand of hair out of my face as I slide down against the wall.

"Don't let me do anything stupid tonight, Ele," I say as she removes the smudged liner from my undereye with a Q-Tip.

"I promise, I won't," she assures me. Vivienne comes back into the bathroom with my refill.

"Unfortunately, we're low on ice," she says apologetically, handing me the room-temperature mixed drink.

"As long as it takes the edge off," I say.

"That's my girl," Ele smiles.

———

Tommy O's is absurdly packed. The three of us hold hands in single file, barely able to squeeze through. Broad backs and elbows shove into me, knocking me from side to side, but I'm sufficiently buzzed and can't find it in me to care. With every foot of progress, we run into another familiar face and scream with glee. By the time we make it to the counter of the bar, I've given at least thirty hugs. Everyone is ecstatic to see each other, and since I was abroad in Spain the second semester of my junior year, it's been over nine months since I've seen most of these people.

Thirty percent of Dornell's student population is involved in the Greek system, which is fucking huge when you do the math, yet somehow, our circle of friends feels no bigger than the number of bodies packed into this shitty, matchbox-sized bar. I'm glad we came out, because even though this bar smells of sour beer and piss like it always does, it's comforting in a way, and admittedly, there's no place I'd rather be on my first night back.

I'm beckoned into a booth and haul myself onto the ledge as a classic eighties song blasts across the speakers. Without question, the last song of the night is always *Don't Stop Believin'* by Journey, and it's sacrilege not to belt it out as loud as humanly possible.

I'm mid-conversation with the girl next to me, another friend from my Delta Gamma sorority pledge class, when an uncomfortable feeling settles over me and chills skate up my exposed arms. My heart palpitates at the eerie sense I'm being watched. I've only felt this sensation once before, when my mom and I helped Monroe clear out her recently deceased grandmother's house, and it's unnerving.

I do a quick scan of the bar, but it's hard to make out faces from my hunched position. It's impossible to hear over the music unless the person you're speaking with screams directly into your ear, so I've been huddled over, listening to this girl tell me about every person she slept with over the summer in painstaking detail, for at least twenty minutes. When I look around, I see so many people packed into this bar that, frankly, I'm surprised the fire marshal hasn't appeared.

"Are you going to after-hours at Sigma?" she shouts against my hair, and like clockwork, the telltale tune of Journey starts to play over the speaker, building to what I know will be a deafening crescendo.

I give her a look that says, "*fuck no,*" but she's insistent. "Come!" she demands. "They're having a big party; besides, we should be there to represent."

Her tenacity is annoying, but I know what she means. In the bizarre microcosm of Greek-system politics, we have to show face at these things lest our lack of attendance be considered a snub. It's also subliminal marketing for our sorority, Delta Gamma, and therefore crucial for the new freshman class to see our faces at these parties, especially Sigma parties.

Besides, I'm tipsy enough to be undeterred by my own anxiety.

Sigma has always sat at the top of the Dornell fraternity food chain. Every guy you hate to admit you want to fuck is in Sigma. They are pretentious, elitist assholes. They all come from money, and like to make it abundantly clear how superior they are, not only to other fraternities, but to all other individuals on this campus, professors and staff included. But girls fucking throw themselves as these guys like they're gods, and it just perpetuates the whole insufferable cycle.

Two years ago, I would have relished going to Sigma after-hours. At the beginning of our sophomore year, all bets were off. Monroe had just spent the worst summer of her life burying her grandmother, and I was newly single. Neither of us could find a fuck to give. Jace and Kieren were low on the Sigma pecking order as recently admitted brothers, and we savored every opportunity to torment them. We were fucking belligerent, flirting with Sigma upperclassmen at parties, rubbing it in their faces, and there wasn't fuck all they could do to stop us.

But when we returned from winter break that year, something changed. Maybe it was the new batch of freshman pledges and the fact that Jace and Kieren no longer had to play the role of indentured servants, but the two of them became monsters. I tried to keep Monroe away from Kieren...

I tried.

The thought makes me vomit in my mouth, just a little, to know my friend was trapped in the vortex of an addict as he descended into madness.

No one knows why Kieren didn't come back at the beginning of junior year. Everyone assumed he went to rehab. He went no-contact, even with Monroe, and truthfully, his absence was a peace she had never known.

We hugged each other goodbye at the end of that semester – Ele, Viv, and I were headed off to various countries around the world, and Monroe would soon start her reign as president of Delta Gamma. It was a bittersweet parting of ways, but it was a consolation to know our time apart would be temporary.

And then he came back.

3
MONROE

Eight Months Prior to Present Day,
Early January, Junior Year,
Dornell University

I feel it in the air.

Thick grey clouds hang over campus like an ominous shroud, threatening to unleash a maelstrom of icy, bitter snow at any second. Nauseating angst climbs up the back of my throat. My fingers quiver. A mixture of fear and longing and something else – something dark and unsettling that I have yet to comprehend – churns in my chest.

No one has said anything, no texts have appeared, and no social media posts have been seen to confirm this feeling, but I just know.

I know it in my bones.

Kieren is back.

I shake out my hands in an effort to expunge some of my

nervous energy. Hopeful freshman women stand in a line outside the Delta Gamma front door, half frozen to death. The bullshit rules of sorority rush dictate the precise time we are permitted to let them enter. Any earlier, and we would be reprimanded with a fine and a strike against our good standing.

I watch the second hand on my phone's clock tick toward twelve. In four minutes and twenty-three seconds, we are finally allowed to begin. The foyer of Delta Gamma is packed with members of each pledge class, ready to cheer like banshees when I swing this door open. It's absurd. All of it, really, but I don't make the rules. As sorority president, I just enforce them. Dammit, I wish I was in Spain right now with Gabi. Why and how did I talk myself into this thankless and unpaid job?

A profanely loud knock rasps against our front door.

"Delivery," a man's voice says outside.

"You have got to be fucking kidding," I grumble. All this buildup just to be foiled by fucking Amazon.

The knocking grows increasingly loud, and unsure eyes around the room meet mine. What's the protocol in this situation? I sure as fuck don't know, yet everyone is looking at me for answers. Fine, fuck it.

I swing open the door, ready to snatch this package with supersonic speed, when I see...

Oh, no.

No...

My mouth gapes open, frozen with both panic and horror. An obnoxiously big bouquet of what looks like three dozen blood red roses takes up the full span of the doorway. The sight in and of itself should be shocking – that many brilliant, bright red roses contrasting against the snow-white backdrop – but it pales in comparison to the face I see holding the bouquet.

His face is fuller than I remember, and it looks healthy rather than sickly and gaunt, like it was the last time I saw him. I quickly calculate how long it's been.

Seven months.

Tattoos swirl up his neck, extending past his coat collar where they hadn't been before. A silver piercing in his right eyebrow catches the light, and as I take him in, I see an almost indiscernible silver nose ring in his left nostril. I can tell by how his coat fits him that he fills it out, a far cry from seven months ago. What in the actual glow up is happening?

"I have a delivery for a Monroe Campbell," he says with a cocky grin that makes me want to eat his face.

He takes a step toward me, his shoe crossing the threshold. I should take a step back. Hell, after the second semester of sophomore year and what I witnessed, I should run. But I am mesmerized by whatever version of Kieren stands before me, and I can't will my body to move.

His hand wraps behind my neck, and before I realize what the hell is happening, he leans down and pulls my lips to his. I hold my breath, everyone holds their breath – the entire sorority behind me, the line of fifty frozen women in front of me. Time stops for all of us as his pillow-soft lips plant firmly against mine. The temperature might be barely above freezing outside, but it's a furnace where I'm standing.

He pulls back, thank God. Thank God he doesn't claim my mouth like a feral animal in front of all these women. I would be mortified.

His amused eyes search mine, flicking down to my mouth and then back up to hold my stunned gaze, and I swear to fuck I see those dark brown eyes of his twinkle.

"I brought you flowers, baby," he says in a whisper that is both embarrassingly loud and softly intimate at the same time.

He straightens, grazing my lower lip with his thumb before

passing me the bouquet. I wasn't expecting flowers to weigh so much and nearly drop the whole thing once he lets go. I have to quickly grab hold with my other hand so the pristine petals don't fall to the dirty, snow-wet ground. I can practically hear the gasps of horror at my near blunder.

He saunters past the line of women with his hands in his pockets while they shamelessly gawk at him. I can't blame them. It's not every day you witness such an over-the-top, romantic gesture from someone who looks like Kieren.

Remembering myself, I plaster a massive smile on my face, realizing it's well past the start time for this round, and usher the awaiting women inside. A chorus of cheers surges to life as the caravan begins. I go through the motions, joining the cacophony of greetings, as I clutch the flowers between two hands.

Finally, once the women are inside, I duck into the kitchen. Our resident chef, Colleen, stands over a stove, stirring something that looks like it could be soup. Or the entrails of a small animal she found dead on the side of the road. You never know with her.

"Colleen, do you have a vase?" I ask, getting her attention.

"Ohhh," she says in her raspy smoker's voice as she admires the roses. "I sure do. You can just set those down on the table in front of you, and I'll get them in some water."

"Thanks Colleen," I say, doing as she instructs.

"Better get yourself a band-aid," she comments.

I give her a confused look. "What?"

She nods at my hands. "You're bleeding."

Two separate cuts, one on my right index finger and one on the palm of my left hand, ooze droplets of blood.

"Shit," I curse, knowing I need to get back out to our living room as fast as possible to give my welcome speech.

"There are some in the first-aid kit behind you," she points out. I hadn't realized we had a first aid kit on the kitchen wall, but given the presence of knives and, well, Colleen, it makes sense. I grab a handful of paper towels to staunch the bleeding before rifling through the first-aid kit.

It all happened so fast. It didn't even occur to me that the roses could have thorns.

4
GABI

Thumping bass loud enough to rattle my teeth can be heard from the Uber as we pull up to Sigma. I climb out of the front seat, thanking the driver as I shut the car door.

My heels are unsteady on the gravel driveway, and I cling on to Ele's shoulder for support. Freshman girls wearing sneakers bound past us, and part of me wonders if we're too old for this scene. After spending a semester abroad and a summer in New York City, my tastes in nightlife have matured, leaving me with zero desire to attend another Sigma frat party. But whatever, we're here.

Two powerful searchlights positioned in the center of the expansive front lawn beam massive halos onto either side of the house, making the familiar grey stone exterior glow. From the street, Sigma looks like a medieval castle. Colorful strobe lights create silhouettes of thrashing bodies that can been seen from the first-floor windows. If I were a freshman and didn't know the type of men living within the walls of this fraternity, I would find it intoxicating.

I *did* find it intoxicating once upon a time, but my naivety, along with my innocence, are long gone.

The girl we came with, Lana, marches straight up to the front of the line and says something to the stern-faced boy playing bouncer. He gives us an infuriating once-over before waving us past.

We walk through the two sets of ornate double doors and into what can only be described as the pits of hell. The Great Room is the first room you enter once inside the fraternity house, but there's nothing great about this room other than its size. It's a massive living room area with walls made up of dark wood panels that hold strange carvings. When Sigma isn't having a party, tattered brown leather couches face each other in the center of the room to give the illusion of civility. When Sigma *is* having a party, like tonight, the furniture is moved into the adjoining room, and the Great Room is transformed into a dance floor.

Having danced in this room more nights than I can count, I thought I knew what to expect from Sigma after hours. Something about the atmosphere tonight, though, is off. It feels heavy and seedy like we've stumbled into an underground nightclub, and not the good kind.

Every single person around us appears obliterated, and that's coming from someone who had more than her fair share of vodka sodas at Tommy O's. Girls, who I assume are freshmen and sophomores because they look like babies and I recognize none of them, trip over each other while trying to dance. Some of the guys look to be equally plastered. Bodies writhe against each other like this is one big orgy, and suddenly our presence here feels very, very wrong. It's not that we're too old or too *'been there, done that'* for a frat party. It feels like we're observing something we weren't meant to see.

Lana drags us through the Great Room and into the smaller, adjoining room where they've set up the kegs.

I turn to Ele, who has her back to me, fixated on the shit show we walked through.

"I think we should leave," I say, tugging at her tank top to get her attention.

She turns around, and her expression reflects exactly how I feel. Viv steps closer, and the three of us form a small circle.

"What the fuck is going on here?" she shouts over the music.

"I don't know, but I think we should go," I shout back.

"Can we go to the bathroom first? I really have to pee," Viv says.

I nod and try to get Lana's attention to let her know, but she's engrossed in conversation, and Viv looks like her bladder is about to explode. We walk through the maze of hallways until we get to the first-floor bathrooms and step into what is fortunately a short line.

"Kasey!" I hear Ele gush from behind me, and I turn to see Kasey and two other girls I'm pretty sure are also members of Delta Gamma exit the bathroom.

Kasey looks... out of it. Like Monroe, she has long, blonde hair and thick, black lashes that frame smoldering bedroom eyes. Unlike Monroe, who has deep, complex ocean-blue eyes, Kasey's eyes are a light shade of vibrant aqua. She has the type of look people pay thousands of dollars to emulate.

As I look closer, I notice her pupils are unnaturally dilated, and as the oldest of three sisters, I feel the immediate need to protect.

Kasey stalls at the mention of her name and looks at Ele

with muddled confusion. In fairness, other than Monroe, none of us have met Kasey in person since we weren't here when she pledged. We've only seen pictures of her on social media and her headshot in the official DG announcement email sent back in January to welcome new members.

"I'm Ele. Eleanor," she states, "I'm Monroe's friend and also in DG."

We can see the wheels turning in Kasey's head, but recognition has yet to click.

"And this is Gabi and Vivienne," Ele says as she points to us.

"Oh my God," Kasey stammers, "You're Gabi? Oh my God, Monroe told us about you. She loves you," she slurs.

The other two girls standing beside Kasey start to fidget.

"Wait," Kasey says, getting uncomfortably close, and I ready myself because I'm sure she's a second from toppling over. "Have you heard from Monroe? Is she back? I really need to talk to her. Like really, really."

"No, I haven't. I'm sorry. Can I help you, though?"

"No," she sways. "Maybe. I don't know."

"Let's talk at our chapter meeting on Sunday. Will you be there? Or tomorrow," I offer, giving her a way out. I'm not sure I should leave her here. "Here, give me your number and I'll text you."

She gives me a sad smile as I dig around my purse for my phone. "Please tell Monroe I need to…" She pauses to hiccup. "I'm scared," she says.

"You're scared?" I ask, my eyes flying up to meet hers. Her eyes glaze over, and I start to panic. "Why? What's going on?"

She shakes her head. "I can't…"

"Kasey," a male voice booms from down the hall. "Let's go."

I whip my head his direction, because I know that fucking voice, and glower.

"Fuck off, Kieren," I call, positioning my body in front of Kasey. "Can't you see we're having a conversation?"

He stalks toward me, flanked by his despicable lackey, Barrett. I despise that man, maybe more than I despise Jace. Kieren stops five feet away and crosses his arms. He looks me up and down with a cocky sneer, and although I remember Monroe telling us he looked different in our group chat, seeing his transformation up close and personal is jarring.

On the surface, the changes to his appearance are subtle – the new tattoos and piercings merely enhance what was already his aesthetic. He's also bigger, taller somehow, in a way that suits him. By the end of our sophomore year, he'd lost a considerable amount of weight, which, in hindsight, is not surprising from a person who allegedly snorted cocaine for breakfast. His frame now looks healthy, and he's clearly put on muscle.

No, it's not the physical changes that give me pause.

It's his eyes.

They're empty in a way that makes him look inhuman.

Chills prickle my skin as I take in his hardened, expressionless face. If we weren't surrounded by people right now, I'd be tempted to reach out and touch him simply to confirm he has a heartbeat.

"Gabi," Kieren says in a disgusted tone that turns my blood to ice. "Who the fuck let you in?"

"Excuse me?" I snap back.

"Jace," Kieren barks, and a towering, menacing figure emerges from down the hall. I cross my arms, pissed off, as Jace fucking Carver makes his way to Kieren's side. The repulsed look he gives me, dripping with venomous hatred, would make most people cry.

But I'm not most people.

"Jace, get these geriatric cunts out of here, and tell which-ever fuckhead let them in that he's cleaning the basement with his toothbrush for the next month."

"Do not fucking touch me," I growl when Jace takes a step in my direction.

"Gabi, it's okay. Let's leave. This party sucks, anyway," Vivi-enne adds.

"Yeah, I know this party sucks ass, but I'll be damned if I let some oversized minion throw me out."

"What the fuck did you say, cunt?" Jace snarls, edging me backward, and it takes me a second to collect myself because this man, who talked about marriage and babies within two weeks of dating, who begged me not to break up with him, who sobbed at my feet, just called me a fucking cunt.

Somewhere in the background, I hear Ele tell Jace to knock it off, and then my back slams against the wall, and I see red. My hand has never moved so fast.

I feel the searing sting across my palm before I realize I've slapped him. His head whips to the side, and I feel a fleeting moment of satisfaction until I watch him slowly turn back to face me.

"That was a mistake," he growls, then picks me up and slings me over his shoulder as if I weigh less than a backpack.

"Put me down," I scream as I claw at his backside in a vain attempt to give him a wedgie. It's childish, I know, but it's my only form of retaliation.

"Where are you taking me?" I demand. I try not to focus on the fact that this is the first time Jace has touched my body since our breakup. He winds through the halls at an alarmingly fast clip, and I start to feel dizzy. Ele and Viv are on his heels, screaming at him with equal vigor.

The sharp clang of a metal door hinge cuts through the commotion.

"Outside," Jace bellows. I don't know where we are, and all I can see is the ground behind Jace's feet as he holds open the door. We've all stopped screaming. What's the point? I remain hanging upside down over Jace's shoulder, and it's not like any of us can physically go toe to toe with him.

"Can you put me down now?" I plead, but in the blink of an eye, I'm back inside, and Jace has pulled the door shut.

He flings me off his shoulder like I'm a rag doll and shoves me into the wall. My head bounces against the hard surface, and I let out a cry.

I hear Ele and Viv pounding on the outside of the door, threatening to call the police.

He presses his body against mine, pinning me in place. "Stop," I grind out as he squeezes my cheeks together and forces my face into an upward tilt. He's so much bigger than me. There was a time when I found our size difference to be thrilling, but now I'm doing everything I can to stop myself from shaking with fear.

"Do not come here again," he growls down at me. "Do you understand? You and your friends are not welcome at Sigma."

"You're pathetic," I snarl through my clenched jaw. "Are you Kieren's bitch now? Is he your daddy? Tell me, Jace, do you suck his dick before tucking him into bed at night?"

Jace squeezes my face harder, but I refuse to cower. I refuse to let this sorry excuse of a man see me beg. That's his style, not mine.

Jace drops my jaw but grabs me by the scruff of my neck, slams open the door, and throws me – not pushes, not shoves, *throws me* – outside.

The force of the door smashes into Ele and Viv, who were standing directly on the opposite side, and knocks them to the ground. My back collides with grass, and I roll to a halt somewhere between eight and ten feet from where Jace launched me into the air.

I roll onto my side, grimacing in pain. Ele and Viv scramble to kneel beside me.

"Oh my God, Gabi, are you okay?" Viv beseeches as she shines her phone light over my body in search of injury.

"I'm fine," I grit, worried I cracked a rib because it hurts to breathe.

"What the fuck?" Ele stammers. "What the actual fuck?"

"He assaulted you!" Viv cries. "Should we go to the police? At minimum, we have to report this."

"To whom?" I snap. "You saw what was happening in there. Look at those girls! Nothing has been done to stop Kieren and his army of assholes so far. Sigma has always been fucking invincible, but this is a whole new level of crazy!"

After a moment, I say, "I'm okay, I just need a minute." I push myself into a seated position. Tears run from my eyes, and I'm not sure if it's the pain, humiliation, or both. "Where are we?" I ask.

The three of us look around our inky surroundings. Music from the party sounds muted, nearly drowned out by the sound of rushing water from the nearby gorge.

"I don't know, maybe it's an emergency exit, you know, in case of a fire," Ele guesses, helping me to my feet.

"I always forget how huge Sigma is. Wait," I gasp, reaching for the nearest arm, "Kasey. What happened to Kasey? Did either of you see?"

"No, I mean, no offense to Kasey, but you were our priority, and we thought Jace was going to strangle you," Ele says.

"Dude, she looked fucked up," Viv adds. "And not just drunk. I mean *fucked up*."

"She said she was scared," I say. "She kept saying she needed to talk to Monroe. And then Kieren..."

"There is no way that was Kieren," Ele says. "That thing in there was an alien wearing a Kieren bodysuit. Did you see his eyes?"

"Dead," Viv agrees over the sound of liquid splashing against grass.

"Viv, are you peeing?" I whisper-shout.

"I had to go!" she exclaims in a whisper-shout of her own. "This place is trash, anyway. Might as well piss on it."

"She's not wrong," Ele agrees with a shrug and a small smirk.

"He made Kasey go with him and Barrett," I say, "but I don't think she wanted to." My words catch in my throat like the truth of what we saw is too horrible to repeat aloud.

"Goddammit," I sigh in frustration. "I was trying to help her, to talk to her, before henchman Jace was tagged in and literally throttled me."

"We've got to find her tomorrow," I continue. "We need to figure out what's wrong and help her, or I'm afraid whatever happened to Monroe is going to happen to Kasey, too."

"First of all, we need to get out of here," Viv shudders, pulling up her shorts. "This place is giving me the creeps."

"The vibes felt rotten, like Sigma is decaying from the inside out," Ele states.

I nod in agreement. "Whatever corruption is going on in there, it's not good, but I'm determined to find out."

5
KIEREN

Eight Months Prior to Present Day,
Early January, Junior Year,
Sigma

"Look at your girl, Jacey, posting more thirst traps," I taunt, never failing to use my favorite nickname for my friend. I know he hates it, but that's his problem.

"Fuck off, Kieren."

I chuckle, because it's so fucking fun getting under Jace's skin, not to mention, it's so simple. Damn it feels good to be back. Only those in my inner circle knew I was returning, specifically Barrett, Harrison, Jace and Sigma's outgoing doormat of a president. Good fucking riddance with that one. He was worse than Knox.

The mere thought of Knox Sterling, who was the president of Sigma when I pledged my freshman year, is infuriating. That motherfucker went out of his way to make my life miserable.

It's a good thing he was only around for one semester. Golden boy Knox graduated in three years and now is in law school at Stanford. Of course, I know his family. Everyone knows of the Sterlings. Now prominent politicians, the Sterlings are decedents of Scottish nobility, complete with a crest of arms, which the asshole has tattooed on his back so he can rub his superiority in everyone's face.

The number of times I caught that prick staring at Monroe when she would come to Sigma for parties would rile even the most tolerant, but he knew better than to make a move, especially after what happened at the Sigma alumni homecoming event my freshman year. I don't give a fuck if I was a lowly underclassman he thought he could squash under his feet. If he touched Monroe, so much as brushed her arm in a chance passing, I would drain the fucking life from his eyes with a smile on my face.

Pushing my memories of Knox asshole Sterling aside, I scroll through the last handful of social media posts from Jace's ex-girlfriend, Gabi. He won't admit this, but I know he's never fully gotten over their breakup. He pined for that girl our entire sophomore year like a sad puppy dog, yet all he could do was watch her have the time of her life from the sidelines. I'll give her credit. She never missed an opportunity to parade her desirability in his face by flirting with any junior or senior Sigma brother who would give her the time of day. *Which was all of them,* I laugh to myself.

She's not my type, but the first time I laid eyes on Gabi, I thought she was objectively one of the most beautiful women I'd seen. Poor Jacey. Every party, every social post, every run-in he had with her on campus just made him angrier and angrier. Just as I had hoped. I think he fucking loathes the girl now, and I'm happy to stoke his ongoing hatred with any silage I can find. I need Jace focused on the big picture.

"Did you read her caption? *'It's true what they say about Spanish men,'* followed by an eggplant emoji!" I quote, feigning judgement at her lewd comment.

"Seriously, Kieren, shut the fuck up," Jace shouts as he stuffs workout clothes into a gym bag. For someone who has been in my circle of friends for years, he should know by now that I love to push buttons, yet he continues to wear his emotions on his sleeve around me like a child. I wonder if he'll ever learn that his volatility makes him easy to manipulate? Well, not my problem.

I raise my palms in supplication. "Easy killer. I forget how sensitive you get over some undeserving bitch who broke your heart. How long has it been? A year-and-a-half? I figured you'd be over her by now."

"I am over her," Jace snaps, which we both know is a lie.

"When was the last time you got some?" I ask.

"Some girl on New Year's Eve."

"What was her name?"

"Don't know. Don't care. Don't remember."

"Sounds like she made a lasting impression," I tease.

I lounge on a couch in the generously sized common area that adjoins my presidential bedroom suite at Sigma. The president's quarters are palatial as fuck and best of all, semi-private. My rooms, *yes, plural,* are at the end of a long hallway, and the common room sits between my bedroom and Barrett's room, creating a natural sound barrier of sorts. The south wall of my bedroom faces the parking lot behind Sigma house, the east wall faces a patch of woods, which border the nearby gorge. It's quite serene really. A hallway separates my quarters from Jace's room. Harrison is in the room one door down from Jace. The most exciting part of this room configuration is that all of us have en suite bathrooms, a privilege only awarded to the seniors who hold executive positions in the fraternity.

It's blissful, really, because I plan to fuck Monroe into the next dimension at all hours of the day and night, and I'd prefer not to have sophomore and junior grunts jerking off to her screams.

Jace stuffs another piece of gym apparel into his bag.

"Not all of us have someone like Monroe wrapped around our pinky finger."

I make a show of looking down at my grandfather's Sigma ring, thinking about how sweet Monroe is going to taste tonight. "She is quite the compliant trophy, isn't she? Well, don't worry, Jacey. Once you fuck some freshman pussy, you'll feel better."

He snorts, which I take as a sign of agreement.

"Speaking of freshman pussy, what's the plan with the Sigma Sinners tradition?"

"I think you mean Sigma Little Sisters. I'm rebranding the name to make it more palatable. I don't think being called a Sinner has quite the lure and wholesome appeal as being called a Little Sister," I explain. Jace huffs a clipped laugh at my ingenuity.

"Anyway," I continue, "the executive team, which, don't forget, includes you, is meeting tomorrow to discuss the rollout to the rest of Sigma. We'll need everyone's buy-in, especially the new pledges as they'll be the ones responsible for recruitment. That said, I've already had side conversations with most of the existing brotherhood. Everyone seems feral and horny, so I'd classify their reactions as excited. The first Full Moon Ceremony will happen next month, and I'm hopeful by then we can initiate a few dozen. Some of the guys have already begun composing their lists."

"Next month, as in February?" Jace questions. "Then why did my brother text me that he's coming for the first Ceremony in March?"

Fucking Reid Carver. I should have known.

"And how is your dear older brother?" I ask, deflecting. "Divorce still beating the shit out of him?"

Jace shakes his head. His relationship with Reid has always been strained. Reid, ever the darling child, and Jace, the unplanned pregnancy that came six years later.

"Fuck if I know," Jace comments as he zips his gym bag. "I hardly talk to the guy."

"Pity," I offer, my insincerity obvious.

No one is supposed to know names. Anonymity affords plausible deniability and must be strictly enforced. If I knew which email address was associated with Reid, I would fire off a scathing note immediately telling him to shut the fuck up if he knew what was good for him.

Clearly, that motherfucker doesn't. Didn't seem to know what was good for him when he married his college girlfriend, either.

"You know, he's not supposed to tell you he's coming here. You're not supposed to know."

"I know," Jace states. "He said as much, albeit in an aloof, ambiguous sort of way. Very Reid-like of him. He texted, '*If you see me at the Sigma Full Moon Ceremony in March, no you didn't.*'"

I huff a mocking laugh. "I don't think you'd recognize him, which I assumed he would know, but whatever," I say. From the renderings I've seen sketched in the lost chapters of the Sigma Charter Book kept in the hidden room, elders present at the Ceremony wear a black, horned mask in honor of our fallen God that covers their entire face. It also seems like black robes are common as well, but judging by the fact that Jace never misses an opportunity to go shirtless, my guess is Reid's the same. The apple never falls far from the tree.

"What's the deal with all this shit anyway and why the fuck are alumni coming?" Jace asks.

"Because it's our fucking tradition, Jace. Our rite of passage as Sigma. We are owed this opportunity. We would have had it if recent pledge classes didn't fuck everything up, get us kicked off campus, and then turn into pussies. Sigma is hanging on by a thread, Jace. By a fucking thread. Don't you remember freshman year when Colin Coates basically threatened to cut off all funding to Sigma if we didn't bring back Sigma Sinners during my presidency? These are not rational people, Jace. They are some of the most powerful people on the planet, people who deal almost exclusively in the currencies of blood and pussy. People who are the sole reason why the two of us grew up living in mansions, even though our fathers barely lifted a finger. And I don't know about you, but I'm sure as fuck not going to jeopardize my future over some faceless cunts who are already begging to get fucked by Sigma dick anyway. If we don't resurrect these traditions that are ingrained in the heritage of our brotherhood, the entire thing collapses."

"I don't know how I feel about *'these traditions'*," Jace responds. "It's one thing to bring back Sigma Sinners, or Sigma Little Sisters, whatever you want to call it. Plenty of fraternities have Little Sister programs that they claim are a way to create mentorship bonds between sororities and fraternities. We all know it's just a sex thing, though. But this other *tradition* my father told me about... I don't know, Kieren, if I have the stomach for this medieval times shit. My father was practically giddy, which is not a good thing."

Fury boils under my skin at his cowardice, and I point an accusatory finger. "I need you to get your fucking head right, Jace," I shout, "because I'm sure as fuck not losing access to my trust fund because you decide to suddenly have a moral compass."

"I do have my fucking head right!" he shouts back. "You think you're the only one with a psychopath father? You think my dad didn't dangle my trust fund over my head if I didn't fall in line?" he yells, pointing to himself. "You know how badly I want to get away from that man."

I raise an eyebrow. "Would you kill for it? For your freedom?"

"Yes," he seethes, quieter now. "I'll do what I have to do, but that doesn't mean I have to approve. These elders, as you call them, are sick fucks."

"Yeah, well, welcome to the world we live in, Jacey. You know, Barrett and Harrison don't seem to have a problem. On the contrary, they seem quite eager."

"Barrett and Harrison are animals," Jace says with a shake of his head. "Are you going to tell the rest of the fraternity?"

"Fuck no, are you crazy? The Ritual of Sacrifice is on a need-to-know basis only."

"You don't think people will ask questions?" he asks.

"I think they'll be too preoccupied by the thought of being balls deep in a fifty-person orgy to notice or care. But, if anyone becomes a problem, I'll deal with them."

I reach behind my back, and I can't help but smile at Jace's stunned and terrified face.

"Kieren, what the actual fuck?" he stammers. "A gun? Really?"

"I don't expect you to understand the pressure I'm under, Jace, or what I stand to lose if the Ritual of Sacrifice doesn't return, but believe me when I say if anyone gets in my way, I'll toss their lifeless carcass off a fucking bridge without a second thought."

"Who's pressuring you? Your dad?" Jace presses.

I like Jace, most of the time, but right now he's getting on my last fucking nerve. Jace and I are friends solely because of our time together at Andover. He latched on to me because of my known wealth and social status, and I brought him into my fold simply due to the pull he has with the opposite sex. It was a mutually beneficial relationship, but if we hadn't attended the same private high school, I wouldn't give him the time of day. Sure, he'd be in Sigma at Dornell and we'd cross paths, but my right-hand man? Absolutely not.

His father is a Managing Director at Citigroup, rumored to be next in line as CFO, but I'll believe it when it happens, if it happens. Notable, but not impressive. A Managing Director's compensation package is around one to two million annually, something any Wall Street lackey can obtain if you stick it out long enough. Come talk to me when you're earning over thirty-million a year and then you'll understand what real pressure feels like; how catastrophic the fall can be when you're flying this close to the sun.

"Drop it, Jace. Now fall in line like a good soldier and shut the fuck up."

"Whatever. I was headed to the gym anyway."

Jace pushes past me, storming away like a little bitch. People claim they want success, they want power, but most are too weak to make the required sacrifice. Jace falls in this category. But you know what? Let him be a coward. Let him continue to live his mediocre life, with his mediocre family, yearning to get ahead but forever lacking the balls.

6

MONROE

I groan, lying starfish style on my bed. My feet ache from standing all day. I can't believe I let myself get talked into running for sorority president. I stupidly assumed someone would run against me, but when no one did, I knew I was fucked.

'It'll look great on your resume, you'll make connections with alumni, and it'll help you get a job,' they said. I mock their words in my head because I'm pretty sure they were desperate, and no one else was stupid enough to step up. I'm so goddamn gullible sometimes.

'And you get to have the large president's room in the sorority house,' they said, like living in a house with thirty under-classmen is something to be desired. Don't get me wrong, I

love these girls, but we're not close like I'm close with Gabi, Ele, and Viv. I also feel like their mom in some ways. Ugh, why do I always feel like I need to be the responsible one? I just can't help my altruism.

The only upside is that all of my meals are free, and Colleen's cooking isn't terrible. Questionable, sure, but edible. Growing up with only one parent who was absent most of the time, I've regrettably eaten worse.

I'm so tired that I didn't have the energy to drive back to my apartment after we wrapped up tonight. The four of us signed a two-year lease for an overpriced apartment in the heart of College Town at the end of our sophomore year. Three months later, we moved in and felt like we were on top of the world. The location is epic – right across from our favorite dive bar, Tommy O's – but it's expensive as hell.

Part of me regrets not subletting my room this semester, while the other three girls are abroad, because I could have used the cash. After taxes and realtor fees, the proceeds from the sale of my grandmother's house after she passed were paltry. Turns out, people aren't dying to live in a derelict, two-bedroom home in small-town Ohio.

If I stick to my budget, the money from the sale will carry me through graduation. I'll still have student loans to contend with once I get my diploma, but hopefully my computer science degree will help me land a well-paying job at a tech company with deep pockets. Maybe I'll move to San Francisco after college. I've never been, but for whatever reason, living in California has been my dream for as long as I can remember, and living across the country means I'll be three thousand miles away from my incarcerated mother. It would be a chance to start over. A chance to reinvent myself.

Perhaps it's not too late to sublet my room. The other three rooms are rented by foreign exchange students this semester –

two from Singapore and one from South Africa – and the patchwork quilt of personalities isn't the most fun to be around. The exchange students seem nice enough, but they've been here for less than a week and each time I'm at my apartment, I either get sucked into a forty-five-minute conversation with the South African or asked if I can drive their motley crew somewhere.

And sure, maybe this makes me an asshole, but I can't play chaperone right now because I'm in the midst of sorority rush, where we have to make bubbly chit-chat with hundreds of freshman girls during the day and then talk the most ruthless shit about said girls at night.

I drag my hand down my face at the memory of tonight's debate. One of the girls rushing Delta Gamma is a legacy – some granddaughter of a prominent Delta Gamma member from a southern chapter – so she's supposed to receive a bid by default. The problem is everyone hates, no, loathes, this girl. Apparently, she's made a name for herself already and has been an asshole to some of the current members at a few frat parties.

And she's not cute, which shouldn't be a prerequisite for joining a sorority, but we're all vain, shallow bitches at heart and unfortunately, people judge a book by its cover. Tonight, one of the existing members called this girl *'brutish and abrasive'* and threatened to leave Delta Gamma if we extend this girl a bid. Personally, I don't give a fuck that she's a legacy. She shouldn't be invited to join if she's been unkind to our sisters.

So, we cut her, and I can guarantee tomorrow I will get a nasty phone call from some faceless hag at DG headquarters, because I've already gotten several nasty calls about our delinquent chapter fees thanks to our unfilled treasurer position. Yet another unappreciated job I'll have to take on. God, the list does not fucking end, does it?

I rub my temples, already overwhelmed, and the academic semester hasn't even started.

Ice cracks against the glass window pane. Oh great, a winter storm. Perfect timing.

Another crack has me seated upright. Was that ice or something else?

This time, I see the small rock hit the glass, and I startle.

I scramble off the bed when a fourth crack collides with the cold glass because if this thing breaks, my already fraying patience will snap. The ground below my second-story window is dark, the light from the streetlamp is too far away to do any good.

Squinting, I think I see the white-blue glow of an illuminated phone screen. I step away from the window to retrieve my phone. I've been neglecting it for the last hour because I just need one shred of fucking peace.

> Kieren: Open the door.

Shit. I completely forgot about him. Rush has been such an all-consuming shit show, that I somehow managed to forget his outlandish grand entrance today.

The clock on my phone reads five minutes past one a.m. Dealing with Kieren and my unresolved feelings is the last thing I need to contend with tonight.

> Me: I can't. You're not supposed to be here. Boys aren't allowed.

> Kieren: Then I'll stand here and throw rocks at your window all night.

I debate what to respond when he texts me a picture holding a rock the size of his fist.

Me: You'll break the window.

Kieren: That's the point.

Me: Go away.

Kieren: This rock leaves my hand in two minutes.

Fuck.

Fuck, fuck, fuck.

Rushing out of my room, I make the hasty decision that letting Kieren inside is less disruptive than him hurling large rocks at my window.

Light chatter seeps under a few bedroom doors as I tiptoe down the hallway. Most of the rooms are silent; nearly everyone is exhausted after four marathon days of rush. It took eons to come to a consensus tonight. Our final list of bids was due by midnight since tomorrow is Bid Day. I told the girls to get some sleep because once formal invites are received and accepted, the real work begins. Yet, here I am, ignoring my own advice and on my way to rip open old wounds.

The first floor of our sorority is empty and quiet – a stark contrast to the state of these rooms twelve hours ago. It's strange and also a relief. I quietly crack open the heavy front door. Glacial air pummels my face as I stand in the doorway wearing only thin sleep pants and a tee. Kieren wastes no time and steps inside, kicking snow off his shoes.

I put my index finger over my lips, indicating we need to be quiet, and then turn to lead him upstairs. Frozen fingers grip my wrist, and I'm tugged backward. I gasp at the feeling of his brittle, cold clothes against my skin, but when I feel his hot tongue in my mouth, my resolve turns into a puddle like the melted snow at his feet.

Our kisses start to grow hungry, because fuck, it's been seven months of me wondering if he's alive or not, of hating him but also wishing he would answer my calls. I've missed him like a recovering addict misses heroin, knowing I'm better without him, but wouldn't one last high feel so good? Touching him, tasting him, needing him like I need air... Goddamn. I burned for this man. I burned for him until there was nothing left.

I couldn't admit the truth to Gabi – not after what Jace did to her. I made sure the nights I snuck out to see Kieren, Gabi was either out partying with Ele and Viv or with another guy. She had a few hookups since her breakup with Jace, but none were serious. I claimed I was in the library and needed to study or pull an all-nighter. It wasn't that hard, especially the first semester of our sophomore year when Kieren was still lucid. It wasn't until the second semester that maintaining my secret relationship with Kieren became impossible. He was out of his mind most nights, and I knew he needed help, but I couldn't reach him.

My hollow threats were feathers against his cavalry of alcohol and pills. Throw cocaine into the mix, and it was over. We were over. I've never been enough for Kieren Hunt. I never have, and I never will.

But fuck, I can't stop. And I hate that the first thing he did upon returning was come crawling back to me. I hate that he makes me believe I'm the missing piece he needs to feel whole. But what I hate the most is how badly I want to believe it's true.

I pull back from his kiss and cup his cheeks; his slight stubble feels scratchy under my fingertips. A lump rises in my throat. My chest clenches. If I allow myself to breathe, I'm going to fall apart.

He places his hands on top of mine, pulling one hand away

from his cheek so he can plant a kiss on my palm, and perhaps unironically, it's the palm with the band-aid.

"What is this?" I ask in reference to the gargantuan ring on Kieren's left pinky finger. My fingertips graze over the ostentatious gold and obsidian ring that's decorated with cryptic carvings. In a way, it reminds me of the commemorative rings professional football players get after winning the national championship.

"Later," he whispers against my lips. "Take me upstairs." It's not a question, nor does it need to be, because without hesitation, I wrap my fingers around his and bring him with me.

Quietly, he pulls his coat and shoes off as I close and lock my bedroom door. I climb onto the bed and tuck my legs under the comforter. He sees this and takes it as an invitation to undress further. I clench my jaw to stop myself from gaping at his body as he strips down to only his black boxers. Whatever training regime he's been up to over the last several months has paid off. I take in his defined abdomen and broad tattoo-covered chest and pray he can't hear how fast my heart beats or see how flushed my skin is with goosebumps.

I hold my breath as he crawls to the top of the bed and tucks himself in beside me. He slides down until he can rest his head on my lap and begins to stroke the top of my thigh. My core heats, and I wonder if the side of his face can feel my temperature change through my paper-thin lounge pants. I run my fingers through his dark brown hair and down the back of his neck, tracing the swirls of his new tattoos. Where to even begin?

"Kieren," I sigh softly.

"I know," he says. "I know."

"Just let me hold you, Monroe. I need to hold you."

I lean the back of my head on the wall behind me and try to

keep it together. Where was this need to hold me seven months ago? I try to stave off my million questions for him, but they're searing a hole in my heart, and it hurts. It hurts so much that I can't help myself.

I internally settle on my first question, arguably the most significant missing piece of the puzzle. "Where did you go?"

"A few places," he responds, gently tracing his hand down my outer thigh and around my backside. I want so badly to rip off these pants and feel his skin against mine. I want to feel that stubble along his cheeks and chin rub my inner thighs raw.

"Did you go to rehab?" I ask.

"No," he answers, pressing himself forward as he lifts my tee.

I whimper at the feeling of his lips against my stomach. He hooks two fingers behind my waistband, tugging it down as many inches as it will give in my upright, seated position.

"Kieren," I push, as his broad tongue licks and sucks at the soft skin below my navel. "I haven't seen you for seven months," I say, swallowing.

He groans, yanking me down the bed by my hips. Hitched breaths catch in my throat, but I press on despite my quickening pulse.

"What happened to you, Kieren? I need answers."

Hungry kisses trail up my stomach as he pushes my tee over my breasts. He repositions himself on top of me, sucking my left nipple into his mouth. My pussy throbs in response, and I feel myself slipping. His lips find my collarbone, the curve of my neck, my jaw, my mouth... His hard erection presses firmly against my center, and the mere thought of him inside me, stretching me, makes my head spin with desire.

"Kieren," I plead, wanting to hold firm, but his name comes

out like a clipped moan when it leaves my lips as he makes his way back down my exposed flesh.

"I don't have any condoms," I whisper, succumbing to the ferocity of my own need.

He glances up at me but doesn't answer. *Obviously, he brought condoms, you idiot,* I think to myself. Kieren Hunt doesn't show up outside my window at one in the morning just to talk.

"Do we need condoms, Monroe?" he asks, pulling down my waistband to flutter kisses against my pelvis. The bite in his tone borders on accusatory as he shimmies further down the bed, fisting the sides of my pants.

"Did you let anyone else fuck this pussy while I was gone?"

I shake my head. "I haven't been with anyone since you."

A pleased acknowledgement rumbles in his throat. "Then we don't need condoms."

I sense he's a second from pulling my pants down.

"But what about…"

"There was no fucking happening where I went, Monroe," he says in a harsh, silencing scold as he positions himself between my legs.

I swallow my racing thoughts.

"I know you want answers," he says, softer now, and I can feel his hot breath through the thin material. "I want to tell you. I will… tell you. But right now, you're keeping me from my favorite meal, and I am very, very hungry."

He rises to his knees, and even though I knew it was coming, I yelp when he yanks my bottoms down over my ass, exposing my bare pussy. A primal growl of approval reverberates in his throat when he sees I'm not wearing panties. Kieren slides off my pants one leg at a time, and my entire body quivers in anticipation.

He lowers himself down, spreading my thighs so wide that

even under the covers, cold air kisses my center. The bridge of his nose grazes my clit, and I feel myself tumble over the edge and into the abyss of surrender when he draws in a long, extended inhale of my scent.

"Monroe." He growls my name on an exhale like an animalistic savage who has just been set free.

"Yes?" I squeak, unsure if I'm still alive.

"Don't scream."

7
GABI

Present Day

The more I think about it, the more I realize nothing about last night makes sense. Kieren's reaction to seeing us was comically overblown. Why was our presence at Sigma after hours an issue so severe that Kieren ordered his underling to throw us out?

And then the way Jace quite literally threw us – well, me – out... The punishment did not fit the crime. Was he always this much of an asshole? I guess he was, although he masked it well. I just wasn't on the receiving end of his wrath when we were dating.

Lying on my bed, I scoff to myself. Dating. Dating is far too casual a word for our relationship. I brought him to meet my parents over winter break our freshman year. We told each other '*I love you*' for fuck's sake.

Checking the time on my phone, I groan. I need to get

going. The problem with going abroad is that you get stuck with a full load of classes in your senior year and aren't able to coast.

"Ahh, goddammit," I cry, rolling onto my side. My left hip sears with pain from where I collided with the ground. I hiss and hobble over to my dresser to pull out a pair of cotton shorts and then make my way to the combined living room and kitchen area where I find Vivienne.

"How are you feeling this morning?" she asks, without looking up from her laptop. I use the ledge of the kitchen counter for support as I limp to the freezer in search of an ice pack or frozen bag of vegetables.

"Angry," I respond to Vivienne.

"Can't say I blame you," she adds. "How's the leg?"

"Look at this thing," I say, hiking up the side of my shorts.

Her eyes go wide. "Jesus! That's a nasty bruise."

"Jace is a fucking asshole," I seethe.

"At least you got a slap in," Viv adds, reminding me of my one moment of triumph.

"I hope he has my handprint on his face this morning," I grumble.

"Maybe we should go slit his tires," Viv suggests.

"Actually, that is a great idea. Do you think a kitchen knife is strong enough to do the job?"

Viv looks at me with concern. "I was kidding. You could get arrested for vandalism."

"Honestly, slitting the tires on his motorcycle would be worth the jail time."

———

And who drives a fucking motorcycle in upstate New York? I seethe to myself as I make the painfully slow trudge toward the campus store. I have a fair amount of class course packets and books to purchase. When is this shit going to be fully digitized? Just because paper is a renewable resource doesn't mean we need to waste it when the digital version is preferred. Not to mention, digital files don't weigh five thousand pounds.

But, back to the motorcycle. What a dumb idea. A month from now, the weather will turn cold, and shortly after that, snow will arrive. I never took Jace for a Neanderthal, but he sure as fuck is acting like one.

I catch myself grinding my teeth at the thought of slitting those tires. God, wouldn't that be satisfying? I'm not prone to violence, but I'm also not completely opposed.

I grab a handbasket and head to the section of the campus store where course supplies are kept. When I see that the packet for the Economics of Advertising course is two inches thick, I grimace. Maybe I should have chosen to pursue a strategy concentration instead of marketing, because the ones for senior-level strategy classes are laughably thin.

I find the course packets I need and toss them into my basket, now irritatingly heavy, and audibly grunt when I try to pick it up. The person standing at the end of the section turns around upon hearing my struggle, and I don't know how I didn't notice him before.

"You," I sneer.

Part of me thinks I should walk away, but that part of me is a pussy. Besides, I wouldn't be walking away, I would be hobbling, and I won't give Jace Carver the sick gratification of seeing how badly I'm injured.

I drop my basket. "What the fuck is your problem?"

It takes a considerable amount of strength and focus to hide my limp. Jace gives me a once-over, then turns around, pretending to be preoccupied by the packet in his hand.

I sidle up next to him, forcing him to acknowledge me.

"What do you want?" he asks without looking at me.

"What do I want?" I all but gasp. "How about a fucking explanation and apology for last night?!"

He puts the packet back on the shelf, which is confusing in its own right because why would you pick up a shrink-wrapped course packet unless you were taking the class? It's not like a book you can open and peruse.

"I don't know what you're talking about," he says. His gruff tone is borderline dismissive, which only enrages me further.

"Seriously?" I ask, raising my voice an octave. "Look at my fucking thigh, Jace. Look at it," I order, pulling up the hem of my shorts to expose the massive brown and purple bruise. His eyes glance down at my thigh without so much as a wince, let alone turning his head to look at the injury *he* inflicted.

"I get it, you hate me, but are you that much of an asshole that you think it's okay to physically assault me? And, for what? For daring to show my face at fucking Sigma?"

"You shouldn't be there," he says, turning to walk away.

"Hey," I say loudly, grabbing the sleeve of his T-shirt. "Get over it. We broke up over two years ago. Move on."

The muscles in his jaw feather. He gives me that look – like he might rip my head off but also start weeping – and my fire ignites.

"What did he do to Monroe?" I say with slow enunciation. Jace shakes his head and scoffs a laugh like he's mocking me.

"Let it go, Gabi," he says as he shrugs his sleeve from my grip.

"No," I say through gritted teeth, stepping in front of him to block his path. Our bodies are inches from each other, and with his height and size advantage, I'm very aware he could plow through me and knock me to the ground with zero exertion on his part whatsoever.

"I need to know what happened to her. I need to understand why my best friend vanished like a ghost, why her phone number is disconnected, and no one can reach her. Please Jace, you must know something," I plead. "Please, if you ever cared about me, tell me what happened."

He gives me another mocking laugh. "You assume your friend is so fucking innocent. Maybe there's a reason she doesn't want to be found."

He takes a step to the side, but again, I block his path.

"What does that mean?" I ask, pressing my hands to his chest. I know I'm not strong enough to block him, but I'm hoping he isn't reckless enough to cause a scene similar to last night's. Jace holds my stare. His soft, dark brown eyes are somber and heavy, as if he knows exactly what happened to Monroe, but something *or someone* is forcing him to remain silent.

"Stay away from Sigma, Gabriella," he rasps with a scowl. I falter at the use of my full name, gazing up at his boyish face, because the only time he would call me Gabriella was when we were...

I swallow the burgeoning lump in my throat.

He quickly sidesteps around me, and I make no move to stop him.

8

GABI

Present Day

I stuff the thick course packets and textbook into my backpack. It's heavy but manageable. Delta Gamma is a solid mile walk from the campus store, but after my unnerving interaction with Jace, I need answers. I've got to find Kasey.

I have no idea how to track down a person who doesn't want to be found. And what did Jace mean by Monroe isn't innocent? Innocent in what? In allowing Kieren back into her life? In being unable to let him go? Like that wasn't obvious. Monroe thinks I don't know about the ongoing relationship she had with Kieren during our sophomore year. She's a terrible liar. I knew she was still sleeping with him. The all-nighters she claimed she had to pull in the library were a ruse to see him. He had a hold over her in a way I can't explain or understand.

When I first met Monroe at Dornell, she was naïve and inexperienced, which was not her fault, given her tumultuous childhood. It's one thing to have a deadbeat dad. It's another thing to have an unstable mom with dubious morals who fell for a mob-affiliated con man and landed herself in prison. Spending her teenage years in Ohio, living with her grandmother, certainly didn't help. It's like Kieren could smell her insecurities from miles away and hunted her down with his money and dominance like she was prey. He was so controlling of her during our freshman year, always present, always around, always listening, and ready to whisk her away to his childhood home in Connecticut to do God knows what the moment she exhibited a semblance of confidence.

Monroe would say Kieren set her free. I would say he exploited her for his own sexual sadism. Jace told me Kieren was known to have a fondness for BDSM, going so far as to chain past girlfriends to the bed. And while I absolutely am not kink-shaming my best friend, a large part of me does wonder how much of their sex life was dictated by Kieren's desires. But, I guess Monroe liked Kieren's brand of bedroom play enough to keep crawling back. Honestly, I think she became addicted. I recall spending hours freshman year researching Stockholm syndrome.

All I know is that things must have gotten unspeakably bad for Monroe to leave in the manner she did. I wonder if there is a way I can check her student status. Maybe she arranged a formal leave of absence with the University, like Kieren had when he was gone the first semester of our junior year. I would feel hopeful if that's the case, because it would mean she intends to come back.

The front door of Delta Gamma is surprisingly open when I arrive, but I'm grateful for the ease of entrance. I shed my backpack as soon as I'm through the door, and it hits the ground with a loud thud. My long, dark brown hair sticks to my sweat-drenched back as I fan out my tank top.

The bottom floor of the sorority is empty, so I assume everyone is either upstairs or out running errands in preparation for classes on Monday. I probably should have waited until our chapter meeting tomorrow to find Kasey – who knows if she's even here right now. Someone must be home, however, and if Kasey's not here, at least I can get her number from one of the girls in her pledge class.

I make my way up to the second floor, peeking my head inside each room I pass. Unfortunately, so far, no one is home. Footsteps creak above my head from the third floor, and I'm relieved that my poorly timed visit won't be entirely in vain.

"Hello?" I ask as I ascend the stairs. "Hello, is anyone here?"

A girl with dark, curly hair emerges from a room at the end of the hall.

"Hey," I say with a smile. I'm sure I'm a stranger to her, and I don't want her to panic. "I'm Gabi, I'm a senior in DG. I'm actually looking for Kasey. Do you know if she's here?"

"Are you Gabi Pimentel?" the girl asks eagerly. I must look at her like I'm surprised she knows my name, because she explains, "We were required to memorize all the members of DG when we joined, and your headshot is so pretty. You kind of stand out."

Her face flushes when I brush off the compliment with a teasing scoff.

"You're too kind. But hey, are you friends with Kasey?" I ask, redirecting the conversation back to my initial question.

"She's my roommate, actually," she offers hesitantly. Her bubbly expression deflates like a balloon at this admission, but I pretend not to notice.

"Oh!" I exclaim, excited by my luck. "Is she here?"

The girl shakes her head. "The last time I saw her was yesterday afternoon."

"So, she didn't come home last night?" I ask.

The girl shakes her head again, and I start to open my mouth when I realize my line of questioning might sound intrusive and accusatory. It's not abnormal to spend the night with someone, certainly not when you're in college. This place is just one big cesspool of unbridled hormones, after all.

"I met Kasey last night at Sigma, and she was about to give me her number when we got separated," I clarify to soften my approach. I don't want to come off as a judgmental senior. What did Kieren call us last night? *Right*. Geriatric cunts.

"She was at Sigma?" the girl asks, her eyes going wide with worry.

"Yeah, why? Is something wrong with that? With her being at Sigma, I mean."

The girl nervously shakes her head. "It's not my place," she stammers.

Shit.

My mind quickly works through ways to get this girl to tell me more.

"What's your name, by the way?" I pivot. "I'm sorry, I've been rude not to ask."

She gives me a shy smile. "Adrianna."

"I love that name," I gush. "My favorite cousin is named Adrianna," I lie, and her smile widens.

"Would you mind if I came inside? When I saw Kasey last night, she looked really out of it, and it looked like she was with this guy named Kieren who used to date my best friend."

All color drains from Adrianna's face.

When I see this happen, I push inside her room so as not to give her an opportunity to turn me away. This girl knows something, and I need fucking answers.

"Shut the door," I say in a hushed voice to Adrianna as I take a seat on the circular rug in the middle of the room and wait for her to join me. Slowly, she lowers herself down with uncertainty and sits cross-legged in front of me. I sense this girl is on the verge of tears, which, as fucked up as it is, I use to my advantage.

I blow out a long, steadying breath. "Monroe is my best friend," I begin, "and I think something really bad happened to her last semester."

"She disappeared," Adrianna interjects. "She stopped showing up to lead chapter meetings. The other Delta Gamma juniors said she stopped responding to emails and texts...It was so strange."

"Did you know she was dating Kieren? You know Kieren, right? I mean, I just assumed by the way you reacted a second ago when I said his name in reference to Kasey."

She nods. "Yes, I mean, I know who he is, everyone does. He's the guy who showed up with a bouquet of roses for Monroe during rush. Kasey and I were so thrilled when we both got into Delta Gamma – it was our dream. We were room-mates my freshman year also."

I can't contain my nerves anymore. I need answers and not a walk down memory lane. "What's going on?" I blurt out.

Adrianna goes quiet, gathering herself, and then shakes her head. Tears fall from her cheeks, and she uncrosses her legs to pull her knees into her chest.

"Hey, it's okay," I soothe when she starts to rock back and forth. As much as I want to smack her and tell her to snap out of it so she can tell me the rest of what she knows, I take a page from Monroe's book and play the empath.

"I know," I say in solidarity. "Something isn't right. I wasn't here last semester, but I feel it, too. When I was at Sigma last night for after hours, even before I saw Kasey, I could sense things were off."

Adrianna sniffs and wipes at her face. "She can't talk about it," Adrianna says. "The only thing I know is that at the beginning of last semester, she got initiated or something."

"Initiated to Delta Gamma?"

"No," Adrianna says, "to Sigma. Not as a brother but... she said it was like being a little sister. She was close with a bunch of guys in the house, not Kieren or his year, but other freshmen. She described it as an honor – like you're given extra special treatment, always get right in for parties, and you can go upstairs, that sort of thing. But then she was there every weekend, *all weekend*. And each time she came back..."

Adrianna trails off and begins to cry again.

"She just wasn't the same," she breathes. "I don't know anything else about Kieren other than what Kasey shared, which wasn't much. She made him sound like a god. She did say once that Monroe was there," Adrianna pauses, and uses her fingers to make air quotes when she says, "looking after the girls."

"Looking after the girls?" I repeat in question. "What does that mean?"

"I don't know. Kasey said she couldn't talk about it. I started to get concerned when she was gone every weekend, but when I asked her about it, she said it was her duty or something. Like an obligation. I told her that was stupid and to just not go the next time, but she seemed genuinely scared at the idea of not showing up."

I pause to take in the information, because what in the actual hell? Is this like a fucking cult or something?

"But I saw what they did to her," Adrianna whispers.

"What do you mean? Did they hurt her?"

Adrianna looks around the empty room like someone might jump out of the closet at any second.

"Please promise me you won't say anything," she asks.

"I promise," I assure her, though I sure as fuck am telling Ele and Viv.

"I think they branded her," Adrianna says in a voice so quiet, I have to strain to hear, even though she's sitting three inches in front of me.

"Branded her?" I ask, nearly choking on the words.

Adrianna nods. "She was getting dressed one day, and I happened to glance over right as she was putting on her underwear. It was this ugly, red welt on her ass. I gasped when I saw it, and she immediately covered herself. I asked her what it was, and she played it off. She said it was nothing. But I couldn't keep my fucking mouth shut, so I kept asking, until finally she snapped. She told me to pretend I didn't see it, to never ask about it again, and to never tell anyone. She said if I tell anyone, they'll find out, and they'll take it out on her."

I suck in a breath and try to process the horrifying concept of a freshman girl getting branded all because she wanted to be someone special to a bunch of feckless frat boys.

A disturbing thought occurs to me.

"Adrianna, did you tell anyone else? I mean, maybe accidentally, after a few drinks or something."

She peers over her knees, now clutched so tight to her chest that I could roll her out of this room like a ball.

"Only a couple of the girls in our pledge class, when they started asking why Kasey wasn't showing up to events." The horror on her face makes me feel like I've stepped into some sort of movie. "I...," she stammers. "They said they wouldn't say anything."

Because a house full of thirty chatty sorority girls isn't a swirling cauldron of gossip...

Right.

9

KIEREN

Seven Months Prior to Present Day,
Beginning of February, Junior Year,
Dornell University

"What do you want, Father?" I ask with annoyance. Up until this point in my life, my father couldn't give two shits about me. As long as my extracurricular proclivities weren't fodder for the amusement of his gossiping country club buddies, he preferred to leave the parenting to my mother, who in turn preferred to hand me off to my rotating door of nannies. It's shocking either of them remembered my name, although I'm fairly certain half the time they forgot my birthday.

Today's phone call from my father marks the sixth phone call I've received from him over the past four weeks, which might amount to more than all the calls he's made over the past four years. After the first call, I was pleasantly surprised, believing his need to check in on my well-being was sincere. After the second call, aggravation began to fester as the reason for his calls became clear. Then, the third call came, and the old man couldn't be bothered to even pretend to care. He wanted to know if I'd set the wheels in motion. X had made good on his end of the bargain, and now it was my turn.

"Kieren," he says gruffly. "X tells me you've been challenging to pin down."

I huff my frustration, because that's bullshit. "I don't know what the fuck he's talking about. I've returned every email and every text."

I've spoken to the man once, and it was clear from our twelve-minute conversation that he was using a voice manipulation tool. His instructions were curt and to the point. I was to reinstate the Ritual of Sacrifice no later than the third full moon of the new year. X would work out the details with my father to reinvest our clients' remaining money, which would save our family from financial ruin, and I was to study the lost chapters of the Sigma Charter. When I asked where I could find said lost chapters, he became irritated, scorning my grandfather for not explaining Sigma's history to me or my dimwitted father.

As much as I enjoyed hearing another person debase the man who sired me, attacking my grandfather who suffers from dementia is where I draw the line. Once it became clear to X that I don't find his snarling threats intimidating, he begrudgingly told me that everything I needed to know could be found in the hidden Room of Sacrifice, which can only be opened with a Sigma Key.

While I understand this X character is to be feared, I also find it difficult to take someone who uses a voice manipulating device seriously. The number of times I had to bite my tongue to prevent myself from calling him Freddie Krueger should be studied by monks.

But, whatever. He gets what he wants, and my family's reputation lives to fight another day. I should be more concerned than I am about how easy this agreement was to strike, but having regard for the welfare of others has never been my strong suit.

"X tells me your responses to his correspondence have been vague and lagging."

"Did he now? I see I'm not the only one doing X's bidding. Has he got you wiping his ass as well?"

"Boy, believe me when I say you'll never see a dime of your trust fund if you keep up this insubordination," my father growls.

"Jesus Christ, I'll text him!" I say, exasperated by my father's whining. Truly, I don't know what more information X needs. He knows the date, the time, the place. I've done everything by the book. Does he need me to book his travel, too? This man is turning out to be a high-maintenance diva.

"See to it that you do," my father barks, before ending the call. Part of me believes I should have strangled him when I had the chance. Playing the part of a puppet on a string is not something I do well.

Playing the part of God, however, is electrifying.

I've always possessed some degree of inherent power, the result of my surname combined with my natural ability to bend others to my will. It's an innate talent, one that doesn't require much exertion to achieve my desired outcome. I usually have control over every situation, which is why I was delighted to read that the individual most critical to the Ritual of Sacrifice is the current Sigma president.

Me.

The lost Sigma chapters were enlightening, to say the least.

X is lucky to be in the room. Now I understand what my father meant last summer when he told me X *'knows about me and my unique position.'* Not only am I president of Sigma's Dornell chapter, but by way of my grandfather's ring that functions as both a key and a brand, I can open the hidden Sacrifice Room, and who knows if every Sigma house has one of these?

Hell, I am likely the one and only person in the nation right now who has access to and can *open* a Sacrifice Room, is the current residing president and therefore able to conduct the Ritual, and, the most important piece of all, has no moral qualms with doing so. If it worked for my grandfather, it can work for me, and I'd say time is of the essence as it seems whatever good fortune my grandfather earned from participating in these Rituals has run out.

Perhaps my favorite discovery in the Sacrifice Room was the masks. There are additional items we will need to procure, but the masks cannot be replicated. Pussy loves a secret society of mask-wearing elites. I won't be surprised if we end up with a waitlist.

I can't wait for Monroe to see me in my mask. It is by far the most sinister. But seeing Monroe in her mask... my dick twitches just thinking about her wearing nothing but the black leather puppy mask I had custom-made. To think I had her mask commissioned months ago, before I realized I would have a mask to wear as well. Some might call it a coincidence, but I call it destiny.

Disappointment drawls a scowl to my lips. My phone sits idle in my car's cupholder, waiting for Monroe to text me back. I let the first few weeks slide. Both of us were busy with rush and new pledge initiation. On top of that, I had a list of other priorities. Now that the full Sigma brotherhood, including all incoming pledges, have been briefed about Sigma Little Sisters, preparations are in motion. I underestimated the feral ruthlessness of the current Sigma members, having assumed there would be some pushback to the idea of resurrecting a tradition that, at its core, revolves around the degradation of women, but I was pleasantly wrong. I heard one Sigma brother describe it as sexual liberation, and you know what? He's right.

Speaking of liberation, I think to myself, as I tug at my jeans, *where the fuck is Monroe?*

I've given her enough leeway. Apparently, the flowers and night we spent together several weeks ago followed by an onslaught of thirsty texts didn't do the trick. She's still hesitant, but I have a plan. Clearly, she thinks she can ignore me, and that's laughably incorrect.

My hands grip the steering wheel, fisting the taught leather.

I. Want. Her.

She was mine before, and she will be mine again.

10

MONROE

Seven Months Prior to Present Day,
Beginning of February, Junior Year,
Dornell University

"Hello?" I answer, but my greeting is cut short by a phone operator who announces, "You have an incoming call from the Federal Correction Institute, Otisville, New York. Do you accept this call?"

"Yes," I grouse because it's my fucking mom. Again.

I wait with annoyance as the line pauses, debating if I should hang up.

"Monroe?" My mother's grating voice rings loud in my ear, and I grimace.

"Mom," I respond, careful not to emit any emotion. I don't want to rile her up, and I cannot afford to let this pathetic excuse of a parental figure drain any more of my energy today.

A delicate, icy-cold kiss lands on my nose. The predicted

snowfall has begun, and we're expected to get six inches by morning. My last class ended ten minutes ago, yet I'm still a mile away from the sorority house.

"How's my rich daughter?" my mom asks. Words cannot express how much I fucking hate this woman.

"Mom, I've told you a thousand times. Grandma Sadie's house wasn't worth shit. Proceeds from the sale after the mortgage was paid off will hardly cover my bills for the next few years. Other than what little equity she had in the house, she had no money. No savings. No hidden bars of gold in her basement like you claimed. So, stop asking me to send you fucking money, because I don't have any."

"You're a terrible liar, Monroe. Always have been."

"Why don't you call your upright citizen of a husband and ask him for money?"

"I'm prohibited from contacting him, and you know that."

"What about his cousins or his sister?"

"You mean the one you snubbed for Christmas? Yeah, I heard about that, Monroe. I got an earful from your Aunt Nikki. She said you didn't so much as call to wish them a Merry Christmas."

I scoff a bitter laugh. "Why would I call her? She's not family. Besides, I don't see her picking up the phone to reach out."

"Where were you over Christmas?" my mom interjects.

"Waiting fucking tables," I sneer.

"Oh, then you do have cash. I'm sure those perky tits of yours made good money."

"I was waitressing, not sucking dick on the corner," I snap.

"Language!" she scolds, which is ludicrous coming from the woman who fucked her way to a prison sentence. My grudge isn't so much with my stepdad – as far as temperament goes, he was always decent to me, and tolerated far more verbal abuse from my mom than he should. But he was involved in some shady shit. I remember being eight and watching him count stacks of cash on our living room coffee table; my mom by his side with a cigarette dangling from her mouth. His *'cousins'*, although I'm not convinced there was any blood relation, were always in and out of the house.

I mostly kept to my room, but when he and my mom were charged with multiple accounts of money laundering four years later, it all made sense. As a twelve-year-old, I didn't fully understand how money laundering worked, but it didn't surprise me to learn my mom had been a willing accomplice. Once my stepdad, Kerry, came into our lives, all of a sudden, my mom started wearing designer clothes and a brand-new white Mercedes magically appeared in our driveway.

She's so fucking dumb. Both of them, actually. Rule number one of being involved with organized crime is don't act like you're involved with organized crime. Don't buy hundred-thousand-dollar cars and Chanel handbags when you could barely put food on the table six months prior.

"Listen, I don't have much time left on my phone card, so just send me some money, will you?"

I sigh. "I'll drop a few hundred in your commissary account. Just give me a few days. Things are really busy at school."

"That's my sweet girl. I knew you weren't completely ungrateful for everything I did for you, after all. And call your Aunt Nikki. She only wants to make sure you're okay, Monroe. She means well. It's got to be scary, being all on your own."

No, it's a fucking delight, I want to yell, but I instead mumble something about calling my stepdad's sister and hang up. Nicole, or Nikki for short, is not my aunt – not by blood – and my personal position on the matter is I owe her nothing.

I'm preoccupied with my seething thoughts when I hear

my name. Turning, I see a black BMW roll to a stop on the street beside me.

"Get in," Kieren shouts from the driver's seat. I debate ignoring him, since that is what he's done to me for the past few weeks, but it's freezing, my fingers are numb from holding my phone, and the idea of a warm car is too tempting to resist.

"Came to your senses?" Kieren asks when I shut the passenger-side door.

I roll my eyes at him.

"I thought you'd ghosted me again," he says.

"Kieren, you're the one who ghosted me! Each time I text you back, you don't respond for days. I'm sorry I was preoccupied with classes and new member events the one time I didn't get back to you right away."

"That's not at all accurate, but okay," he snips. I think he's joking, but I can never tell with him. "Do you have somewhere to be right now?" he asks.

"I was headed to DG."

"Hmm. Well, now you're headed home with me to Sigma."

"Only if you're going to give me answers," I complain.

He rolls his neck and sucks his bottom lip between his teeth. I can't tell if he's frustrated or contemplating telling me the truth.

"I'm not getting out of this car until you tell me why you didn't return to Dornell last semester," I say in my most defiant tone.

"You forget that I'm significantly stronger than you," he says with an unamused smirk.

"Fine, I'm not fucking you until you tell me what happened."

"Again, you forget that I'm comically bigger and stronger than you, and that you also happen to desperately want my cock."

I scoff. "You wouldn't."

"I wouldn't what? Pin you down on my bed, put restraints around all your appendages, and fuck you until you forget your name? Pretty sure I've done that countless times before, Monroe. In fact, I bet your pussy is wet right now just thinking about how good it would feel to be tied up with my cock buried deep inside you."

He leans his head back on the headrest and groans. "Fuck, now I'm getting hard imagining you spread open and helpless," he says, adjusting the front of his pants as they strain to tent around his obvious erection.

"Give me what I want, and I'll give you what you want," I banter.

He grunts a laugh. "I don't think it works that way, Monroe. Not when you want my cock just as badly as I want your pussy."

"What makes you think I want it as badly as you do, Kieren?"

He looks at me with a cocky grin. "Touch yourself."

"What? No!"

"Then I'll do it."

His hand shoots across the center console and paws wildly at my buttoned coat. His erratic movements cause the car to lurch violently to the right, and I scream.

"Fine! Fine, Kieren. Jesus, just don't kill us."

I pull at my layers of clothing until the waistband of my jeans is exposed, and I unfasten the top button. I slide my frigid hand down my pants, tensing at the cold, until two of my fingers reach my hot center, already slick with the beginnings of arousal. I close my eyes and lean back, playing lightly with my clit before sliding my fingers down to my wet entrance.

"That's enough, Monroe," Kieren commands, but I ignore him.

"Give me your fucking hand," Kieren barks, ready to yank my pleasure away.

I reluctantly pull my hand from my pants and extend it in his direction. He snatches it like a greedy child and presses it to his mouth, smearing my arousal across his lips. He smiles at me with animalistic delight as his tongue darts out to lick up my taste.

"I hate you," I huff.

"Tastes like it," he grins, popping both my fingers into his mouth then languidly sucking them clean.

He releases my hand, and I cross my arms over my chest as we approach the statuesque stone castle that is Sigma. We pull into the long driveway, and I hear the familiar crunch of gravel under his tires. My throat constricts with hurt as Kieren guides his car into a parking spot at the back of the fraternity.

I still don't have answers.

He turns the car off and unclips his seatbelt, readying to jump out, but I don't move.

"What's wrong Monroe?" he asks. He repeats the question, but I refuse to look at him.

"Talk to me," he demands, gently pulling on the collar of my coat. I shrug him off, furious.

"How can you be so nonchalant about what happened to you? What you put me through our sophomore year was unforgivable. You were horrible to me."

"I know," he admits. His accountability takes me by surprise.

"By the end of the year, I hardly recognized you. Honestly, I was worried you would overdose."

"If you were so worried, why did you leave?"

"Why did I leave?" I ask incredulously, my voice rising an octave. "Because I couldn't stomach watching you destroy yourself."

His laugh is cold and bitter. "Everyone claims they care until you're standing alone in your bathroom at three a.m. with a razor to your wrist. I was fucking suicidal Monroe and you abandoned me."

Tears land on the collar of my camel-colored coat. "I didn't abandon you," I say, shaking my head. "I was there, Kieren, but you pushed me away."

He reclines his head against the headrest of his seat again and closes his eyes. I watch his Adam's apple bob in his throat as he swallows.

"You left, Monroe. You were all I had, and you left. You don't know what goes on in my head," he says quietly.

"Then tell me," I plead.

"My dad tried to kill himself," he says out of the blue, and for a moment, I forget to breathe. "It was right after finals in May of last year. I got the call from my mom. Obviously, I left right away. I'm surprised I even made it to the hospital. I had taken a fuck ton of molly earlier that day to celebrate being done with exams, planning to trip my balls off, and then got the phone call and did three lines of cocaine to sober up before driving to Connecticut."

I want to scream at him for being so reckless, but I force myself to be still because this is the most vulnerable Kieren has been with me in ages.

"Honestly, the thought did cross my mind that I would get killed in a car accident, but at that point, I didn't care. You had given me your ultimatum. I think by then it had been three weeks since I last saw you, so what difference did it make if I lived or died?"

"But somehow, I made it to the hospital. Staggered in like a strung-out junkie. My mom was a wreck, but she took one look at me and got me admitted. I spent a week puking my guts out. My dad was in a medically induced coma during this time, so my mom would go back and forth between our two hospital rooms. Once I was stable, we moved my dad home and were told he needed twenty-four-seven observation. My mom would sit with him for a few hours during the day, but it was mostly just me and the nurses. It took him another week to be fully coherent again. I'd say this was around mid-June. I thought about coming back in the fall, but there were things I needed to take care of for my family. Dornell granted me a leave of absence, no questions asked. It took the rest of the summer and most of the fall to get things in order, but I managed."

He pauses, and the interior of the car is pin-drop quiet.

"Kieren, I'm so sorry," I offer. My words catch in my throat; my heart breaks for him and what he went through last summer. I failed him because I wasn't there when he needed me the most. It breaks me that he had to go through such a devastating ordeal alone.

"I would have come," I say, even though I know it's too late.

"I know you would have. That's why I didn't call or text. I was weak, and I knew if I heard your voice, I would beg to see you. Even if you were the one who left, you didn't deserve what I put you through. I was a shell of myself, but I knew that much."

"And I loved you anyway," I admit, because it's true. I was in love with him, despite what it cost me.

"You did," he agrees. He turns to look at me, his eyes glassy with unshed tears.

"I want you back, Monroe. I need you. I can't stomach the thought of existing on the same campus as you and being unable to call you mine."

I huff with uncertainty. Letting Kieren Hunt back into my life is a massive gamble.

"How's your dad now?" I deflect.

"Better," Kiren says, nodding his head.

"Are you sober?" I ask.

"I'm trying," he admits.

He turns to look at me with pleading eyes. "Please. I need you. You're the only one who has accepted my faults. You're the only one I trust with my demons. Tell me what I have to do to make this right. I'll do whatever it takes if it means I can call you mine."

11

GABI

Present Day

"Ele, I need you to get the fuck in your car and come pick me up immediately."

My hips and arms swing wildly, and I must look borderline deranged walking at this speed, but Adrianna's secrets are burning a hole in my pocket, and no amount of power walking will get me back to our apartment fast enough.

After what feels like an eternity, a car lightly taps on its horn as it pulls up next to me.

"Jesus, what took you so long?" I huff as I climb into the back seat of Ele's Subaru. Sweat pools at the base of my bra and runs down my temples as I struggle to shimmy off my heavy backpack.

Ele and Viv have their windows down, and I crinkle my nose at the faint smell of marijuana and sunscreen.

"Where were you two?" I ask accusingly.

Viv turns around, and I see my annoyed scowl reflected in her oversized designer sunglasses. "We went for a swim in the gorges."

The mention of the gorges makes me remember all the times the four of us went swimming together and how Monroe would fearlessly jump off the high cliffs into the water. I've never met anyone as courageous as she was, *is,* when it comes to heights. God, the thought of those happier, simpler times makes my heart hurt.

"We were going to invite you," Ele chimes in from behind the wheel, "but you left in such a foul mood, we figured you wanted some time alone to stew."

"Whatever, there are probably dead bodies in that water, anyway."

"Okay, morbid," Viv states, holding a cigarette between her teeth. Two seconds later, the smell of smoke blasts me in the face, and I'm torn between finding it repulsive and soothing.

"Well, while you two were out on a joy ride, I was doing reconnaissance. I went to DG to find Kasey. She wasn't there, but I had quite the interesting chat with her roommate, Adrianna."

I retell every bit of Adrianna's overshare, down to the last detail, and watch as my friends' faces change from curiously intrigued to stunned and disgusted.

"And, as if that's not crazy enough, I also ran into Jace at the campus store, and he was more cryptic than ever."

"Wait, hold on," Ele interjects, shocked, "can we go back to the part about the fucking brand? You know, the whole seared flesh bit. Is that for real?"

"Adrianna says she saw it with her own eyes!"

"And you trust this Adrianna person?" Viv asks skeptically.

"I guess, but I mean, who would make up something like that?"

"That makes me deeply uncomfortable," Ele states.

"It's disgusting," I agree. "But leave it to the all-mighty Sigma to come up with something as diabolical as recruiting girls under the guise they're going to part of a special little sisters thing only to brand them like property."

"How does something like this even happen in this day and age?" Ele asks, infuriated. "At a fucking Ivy League school, no less. God, the world is so sick."

I swallow and lean back against the seat. Students walk in front of the car while we wait at a crosswalk. A group of girls in lively conversation smile gleefully. Sticky, humid air clings to my clammy skin as unrest settles in my stomach like lead.

"We need to confront Kasey tomorrow after the chapter meeting," I state. "Something very wrong is happening at Sigma, and we need to figure out the truth."

———

The silver tongs in my hand squeeze into the firm white flesh of another overcooked and under-seasoned chicken breast – one of Colleen's Sunday dinner specialties. I'm pretty sure Colleen has been Delta Gamma's resident chef for longer than I've been alive, yet the woman cannot cook a decent meal to save her life. Next to the chicken is a banquet serving tray of green beans swimming in a questionable, watery sludge, which should have taken the prize for worst dish of the night, but was upstaged halfway through dinner service when Colleen brought out a tray of lukewarm tofu smothered in marinara.

"I was really hoping for lasagna," Ele confesses in a low whisper as she cautiously places three green beans on her plate. Although I echo her sentiment, because lasagna is one of

those dishes that seems impossible to fuck up, I'm too preoccupied with scanning the room for Kasey to respond.

Ele and I sit across from each other at the end of a long
wooden dining table in the back of the room. We're the only
seniors here, and our presence sticks out like a sore thumb. By
comparison, the rest of the sorority members at dinner appear
to be sophomores living in the house. Most seniors live in
College Town, where there are restaurants aplenty, and under-
standably, have opted to eat elsewhere. Ele gags on a bite of a
green bean and covertly spits it out in her napkin.

"I can't," she states.

I push my plate away in agreement. My stomach is in no
mood to ingest food. We clear our untouched plates and head
into the living room, where the chapter meeting will be held.

Minutes tick by, and members filter into the room from
dinner in a slow procession. A few juniors I recognize have
arrived and sit across from us in the matching set of armchairs.
Everyone is on their phone, scrolling.

Younger, sophomore members sit cross-legged on the floor,
facing one direction. The front door opens, and a petite girl
with mousy-brown hair steps inside carrying a notebook. It
takes me a minute to place her, and then I remember she's in
the pledge class below mine.

I hinge forward to get Ele's attention. "What's her name?" I
mouth.

"Dana," Ele whispers back. She leans closer. "She's the
Secretary. She took over when Monroe disappeared."

"Oh," I say quietly.

I study Dana as she makes her way into the living room
from the foyer. If Monroe had a polar opposite, it would be
Dana. Monroe isn't particularly tall, and if I had to guess, I'd
put her somewhere around five and a half feet – same as me.
It's the way Monroe carries herself, the way her presence lights

up a room, that is of stark contrast to Dana, who I watch scuttle inside like a terrified kitten.

She meekly takes her place at the head of the room, but none of the members notice. Several uncomfortable seconds pass as poor Dana attempts to garner everyone's attention. The room is a cacophony of voices, and to no surprise, she fails, and my hangry frustration gets the best of me.

"Everyone shut up!" I shout. "Chapter is starting."

Ele cocks an eyebrow at me and I shrug. I'm annoyed. I have yet to spot Kasey, and I want to get this stupid meeting over with so I can find her, convince her to tell me everything she knows, and leave.

Roll call begins, and I slouch into the winged armchair. I'm never coming to one of these chapter meetings again. I've done my time, and besides, what will they do? Kick me out? I'd like to see them try.

I'm picking at my cuticles when a loud, demanding knock at the front door interrupts opening announcements. Dana looks around, uncertain of what to do. Another forceful knock rattles the room, and I spring to my feet, because Jesus Christ, someone has to open the goddamn door. I'm also five seconds away from falling asleep in my chair and need the distraction.

I swing open the door, and my eyes go wide.

"Good evening," one of the officers begins. "We were asked to do a wellness check on a Kasey Morelli. Does she live here?"

I fumble over my next words. "She lives here, but I don't know if she's here right now."

"May we come inside?"

My mind races. What's the protocol here? They're police, but do I just let them in? Are they going to try to search the place, and if so, don't they need a warrant?

I freeze, staring at them as I think through what to say.

Finally, I settle on, "Sure, come in. We're in the middle of our weekly chapter meeting."

The two officers step inside, scanning the multitude of pledge class pictures on the foyer walls, and the living room goes silent.

Finding my voice, I address the fifty gawking faces staring back at me.

"The officers are here to do a wellness check for Kasey. Has anyone seen her?"

Hushed whispers hot potato around the room, and I sense the two officers now standing on either side of me.

"Anyone?" I ask again.

"We got a call from her parents," one of the officers says, and I'm taken aback by how his voice fills the space. "Apparently, yesterday was her birthday, and they couldn't get in touch with her, which they said was unusual for their relationship. Then, when they couldn't reach her again today, they called us."

"None of us have seen her since Friday," a voice peeps from the back of the room.

"Since Friday?" the cop clarifies. "What time on Friday did you see her?"

"She was at dinner here on Friday," another voice says. "She said she was going out, but she hasn't been back since then."

"Did she say where she was headed?" the second cop asks.

A few girls answer with *'no'* and I am floored.

"She was at Sigma on Friday," I answer, hoping the girls in the back hear the brash, clipped tone of my response. "I ran into her there. I saw her briefly, and we only talked for a few seconds before she was pulled away by one of the guys in the fraternity."

I want to say more, like she appeared to be out of her mind and possibly on drugs, but I don't want to out her in front of the entire sorority or the police.

"Do you remember the name of this guy?"

"Yeah, Kieren Hunt." I swear I hear hushed whispers when I say his name.

"Does anyone have her number?" the shorter of the two officers asks. "Has anyone tried calling her?"

"We've texted her, but she hasn't responded," says a voice in the back. I crane my neck to figure out who this person is, but I can't see around the many clusters of heads all doing the same.

"Can you call her?" the officer asks.

Seconds pass before the girl confirms, "I'm calling her now."

Everyone waits with anticipation. "It went straight to voicemail."

Worried chatter balloons from the room, and I have to silence the crowd once again. I feel like Judge Judy up here.

"What else can we do to help?" I ask the officers.

"Just call us if anyone hears anything. We'll leave our cards. If she does show up, please tell her to call her parents immediately."

The officers turn to leave, and the room descends into chaos. I follow the two men as they head for the door.

"What happens next?" I ask. "Is she formally a missing person?"

One of the officers gives me an infuriatingly nonchalant shrug. "These situations happen all the time on college campuses. A girl goes on a bender with her boyfriend, doesn't call her parents for a few days, parents get spooked and they call us. Things usually resolved themselves after a week."

"A week?" I gasp. "But what if something awful did happen? What if she were taken?"

"If she doesn't show up in a week, and the parents still are unable to contact her, usually that's when we open an investigation."

"Look, last time you saw her, she was at a frat party with a boy, right?" the taller officer reasons like it's supposed to ease my paranoia. "She's probably still there with him, you know, as girls are known to do at these fraternities."

"No, I don't know," I snap. "What is that supposed to mean?"

The officers exchange knowing glances, and I have to actively tell myself not to rage-scream at them. "Just, call us if you hear anything, okay?"

I'm handed a set of business cards and then watch in utter dismay as the two cops leisurely walk down the stone path and back to their parked cruiser.

"Wait!" I call after them, bounding toward the sidewalk. "Are you going to stop by Sigma to see if she's there or investigate?"

The two cops give each other an odd look as if they're mocking my question.

"If we don't find her after a week and they open an investigation, we'll swing by," the taller officer says in a cocky, dismissive tone. "Now, if you don't mind miss, we'll be going."

Stupefied, I stand on the sidewalk as they pull away. What in the actual fuck was that? They literally implied Kasey, who was last seen at Sigma forty-eight hours ago, is probably still at Sigma, whoring it up, *'you know,'* like *'girls are known to do.'*

A girl is missing.

A girl is fucking missing!

My fingers shake as I pull my phone from my back pocket

to text Ele, because fuck that. If the cops aren't going to give a shit, then we're taking matters into our own hands, and all I need is a single excuse to burn that entire piece of shit fraternity to the goddamned ground.

12

MONROE

Seven Months Prior to Present Day,
Early February, Junior Year,
Sigma

"Puppy, I missed you," Kieren groans as he lowers himself beside me on the bed and nestles his face against the curve of my neck. "I didn't appreciate that you were too busy for me."

I huff at his inaccurate retelling of events. "Kieren, I wasn't the one who was too busy."

He licks up my neck, landing on that soft spot right below my earlobe, and sucks a kiss like he is a vampire ready to rip into my flesh. My body warms with desire as his lips trail my jawline.

"That's not how I remember it," he whispers playfully. "What do you have to say for yourself?"

I writhe under him, my oversized white button-down and

jeans feeling suddenly too hot. I want them off. I want that stiff erection of his currently grinding against my pelvis to push apart my walls.

Finally, I cave, knowing what he wants to hear. "I'm sorry," I whisper as his lips plant lingering kisses down my sternum while he effortlessly unbuttons my top. When the last button is undone, Kieren flings open my shirt and hovers above me.

"So fucking pretty," he rasps, admiring the soft lilac lace bralette that can barely contain my heaving chest. "It's a shame I'll have to punish you for ignoring me."

His fingers dip under the lace fabric covering my right breast and pitilessly twist the delicate skin of my nipple. I moan, arching into the pain.

"The problem with punishing you, Monroe, is that you like it too fucking much," he says, squeezing harder.

Cold sweat begins to prickle my skin. "Kieren, please."

"That's right, puppy. If you want me to show you mercy, you'll need to beg."

"Please, Kieren, ple..." My breath hitches as his warm mouth envelopes my aching nipple and his wet tongue laps soothing strokes against the throbbing bud.

He pulls back, releasing my breast. The soft lace now feels painfully rough as it moves back into position.

"Stand up and undress yourself."

I press myself upright and push off the bed. My already unbuttoned top slides off my shoulders with barely a nudge and pools around my feet. I pull open the top button of my jeans, then the next, then the next, as Kieren leans back on his elbows, watching me with a devilish grin. I slide my thong down my bare legs and then kick it to the side. Finally, I pull my bralette over my head, freeing my bound breasts, and let it fall from my fingers.

My heart races as I watch Kieren drink me in with a

ravenous hunger. I can feel my elevated pulse beating between my legs as I stand naked in front of him. The urge to crawl over his body and straddle his face becomes irrepressible. The beating at my center has turned into throbbing, and I don't know how much longer I can stand here before I drop to my knees and plunge my fingers into my pussy simply to feel a sliver of relief.

Having Kieren in my bed at the start of the semester helped to take the edge off, but it wasn't enough. Despite how I thought the night would go, I ended up becoming too paranoid to let him fuck me in my room at the sorority. The walls are ultrathin, and I feared my quiet moans would quickly divulge into primal screams that not even the densest of pillows could stifle. I could barely contain my volume when he sucked my clit and stretched me with two fingers. Penetrating my aching pussy with his cock would have resulted in me waking the entire sorority. He begged, but I held firm, offering him my mouth instead.

But fuck, I am desperate.

The nights I spent touching myself while riding my vibrator until the battery died did nothing to quench my need. I couldn't get myself there – not in the same way that Kieren can. I bought the thickest and most powerful dildo I could find and fucked it until my pussy went numb, only to give up in frustration.

I am desperate to feel myself spasm with a force powerful enough to drain my consciousness. I want aftershocks that quiver down my spine. I want to be soak-the-bed drenched. I want to feel that euphoric sensation of free-falling as I topple over the edge.

During the months he was gone, I chased his unnatural high that's proven impossible to recreate. I willingly took his drug, thinking he wouldn't fundamentally change me, only to find out that I'm now irrevocably and devastatingly ruined. I am positive no man will ever be able to compare, which is why looking elsewhere didn't cross my mind. How do you tell someone you like to be lightly tortured during sex – that pain and restriction and degradation get you off?

Maybe it stems from my less-than-ideal childhood, or maybe I'm just a masochist who fell in love with a sadist. I know Kieren will never love me like I foolishly hoped he would when we first met. Boys like him, with his wealthy upbringing and societal status, don't fall for broke, riff raff like me. He told me this once, although he pretends not to remember. I'll never be his wife or fiancée or even his girlfriend – at least not the kind he would take home to meet his parents. We are like Romeo and Juliet on a runaway train, destined for disaster.

So here I stand. Naked and silently begging. Prepared to offer him all of me, give him everything I am, in exchange for what I know will only amount to a splinter of him in return.

Kieren stands, drawn to my desperation like a moth to a flame. His broad hand wraps around my neck, forcing my gaze upward. Our eyes lock, and I watch the subtle widening of his pupils as his countenance shifts. A slow pressure builds against my windpipe. The left corner of his mouth quirks ever so slightly upward. The change would be imperceptible if it weren't for his eyes – eyes that now stare back at me, soulless, cruel, and ravenous— just like I want.

"Get on your knees, puppy, and beg."

The hand around my throat snaps to my shoulder, shoving me to the ground in half a heartbeat. I drop without a fight, colliding with the concrete floor like a sack of stones.

Seconds pass as I collect myself.

"Please Kieren." My voice is breathy, but resolute. I should have done better.

Kieren huffs a knowing laugh like his prey just stumbled right into his trap.

"Monroe, Monroe, Monroe, what are we going to do with you?" The tone of his voice is borderline deranged as he walks to the closet six paces behind me. Sounds of suitcases being unzipped fill me with both dread and need – a need that over-powers my better judgment as my fingers snake down my center and part my soaked pussy. I knew I was wet, but as soon as I feel my dripping arousal, a primal urge overtakes my brain and I sink two fingers inside my hot cunt.

A regrettable gasp slips from my lips as I hinge forward and ride my own fingers.

"What the fuck are you doing?" Kieren booms, catching me pleasuring myself. He crashes to his knees in front of me and rips my hand away from my core. I whimper, pleading, as he fists my wrist and examines my two outstretched fingers. Without warning, he yanks my hand to his mouth, wrapping his wet tongue around my index and middle fingers, and groans.

I'm frozen, transfixed, as Kieren's eyes flutter shut and he sucks like he can't help himself. My breath hitches when his eyelids fly open and he glares at me with unhinged vitriol, furious that I made him lose control.

"Goddammit!" he yells, flinging my hand away. It bounces limply against my torso.

"I'm... I'm sorry," I stammer. "Kieren, please, I'm sorry. I couldn't help it."

"You will be punished for such blatant disobedience. You don't get to come until I say you can come. Do you fucking understand me?"

My voice cracks when I try to speak.

"I thought I trained you better than this, but it seems you

need another lesson because you've forgotten how to behave. Isn't that right, Monroe?"

I nod.

"I asked you a fucking question. Do I need to repeat myself?"

"Yes," I yearn with agreement, desperate for him to do his worst. "Yes, I need another lesson. Please train me again. I want to be good. I want to be so good for you, Kieren."

The screech of a stepstool against the concrete floor makes me shiver, and then I hear them.

The chains.

He must have brought them here from his parents' house in Connecticut, because we didn't use them during our sophomore year when he shared a suite with Jace. I suppose now that he's president of Sigma and has this massive room all to himself, all bets are off.

I make the mistake of glancing up at the sound of metal links rattling through a loop in the ceiling. Quickly, I look away before I'm caught. Hanging chains sway in my periphery as Kieren lumbers down the stool and crouches in front of me. Leather cuffs are fitted snugly around my wrists and then hooked together by a carabiner clasp. Kieren tests the efficacy of the clip by forcefully pulling my wrists apart and then grins when it's clear I'd be unable to separate them on my own.

He reaches for one of the chains and then hooks a second carabiner through the last link before attaching it to my bound wrists.

"Open," he instructs, and I pop apart my lips.

Kieren positions a silicon ball gag in front of my mouth and shimmies on his knees to pull the straps tight around my face before securing the buckle at the back of my head. He stands and wastes no time removing his heather-grey T-shirt and jeans.

I look up at him from my subjugated position. Saliva fills my mouth at the sight of his strained erection. The memory of his taste when I sucked him dry a few weeks ago causes more saliva to build and drool shamelessly spills over my lower lip. He pushes down his boxer briefs and kicks them aside as he fists the base of his cock, positioning himself mere inches from my face. I inhale his heady scent as I visualize his thick cock breaching my entrance. My pussy throbs in response, desperate for his girth.

Before I can register the movement, he taps my cheek with the side of his cock, then reels it back and slaps me with its length. It doesn't hurt, but still I wince.

"As much as I want to fuck your mouth and spray your face with my cum," he rasps from above, "it seems I need to teach these deviant hands of yours a lesson."

He steps back, and I hear the pull of the chain through the metal loop. My hands rise, then arms, then, when the pull at my shoulder sockets begins to feel painful, I push to my feet.

I glance up at my arms overhead. A flicker of thought crosses my mind, and I wonder how long I can have my arms like this before they go completely numb.

"Oh, you know what?" Kieren asks rhetorically, although it's not like I could answer with a ball gag in my mouth. "I almost forgot your blindfold."

Soft silk fabric covers my eyes a second later, and the sensory deprivation makes my pussy ache.

Kieren's thumb brushes against my left nipple before rolling it between his thumb and forefinger with a level of restraint that can only mean the worst is yet to come.

A clipped moan bubbles up my throat a moment later when I feel the intense squeeze of the nipple clamp. It takes several labored breaths to ease into the pain. Somehow, once the second nipple clamp is in place and the pain is evenly distributed between my two breasts, the intensity is more tolerable. The nipple clamps start vibrating, and the sensation spiderwebs across my chest and down my abdomen.

"Oh God," I moan against the gag, although I'm sure the words sounded more like garbled cries.

Without warning, the vibration ratchets to the point of being unbearable, and I scream like a pig headed for slaughter. Kieren chuckles like a man possessed as the intensity returns to the original level. Tears prick the corners of my eyes as I heave through my nose.

"If you're going to beg for mercy, Monroe, you better make sure it's my name that leaves your lips."

I growl my displeasure against the gag.

"Oh, I'm just getting started, puppy," Kieren says with an unnerving huff of a laugh.

"Since you seem to think you can come without my permission, we're going to play a game." My body goes rigid when I hear the word *'game,'* because Kieren's definition of game usually revolves around his favorite theme of *'how much pain can Monroe's body take?'*

Fingers wrap around my left ankle. "Lift up your leg."

I do my best to follow his instructions without losing balance. With my wrists bound and pulled taught over my head, I can't topple to the floor, but I'd like to avoid awkwardly flapping around like a fish strung on a line. The sole of my foot connects with skin, and I visualize it propped on the top of Kieren's shoulder. The stretched position spreads my labia, and I feel the cool waft of air against my exposed pussy.

"Good girl," he praises, running the smooth palm of his hand up and down my calf in a slow, soothing motion. "Do you know what I see from this vantage point, Monroe?"

I could wager what I expect would be an accurate guess, but instead, I shake my head like a good submissive.

"I see your greedy, pink little pussy and it's soaked. It's begging to be fucked."

A stream of warm air flutters between my legs, and the scant stimulation is enough to elicit a quiver.

"Goddamn, your pussy is already swollen, Monroe. You were such a good girl to deny yourself while I was gone. Is my puppy ready to begin the game, or shall we give her more time?"

I'm unsure if he's expecting me to acknowledge this question or if he's having a one-sided conversation with himself again, but I nod my head regardless.

"The rules are simple."

A faint humming noise permeates the bedroom.

"You don't come until I say you can come."

His smooth thumb at my apex pulls my labia further apart.

"Because I'll know if you do," he says in an unhinged sing-song voice that's an octave higher than his usual pitch.

"Because I'll see it," he says, switching his voice to a guttural growl. A rough tug at my clit makes me whimper.

"And I'll smell it." Another tug.

"If one drop of cum leaves your tight cunt without my permission, you'll spend the entire night in a cage. Am I clear?"

I have no idea what he means by 'cage', but I nod vigorously as my entire body shakes.

The words "let's begin" are all the warning I get before my back arches on instinct at the firm sensation of a wand vibrating against my clit. A muffled cry bubbles up my throat because it feels like the vibration from the clamps and the vibration from the wand have joined forces, meeting deep within my core and are rumbling down my channel with the force of a thousand tidal waves.

It mercilessly pounds for a few seconds, then stops, and I'm left with an indescribable feeling of anguish, like my orgasm is stuck inside me, blocked by an invisible obstacle. My stomach cramps, and I wonder if this is the female equivalent of blue balls.

Again, three seconds of pounding followed by what feels like an eternity of agony. I plead against the gag.

"You're going to have to do better than that, puppy, if you want to come. Tell me, who owns you?"

I don't know why I withhold the answer I know he wants to hear.

"Who fucking owns you, Monroe?" he shouts, holding the wand millimeters below my clit. The flutter of pulsing air against my sensitive flesh is agonizing.

"You," I attempt to scream. Drool runs down my chin, but I don't care.

"Not fast enough, puppy," he scolds, pressing the wand true.

I crest, then stop. Crest, then stop. Each round of stimulation edges me closer and closer. Each time, Kieren repeats the question, "Who owns you?" Each time, I scream the answer he wants against the gag, tugging down on the wrist restraints even though I know it's fruitless. The denial is agonizing, and I feel like I might pass out. If it weren't for the blindfold, I'm convinced I would see bursts of black around the corners of my vision, like I do when I stand up too quickly because, of course, I've turned out to be a pain junkie who also has an iron deficiency.

Both my core and stomach scream for release, and just as I decide I'm going to give in to my orgasm during the next round, regardless of the consequences, the tension holding my wrists above my head disappears, and my elevated foot drops. I collapse against Kieren like I don't have a solid bone in my body.

His cool hands atop my molten skin roughly position me

chest-down, causing the nipple clamps to scrape against the hard floor. Blood rushes into my numb arms, now stretched in front of me. A forceful yank has my ass in the air, the clamp around my clit is removed, and before I can gather myself, the crown of Kieren's thick cock is at my entrance, slamming inside me a heartbeat later. Immediately on impact, I start to quiver.

His fast thrusts pummel me at a dizzying tempo. Algedonic pressure dances up my spine with each ram of his groin. "Don't you dare come, Monroe. Don't you fucking dare," he snarls like a fraying madman standing on the precipice of no return.

Fuck, he's going faster. Each thrust shakes my already swollen clit. Each slap of his balls threatens to send me over the edge. High-pitched screams that sound like a hyperventilating hyena chafe my throat raw. Oh fuck. *Fuck, fuck, fuck.*

An arm hooks around my waist, frenzied and rough, as I register the weight of his torso leaning into me. Slick fingers press firm against my clit, jostling with each drive of his hips to create the perfect rub of friction. My core winds into a torturous tremble, and I don't think I can control it anymore.

"Now, puppy!" Kieren yells, pinching my engorged clit with the force of a thousand clamps, knowing this last bit of pain will be my salvation. And my ruin.

Inexplicable pleasure crashes down my core like a launched rocket. I unleash a scream so visceral that spittle flies everywhere, and my voice gives out. My pussy clenches and pulses with a strength I can feel in my teeth. My contracting walls must feel like a vice because Kieren sounds like he can barely breathe. He stutters the word "fuck" and follows it with clipped, breathy pants as he collapses against me.

Only when he's completely drained do I feel Kieren pull out. I have the faint awareness that our combined releases run down my inner thighs, and the vibrating clamps are still attached to my nipples. My brain makes a mental note that my wrists remain bound, I'm covered in my own saliva, and I'm lying face down on a concrete floor with my ass in the air.

But then my mind pushes all that aside, compartmentalizing the pain, and I... just... float.

My body is weightless with ecstasy, untethered and set free by satiety. I am nowhere and everywhere all at once, and I never want this sensation of unadulterated, unholy bliss to end. The heaviness of life dissipates, and I remember why I first fell in love with Kieren, my uncut gem.

I remember us.

He set me free, even if he took part of my soul in the process. And now, I want to feel free once more. For him. For this. For us.

13
KIEREN

Seven Months Prior to Present Day,
Early February, Junior Year,
Sigma

Her nipples, still raw and puckered from the clamps, press against the side of my ribcage, and I have to actively resist the urge to roll her onto her back and suck one into my mouth. Getting Monroe cleaned up was a Herculean effort. Even after I removed the wrist restraints, ball gag, nipple clamps, and blindfold, I could not coax her off the floor. Her glassy eyes reminded me of my own during my ketamine days, sophomore year – seeing but not seeing at the same time. She had dissociated almost to the point of unconsciousness, and it made me so goddamn proud to know it was my dick that fucked her into oblivion.

It's difficult to describe the unbridled need I feel toward Monroe. From the moment I first laid eyes on her at the

Sigma return-to-campus barbecue our freshman year, I felt an uncontrollable need to own her. It was as if the Universe had planted her at that barbecue specifically for me to find. There she was, standing alone at the edge of the crowd, admiring the trees like a princess in a goddamn Renaissance painting.

Sometimes I forget how perfect she is for me. *I did forget.* Most men my age aren't actively practicing hardcore BDSM to the point of owning an entire arsenal of accoutrements. Whether it's intrinsic to my DNA or the product of having too much alone time as a teenager, I've always found the act of controlling someone's pleasure to be alluring. Once I got into high school, I began to dabble, although at first, finding willing participants was a challenge. But the more entrenched I became with wealthy Manhattan socialites, the more my pool broadened. Those raised in New York City seemed to mature more rapidly than the rest of us. A person who grew up in Manhattan has lived three lifetimes by the time he or she turns eighteen, and in my circles at least, that included sexual experiences. Even so, finding someone who is comfortable with experimentation and finding someone who enjoys pain play are two different quests. Submission is not enough. I want someone who needs this kind of stimulation to find release, because that means they need me.

The first time I pinched Monroe's clit and felt her spasm around my fingers, unable to control herself, I knew I had found my diamond in the rough. She was so innocent and curious when we were freshmen, ripe for the picking. I claimed her. I trained her to perform to my liking. I molded her into the deviant pain slut she is today, and everything was so fucking perfect until I lost my mind toward the end of our sophomore year, which, admittedly, I knew at some point would happen. You can't join the most notorious and powerful fraternity on the fucking planet and not expect to lose yourself in the process.

But by then, I had already allowed her into my world. Letting her go was never an option. Mine until the bitter end, if only the bitter end weren't right around the corner. I can't marry her. I can't even date someone like her in the eyes of my father. Never once while I was home, fixing my father's mess, did I mention Monroe, and it infuriates me that I was bequeathed such an impeccable gift, only to find out that I couldn't keep her.

Now her body is curled against mine, asleep, and I can't quiet the rage festering in my mind. This situation Monroe and I have will get bleaker by the day, although I don't think she's aware. How could she be? I haven't and will never tell her the truth, because if I did, she would abandon me again, and I'm far too ensnared by my obsession with her to let that happen.

Perhaps this obsession should be worrisome, but the problem is, I can't find it in me to care. Monroe was put on this earth *for me*. The way I see it, she is rightfully mine, even if I know there is no future for us after graduation.

But the thought of someone else owning what's mine, fucking her, claiming her, filling her pussy with their cum... I can't. The thought makes me want to rip my fucking hair out. I want to cage her for an eternity, locked away from the rest of the world. I want to stroke her silky blonde hair, glide my fingers across her smooth, supple skin, tilt her chin upward so her pleading ocean blue eyes, brimming with unconditional love, can find mine while she kneels obediently at my feet.

My perfect pet.

Mine.

She's mine, and no one gets to have her other than me.

And herein lies the problem.

What to do?

We graduate in sixteen months, a thought that should feel comforting. Plenty of time to own her, to fuck her, to tie her up and do the most depraved things to her body until she collapses in a pool of her own drool like she did today. And goddamn. Sometimes, I convince myself I need this woman like I need air. I need her so badly, I want to scream. I want to rage. Calling her mine drives me to madness, and I fucking love every second of her insatiable high. I want to inject her into my fucking veins like heroin, because that's what she is to me, and that truth is a secret I'll take to the grave.

I can't graduate and simply end things with her – watch her walk off into the sunset, knowing she'll eventually end up with someone else.

No.

But I don't know what to do.

Monroe doesn't know it yet, but she plays an important part in my plan for Sigma Little Sisters. She's the ultimate status symbol given her position as president of Delta Gamma, the perfect endorsement to have by my side. It might take convincing, but she'll partake in the process. Of course, this means I'll have to tell her about said plan. Well, not all of it – only the parts she needs to know. She's already asked about my grandfather's ring so many times that it's starting to get fucking annoying, so these scraps of information should satiate her curiosity.

I just have to make it through the next four months, get to summer break, then I'll be able to think clearly about what to do with Monroe without the noise of my father and this nefarious X character breathing down my fucking neck. If anyone can pull this off, it's me. I was made to play this part, and as long as Monroe complies, we'll be the picture-perfect example.

The king and his queen, leading the sheep to slaughter.

14
GABI

"This is an exceptionally bad idea, Gabi. In fact, this might be the worst idea you've ever had," Ele barks as I swing open the door to our apartment.

"Oh my God, can you keep it down?" Viv groans from the couch where she lies with a washcloth and cold compress over her eyes.

"Sorry," Ele says in a hushed shout.

"Let's go to my room," I say to Ele, rolling my eyes and grabbing her hand.

"No, I want to hear," Viv groans again like she's dying, although I can't imagine the pain of a migraine is pleasant. "Just stop screaming," Viv adds.

"I wasn't screaming," Ele protests. "I was simply talking with emphasis because *Gabi* wants to break into fucking Sigma and get herself killed."

"Okay, that's a bit dramatic, don't you think?" I scoff. "Besides, they won't catch me. I'll be in and out like a thief in the night."

"Right. Until they do catch you and throw you in their basement with the other girls you claim to be down there."

"Sigma's keeping girls in their basement?" Viv croaks.

"I don't know," I admit. "But the cops made an appearance at chapter tonight looking for Kasey, because apparently, Kasey is missing now, too. Although the cops could not give two shits. They only came because they got a call from Kasey's parents."

"Whoa, slow down," Viv says. "Kasey is missing, and the cops are looking for her?"

"Kasey didn't answer the phone this weekend when her parents tried to call her, so they called the police, who came to DG tonight looking for her. No one has seen her since the Sigma party on Friday. But when I told the cops this, and they realized she was at a frat party with a guy two days ago, they immediately brushed aside any concern. In fact, they basically implied Kasey is just whoring it up at Sigma and ignoring her parents, you know, '*like girls do*,'" I say, using air quotes.

"Literally, this country does not give a shit about women," Ele grumbles from the chair at the base of the couch.

"It's not just this country," Viv pipes in, her corpse-like position unfaltering.

"Side note, did we ever get this couch cleaned after the exchange students moved out?" Ele asks.

I huff a clipped laugh. "What do you think?"

"My hair co-mingling with random bodily fluids is not what I want to think about right now," Viv groans. "Can you stick with the story and go back to the part where Gabi thinks it's a good idea to break into Sigma?"

"I never said it was a good idea! I said we should go there

to see if Kasey is indeed still inside. I mean, who knows? What if they are keeping girls in their basement? Would it be that much of a stretch given the psychopath who currently resides as Sigma's president? What if Monroe is in there? What if she's been in there the entire time, held captive? What if the other girls who went missing are still in there? We have to see! We know they are doing some shady shit, and we have to see with our own eyes what the fuck is going on!"

"No, see, this is where you lose me, because I never agreed to this, and you keep saying '*we*' as if stress testing your conspiracy theory is some group project," Ele complains. "I'm not setting foot inside that place. Not after what happened to you. Are you crazy? Do you not remember getting thrown out by your ex-boyfriend a mere two days ago?"

"Didn't you also say Jace warned you not to come back?" Viv mumbles.

"I don't give a fuck what that roid-head said. Since when do we take orders from men, especially shitty men who are known to be *liars*?" I ask through gritted teeth.

"Okay, let's say we do agree to go along with this insanity. What's the plan?" Ele asks.

"Sneak in through a window," I say as if that part of the plan should be obvious.

Ele grunts a frustrated sigh. "Great plan, Sherlock. Fool-proof. And then what?"

I press my lips together and squeeze my eyes closed, because I don't fucking know. I'm not a goddamn burglar.

"Okay," I say with resolve, resetting the tone of the conversation. "We find an unlocked window on the first floor."

"But what if there isn't one?"

"That place has like a bazillion windows. One of them will be unlocked. I sneak in around three or four in the morning during a weeknight, right? Because chances are, everyone is asleep at that time."

"You're forgetting thirty-some people live there," Viv croaks.

"Sure. Maybe some of them keep odd hours, but they probably are up in their rooms, not on the first floor. I sneak in and make my way down to the basement. All I need to confirm is whether or not their basement has been turned into a freak petting zoo of missing girls, and then I'll get out."

"Even if Kasey and Monroe are still at Sigma, why do you assume they'd be in the basement? What are you expecting to find, like a pod farm from a sci-fi movie?" Ele challenges.

"I... I don't know!" I stammer in frustration. "Do either of you have any better ideas? We can't just sit around and do nothing! The cops obviously aren't going to do shit. Come on, we saw Kasey there on Friday night, and she looked loopy as fuck! She told us she was scared! We all saw Mad Max Kieren basically strong-arm Kasey away while losing his shit over the two-minute conversation we managed to have with her. It was like he was worried she'd tell us something he didn't want us to know. Shit is not okay!"

I take a breath to steady myself. "Two women, well, four if you count Kasey and Monroe, have gone missing at Dornell this year alone. And I know this is a very stressful university, and I know the statistics are bad for incidents where students take their own lives, but I can't shake this gut feeling that these disappearances are connected. This ties back to Sigma in some way. I know it does. These young girls, they remind me of my sisters. If one of them went missing, and the University and law enforcement ruled it a suicide without proof of a body, I wouldn't be able to sleep at night. I would chase every lead or crazy conspiracy theory I could find. Call me insane, but I wouldn't be able to live with myself."

Silence permeates our apartment. I slump down into my chair and fight back tears of hopelessness.

Ele exhales a long sigh. "Fuck, well, I can't believe I'm asking this but, when do we do this?"

My eyes flick up to hers with disbelief.

"I'll go too. Ele can be the getaway driver. I'll be the look-out," Viv agrees.

My wide smile bounces between them, and I open my mouth to speak, but the words catch in my throat. I suck my bottom lip between my teeth and swallow down the emotional lump threatening to undo my conviction.

"Thank you," I manage, but it's not what I wanted to say. It's not what I would have said if it were her. Because I would never have to convince Monroe. Never would I feel the need to plead my case. She would already be downstairs, heading for her car, going to fill up the gas tank, and telling me, *'Ride or die, Gabi. Ride or fucking die.'*

15

MONROE

"I've already told you a thousand times, Monroe. It's an initiation."

Kieren threads a string of what looks like a black leather bikini top under my breasts. The material digs into my ribcage as he ties the bottom ends together along the middle of my back. Next, he tightly cinches the top two strings around the nape of my neck. I frown when I look down at the leather triangles, which are barely big enough to cover my nipples.

I huff in frustration. "But you haven't told me what exactly happens at this initiation, and now you're dressing me in BDSM lingerie."

"I'm dressing you this way because all the Little Sisters

getting initiated will be in their bras and underwear, and it would be weird, not to mention prohibited by the Sigma initiation rules, if you were fully clothed."

"What initiation rules? Who made up these rules, and why only a bra and underwear?"

"Jesus Christ, Monroe. I fucking told you. Anyone initiated must bear and offer their whole and true selves to the Brotherhood, and such purity of form cannot be tainted or obstructed in any way, including by material coverings. I didn't make the rules. The rules are outlined in the Sigma Charter, which was written centuries ago by Sigma's founding members. I'm sure your sorority did something similar when you initiated new pledges."

"I guess, but it was different. It was a born-again thing, and everyone wore white. And it was all women. What does '*bear and offer*' mean?" I ask, recalling words from his lecture.

"Use your imagination," he answers gruffly.

I huff a grumble at his lack of information.

Kieren drops to his knees and unbuttons my jeans, pulling them and my underwear down my legs as he helps me step out one foot at a time.

"Should I be nervous?"

"You'll be with me the entire time, so no."

Kieren cups his hands around my backside, pulling me into him. He plants a lingering kiss below my pubic bone, inhaling my scent.

"Fuck, I wish there was time to eat this pussy before the Ceremony." His warm breath caresses my center. "Maybe just a taste," he growls. My breath hitches as his wet tongue parts my labia and works broad strokes against my clit. Restrained sucks turn hungry and I worry I'll lose my balance. The intimacy ignites something feral within my bones, and I fist his hair, yanking him closer so I can grind my clit against his face. Just as I feel the build of my orgasm, he shoves me away as if I've done something wrong.

"Kieren," I plead through gritted teeth.

"Don't you ever grab me like that again, Monroe. Don't you ever undermine my control. You know better."

I swallow my defeat and avert my eyes as he slips a black leather G-string thong over my feet. I study him as he pulls it up my legs and into place. Despite the dimly lit bedroom, his dark eyes glimmer with ferocity. The air around him feels different – charged, in a way – like an electrical current crackling with heat. It's not excitement or anxious energy I sense, but I can't put my finger on it either.

He wraps a black lace skirt around the curve of my waist, although skirt is a generous description for this scrap of fabric, and ties the strings together in a bow. The lace pattern is near transparent, leaving nothing to the imagination.

"Almost ready," he comments.

I turn to look at myself in the full-length mirror propped against the wall, and gawk with a mix of horror and amusement. Pivoting on the balls of my feet, I see my backside is on full display save for three shoestrings of clothing, the lace wrap skirt doing nothing to conceal my naked form. Discomfort bubbles in my throat, and anxiety rips through my stomach.

"Kieren, I don't like this. I don't want to…"

"You don't want to what?" Kieren barks, standing behind me now with a leather mask in his hand. "If you're going to leave me again, then fucking leave now, Monroe. You want to leave me on the most important day of my life, then go! Go now. Because there is no turning back after you're initiated. Betrayal and defection are punishable by death. If you run after tonight, I'll be forced to track you down, and I'll have to fucking kill you."

"Why are you being so dramatic?" I scoff, holding his gaze in the mirror.

"Because this is dramatic," he answers, stepping between me and the mirror. "This is a big fucking deal for me, Monroe. I've been working toward this moment for three years. For my entire life, really. I need you to take this seriously. You're the president of the most prestigious sorority on campus. These freshmen women know you and look up to you. Some of them are probably in your sorority. I need you by my side. Please."

Kieren's pleas pull at my heartstrings. I've already abandoned him once. I don't want to let him down again.

I nod my complicity.

"Thank you," he says softly, followed by a kiss on my forehead. Rarely is Kieren ever this vulnerable, and it makes me ache for more. What I wouldn't give to be loved by him. Truly loved. I know I would bleed myself dry if it meant I could earn this man's genuine affection, and that honesty terrifies me. Despite all he's put me through, I'm afraid I've fallen in love with him again.

I don't know why I crave him. It's more than physical. It's an overwhelming need to have his approval, his warmth, his acceptance, or otherwise, I feel like I am nothing. I am worthless. Discarded. Unwanted and unloved.

I feel like I am no one.

And I have always been no one.

I fight back tears because this isn't the time. Turning to face myself in the mirror, Kieren lifts the mask, pulling it tight against my face as he ties the leather strings behind my head. I take in my reflection. The mask covers the top half of my face with a singular, thick black strap that originates at my forehead and runs along the middle part of my hair. It's sturdy, not like a cheap masquerade mask you see people wear during Halloween. The grommet details and Sigma symbol atop the third eye give it an edge, but the detail that stands out the most are the pointed, dog-like ears.

"It's beautiful," Kieren breathes in admiration, standing at my back with his arms wrapped around my chest.

"I guess?" I agree warily.

"Or maybe it's just beautiful on you. I had it custom-made."

My brows furrow as I can't help but mentally calculate the time it might take to commission such a piece. Months? Which means Kieren has been planning this for...

"I'm so lucky you're mine," Kieren rasps, interrupting my thoughts. He turns me around by the shoulders and takes in my finished appearance.

"Fuck," he growls, raking his eyes up my exposed torso and onto my breasts. "So goddamn perfect."

"Kieren," I hear a male voice call from outside his door. "You ready?"

"Five minutes," Kieren bellows back.

His hands leave my shoulders and I take another look at myself in the mirror as Kieren disappears into his walk-in closet. I'm about to make a comment about my lack of footwear when I see him emerge, and I freeze.

My entire body goes rigid.

Kieren has on black, low-slung dress pants that accentuate the V-shape of his abdomen, a matte black, hooded robe currently open in the front exposing his swirls of tattoos, and a mask that looks like it was resurrected from the pits of hell.

My eyes immediately flick to his grandfather's bulbous gold ring on his pinky, and then back up to his gold mask in terror. Frankly, I wonder if I'm hallucinating because it looks like the ring and mask are personifications of Kieren himself instead of ceremonial accessories.

"Kieren?" I ask quietly. Did I just become the main character in a horror movie?

The gold mask with whirls of ancient lettering and gold horns triggers thoughts of a demon cow – like the bulls I would see in pastures back in Ohio. The mask tilts down and cocks to the side.

"Do I scare you, Monroe?" he asks, and I shudder because I swear, even his voice sounds different. If this were Halloween and our outfits were meant to be costumes, I would marvel at his demonic transformation. But it's not Halloween. And these aren't costumes.

Suddenly, my mouth is too dry to swallow. Speaking is too terrifying, because it dawns on me that *I'm in a fucking cult.*

My eyes flick to his bedroom door, and his hand shoots to my wrist a second later.

"Too late," he says with a low chuckle.

A hand dips into his pocket, and he pulls out a pill.

"What is that?" I stammer.

"Take it."

I shake my head, and try to twist my wrist free, but he's too fast. His hand snaps to my jaw and squeezes.

"Open," he commands.

"No," I say through clenched teeth. "Tell me what it is first."

"Molly. Just a small dose. It'll take the edge off."

My eyes plead with the mask in front of me. "Are you lying?"

"No. I promise you Monroe. You're supposed to take enhancements at these Ceremonies. It's even written in Sigma's Charter. You'll enjoy the festivities more, trust me."

I'd really like to get my hands on this so-called Charter. What the fuck else is in there, anyway? Demon worshipping?

I sigh a loud breath of surrender. "Okay," I huff with resignation and open my mouth. He places the pill gently on my tongue and holds my jaw closed until I swallow.

"Show me," he demands, squeezing my jaw open. I timidly stick out my tongue as proof.

"Good girl. Now let's go."

16

MONROE

Seven Months Prior to Present Day,
The February Full Moon Ceremony,
Sigma

Nothing could have prepared me.

I follow Kieren through the eerily quiet halls of Sigma. His fingers intertwine with mine with a tightness that feels both possessive and protective. My heart pounds in my chest as we weave through the maze of corridors and down flights of stairs until we finally reach the dimly lit stairwell that leads to the basement. Fear churns in my stomach. We descend the steps and halt at the closed door. A downdraft of frigid air snakes over my skin, and I visibly start shaking. I bite my lower lip to steady my chattering teeth, but it's useless.

Kieren raps a specific sequence of knocks against the heavy wood door, and it swings open. Warm air immediately billows into the stairwell, and for a fleeting moment, I have the stupid notion that all will be okay.

We step into the basement, and my stomach drops.

Maroon floods the space: in the drapes that hang on the walls, the color of the floor, the strange furniture, and the light illuminating the room.

Everywhere I look is doused in blood red.

Kieren strides toward an elevated stage where a singular chair is placed. No, not a chair. A throne. A gold and black ornate throne carved with ancient lettering and one large Sigma symbol in the center. It's otherworldly.

Kieren easily scales the elevated platform in one step, turns, and hinges from the waist to lift me up.

"Kneel," he commands and points to the space beside the throne. "Here."

I should refuse. I should tell him to go fuck himself, but in this moment, my better judgement gives way to fear and I drop, kneeling beside the throne of my keeper. My eyes dart around the room as Kieren lowers himself onto the seat, assuming his position of power. Men, I hadn't initially noticed, stand at attention around the rim of the room. All wear black pants and no shirt. All have on the same black demon animal mask covering the top half of their face emblazoned with a gold Sigma symbol in the middle of the forehead. I squint, attempting to focus. It must be a horned goat or sheep. I realize dark maroon curtains hang from different spots in the ceiling, partitioning off chambers and private pockets within the large room. A soft noise, maybe music of some kind, plays in the background, and I find the sound strangely comforting.

"Bring in the Sinners," Kieren booms. His voice cuts through the stagnant air, and five seconds later, the basement door creaks open.

A woman, naked save for her baby-blue lace bra and

matching panties, stands in the doorway with a black cloth bag over her head. Black leather cuffs bind her wrists together in front of her. A masked man grips her arm and carefully guides her forward. My nails unknowingly dig into the skin of my thighs as I watch woman after woman, all dressed the same, all with bags over their heads, being led inside the basement.

What the actual fuck?

One after another, the procession walks in a straight line. I count at least fifteen. Maybe more. They are positioned shoulder-to-shoulder, facing Kieren. Once the last woman is brought in and properly stationed, the basement door shuts.

"Kneel," Kieren commands.

The women awkwardly get down on their knees.

"Nominating Sigmas, step forward."

Masked demon goat men push off the walls.

"Take your position behind your Sinner."

Masked men filter behind the rows of women until the ratio is one to one.

"Remove the sight restraints," Kieren commands.

In a smooth, cohesive motion, the bags are removed.

I try to study each woman's face, but it's difficult to discern identities because each wears a black lace eye mask. The lace pattern is not dense enough to limit their sight, but sufficiently gauzy to create a haze, much like the pattern of my tiny lace skirt.

As I look down the line, expecting to see expressions of fear or panic, I'm surprised to find a mix of grins, smirks, and even a few closed-mouth giggles. I don't know what these women have been told about the initiation Ceremony. Kieren has described it as a little sister's program, and that it's considered an honor, but I've also heard him call it different things. He's called it Sigma Little Sisters, which sounds innocuous, but he also keeps referring to the women as *'Sinners.'* Yet, as I continue to scan their faces, no one seems frightened. In fact, some fight to stop themselves from bursting into laughter.

What the fuck is going on here? Coming from someone who is usually the most gullible person in the room, I'm fucking terrified. Is it the drugs? Did they also take molly? And if so, why the fuck isn't mine working?

The strange background noise stops, and the room goes silent.

Kieren stands.

"Sinners," he booms, addressing the women. His voice is stern and unwavering.

"You are the selected few, brought here today by the hands of the Sigma brothers who deem you worthy. Tonight, you shall become part of something bigger. Tonight, you shall become part of Sigma's legacy. Tonight, you shall be taught our traditions – traditions we have fought to keep secret. Secrets, which if shared, could put the Sigma Brotherhood at risk."

"Sinners, I ask you, do you present yourselves true, and do you swear that you are not here with ill intent?"

"We swear."

I blink my surprise at the sound of unanimous female voices who answer without hesitation or smidgen of trepidation.

"Do you swear yourselves to the Brotherhood? To come when called upon? To serve our Sigma brothers?"

"We swear."

"Do you swear to withhold yourself from relations outside of the Brotherhood? To abstain from carnal desires with non-members? Do you swear to offer yourselves fully to the Brotherhood, mind, body, and soul?"

"We swear."

"And lastly, do you swear your loyalty? Do you swear to

keep our secrets? To never speak of what happens within these walls of Sigma to anyone, not friends, not family, not your closest confidants?"

"We swear."

"Repeat after me: I swear my soul to Sigma."

"I swear my soul to Sigma."

This time, it's not just the women who repeat the chant, but the men too. I'm unsure if I'm meant to do so as well, but I don't move my lips. Instead, I bow my head, praying my disobedience goes unnoticed.

"The spilling of Sigma's secrets is punishable by death."

"The spilling of Sigma's secrets is punishable by death."

"A death which I will gladly accept should I prove disloyal."

"A death which I will gladly accept should I prove disloyal."

"Should I be called upon in the name of Moloch, I offer my soul as sacrifice."

"Should I be called upon in the name of Moloch, I offer my soul as sacrifice."

My lips quiver, my hands have gone clammy because what in the actual cult have I unknowingly joined? Not a single peep of dissent.

"Congratulations, initiates, for you are no longer Sinners in the eyes of Sigma, and later tonight, after you receive your brand, you shall from now on be known as Sigma Little Sisters, binding your soul to the Brotherhood."

Kieren pauses and then shouts, "Let the Ceremony begin!"

Trap music fills the space, a jarring contrast to Kieren's broadcast. Women are helped to their feet. Wrists are unhooked, but the cuffs remain, as do the lace masks. Men and women mingle, some lounge on furniture around the room, and some sit on pillows strewn across the floor. Cups begin circulating with what I assume is alcohol. I make the mistake of glancing to my right and see a masked brother standing against the wall while a woman kneels at his feet. Another masked brother kneels behind the woman, stroking the woman's ribcage as she unzips the standing man's pants. My eyes flare wide when I see his cock spring free. The woman grasps the base of his shaft while she licks and sucks at his tip. The man's head tilts backward, and I can hear his moans even from where I'm stationed. The man kneeling behind the woman now fondles her breast with one hand and fingers her pussy with the other. She rocks into his fingers, releasing moans of her own, as she deep-throats the cock in her mouth.

Heat spears my core at the sight, but I remain kneeling because, honestly, I don't know what else to do. My initial shock has subsided, and now I'm flooded with self-consciousness. I'm a voyeur watching an orgy unfold, and I have to mentally shoo away my traitorous fingers every few seconds because they keep drifting toward my center.

"Puppy," Kieren says, keeping his voice at a volume only I can hear. "Come sit on my lap."

My body feels fuzzy as I stand. My legs tingle with dissipating numbness.

I sit at an angle as Kieren wraps his arms around my waist, and I lean into him, fighting the urge to curl against his chest like a child. His dress pants are tented with the beginnings of an erection, and I have an overwhelming urge to unzip them. His right hand slides effortlessly under the leather triangle of my bra, and he begins to knead my right breast, stroking and squeezing and twisting my nipple between his fingers. I arch into the heightened stimulation and almost don't notice his other hand pushing past the elastic band of the thong. Thick fingers tease at my clit before dipping inside.

"You're soaked, puppy." The first two pumps of his fingers are reserved, but that doesn't last. I writhe against him as he buries his fingers to the knuckle.

"You're so fucking turned on by this, aren't you?"

His right hand greedily slides across my chest, and in the process, exposes both breasts. The triangle top might as well be on the floor, but I suppose that was the point.

"Turn around and fuck me," he growls through his mask, removing his fingers from my pussy. The unexpected and immediate absence of pressure almost brings me to tears.

A momentary flicker of hesitation passes through my consciousness. Am I really doing this? I guess so.

I climb around to face him and shamelessly tear his zipper apart. It takes effort to pull his boxer briefs over his fully erect penis, but at last, I have him freed. Using the head of his cock, I push my thong aside and once it's aligned with my entrance, I sink down on his length, and goddamn... nothing has ever felt so good. I pant unabashedly as I grind myself against him until I feel the firm resistance of his pubic bone against my clit. The teeth of the zipper scratch the insides of my thighs in a way that feels strangely good. If I could feel my quads, which I can't, I'm sure they would be on fire with the amount of bouncing I'm doing.

Is this why people caution against having sex on ecstasy – because nothing will ever feel as euphoric again? I don't even have the benefit of the clamps or our usual pain play to heighten my pleasure. But in this moment, I don't need them. I want to savor this feeling. I want to remember how good the veins of his dick feel as they glide against my walls, because I can fucking feel each and every one of them. The overwhelming urge to cry surges behind my eyes, and more than anything else, I need to kiss him.

I can't bear to look at the sight of Kieren's demonic mask. It feels wrong. I try to lift it, but he shakes his head.

"Please kiss me. Please." My words sound more like a sob than a beg.

"Please," I ask again. I hear my voice growing desperate as if I'm having an out-of-body experience, and I physically feel my heart start to break. I might have started crying. I don't know. But as soon as I see Kieren slide his mask back, exposing the bottom half of his face, my lips crash against his. I kiss him with more hunger and desire than I've ever felt before. I cup his face as best I can despite the interference from both our masks, and relish in the heat of his skin, damp and sticky with sweat. The pad of my thumb skims over his slim silver nose ring and brushes along the ridge of his cheekbone. I want to memorize the feel of his face in this moment. His tongue fills my mouth, and this taste alone could satiate me for a thousand years. The swirl of bodies around us blurs until it's only me and Kieren, cocooned in a vortex of blood red clouds, and I crest with the beginnings of an orgasm.

I mean to tell Kieren that I'm going to come, but when I open my mouth, something completely different tumbles out.

"I love you."

My core tightens, and my orgasm builds to that sinfully delicious tipping point of inexplicable pleasure. I grind against him, harder and harder, reaching for his hand, fumbling with his fingers, pressing two firm against my clit as the room spins faster.

Nerve endings quiver from my clit back to my entrance. The shake of my orgasm builds with momentum and intensity deep within my core, my breath catches in my throat, and then that blissful feeling of descending release sends me over the edge. "I love you," I cry out, unable to control myself as my pussy pulses with sweet relief. Kieren's cock gushes hot cum inside me a second later, and slowly, once the chaos around me settles, I come to a stop. A genuine smile spreads across my face as I plant soft pecks against his lips. I've never thought myself the type to enjoy sex in public, and yet I've never felt so liberated.

"I love you Kieren," I whisper against his skin, my mind still effervescent with elation.

But he doesn't say it back.

Seconds pass, and he doesn't say it back.

A sobering tightness constricts in my chest. My palms are still pressed against his cheeks. His flaccid cock twitches inside me, expelling the last drops of his release. Cum leaks from my pussy, soaking through my thong. Confused and dizzy, I pull back to look at him, the expressionless, bottom half of his face is all I can see. His lips are pressed together in finite resolve, and it occurs to me... He's not going to say it.

The beginnings of a smirk tug at one corner of his mouth. I watch, frozen, as his hand lifts to pull his mask back in place. But, he pauses. His mouth opens to speak, and each beat of my heart thunders in my ears.

"I know," he says.

And with those two words, that beating, foolish heart of mine shatters.

17
GABI

Present Day

"Viv, turn that light off! Someone might see us," I scold.

"Seriously Viv, it's Saturday night. You don't need to do homework right now," Ele agrees.

Viv huffs her annoyance. "We've been here five nights already, and nothing has happened! I don't know why we had to come back after the first night, when you didn't find anything. You'd think breaking and entering one time was enough. Now you're just asking to get caught!"

"I told you Viv, something felt very off in that house. There were zero signs of life, and the one room I needed to scope out was locked."

"It was also three in the morning on a Tuesday," Viv argues.

"Yeah, but why have your basement locked?" Ele debates. "The basement at DG isn't locked."

"Maybe they have expensive DJ equipment down there they don't want stolen," Viv suggests.

"Viv, whose side are you on?" I snap.

"I'm sorry, I'm just tired! And completely behind on class-work. Also, why are you giving me a hard time about my minuscule reading light? Do you see that full moon?"

I glance up at the saucer of brilliant light and have to admit Viv is right. The road in front of us is illuminated with silver moonlight, which is both helpful for our mission and harmful.

I sigh a grumble. "You didn't need to come tonight," I remind her.

"Oh sure, leave me behind to miss all the action."

"Reconnaissance isn't for the weak of heart, Viv. You can't have it both ways. Besides, Adrianna said that Kasey was gone every weekend, so maybe that's when whatever messed up shit they're doing at Sigma goes down."

"Nothing happened last night," Viv reminds us.

"Does Friday night count as a weekend, though?" Ele ponders, bringing a pair of binoculars up to her eyes. "I don't know. One could argue either way."

"Are there any more snacks?" Viv asks.

"Some Takis," I offer.

"Not in the mood," Viv grumbles. "Can we all agree that if nothing happens in the next hour, we'll go for a snack run? I could kill for a bag of Nerds Gummy Clusters right now."

"Yes, I second this motion," Ele adds.

Sighing, I lower my pair of binoculars. Not a single car has driven into or out of Sigma tonight, which feels odd for a Saturday. Shouldn't there be a caravan of people coming and going? It doesn't make sense, but then again, it's been like this every night of the week. Don't these guys need to go to study groups or the library, at least? Does no one do late-night munchie runs anymore, or stumble home drunk at two a.m.?

"Fuck it, let's go get snacks now. I'm hungry," I concede.

"Now you're talking," Ele grins. She rummages around the two front cupholders. "Where the hell are my keys? They have to be here somewhere. Ah, found them. Okay, let's..."

"Whoa, hold on!" I jump. "Headlights!"

The three of us crouch down on instinct as high beams emerge from the back parking lot and jostle down the driveway.

"They're leaving!" Viv whispers loudly.

"Whose car is that?" Ele asks as she peeks over the dashboard at the car now turning onto the street. "What college kid drives a big ass black SUV?"

"You forget they're all rich," Viv says.

"I know, my point exactly! Rich kids get driven around in black SUVs. They don't drive them. Should we follow it?" Ele asks.

"You two follow it," I whisper. "I'm going to stay and try to sneak in again. "

"No, Gabi. Enough with the suicide mission," Ele hisses, but my hand is already on the door handle. I gently open the car door and slide out. "Follow it!" I whisper-shout. "Hurry, before it gets too far away!"

I quietly shut the door before I change my mind, and slink around the car with cat-like movements. The brush alongside the road is thick enough to provide sufficient cover as I cut a wide path around Sigma house. Next comes the most treacherous part. A stretch of grass stands between me and the hedges planted along the house's perimeter. Even with my all-black femme fatale outfit, it's light enough outside, thanks to the full moon, to see a human-sized figure darting across the lawn.

The decorative gables and Gothic spires cast a patchwork of moonlit shadows ahead. I study the windows facing me for signs of movement, and when I see none, I bolt. Small branches snag the fabric of my black athletic zip-up as I force my way through the five-foot-tall hedge. Sharp twigs scrape the exposed skin of my hands and face. Some snap noisily apart as I continue to push past. The sound is loud enough to raise concerns, but I pray it gives off more of a medium-to-large animal foraging for food vibe than a human burglar.

Once I make it to the back of the hedge, I press my front torso flat against the exterior stone wall. I shuffle sideways from window to window. Unkempt branches dart out every few feet like barbs. No windows on the west-facing side of the house are even the slightest bit ajar, which means I have to continue the process on the south-facing side that borders both the back yard and the parking area. I slither around the south-west corner. The sound of gravel churning under tires fills the night air seconds before headlights come into view.

Sharp sticks rip at my shirt as I drop into a crouch. The hedge is thick with leaves, making it impossible to see, so I force my way inward until I have a clear vantage point. I try not to think about the millions of spiders and bugs crawling on me, likely readying an attack against the invader who smashed their home like a wrecking ball.

The slender porch in the back of Sigma house is brightly lit with porch lights. From where I'm crouched, the elevated porch obstructs my view of the parking lot, but I have a perfect side view of the porch steps.

"What the fuck?" I catch myself whispering aloud.

Figures approach, wearing long black cloaks and full-face black masks with tall... horns? I squint to get a better look, but details are hard to see in the dark. What in the satanic ritual shit is this? My pulse skyrockets, and I have to remind myself to control my breathing.

One... two. Three, four, five.

Five of these demonic figures just entered Sigma. Is this a twisted take on a themed mixer? I mentally strike that idea because it's approaching midnight, and mixers always start around nine-thirty or ten p.m. Plus, if they were having a mixer, music would be playing, voices would be shouting, and there would be people standing outside.

Fuck, Gabi, this is it. It's happening, I tell myself. I have to get inside. My phone vibrates with a text from within my jacket pocket. I glance up to see if any more figures are approaching the back porch, and when I see none, I decide it's safe to take out my phone.

> Ele: Black SUV headed back your way. Went to two freshman dorms. People got out then more people got in. Couldn't get a good look. Too far away. Returning to idle spot.

Shit, okay. Do I wait it out in this bush or try to get inside? The back door seems open, and with some luck, I can slip in that way.

Just as I gather my courage, I hear the thunk of car doors closing.

"Jesus," I whisper at the sight of men dressed in head-to-toe black, wearing black balaclavas, escorting figures who look a hell of a lot like women in pajamas with black cloth bags over their heads. And there are a lot of women. I try to count but lose track. They all have their hands out in front of them as if they've had their wrists bound together.

What in the actual fuck is happening?

I unzip my other jacket pocket and take out my ski mask – one I wear when I actually go skiing. It's regrettably not black but rather hot pink, which in hindsight was really fucking dumb. Sharp branches fight me as I pull this thing over my head and push my way out of the hedge. Crawling on all fours is my best bet at going unnoticed, so I scurry along the ground, being careful to stick close to the bottom of the hedges.

Do I crawl up the back porch steps? That seems like a bad idea. It's too bright. But I don't know if I'm tall enough to reach the ledge of the porch. I'd need a boost.

I stand on my tiptoes until my fingers curl around the lip of the ledge. Maybe I can scale it on my own like a rock climber if I put my foot... right... here...

The back door bursts open, and I panic, whirling around to press my back into the side of the structure.

Please don't look over the side. Please don't look over the side, I repeat in my head.

The sound of a lighter striking to life accompanies the smell of cigarette smoke.

"I fucking hate doing watch duty," a male voice says. "Max and Brody got stuck with the front door."

"How many more of these will there be?" a different male voice asks.

"The initiation ceremonies are once a month, right? Every full moon," the first male voice either asks or confirms, but it's unclear.

"I'd give anything to sink my dick into some pussy right now. Too bad it's not a regular weekend or we could order these sluts to beg on their knees."

I think it's the first male voice again, but they both sound similar.

"Too bad we're not Kieren. That guy can have all the pussy he wants."

"Psshhh. I wouldn't want to be him."

I've lost track of which voice is saying what, but it doesn't matter.

"Why not?"

"They say he lost his fucking mind after his girlfriend left. Like, truly. The guy is mental."

"That hot blonde girl? She's still not back?"

"She ran, bro. You heard the rumors about what he did to her, right?"

"Yeah, but there's no way that's true. You'd have to be out of your mind crazy."

"I'm telling you, bro. He's off his rocker. I avoid that guy at all costs, dude. I see him in the hallway, and I walk the other way."

"Speaking of crazy, I hear Barrett and Kasey are on the outs."

"Really? She's been here all week, or at least, that's what I heard."

Here all week? That would explain things, and I hate that those fucking cops were right.

"Jonah said that Barrett is still pissed she cheated on him over the summer."

"Weren't they on a break?"

"Who knows, but you know Barrett. That guy's an asshole."

"Fair point. Have the elders arrived?"

Elders? I think to myself, pondering the new terminology.

"Yeah, about fifteen minutes ago. You didn't see them? Hard to miss them in those masks. How can they fuck in those, anyway? Has to be hard. With those horns? Shittttt."

Both guys snicker at the joke, and I wonder if they are talking about the masked individuals I saw exit the SUV. The description fits.

My head spins as they banter, and I become more confused by the second. Unable to follow along, I plot my extraction plan. The options are grim. It sounds like guards are stationed at the front door, so that rules out testing those windows, and I won't be able to get to the other side of the house, given the guards at both the front and back exits. The only way out, as I see it, is to go back the way I came.

I draw in a steadying breath and take a step. Then another, then another. I'm careful to stick close to the hedges so I can remain shrouded in their shadow. Three more steps and I'll be around the corner.

Crack.

I freeze at the snap of a large stick under my foot.

"Hello?" I hear a male voice call, followed by, "Turn on your flashlight."

Fuck.

Run.

I take off at a full sprint around the corner of the house and beeline it for the trees and brush that line the street. My mind tries to calculate the trajectory I should head to avoid coming into view of either set of guards. I end up running a diagonal line moving westward until I reach the cover of trees. I bound through thickets of low-growing vines and leaves, and stumble over tree roots. My feet hit the pavement at full speed, and I sprint toward Ele's car parked twenty feet ahead.

Skidding to a halt, I grab the door handle and throw myself inside the car.

"Go! Go! Go!" I scream, turning to keep watch out of the rear window.

The engine roars to life just as Ele slams her foot on the accelerator. Tires squeal for purchase. Flashlights bounce in the distance.

"Go!" I scream again.

The car leaps forward and zooms at lightning speed in the opposite direction of Sigma.

Only when it's clear we've outrun the flashlights do I take a breath.

"What the fuck happened?" Viv shouts from the backseat.

"I'll tell you when we get home. Don't slow down," I pant. "They'll catch us."

"Headlights!" I scream at the beams reflecting in the rearview mirror. "Drive!"

18

MONROE

Consciousness seeps into my mind like a dripping faucet. A nightmare skates around the edges of my memory. Flickering moments burst into view, so visceral, they could be real.

Jace and Barrett holding me down.

The sound of a lighter flicking to life.

The sear of white hot metal against my skin.

The smell of burnt flesh.

The feel of my saliva running down my chin as I scream against the ball gag.

The silent cry of my broken heart.

Awareness returns to my limbs. Something uncomfortable

and cumbersome is around my ankle. My head is a boulder atop my neck, too heavy to lift, too disoriented and dizzy to think.

The room where I lie is cloaked in soft darkness, and it takes my eyes several minutes to adjust.

"Kieren?" I croak, reaching my arm out when I don't get a response.

"Kieren," I say louder.

A groan surfaces from the other side of the bed.

"Kieren," I whine.

He gives me a muffled, "What?"

Sensing I'm on my own, I muster the willpower to roll onto my side.

Excruciating pain radiates from my left ass cheek, and my body seizes. I can't roll to the left or right. I can't move my legs. I'm frozen like a stone.

"Kieren! Help me," I scream.

He scrambles onto his knees.

"What's wrong?"

"It hurts! Something is wrong. Please, I need you to lift me up!"

He climbs over me and throws the covers off my body.

"Pull me up!" I shout.

He lifts me by the armpits, and finally, the fire-burning sensation in my glute dulls to a throb. A chain clangs to the floor, attached to the cuff around my ankle.

"What the fuck?" I falter as the realization that I've been chained to the bed the entire night slaps me in the face.

Twisting my torso, I peer over my shoulder. A square patch of gauze the size of my hand is secured to my ass with medical tape. Mistakenly, I graze the patch with my fingers and hiss with pain.

"What happened?" I ask, turning back to face Kieren.

"What do you mean '*what happened*'? You were initiated."

"But what is that on my ass?" I wail, pointing to the bandage.

Bile rises in my throat, and I fear I might vomit.

"Did you drug me?"

"We had to sedate you. It was for your own good."

"*With what?*"

"Ketamine."

"Ketamine?!" I shout.

"I tried to give it to you before the Branding Ceremony to ease the pain, but you refused to open your mouth. You're so goddamn stubborn sometimes."

"Branding Ceremony? What the fuck did you do to me?"

"First of all, watch your fucking tone. You knew what you were getting into. I didn't see you complaining when you were high on molly and riding my dick last night. You knew you were getting a brand. It was in the oath you took. And guess what? I fucking branded you."

My hand rears back on instinct, and I slap him across the face.

Slowly, he turns back to look at me. His nostrils flare with cold fury, his jaw muscles clench with rage as he levels me a look of disgust. But like an indignant fool, I remain standing at the foot of the volcano, daring it to erupt.

"Slap me all you want, Monroe, but what's done is done. You're mine now, from your flesh to your soul. I own every fucking inch of you. Sigma owns every fucking inch of you, from now until forever. Hide and I'll find you. Run and I'll catch you. Do you know what happens to Sinners who dissent, Monroe? Do you remember the words from your oath?"

His wrath twists into a victorious sneer. Tears of betrayal stream down my devastated face, yet he watches them fall, emotionless and unfazed. I try to step around him, to leave, but he grabs the back of my neck, forcing me against his warm chest like a helpless, bound mouse.

"Don't make me put you in a cage, puppy," he breathes into my hair as he plants a lingering kiss atop the crown of my head. "But if you ever try to leave me, I'll have no choice."

19
GABI

Present Day

"This spot is far enough away from our apartment. Park here," I instruct Ele, pointing to the open space between two parked cars.

After driving in chaotic circles for the last forty-five minutes to shake whatever car was or wasn't on our tail, the fear we all initially felt has morphed into a mix of emotions. Ele is fuming. That much is clear. Viv has settled into a quiet, pensive mood, which is never a good sign, and despite my innate urge to return to the scene of the crime and double down on our spy efforts, I've kept my mouth shut.

Ele parallel parks her light blue Subaru and switches off the ignition with intention. I brace myself for what I know is next.

"What the actual fuck was that, Gabi?" Ele shouts at me, her voice especially damning in the close confines of the car.

"You want to tell us why we were getting chased like criminals in a goddamn witch hunt?"

"They heard me," I admit. "I was crouched against the porch, and two Sigma guys were outside talking. I overheard them say they were on guard duty. You don't understand what I saw."

"Well then, enlighten us," Ele snaps.

I angle my body in the front passenger seat so that both Ele and Viv are in my line of sight before launching into a recount of the horrors I witnessed.

"What exactly did these satanic masks look like?" Viv asks from the back seat. I take out my phone and type *'black horned demon mask'* into the search bar. Several images populate the search results.

"Kind of like this," I say, clicking on a strikingly similar image from a seller on a retail site known for handmade goods. I hand my phone to Ele who leans back so both she and Viv can see the screen at the same time.

"Full face demon mask. Black horned demon, Halloween parties, demon masquerade..." Ele mumbles, reading the product description aloud.

"Admittedly, that is terrifying," Viv states.

"That is some cult shit right there," Ele agrees, handing my phone back.

"Yes!" I say, emphasizing the conclusion that these masks do trigger thoughts of a satanic cult. "Plus, they were wearing floor-length, hooded black robes. Then all the women with bags over their heads. I mean what the fuck!?"

"Also, those guys on guard duty mentioned Kasey. I guess she was at Sigma all week with Barrett, but maybe they're on the outs because apparently she cheated on him over the summer. Oh, and something about elders."

"Elders?" Viv interrupts. "Like old people?"

"Nothing you just said makes any sense," Ele reasons.

"No, it doesn't," I say, furrowing my brow as I think through what I overheard. "Also, if she was at Sigma all week, why wouldn't she just answer her phone when her parents called, or text them back?"

"So, in conclusion," Ele begins, her tone mockingly playful, "basically, Sigma may or may not be running a satanic kink club for grandpas. And we almost got caught by a bunch of cult fanatics. Cool. What a steaming hot dump of malarkey."

"They're going to figure out it was us," Viv adds.

"How?" I ask in challenge.

"Hello?" she gestures with her hands, as if the reason should be obvious. "Could we have picked a more conspicuous getaway car? How many Subaru cars of this same color do you see driving around campus?"

"I don't know! It's a hippie college town. It has to be filled with Subarus!"

"Jesus, Viv's right," Ele laments. "But not this color, Gabi! We might as well have left our calling card on the ground. Dammit, this is so fucked. You know what? A secret satanic sex club for old men is an immediate no for me. Immediately no. I'm out."

Her words pin me like a cornered animal, and I lash out. "Are you fucking kidding me? Did you even listen to a word I said? We have to expose this shit! If not us, then who?"

"Do you hear yourself, Gabi? You sound absurd! Listen, we know Sigma is doing fucked up shit, right? Obviously, corralling women and bringing them to a party wearing only sexy pajamas is fucking gross, but so what? Okay, so some dudes got out of an SUV wearing weird-ass masks. Is this probably some strange sex thing? Yes. But do we need to go poking around where we don't belong? Absolutely not. Those guys said Kasey was at Sigma all week, so drop it! Let them have their orgy parties. Who cares? Did anyone have a gun held to their head, because if not, they're all consenting adults. It may not be our cup of tea, but don't yuk someone else's yum."

"How can you be so dismissive?" I gawk.

"Is this about Jace?" Viv abruptly pipes in from the back seat.

Ele's gapes at me, and I can see the wheels turning in her head. "Oh my God," Ele gasps, like she's just solved the puzzle. "This *is* about Jace, isn't it? This is about Jace participating in something you disapprove of, and you want to out whatever Sigma is doing so you can drag Jace over the coals?"

"No!" I stammer. "I could care less about where Jace sticks his dick. Are you serious? Why aren't you listening?"

"No, you listen, Gabi," Ele says, turning stern as she points a finger at me. "If you want to keep running around, playing your little Sherlock Holmes shit, then be my guest. But I worked my ass off to get into this school, and I'm not going to fuck it up in my last year over some bullshit frat trying to have secret kink parties. Plus, if we get caught, you know those Sigma assholes will press charges, and if that happens, my career will be dead on arrival. I love you, Gabi, but I don't want to be dragged into your circus of revenge. I'm sorry."

"She's right, Gabi. I'm sorry, but I can't risk it either. My parents would literally disown me if I managed to get myself arrested and not graduate."

"Guys," I stutter. "You're wrong. This is not about Jace."

"Listen, for your own good, let it go," Ele says. "Make no mistake, I'm not condoning whatever fucked up shit Sigma is doing, but this feels beneath you, Gabi. You're better than this, and you're better than Jace. This is not the hill to die on, trust me."

They're wrong. I know they're wrong, but I know it's pointless to contest. Hell, I'm even starting to doubt my own motives. Is my need to know the truth subconsciously about Jace?

I mutter, "You're right," and reach for the door handle.

The ruckus of drunk reverie grows louder the closer we get to our apartment. Swarms of people linger on the sidewalk outside Tommy O's, likely making plans for after hours. The three of us walk solemnly in a single-file line, dodging and weaving around groups of passersby. I lag several feet behind my two friends, numb and dejected.

Only once before have I felt this isolated and disowned, and that was in high school. Is this how Monroe felt last semester when we were gone? Did Kieren force her to partici-pate in weird, Sigma cult-y sex things against her will? When I saw Jace at the campus store, he made a comment about Monroe not being innocent. Was she in over her head, or a willing participant?

A sickening image of Monroe being forced to do sex acts under duress pops into my mind, followed by an even more disturbing image of Monroe's body lying dead in a gutter. Monroe may be easily susceptible to Kieren's spell, but she's no weakling when it comes to standing up for what's right, and that's what scares me. There's nothing *wrong* with secret sex parties, even if they are considered taboo, so if Sigma is only guilty of throwing orgies, then why would Monroe have gone missing? It doesn't add up.

I reach for a kernel of doubt, but my gut tells me I'm right, and if I have to walk this road alone to uncover the truth, so be it. I know Monroe wouldn't have gone down without a fight, and neither will I.

20

KIEREN

Six Months Prior to Present Day,
Early March, Junior Year,
Sigma

My phone falls to the floor with a plunk. Where the fuck is Monroe? I've texted her ten times in the last hour.

This is not what she promised.

She promised to behave.

She promised not to run.

And what the fuck is she doing? Running.

Fucking disobedient fucking bitch.

How does she not understand all that I have riding on the success of these Full Moon Ceremonies? I need her full commitment. Physically, mentally and emotionally.

I should have just told her I loved her. I should have just said it back. It wouldn't have been a complete lie. I do love her in my own way. I especially love the feeling of owning her. The way she yields control of her body, trusting me with her needs, is intoxicating. Having that much power over someone, bending her to my will, makes the darkest parts of me come alive.

And now she's fucking disappeared, again, just like she did at the end of our sophomore year. She's going to abandon me.

Not this time, Monroe. Not this fucking time.

The March Full Moon Ceremony with attending elders will be the first Ceremony held this century at the Dornell chapter. Last month's Ceremony was just a dry-run, a means to recruit Sinners to tap for the Ritual of Sacrifice. Finally, the ancient tradition will return and reclaim its rightful spot in the legacy of this fraternity, just as X and my father want. Maybe then, they will finally shut the fuck up.

The hours I have spent organizing and preparing for this have been a sacrifice in and of itself. Not that I care about my classes. Convincing new pledges to trade scrubbing toilets for ghost writing my papers and completing my homework took no effort whatsoever. Besides, they're all terrified of me, with good reason.

So, for Monroe to pull away now?

Over my fucking dead body.

If only I could find her. She's never at her sorority, nor do I know her class schedule. I'll be six feet under before I set foot in the Engineering Quad, so if my plan to coax her back to me doesn't work, I'll be forced to send in reinforcements. I'm not above using extreme measures to get what I want when it comes to Monroe.

I reach over the edge of the bed to retrieve my phone so I can text Barrett. He's our social chair and loyal as fuck. He told me in confidence that his family needs this to happen just as much as mine. Plus, he's a bigger sadist than I am, so getting him on board to help with some of the more uncouth parts of these Full Moon Ceremonies has been a walk in the park. It's amazing how dangling even the smallest carrot of power can motivate a man. Barrett, Harrison, and even Jace who just stood at the edge of the room with a scowl on his face, are now revered as gods. Untouchable. Women will claw their eyes out simply to get a taste of these men, but they'd be remiss to forget that power can be taken away just as quickly as it can be given. Power is an illusion, after all. I have my dear father to thank for that knowledge. Fucking prick.

Five elders will be in attendance this Saturday. One of which is X himself. I'm so over this self-important mother-fucker. I know he's exceptionally powerful, a kingmaker, and someone you don't want to piss off, but Jesus Christ. I wonder if I'll have any humanity left by the time this is over. This bloodthirsty motherfucker might just be Moloch himself.

He expects an offering at the Full Moon Ceremony. I have a candidate in mind, one who I'm told has been running her mouth around campus, and I plan to turn her into a lesson. I'll make the disloyal weep for a mercy they'll never find. Not from me. People go missing all the time, right? Especially on college campuses, where they just might wander off drunk and fall into a gorge.

Actually, it's kind of fun getting to play God. It suits me.

I type out a text to Barrett telling him to set up a mixer between Sigma and Monroe's sorority this Thursday. I'll lure Monroe out of hiding, and once I catch her, I'll cage her. She'll be there for the next Full Moon Ceremony, come hell or high water, because I don't plan on letting her out of my sight until the curtain drops.

21

MONROE

Six Months Prior to Present Day,
Early March, Junior Year,
Sigma

"You don't seem happy to see me, baby," Kieren rasps against the hair covering my ear. I give him a scathing side-eye glance before refocusing on the drunk debauchery unfolding on the dance floor.

"And why do you think that is, Kieren?" I sneer without turning my head to give him the acknowledgement he wants. I take a sip of my absolutely vile vodka soda through one of those skinny black straws and cross my arms.

"Monroe," he says as he steps directly into my line of sight, cupping my face with his hands so I have no choice but to look at him. "Stop pretending you don't love me."

Fury crackles under my skin at his audacious remark. I

glare up at him with what I hope is enough venom to stop a beating heart.

"Stop pretending you do," I bite back. "Oh wait, you don't."

He rolls his eyes in a way that says, '*Here we go again,*' and I fight back the urge to punch his throat. He leans forward to kiss me, but halts when I abruptly turn my head to the side.

"Seriously? I can't kiss my girlfriend now?"

"I'm not doing this here," I snap. I've been plotting this fight since I left Sigma the morning after the Full Moon Ceremony.

"Fine, then come upstairs."

"Why? So you can fuck me?"

"If you want me to fuck you Monroe, I'll happily fuck you. But it's obvious you need to get a few things off your chest, so why don't we start there?"

My feet press into the floor like magnets on metal. In my peripheral view, I can see Kieren staring down at me, waiting for my response. Waiting for me to cave.

"Come on, Monroe. Don't be like this. Besides, I have a birthday present for you."

I shift on my feet, unsure if this is a genuine attempt at reconciliation or a trap.

"I don't forgive you for what you did," I say.

"Fine," Kieren huffs in aggravation. "Again, I *apologize*. I thought we were on the same page."

"We were very much *not* on the same page."

"Okay! I know that now, and I'm sorry."

"You permanently damaged my..."

Kieren cuts me off with a silencing finger over my mouth. "Not here," he growls. "Upstairs."

His hand finds mine, and he all but drags me away from the mixer. I follow him through the halls, fixated on the pull of his

Henley across his broad shoulder blades, and realize this is the moment I start to lose myself. This is the moment where my brain can't sort through feelings of wanting to be his, hoping this time will be different, and wishing I wasn't so goddamn weak.

Because, I'm not weak. I have survived so much worse in my almost twenty-one years of life, from my father abandoning me when I was three, from my mother being the most selfish piece of shit on the planet, from moving in with my grandmother at the age of twelve when my mother went to prison, so what is it about Kieren that makes me abandon my fire? What voodoo hold does he have over me?

Kieren unlocks his bedroom door as I wrestle with my thoughts. A small voice in my head tells me it's not too late, but when the door swings open and Kieren's hand rejoins mine, I follow him inside like a wraith.

It takes several moments for my eyes to adjust to the shadowy room. Ambient light from the glow of Kieren's computer screen casts a somber hue across the space. Memories of the Full Moon Ceremony flicker in my mind as Kieren sits on the edge of his bed and pulls me onto his lap. I straddle him, just like I had done when he sat masked and pompous on that hideous throne, and the sinking feeling of crestfallen rejection settles into the pit of my stomach.

I can't make eye contact. I can't pretend what happened last month didn't emotionally gut me.

"Are you not even going to look at me? Monroe, I thought you understood that you had to get a brand to be initiated. I thought you understood how important this tradition is to me. You said you wanted to be a part of it, and you promised you wouldn't leave me again."

"I told you I loved you," I blurt out. Tears well in the

corners of my eyes. "I don't care about the stupid brand. I mean, it's fucked up, but that's not what hurts. I told you I loved you, and all you said was '*I know.*' Do you have any idea how awful that made me feel? How stupid? And after I went along with your dumb fucking Ceremony and fucked you in front of like sixty people, you couldn't find it inside that black heart of yours to say it back?"

My vision blurs with unshed tears, and as much as I don't want Kieren to know the extent of my hurt, I surrender my pride and blink them free.

His fingers are gentle as he wraps them around my neck, caressing my jawline with the pad of his thumb. He leans his forehead against mine until our noses touch.

"You are everything to me, Monroe, but you need to give me time."

I suck my bottom lip between my teeth to stop it from trembling.

"I don't know how to do this," he continues. "I want to believe this is real, I want to open my heart to you, but every time I reveal a piece of myself I've kept hidden, you run. And I can't give you all of me until I know for certain that you can accept my flaws. I'm not convinced you have what it takes to love someone like me, and I'm sorry if saying that upsets you. You love what I can give you, but I don't know if you truly love who I am. But I'm trying to be vulnerable, Monroe. I've told you, I'm trying."

Guilt punches me in the gut. Blood drains from my limbs. An unexplainable heaviness sinks into my heart, and I want to crawl into a hole and die.

"I don't love what you can give me," I whisper in argument.

"You don't love having me at your every beck and call? You don't love how I'll do anything to please you? You don't love being chained and whipped and fucked until your eyes roll to the back of your head? You don't love being able to use me when you need to get off, only to jet the next morning and ignore me for weeks? Because you know I'll come crawling back, like I always do. You don't love how I'll reduce myself to a beggar because I'm so out-of-my-mind pussy-whipped for you?"

I fist my shirt above my heart, tugging it toward my neck, disgusted and ashamed to hear that's what Kieren thinks of me.

"That's not how it is, Kieren, and you know that," I manage as I hold back an onslaught of tears.

"Monroe, I have never felt the way I feel about you with anyone before. I need you. I can't breathe if you aren't here. I would do anything for you, because despite what you tell yourself, I do care about you, and as much as it terrifies me, I do feel love for you. Sometimes, it's so overpowering, I can't think straight, which is exactly what happened at the last Ceremony. I was overwhelmed. I didn't expect you to have those feelings for me again, not this soon at least. I thought we both needed more time, so when you told me you loved me, it caught me off guard. Also, forgive me, but you were very high and I figured it was the drugs talking. I didn't want to say it back, only to find out that was the case. It would break me."

"I'm sorry," I whisper. "You're right, I'm sorry."

I've been unabashed with my needs, and the thought of how despicably I've acted crawls across my skin like spiders.

Kieren heaves a bemoaned sigh. "I got you something for your birthday. It's a bit early, but I thought maybe you might like to wear them at the next Full Moon Ceremony."

He makes a motion to stand, and I slide off his lap.

The top wooden desk drawer slides noisily open, and

Kieren retrieves a small box from inside. Kneeling before me, he hands me the delicately wrapped present adorned with white silk ribbon tied into a perfect bow.

"You didn't need to get me anything," I swallow.

"I wanted to. Open it."

Carefully, I untie the ribbon and peel apart the taped edges. My eyes go wide at the teal blue box.

"Kieren, I don't know what this is, but whatever it is, I can't accept it."

"Monroe, please," he pleads. "It's a pretty big deal to turn twenty-one. Plus, I wanted to make it up to you for being such an ass at the last Ceremony. You'll participate in the next one, right?"

"Yes, of course." My voice shakes as I pop open the teal jewelry box and gasp.

"Kieren, I can't. I can't accept these! It's too much! I don't deserve this."

He leans forward and gives me a lingering, sensual kiss.

"I've been fantasizing about fucking you in nothing but these diamond earrings for weeks," he grins against my lips.

"Oh my God, Kieren," I stammer, wiping away tears. "Thank you. No one has ever given me something so nice."

Kieren tucks a strand of hair behind my ear. "Put them on, baby. I want to watch them sparkle while I fuck your mouth tonight. Unless, of course, you're still mad at me."

I huff a breathy chuckle as I secure the first earring back. "When has that ever stopped you?" I slide the stem of the second diamond earring into place, tilting my head side to side for his approving grin.

"That's true," Kieren says, rising. His thumb parts my lower lip, his gaze turns lust-filled, and with an upward quirk of his lips, he answers, "Never."

"Kieren, are you getting a pet?" I ask, just now noticing the large animal cage in his room. I'm not sure how I missed such an eye-soar. Kieren, of all people, should not be made responsible for the life of an innocent animal, but maybe Sigma is planning to get a house dog that is looked after by all members.

"I already have a pet, baby," he smirks. "It's you."

22

GABI

Present Day,
Mid-September, Senior Year,
Dornell University

B ehavioral Economics is not my favorite class by any stretch. And I get it, the professor is highly acclaimed, and fan-boy students jockey over who gets to sit in the coveted eye-level seats in the first few rows of the auditorium, but I just don't care.

I'm here simply to check a required course off my list so I can graduate. It aggravates me how economics classes in general tend to be dominated by students of the opposite sex. Even if the class roster is evenly distributed among genders, something about the subject of economics makes the men go feral. Once they step foot into the auditorium and the lecture begins, they morph into the most aggro, masculine version of themselves; it's bizarre. Like chill out, Adrien, we all know you know the answer, okay? We get it. Stop debating with the professor as if you know more than he does. It's obnoxious.

I flip open my laptop and scan through recent, unread emails. Sometimes, if I'm feeling particularly bored and am in the mood to depress myself, I'll open up my text message history with Monroe on my computer. The photos are especially torturous.

My fingertips hover over the mouse trackpad as I debate what amount of memory lane I can stomach today, when I sense him. The heavy aura of Jace's presence settles around me like an ominous cloud as I hear him take a seat directly behind me. Every train of thought I had prior to this moment vacates my brain. I knew he was in this class, but he's never sat anywhere near me. To sit this close feels deliberate.

His shins press into the back of the plastic auditorium seat, and even though I can't feel it, I imagine strands of my long, dark brown hair skimming the tops of his knees.

I swallow, motionless with anxiety. With shaky fingers, I navigate through browser tabs until I get to the document I use to take class notes. Picturing him staring over my shoulder, scrutinizing each word I type, renders me immobile, and I don't know how I'm going to make it through a ninety-minute lecture under such extreme tension. I debate turning around to scowl at him, but I know that would only satisfy his already overinflated ego.

The minutes painfully tick by, and I've managed a few lines of pathetic notes by the time class ends. Standing, I force myself to methodically pack up my belongings, refusing to glance in his direction. It's obvious to both of us that I can see him. He's close enough that I can see the thread pattern of his jeans. Of course, I know he's there. I can feel him glaring at me, as he likes to do, and as I like to do, I choose to ignore him.

When he has yet to move by the time I've returned my

laptop to its sleeve and zipped my backpack closed, my annoyance gets the best of me. The auditorium is nearly empty save for the regular crew of sycophants accosting the professor after class as he tries to leave.

"What?" I snap at Jace, finally indulging his bullshit standoff.

He blinks slowly, looking up at me with only his eyes. I'm not sure if he thinks the look he's giving me is intimidating, but it's not. It's comical.

"Whatever," I huff, tossing on my backpack. I begin walking to the end of the row, and he jumps to his feet, trailing me like a shadow. I quicken my pace, my stride almost a jog, as I make a beeline for the auditorium door.

The clang of the metal push bar reverberates loudly as I slam myself against it, throwing open the heavy exit door with what I hope is enough force to bounce off the wall and hit Jace in the face when he tries to pass through. I hear the same loud clang three seconds later and know I've only got a five-step lead on him. I'm practically running when I reach the exterior building doors, and race down the short flight of stone steps as fast as I can without tripping. I veer off to the right, convinced I've successfully escaped, when his large hand snags the strap of my backpack, and I'm yanked to a stop.

"What the fuck is your problem?" I shout, whirling around.

"You're my problem!" he sneers, tugging me into him by the strap of my backpack.

I grab his hand and try to wrench it free. "Get the fuck off me! Did you follow me just to threaten me again, you fucking ogre?"

"I'm here to do more than threaten you," he growls, his towering frame hunched, his face mere inches from mine.

"You know what's dumb, Gabi?" Sirens blare in the distance. Jace's dark brown eyes bore into mine, and I forget how to breathe. "Wearing a fucking hot pink ski mask while you're trying to break into someplace you don't belong."

I shove him away, taking several steps backward. "What are you talking about?"

He gives me a vicious grin and closes the small distance I managed to create. "I wish we would have fucking caught you. You know what Sigma does to people who get caught? Especially whores like you?"

"Whores like me? How original," I cackle. "You should look in the fucking mirror, Jace. God, your jealousy is disgusting. All this rage simply because I got tired of fucking you," I tsk. "It's pathetic."

"Is that right? Why don't you go whore yourself out some more, Gabi? Or have you run through all your options and now no one wants to fuck used goods?"

The urge to slap this man is so overwhelming that my fingers tingle.

"You have *no idea* what you're talking about, Jace. No idea!" I scream, pointing a finger in his face. "You have no fucking clue, do you?"

"No clue about what? About how you used me for social clout and then discarded me like a piece of trash once you got tired of riding my dick?"

"I swear to God, Jace Carver, if you don't shut the fuck up, I'm going to slap you!"

"Slap me!?" he mocks, throwing his head back in fake laughter. "Do it. I dare you to touch me again."

Tears sting the corners of my eyes, and I know I've got thirty seconds before they fall.

"You were a waste of time, Jace," I glower, because he was. *Fuck this cheating excuse of a man.*

His eyes snap back to mine, his expression one of animalistic wrath.

"And you were nothing more than a mediocre fuck."

I force a feigned smile. My lips quiver. "Oh, I know Jace. I know I was nothing more than a mediocre fuck to you, so why don't you tell me something I don't already fucking know!" I scream.

The shrill volume of my voice stuns us both, and for a moment, we both stand down as if we forgot what we were fighting about in the first place.

"If you get caught at Sigma again, you're leaving in a body bag," Jace says with terrifying steadiness.

"Yeah? Well, I guess I'm a dead girl walking."

I spin around, my eyes so full of tears that I can't see. I'm sure Jace is thrilled with himself for making me cry, but I could not give less of a fuck. That man is the worst person on the entire goddamn planet. My phone vibrates in my hand, and I look down to see an incoming call from Ele.

"Hello?" I answer.

"Gabi," she gasps my name, and I know right away something is very wrong.

"Ele! What's going on? Are you okay?"

"Gabi, what I'm about to tell you is very upsetting."

"What?!" I shout. "Just say it!"

"A body was found floating under the footbridge. People are saying it's one of the girls who went missing last semester, which would mean the cause of death is what everyone originally suspected. As horrible as that reality is to accept, it wasn't Sigma, Gabi."

My fervent walking comes to an abrupt halt. "Oh my God," I breathe, "that's awful."

I wince at how disingenuous I sound.

"You sound disappointed," Ele comments.

Conflicted feelings twist inside my gut. "No. No... it's horrible. Jace threatened me after class today and I'm just rattled. Is there anything we can do?" As if by instinct, I turn around expecting to see Jace, only to find him gone like he never was there at all.

"Jace threatened you again? Because of Saturday? See Gabi, even more reason to leave Sigma and those lunatic assholes alone. By the way, there's going to be a vigil held tonight," Ele shares. "We should go."

"Right. Of course," I agree, but the distance in my voice is apparent. I opt not to answer Ele's questions about Jace's threats, knowing if I do, it will confirm Sigma knows we were snooping, and I can't take any more grief.

I tell Ele I'll meet her back at our apartment and end the call. Streaks of tears linger down my cheeks. Maybe Ele and Viv are right. I should let my theory go. Monroe's gone and doesn't want to be found. Not by her best friend, not by anyone.

A fresh wave of hot tears rips from my eyes. How could my supposed best friend toss aside the last three years with such irreverence? This isn't like her. I mean, fuck, she didn't leave Kieren, and he's a monster. I refuse to believe she would leave me without an explanation.

But the evidence debunking my theory increases by the day, and on top of that, I don't have the strength to survive another Jace encounter. He's gotten under my skin, and yes, we hate each other, but there's only so much cruelty a person can take. I'm not whoring myself around, nor have I ever, not that my sex life is any of his business. I can't take any more of his abuse. It's mean for the sake of being mean, and I don't deserve to be the punching bag for his anger issues.

God, what happened to him? He's become unrecognizable.

You know what, it's fine, I think, as I pull myself together. I just need to see what's down in Sigma's basement, and then I'll let this go, once and for all.

23
MONROE

Six Months Prior to Present Day,
The March Full Moon Ceremony,
Junior Year,
Sigma

"Kieren, please don't leave me. Can't I just stay with you like last time?" I hate how whiny and desperate I sound when it's clear Kieren does not give a fuck.

"I have business to take care of downstairs before the Ceremony begins. I need you to wait in here with the other girls," he explains, pushing me backward across the threshold of the doorway. I stumble slightly, embarrassed to have been scolded and treated with such little regard by my own boyfriend in front of others.

Jace and Barrett stand on either side of the door, already dressed in what seems to be the standard Sigma Ceremony outfit of black pants, no shirt, and a demon goat mask covering the top half of their faces. I still haven't decided if their costumes are ridiculous or petrifying, but right now I'm leaning toward ridiculous.

I can't believe *this* is the *sacred tradition* Kieren ranted and raved about in years prior – the tradition he couldn't wait to resurrect because it would propel him to a level of greatness that *'Sigma hasn't seen in decades.'* I mean, seriously? It's just a big orgy. What's so great about that? The secrecy? The fact that Dornell would immediately kick Sigma off campus if University administration found out?

As wrong as it is to admit, I understand the appeal, especially for the freshmen who are initiated as Sigma Little Sisters. I guess if you aren't into group sex, sex in public or a non-judgmental and sexually liberal person in general, this would be a nightmare. Also, from what I remember from last time, this is not a heterosexual affair. This is complete and utter hedonism. I recall duos and thrupples and groups that looked like a free-for-all. Honestly, it's freeing. Personally, I'm not into multiple partners, but I appreciate that many people are, and as long as all parties consent, it's hot as fuck to watch.

But, that's the thing. Is everyone here a consenting party?

Kieren told me there's a nomination process for initiates, so obviously, you wouldn't nominate someone who wouldn't enjoy the Ceremony indulgences. Those who are initiated have to get a brand, for fuck's sake. You really have to be committed from the outset. He also told me that the freshmen are willingly taken from their beds at midnight, and are told to wear nothing but lingerie to bed, so, they must know, right?

Turning around, I scan the room. Girls in different patterns and colors of lingerie similar to my own black lace bra and thong sit in groups, chatting, laughing, and sipping drinks from red plastic cups. Everyone has on the same black lace eye mask I remember from the last Ceremony. There are no black bags over any heads yet, and no one seems nervous or anxious. Maybe I'm the overthinking prude? Sigma is, after all, the most elite fraternity on campus. Perhaps some of these women will end up dating men in the house, like Kieren and me.

I slide down the wall against my back and try to relax. The pill Kieren gave me has yet to kick in fully, but I feel the beginnings of a bubbly haze creep along the edges of my mind.

Three bodies rise near the back of the room and float toward me. Blinking, I wonder if I'm seeing apparitions or actual humans.

"Can we sit with you?" one of the women asks.

"Of course," I answer, straightening my posture as the three women lower themselves into cross-legged sitting positions.

"You're Monroe, right?" one of the girls asks. She looks strangely familiar.

I nod, reaching for words that do not come.

"I'm not sure if you recognize us in these masks. We're actually in your sorority."

"Oh my God, that's why you look familiar. I'm so sorry. I'm very out of it," I apologize, mortified that I didn't immediately recognize them after the multitude of hours I spent overseeing the initiation of new sorority members.

"Don't worry," one of the women chuckles. "We all are."

"I'm Kasey," she offers. I study her long, blonde hair that flows in waves around her shoulders. Even with her face partially obstructed, it's obvious she's stunning.

"Yes, of course, Kasey!" I say, repeating her name more for my benefit than hers. Even more embarrassing is the realization that Kasey is my Grand-Little and part of my sorority lineage. I really need to do better.

"This is Morgan and Lilly," Kasey says, referencing the two other women. They each give me a cute wave.

"We were so obsessed with you during rush by the way," Morgan gushes. "Everyone was. You just seemed so cool and confident."

"It's true. You're the reason why I wanted to join DG. That, and you're freakishly beautiful," Kasey adds.

I huff a laugh. "I'm not. You should see my best friend Gabi. She's abroad this semester, but she's the textbook definition of beautiful."

"No, Monroe, you are like so hot," Lilly says. "Morgan and I were both there the day during rush that Kieren brought you those roses."

"Oh my God," Kasey exclaims. "It was all anyone would talk about!"

"Is he your boyfriend?" Morgan asks. "Is that why you wear a different mask from the rest of us? Because you're his?"

Despite Kieren shoving me into this room mere minutes ago, I can't stop myself from grinning with pride when I tell her, "Yes."

"He's gorgeous," Kasey fawns. "Does he share you?"

I cock my head in confusion. "What do you mean?"

"Like, at these things. Does he share you with other guys?"

"Umm, no," I respond. An uncomfortable feeling twists in my gut. "Do your guys... *share you*?"

"Yeah, but I mean, thank God, because I don't really like the guy who nominated me that much. Actually, last time I ignored him entirely," Kasey says.

The other two girls giggle. "Yeah, you did!" Morgan jeers. "You went off with Barrett and Trevor and poor Wesley was so fucking pissed!" Morgan and Kasey laugh uncontrollably, and I find it within me to laugh along despite my unease.

"And are you... cool with that?" I ask cautiously. "The sharing? Or, the group stuff, rather?"

"God, I love it," Lilly breathes. "I love it all. I love the attention. I love how these guys treat you like goddesses."

"Same. Oh my God, last Ceremony, I fell asleep in Barrett's bed, and when I woke up the next morning, he was going down on me! He got me off twice and then took me to get pancakes!" Kasey squeals.

I try to make my conspiratorial laugh sound genuine. "So, you like it then?"

"Obviously we can't talk about it because it's like a secret society and all that," Morgan begins in a matter-of-fact tone, "but let's just say people kind of know about it thanks to you know who and everyone is so envious."

"Everyone wants to be a Sigma Little Sister," Lilly agrees. "Not only are you like royalty around campus, but you also get to have the most unreal sex, like guaranteed unreal sex, every weekend, and not even have to work for it, or feel, you know, like you're a slut."

"And the guys are so hot," Morgan concurs.

"Barrett is so hot," Kasey smiles.

I try to focus on their banter but all I can hear are the words *'so hot'*.

"You have a crush," Morgan says in a sing-song voice, giving Kasey a playful nudge.

"Wait, what do you mean *'you know who'*?" I ask, circling back to the snippet of conversation stuck in my brain.

Morgan shakes her head. "I shouldn't say anything. I don't want to get anyone in trouble."

I let the thread drop, deciding the less I know, the better. I don't want these women to think I'm here as a spy.

Before I can stop myself, I blurt out my biggest concern. "And you're okay with the brand?" I ask, touching the circle of raised skin on my derrière. As soon as the question leaves my mouth, a sense of guilt consumes my thoughts. I shouldn't have asked. I'm supposed to be Kieren's ambassador. I can't let my hesitation and insecurities show. I'm supposed to make these women feel at ease.

"Maybe it was because I was really fucked up, but honestly, I didn't even feel it," Kasey says, rolling her eyes mid-sip, and I exhale my relief.

"Andre said I screamed, but I don't remember," Morgan adds. "That's probably why they did them upstairs in the bedrooms."

"Mine's totally healed," Lilly says. "I catch myself touching it all the time. It's so cool. It's like this secret thing I have that no one else can see unless you're one of us."

'One of us.' I mentally chew on Lilly's words, at the pride in her voice to be part of an elite secret society, even if it's rooted in sin.

"Do you have a lot of friends who are abroad?" Kasey asks.

"All my close friends are, yeah," I say. "It's hard. I miss them, especially Gabi."

Light floods the room as the door opens, and everyone looks up with attention.

"Monroe," one of the goat men calls. I'm pretty sure it's Jace, but he's backlit from the light in the hall, so I'm not entirely sure. "Kieren's ready for you."

I reach for the hand extended in my direction and grab on. I turn to look at the three women, unsure of what to say. It seems inappropriate to tell them I'll see them inside the Ceremony room, since anonymity, even if partial, feels important. Telling them I'll see them later also feels... weird. I settle on, "Have fun," and give them a wink I hope they see through my leather mask before finding Kieren waiting for me in the hall.

———

I watch as the procession of women filters into the blood red Ceremony room, kneeling in two parallel lines. Anxiety churns in my stomach – a different anxiety than I felt at the beginning of the last Ceremony. Something tonight feels off balance. Men wearing different masks sit on cushioned chairs in the back of the large room, partially hidden by a curtain hanging from the ceiling. These masks are markedly different from the demonic goat masks worn by all the other men in the room outside of Kieren. They are full-faced, completely black save for the same gold Sigma symbol in the middle of the forehead, with longer, black, demonic horns. Maybe the different masks are meant to signal a different status of fraternity member? Maybe they are worn by other seniors? But why then, wouldn't Jace, Barrett and Harrison – Kieren's core group of henchmen – be wearing them as well?

The last woman in line enters the room and kneels. Kieren, in all his glory, stands from his elevated position on the dais to begin his opening address. I remain kneeling beside the ornate throne as his voice booms over the otherwise silent space. The straps of my own mask feel tighter tonight, digging into the back ridge of my head. I fight the urge to fidget as Kieren speaks.

His words sound similar to the proclamations said at the last Full Moon Ceremony, but this time, he acknowledges the return of already initiated Sinners, now called Sigma Little Sisters. We repeat after him in a cohesive mumble, agreeing to never spill Sigma's secrets, and if we do, to accept we must pay for our sins with blood. I wonder, is there any weight in these words? Kasey and the other two women admitted that people outside these walls are aware of the Sigma Little Sisters tradition, and even if one of the women did talk, what secrets, exactly, are we keeping? I keep coming back to the notion that the word 'tradition' is just a glamorous title for 'massive orgy.'

Kieren ushers in the start of the night, and, like last time, the lights dim, drinks circulate, and the room transforms into an underground sex club. I can tell improvements have been made to the setup of the basement. Curtains hang with purposeful organization from the ceiling, partitioning off sections and areas to create semi-private rooms within the room. It's difficult to discern exact detail from where I kneel, but I think I see beds, cushioned chairs, and various BDSM props tucked within each alcove. My vantage point affords a direct line of sight into one of the nooks.

A woman wearing a blood red silk bra and matching underwear straddles a masked man sitting in a chair. She writhes seductively on his lap as he fondles her breasts. Adjacent to the chair, a woman's torso hangs half off the bed, the tips of her fingers skim the floor. Her legs are spread impressively wide as another woman feasts on her pussy while simultaneously getting fucked from behind, doggy style, by a man in a mask. Both women, especially the one hanging off the bed, moan loudly enough to be performative. A semi-circle of voyeurs has formed around the bed, some stroking themselves, some with a partner.

My own arousal pulses between my legs, and I look up at Kieren, wondering if I can go ahead and climb onto his lap or if I need to wait for his signal. To my disappointment, his gaze appears fixed on the hedonistic entertainment. The last time I touched myself without his permission, I was bound, chained, and edged until I almost passed out. Not that I didn't love every second of it, but I prefer to receive that type of punishment in private, and it doesn't seem like leaving to go upstairs is an option.

The sight of two women being led to the last partition, where men with the special masks sit, catches my eye.

"Monroe," Kieren barks. I crane my neck like a servant

looking up at her king. "Get up here," he commands without turning his head. I climb onto his lap, facing him, but I can't shake the icky feeling occupying my mind.

"What's wrong?" he asks, stroking the side of my ribcage with his thumb. His gravelly voice is as intimidating as it is provocative, yet I can't seem to jumpstart my body.

"I don't think the molly you gave me is working."

Kieren calls the name of someone I don't know, and seconds later, a masked man is at his side, handing him a small cup that reminds me of the ones used for mouthwash.

"Put this under your tongue," Kieren says, placing the small lozenge in my hand.

"What is this?" I ask.

"It's safe, just take it."

"Kieren..." I protest.

"Now is not the time, Monroe."

His dark eyes, the only part of his face not concealed by his terrifying, god-like demon mask, are cold and unforgiving.

"Fine," I mutter, and put the tablet under my tongue.

"Let it dissolve," Kieren instructs as he tucks two fingers under the base of my thong. I exhale a soft moan and will the tension in my shoulders to slacken. I swivel my pelvis in small circles, feeling myself grow wet.

"Good puppy," he praises. I increase my pace when a commotion directly at my back thwarts my progression.

"The show's starting," Kieren says. "Turn around."

His hands around my waist indicate he wants me to switch my straddle to face outward. Once I've changed my position, I see onlookers have loosely gathered around a low table now stationed horizontally in the center of the room. If it weren't for the black leather padding affixed to the top, it would be an average coffee table.

A woman waltzes to the center of the room, hand-in-hand

with a masked man, and climbs on top of the table. At first, she leans back onto her elbows and plants her feet on the tabletop, seductively spreading her knees apart. The man shakes his head, and in a movement that makes me gasp, flips her onto her stomach and pulls her ass in the air until it's flush with his crotch.

My breath hitches when I realize... he's going to fuck her. For a heartbeat, those watching are transfixed. He unzips his pants, pulling out his hard cock to align it with her pussy.

The heat between my legs throbs. Pinpricks of sweat form along my temples and collarbone while beads of moisture form under my breasts.

Kieren's hand fumbles with his dress pants under my base. I lift myself up to give him more space. His stiff erection grazes my ass, and I reach between my legs to move his cock into position. I sink down just as the masked man in the center of the room spears the woman's pussy from behind. She screams in pleasure. Every merciless ram of her pussy feels magnified by the power of ten as I bounce myself on Kieren's length. Whatever tablet Kieren gave me has kicked in, and my entire body is on fire. It's like I'm starring in a twisted porno, where I watch myself get fucked while feeling myself get fucked at the same time.

The woman's clipped screams have turned primal as she begs him to fuck her harder. I wish it were me. I would give anything to feel what she's feeling in this moment. I increase my intensity, but it's difficult at this angle, which feels more tantric than raw, and I don't want tantric right now. I want Kieren to bend me over the arm of his throne and fuck me like an animal until I scream for mercy.

I place one of his hands under my bra, hoping he'll get the hint that I want him to pinch my nipple, and his other hand at my clit. The woman pants a warning to her partner, and I want to come with her. I want to explode when she explodes. The tightness of my release has been building in my core since this show started, but I need more stimulation or I won't get there. My fingers press against Kieren's, squeezing his together, and as I draw my next breath, he pinches my swollen clit like a savage.

I gasp and hinge forward so quickly, I almost fall off the throne. My climax breaks free and ruptures down my core. My thighs struggle to hold me upright as my body shakes with waves of aftershock. Slippery cum coats the inside of my thighs from Kieren's release, and truthfully, I had forgotten he was under me.

I inhale and exhale with intention to slow my racing heart. Edges of surfaces and people blur like I'm looking at my surroundings through a filter. The blood-red room somehow looks more vibrant. Bodies and colors coil together like a medieval painting – a painting that I'm either admiring from afar or participating in like it's the Last Supper. Reality feels fluid. Time is suspended.

I rise on my knees and pause at the absence of pressure. Cum leaks from my pussy and coats my fingers when I slide my thong back in place. Not being able to see Kieren's face makes me feel adrift without an anchor, lost, and I awkwardly reposition myself on his lap so I can curl into his chest. He's tucked his dick back into his boxer-briefs but his pants remain unzipped. Neither of us speaks. The arm he has around my waist is the only tether that grounds me, but his body has gone rigid like a stone statue. I'm not even sure it matters to him that I'm still here. He looks straight ahead, his gaze locked on the back of the room, and the notion of rejection clouds my consciousness. But at the same time, I'm also not sure if my observations are simply a warped manifestation of my mind from the psychedelics I took. Is any of this real? Am I real?

In my periphery, I see a billowing black robe stalking toward us in slow motion. A monster. The full-face mask is satanic – black with the gold Sigma symbol like the others but with swirling gold details like those on Kieren's mask. And those horns... Terrifying gold horns curve in toward each other like a demon bull. Its decorations differentiate it from the rest in a way that signals higher stature. I sense Kieren's muscles tense as this figure approaches, which confirms my fear – that this isn't a hallucination, but real.

I stare, frozen but hyper-aware.

"Are you sharing your pet?" a deep voice rumbles. It sounds almost inhuman. My eyes flick across the ceremonial garb in search of skin. Black gloves peek out from under long black sleeves, and I spot a large, black and gold ornate ring nearly identical to that of Kieren's. My gaze drags up his strangely covered body. Does he also have on a balaclava under his mask because I can't find a millimeter of bare skin? In my haze, I try to focus on the eyes and recoil. Demon red.

What the fuck?

Wait, *am I hallucinating?*

He's wearing colored contacts, right?

"No," Kieren growls, and I exhale a shaky breath of relief because I'm not a fucking object to be passed around. It's fine if anyone else wants multiple partners, but I don't.

"We will talk about this," the voice scathes. "It's time."

The figure turns abruptly, flowing toward the back of the room until it stops at the wall and... opens a door. A door I didn't even realize existed. The figure slips behind the gap and disappears. I can't tell if I'm imagining things, but did the lights in the room get dimmer and the music get louder?

"I have to go take care of something," Kieren says, and without explanation, moves me off his lap.

"Kneel here and wait for me," he commands, pointing to the floor beside the dais.

"Why? Kieren, where are you going? Why can't I come?" I stammer, stepping in front of him as he zips up his pants.

"Move," he says in a jarringly harsh tone, pushing me aside like I've done something wrong.

"Kieren, wait!" I protest, grabbing the waistband of his pants. His dark, scornful eyes flick from my hand to my face as if I'm a filthy beggar who dared to touch the body of a royal. I feel my hand drop to my side even though I don't remember letting go. Hurt fills my heart like lead, radiating its heaviness outward with each sorrowful beat.

I watch his backside as he walks away, stopping in front of one of the partitioned, private areas. A few seconds pass before a disheveled masked man comes into view. Kieren points toward me, and the man nods. Kieren continues his march toward the back of the room, opening the same hidden door the others went through, and flags down another masked man I see standing against a wall. I think this second masked man is Jace because not that many men in this fraternity have light brown, tattoo-covered skin. Jace moves to follow Kieren when one of the black satanic figures suddenly appears from behind a curtain and grabs Jace's arm.

I narrow my eyes at the odd exchange. Unlike the others, this one isn't wearing a shirt and has a very large, singular tattoo on his abdomen. My eyes are unable to focus on the design, but I see that this figure is holding Jace back, shaking his head. If words are spoken, I can't hear them. Kieren watches the exchange and barks something at Jace and the other man. Jace whips his head in my direction.

"Barrett," I hear Jace boom over the moans and music. Barrett turns around, already a few steps away from my position on the dais. Jace says something I can't discern, but I assume it has to do with switching places. Barrett walks quickly to the back of the room. Stupefied, I see a woman, blindfolded with her hands bound in front of her, emerge from behind the last curtained area with two fully clothed satanic figures on either side, guiding her through the hidden door. Barrett slips in behind them, and the door closes as if it were never there.

"Let's go, Monroe."

My attention snaps to Jace who now stands in front of me.

"You're coming upstairs with me."

I hesitate. Did anyone else see what I saw? Am I imagining things? I don't trust my brain to convey an accurate depiction of reality.

The room continues churning like a sick carnival ride. Jace grabs me by the elbow, and I'm forced to follow. Dizzy and nauseated, I give the back of the room one last glance, but see nothing. They've vanished without a trace.

24

KIEREN

Six Months Prior to Present Day,
The March Full Moon Ceremony,
Junior Year,
Sigma

Carefully, I turn the pages of the ancient text, flipping until I get to the lost chapters of the Sigma Charter. I take care to watch the placement of my fingers so as not to tear any of the centuries-old paper. Barrett guards the interior door. It should have been Jace, but fucking Reid Carver got in the way. It had to have been Reid who intervened because what other idiot would opt to go shirtless with such a distinct chest tattoo? So much for anonymity, dumb fuck.

Tonight's offering lies motionless on the sacrificial table, faceless, nameless. The first in decades, perhaps even a century. X, the elder wearing the gold-horned mask, reaches inside his robe. Every inch of his skin is concealed. Even the true color of his eyes has been replaced with red contacts. This is not his first rodeo, far from it based on his preparedness, and that realization is both concerning and irksome. For how long and where has this motherfucker been practicing the Ritual of Sacrifice? Surely not here at the Dornell Sigma chapter. Does he have access to other Sigma chapters around the country? Just how deep does his web of blackmail extend? One thing is for certain, this is one sick motherfucker, but I suppose now I understand how he's so wealthy and powerful. Maybe these sacrifices actually do work. Maybe Moloch and his blessings are real. Only time will tell.

The steel blade that emerges from his robe gleams in the moonlight shining in through the large, round window carved into the stone ceiling. I'm surprised others haven't noticed this window from the outside and wondered where it led, but, seeing as it's flush with the ground and well concealed behind expertly placed hedges, it makes sense. Lit candles perch on shelves that line the small, rectangular room and flank the steps of Moloch's shrine. A modest golden statue of the fallen deity sits at the helm with outstretched arms and open palms ready to accept the blood offering.

Two other elders have opted to partake in the Ritual, although I do not know their identities. That is the way of the Sigma. Although anonymity offers modern day protections, the elders remain hidden under ceremonial garb to remain modest in the eyes of Moloch, who, according to the lost chapters of the Sigma Charter, has always believed faces revealed to him are done so in vain. He does not bestow His gifts unto the braggart. Only the humble who gladly take up the blade in His name and understand that His gifts are not owed but earned.

The elders wait for me to begin. I look down at the woman on the table, unconscious from the chloroform. She will not suffer, which is more than she deserves for spilling our secrets. I should feel remorse for the crime I'm seconds from committing, but I don't. I feel invigorated. Excitement pulses through my veins like electricity. To have this much power, to take a life with absolutely no repercussions, to feel my own lifeblood fortified with that of another, fuck...

I get it. I fucking get it.

And I want more.

Bestow unto me all your blessings, Moloch, because you've turned me into a believer. I will happily commit sins in your name, if it means I can feel this rush of power, of knowing everything is right in the Universe and I'm exactly where I need to be, once more.

I draw in a deep breath to recite the Ritual as only I, in my position as chapter president, can do, because this is my fucking house and I am its keeper.

It's time to play God.

"Blessed be thy Sigma Brothers who join us on this special night during the full moon to bear witness to the sacrifice made in thy name of Moloch, our God, who resides over the strength and fortune of The Brotherhood."

"Moloch, who hath wrongfully borne the shame of those who hath not the courage to live righteously and true in this world and are therefore not worthy of His blessings. Tonight, we defend His greatness, fortified with blood."

"Tonight, we honor Him. We honor the blessings He hath bestowed upon The Brotherhood, upon the Sigma who came before and those who shall come after."

"Tonight, we worship Him, for all He hath done and all He hath given. We worship the greatness He bears, in mind, body and spirit, and the greatness He chooses to share with those in The Brotherhood He deems worthy, for it is His choice and His choice alone."

"Tonight, we call to Him. We ask Him to continue to bestow His blessings, and in exchange for His selflessness, we offer to Him a Sacrifice."

"Tonight, we beckon Moloch, our God, to present Himself with outstretched arms so that He may receive our Sacrifice presented unto Him by those in this room."

"Once He hath appeared, a Grand Master of The Brotherhood, who presides over this Sacrifice in His honor, shall awaken the palms of Moloch with flame so that He may receive our blood offering, for only a blood offering from a Sigma who hath been pledged in service to The Brotherhood shall be considered worthy."

"And it is through this blood, most pure and worthy, that Moloch's greatness may be restored, His disbelievers conquered, and His blessings continued."

"Once the sacrificial blood hath met flame, and all liquid is burned, so it shall be."

"So it shall be," the elders chant.

"He shall rise, His power and greatness restored fully, and with His continued blessings, those who worship Him shall rise as well."

"All hail Moloch," the elders respond in unison.

"And so, the Ritual of Sacrifice begins."

25
MONROE

Six Months Prior to Present Day,
The March Full Moon Ceremony,
Junior Year,
Sigma

"Jace, slow down," I huff as I struggle to keep up with his gargantuan strides. Jace slows enough for me to walk beside him.

Cold, sobering air kisses my skin as we walk silently through the halls of Sigma. I try not to think about the fact that I'm practically naked with cum running down my inner thigh, walking next to a shirtless Jace, while both of us wear bizarre masquerade masks.

"Who were those men in the back, Jace? The ones who wore the masks with tall demon horns?"

"Elders," he answers curtly, like he wants me to drop the subject.

"Who are 'elders'?"

"Alumni."

I furrow my brows in confusion and disgust. "Alumni?"

"The less you know, the better."

I don't know what to do with this response, but I need answers, so I redirect my line of questioning to keep him talking. "Are more women getting initiated tonight? You know, branded?"

"After Kieren is done with whatever he's doing," Jace says, stone-faced.

"Why does Kieren have to be the one to do it?" I pry.

"Because it's his ring."

"The...," I fumble for words, because, *what?*

"What do you mean '*because it's his ring*'?" I clarify.

"The brand. It's his ring. Don't you remember?"

"Not really," I admit, searching my memories from that night.

"It was his grandfather's ring and supposedly can only be used by someone in his family's bloodline."

I sense aggravation and annoyance in Jace's tone as he opens the door to Kieren's presidential suite.

"After you," he says. The common room is eerily dark. I scrunch my nose at the faint smell of alcohol and weed, permanent fixtures at this point. Jace pulls out a set of keys from his pocket, jiggling one into the keyhole of the bedroom. "I have to lock you in here."

I scoff, but I don't bother to argue. "Whatever."

"It's for your own safety. Kieren doesn't want any lust-hungry guys to find his trophy. Who knows what some of these heathens would do if they found you alone."

The thought of horny, masked frat guys coming after me like bloodhounds in The Purge makes me shiver.

"Hey, Jace," I ask before he can shut the door. "Why did

Kieren and the alumni go into that back room with that blind-folded girl?"

"You didn't see that," he snaps, trying to close the door.

"But I did," I say, pushing my body into the gap of space. "Are they going to have sex with her?"

"I'm going to say something, Monroe, and I need you to listen carefully. If you value your life, do not ask questions about what happens in that room. Erase whatever you think you saw from your memory."

I falter at the warning and forget myself. Jace forces the door closed, and I stagger backward. Deadbolts turn, locking me inside with a clang, alone with my own thoughts.

My life? What the fuck is going on in that hidden room?

The rattle of the door slamming shut jostles the room, and Kieren's laptop screen flickers to life. His email is open. Curious and irritated that I'm locked away, I pad over to his computer. My eyes struggle to focus, and I have to blink several times before I can read the words on the screen.

An email received two days ago with the subject "full moon" catches my eye, and I click on the row.

From: x@sigma.me

To: kierenhuntIII@gmail.com

Subject: full moon

Body of the Email:

fine but we will speak on this.

I expand the correspondence to read the full exchange in descending order by date received.

From kierenhuntIII@gmail.com: *no.*

From x@sigma.me: *a disloyal is not preferred. find another.*

From kierenhuntIII@gmail.com: *a disloyal.*

From x@sigma.me: *what is the Sinner's status?*

From kierenhuntIII@gmail.com: *yes.*

From x@sigma.me: *has the offering been pledged to The Brotherhood?*

From kierenhuntIII@gmail.com: *yes.*

From x@sigma.me: *have you secured an offering?*

"What the fuck?" I whisper. Nauseating anxiety coils in my gut. *An offering?*

An offering for what? My thoughts jump to the conversation with Jace. Kieren's ring is the brand? *But how?* I step toward the mirror and twist my torso to see the design of the brand in my reflection. This doesn't look anything like the top of Kieren's ring.

I dart back over to the laptop and do a search for the email address 'x@sigma.me'. Hundreds of emails populate the email search results. I click through the pages to understand how far back the correspondence goes until I find the date of the first exchange – June 26th of last year.

I click on the row.

From: kierenhuntIII@gmail.com

To: x@sigma.me

Subject: hello

Body of Email:

Dear X,

By way of introduction, my name is Kieren Hunt III, son of Kieren Hunt Junior. I'm contacting you at the direction of my father. I'm told you are expecting my email. My family has come under duress, as I believe you are aware, and I'm told you may be able to help. May we set up a time to speak?

Regards,

Kieren Hunt III

. . .

My eyes scan the flurry of back-and-forth responses, but I would need hours to read the entirety of their email exchanges. Who the fuck is 'X' and what did Kieren mean by his family has come under duress? What kind of help does this X person provide? Is he a medical professional?

Kieren told me about his father's suicide attempt – could his email have something to do with his dad's health? But then, how do you explain the first email exchange I read about an offering? What does any of this mean?

The fluttered beep of a car unlocking in the back parking lot pulls my attention from the screen. I scurry to the window and open the curtain just enough to see outside. Two of the men wearing the full-face satanic masks open the back doors of a large, black SUV and climb into the back seat. Two other men wearing black balaclavas carry a bulky, long object, open the trunk, put the object inside, close the trunk, and settle into the driver and front passenger seats. Seconds later, more men in the full-face satanic masks get into a second black SUV. Both car engines roar to life. The first SUV reverses out of its parking spot, then drives off. The second SUV does the same less than a minute later.

So fucking strange. What time is it? Is the Ceremony over? I dash back to Kieren's computer to see that it's almost three a.m. My hand rests on the mouse trackpad, ready to resume my snooping, when heavy footsteps can be heard marching down the hall. The door to the common room opens, and I slam the laptop shut. I've barely scurried onto the bed and under the covers when a key turns in the lock.

I squeeze my eyes closed, pretending to be asleep. Did I close out of the last email exchange with 'X'? Shit, I pray I did.

The thunk of Kieren's mask hitting the floor is followed by sounds of clothes being aggressively stripped off his body and discarded into a heap. His first stop is the bathroom. A stream of urination landing in the toilet bowl is starkly loud in the otherwise silent room. The loud whoosh of flushing precedes the squeaking turn of the sink tap.

He's coming back.

The mattress dips under the pressure of his body, and it takes every bit of energy I have left to steady my breathing and maintain my ruse. Smells of sweat and rancid char permeate my nostrils. Kieren collapses beside me, and the rank scent of him is like the human version of curdled milk. It's so awful, I bury my face into the pillow, hoping the fibrous filling will filter away some of the stench. I should have taken off my bra and underwear. I should have cleaned myself up, but I didn't, and now I'm trapped, wide awake, under the weight of his arm.

Sleep finds Kieren in less than two minutes. His heavy breathing is hot against my neck. Thoughts swirl in my mind, and I can't make them stop. Minutes pass, maybe an hour. I stare at the blank wall in front of me, unable to quiet the nagging voice in my head.

Get up, Monroe.

Get up and find that hidden room.

26

KIEREN

Six Months Prior to Present Day,
The March Full Moon Ceremony,
Junior Year,
Sigma

"We need to speak," the unmistakable metallic voice snarls at my back as I open the door to leave the Sacrifice room. Tonight's offering has been wrapped in black cloth, and I motion for Barrett, who has been standing guard in the adjoining foyer-turned-closet.

"Footbridge," I instruct, and Barrett nods, having already been briefed on logistics. The uncharacteristically warm week we've had must be another one of Moloch's blessings. When I checked the water under the footbridge yesterday, I was surprised to see it flowing freely.

"Take Harrison, but clear the Ceremony room first and get everyone upstairs. The newly initiated must receive their brands," I reiterate. Barrett's already familiar with the order of events, but I find it necessary to remind him, since I assume he's spent the better part of the evening thinking with his dick and not his brain.

Barrett's eyes focus on the scene behind me, before giving me a curt nod and exiting through the door to the hidden room. The presence of X lingering in my personal space, waiting for an audience, gnaws at my patience, and I want nothing more than to spin around and tell him to get off my dick.

"Yes," I acknowledge, slowly turning to face the demon clown. We match each other in height, but I have no doubt who would prevail in hand-to-hand combat. I doubt his ridiculous outfit affords him much mobility.

"You have a pet," he states.

My jaw ticks with ire under my mask as my hands inadvertently curl into fists.

"Leave her out of this," I growl.

"Will she be shared next time?" he asks. The other two elders in the room now stand at rapt attention.

"She's mine," I bite out. "Leave her out of this," I repeat.

"That is not in the way of the Sigma. All Sinners must be shared," he says dismissively.

"When will you offer her?" X asks.

My eyebrows flare up with an amusement I wish this asshole could see.

"She's not up for offer," I snap.

"Wrong," X responds, drawing out the word. "Moloch does not want dissenters. Moloch wants purity of soul. Those who are the most precious to us must be offered. It is the way of the Sigma. It's why we cultivate and care for our Sinners, just as your grandfather had. Ask him."

"My grandfather has dementia, you fuck," I spit.

X takes a menacing step toward me, but I don't back down. Never will I cower to this fucker. "All that has been given can be taken away," he warns.

"She will be offered," he states as if he alone has the final fucking say in the matter.

"You'll have to pry her out of my cold, dead hands first, and good luck with that, because I'll take you down with me in the process. Two can play your death dance game."

"Does your father know about your pet?" he pivots, and his change of subject catches me off guard. My response is too slow, and as such, I've revealed my cards.

"No, he doesn't, does he?" X confirms with a sickening uptick in tone. "And you don't intend to tell him. Interesting."

I glare at X. If he didn't have my family's nuts in a vice, I would rip his fucking mask off and end this charade.

"Next month," X says, as if it's already been decided.

"Come after her, and I'll blow the door of your little blood sacrifice operation wide open."

X laughs like I've made an empty threat, treating me like a fucking child, just like my father. I imagine the conversations those two have had about me, and the skin under my mask singes with rage.

"I'd like to see you try, boy. She can't hide behind you forever. You will offer her or our deal is off."

I turn, abruptly leaving X and the other elders behind in the Sacrifice Room. I'm over fucking pleasantries.

Fury billows behind me like a cape caught in the wind as I stride through the now empty basement used for the Ceremony. I want to kill him. I want to go upstairs and get my fucking gun and blow a hole through his fucking head. The goddamn clown. He thinks he can threaten me. He thinks he can come after what's mine.

The thought of this farce of a man hovering over Monroe's

lifeless body, spilling her blood, playing God, reaping the benefit of my toils...

I want to burn him.

I'm the only God here.

How dare he?

When are these assholes going to learn that they can't *fuck with me?*

Resentment seeps into my veins, and even though I know it's misplaced, I can't help but feel so fucking angry with Monroe. She's in the way. I cannot have X dangle her over my head. This was not part of the agreement, and she was never meant to be collateral used against me. My father already has weaponized my trust fund. I can't have this sick fuck of a human weaponize Monroe, too.

X and my father will force me to choose. I know they will.

Dammit, Monroe. Seething, I clench my jaw as I get sucked down into a whirlpool of my own rage and misery.

They say love and hate are two sides of the same coin. I will hate myself for wanting to love you, won't I Monroe? It's the inevitable outcome of this fucked up situation. But, here we are. The house wins again.

The house always fucking wins.

27
KIEREN

Present Day
Mid-September, Senior Year,
Sigma

How the fuck does this happen? Who fucked up?

A body was found and I was promised this would never happen. Weights were used. All precautions were made.

My paranoia starts to get the best of me.

Fuck.

"Fuck!" I scream loud enough to rattle the windows of my bedroom.

But then I sink back onto my bed, laughing.

"So stupid," I laugh as I draw in a breath.

"So stupid, stupid, stupid."

"Where the fuck did you go, Monroe?" I grunt, grinding my

jaw so tight that it throbs in pain. "Your friends were here the other night, probably looking for you," I say to my empty room. "I couldn't stand to see their fucking faces."

Goddammit, the pain.

Fuck that stupid car accident, I scream inside my mind. If I had only made better decisions four years ago. My TMJ issues will never go away, will they?

I stand and walk over to my desk. The bottle of prescription pain pills is already half empty. I pop one, swallow it, and then open a second pill bottle that contains my ketamine lozenges.

Flopping back onto my bed, I let my head hit the pillow as the tablet dissolves under my tongue.

In the corner of my room, the space her cage once occupied sits empty. I don't know how I'm going to preside over another Full Moon Ceremony without her. I could hardly stomach the Ceremony last week. Leaving the dais to fornicate with the peons was out of the question. I forced myself to sit and watch as long as I could before telling Jace to come find me when X and Barrett were ready.

Going up to my room I feared would not end well, so I sat in the dank stairwell that leads down to the basement and remembered. I'd sell my left nut to go back to the night of the first Full Moon Ceremony and experience that side of Monroe again, high on ecstasy, riding my dick like a fucking carousel. Her pink, rosy cheeks and beaming, ear-to-ear smile as she came undone... And when she told me she loved me. The memory of her crestfallen face when I didn't say it back plagues me more than I'll ever admit.

I searched for you all fucking summer Monroe.

You better keep fucking running, because I'll find you.

And you know what happens when I find you.

You did this to me.

If I could cry, I would. But I can't. I feel nothing. Numb.

Numb like my broken heart, I chuckle to myself.

Never again, Monroe, will I be so careless.

When I find you, you're coming home with me, and I'm going to keep you until the day you fucking die.

28

GABI

Two weeks have passed since a body was found floating in the gorge.

Three weeks have passed since Kasey went missing, and I haven't heard a peep about any police investigation. Do they honestly believe she's simply on a bender with her boyfriend, and therefore aren't concerned? That seems preposterous!

Ele, Viv, and I continue to tiptoe around the explosive conversation we had the night I almost got caught trying to break into Sigma. I guess it's easier to sweep it under the rug, but at some point, I'll have to address the rift I've caused.

I don't dare tell them I've planned one last-ditch attempt to discover what is or isn't hiding in Sigma's basement. Eying my reflection in the mirror, I slick my hair back into a low bun. The light-brown wig I bought looks more realistic in person, which is a pleasant surprise. Combined with a pair of thick-framed, faux glasses, I like to think I will look almost unrecognizable.

What's wild is I've spent a fair amount of time researching Sigma and have gone down several eye-opening online forum rabbit holes. Apparently, it was common in past years for fraternities to have a tradition called *Little Sisters*, where women would get paired with fraternity members who were supposed to act as big brother mentors. In reality, it seemed like it was really about the sex.

At certain fraternities, but not all, it was understood that Little Sisters had to sleep with a designated number of fraternity brothers to maintain their honorary status. If that doesn't scream cult to you, I don't know what does. Sometimes, these *'mentorships'* led to relationships and even marriages, so maybe there are a few happy endings, but overall, it was just a group sex fest. Which, you know, no judgement, as long as it's consensual. I can practically hear Monroe's voice in my head say the heteronormative ways of the past are tiresome anyway. She was always accepting of people's differences. *Is accepting*, I correct myself.

I place the wig on top of my head and straighten it into place.

Sigma's take on this tradition, however, seems to be much darker. For every hundred or so forum threads, a comment regarding demonic human sacrifice would percolate and immediately be shut down as blasphemy, dirty rumors, or the occasional: *Watch your fuckin back. No one is anonymous, even on the Internet.*

I comb out the strands of shoulder-length, mousey brown hair.

It might all be hearsay, but where there's smoke, there's fire, and after what I witnessed three weeks ago, I think there's a fair amount of fire burning in that hellhole.

I swipe baby-pink lip gloss along my lips and pop them together. The look is giving '*shy girl who secretly likes to get railed while handcuffed to the bed,*' and I think my vibe will fit in perfectly at the Sigma mixer tonight.

An email went out earlier this week to the members of my sorority letting us know this mixer was only for freshmen and sophomores. Seems suspicious, doesn't it?

My outfit tonight is an unassuming black tank top, basic jeans, and sneakers – a look that will blend in with the other freshman and sophomore women. I grab my most modest bag and throw my phone, keys, and lip gloss inside.

"Excuse me, who are you?" Ele asks from across the living room.

I try to ignore her, but she's off the couch and steps away from intercepting me in a heartbeat.

"Relax, Ele. It's just me," I say, turning around to face her with a guilty look.

"Gabi? What the fuck? Why are you *wearing* that?"

I shrug. "Thought I'd try something different."

"Hold on," Ele says as she crosses her arms. "Where are you going?"

Again, I shrug. "Just... out."

"*Out?*" she challenges.

"Sorry, I have to run, my Uber is downstairs," I say.

"Gabi," she shouts, grabbing my arm. "Where are you going?"

I sigh in frustration because there's no use in hiding the obvious.

"You know where I'm going, Ele. Don't try to stop me."

29
MONROE

I stir to the loud sound of gravel crunching under tires and headlight beams backlighting the closed curtain. Even from three stories up with the windows shut, I can hear the comings and goings of cars since the parking lot and driveway are immediately below both external-facing sides of the bedroom. What time is it, anyway? The room is still dark, so it can't be sunrise yet.

Kieren lies like a corpse beside me, face turned sideways on the pillow, softly snoring. Sometimes I catch myself staring at him while he sleeps, admiring his beauty, and I hate that he's so fucking gorgeous. I hate that he became even more gorgeous when he got his eyebrow and nose piercings. I hate that he has this hold over me, and that I so desperately want to please him, to be good for him. I crave his praise and affection. I yearn to be loved by him like a normal person. It's all I wish for. Why can't I be enough? I've given him so much of myself. Why won't he do the same?

Quietly, I climb over his body. I'm desperate to relieve myself and curious who is driving into Sigma's parking lot at such an hour.

Pulling back the curtain, I watch the passenger's side door open. Harrison steps out. I'm shocked to see his full, unconcealed face. The driver's side door opens, and in similar fashion, Barrett exits the vehicle. No ski masks, and most interestingly, no one else. I suppose it makes sense that the Sigma alumni, or 'elders' as Jace called them, have arranged other accommodations. I can't blame them for not wanting to spend the night in a disgusting frat house.

Swiping my phone from the edge of Kieren's desk, I tiptoe into the bathroom and peel down my underwear, regretting my lack of foresight to preemptively set out a change of clothes. I startle at the sound of a door slamming shut down the hall, then another.

Despite the noise I'm making in the bathroom and whatever is going on outside his bedroom, Kieren hasn't stirred.

A feeling pulls me to the door like gravity. Unlocked. Kieren never leaves his bedroom door unlocked at night, even when we're inside. My brows knit together, puzzled by this discovery. Twisting the knob, I silently open the bedroom door just enough for my slender body to slip through. A strip of yellow light seeps under the common room door. The hallway is always lit, no matter the time of day, and I squint as my eyes adjust to the harsh florescent lighting.

I pad quickly down the corridor, still in my black lace thong and bra. The coast is clear, so I keep going. I round a corner, then another, then another. I ever so delicately lean into the metal bar of the heavy stairwell door and hold the handle once I'm on the opposite side so the sound of the door closing is only a hissed whisper.

My thighs pump rapidly as I race down the stairs on tiptoes. This time, I notice the filth coating each step, filth that now has transferred to the soles of my feet. I definitely should have showered.

The first floor is empty. Through the windows, I see the sky outside is pitch black.

My heart beats in my throat with nervous fear as I reach the final set of stairs leading to the basement. I creep down to the last step and place an ear against the door to listen. Quiet.

Slowly, I turn the nob and peek inside. A few scant lights remain on, providing just enough visibility to navigate the space. Curtains hang heavy from the ceiling. Some have come unfastened in spots, falling in on themselves. Overturned furniture looks strange and out of place, like a trashed hotel room. Red plastic cups are haphazardly strewn across the floor. I trip when my right foot collides with a cup half-filled with liquid, knocking it over.

I reach the back of the room and run my palm up and down the wall while holding my phone in the other. Where is this door? I know it's here.

My index finger snags on a divot. Such a shame to paint these wood panels, they were probably here when Sigma was originally constructed. I curl my finger into the barely discernible notch and tug. Hinges on the other side of the wall creak. The hidden door drifts open as if propelled by an invisible wind.

Behind the door is a dank, cave-like space that reeks of spoiled, charred meat. What the fuck is that smell? There must be a dead animal in here. With trembling fingers, I lift my phone to pan the small space with the flashlight, expecting to see a hidden room of horrors.

But... It's a closet.

Random chairs, random party decorations, random shit...

Is this like that movie where kids walk into a wardrobe and stumble upon a portal to a secret world? Or in the case of Sigma, a portal to hell?

I study each pocket of miscellaneous items for clues.

Jesus Christ, the smell. Where is that coming from?

A draft of frosty air wafts over my bare toes. Strange.

I point the flashlight at the floor and study the wood paneling. It's ever so slightly ajar. Dropping to my knees, I run my fingers between the two wooden boards and feel that one board is protruding just a bit. I trace the line, up, up, until I'm standing eye-level with a circular indentation in the wood that looks an awful lot like...

... my brand.

Fingertips of my left hand trace around the smooth scars on my left ass cheek while I examine the small design carved into the wood.

It's the same...

The brand, or the ring, rather, is a...

"What the fuck are you doing?"

I jump and let out a scream. My phone clangs to the floor. I drop to retrieve it when Kieren grabs me by the hair, hauling me to my feet.

"Why are you down here?!" he booms in my face.

I clutch my phone close to my body as he yanks me from the small room and out into the basement. When he realizes I still have it, he snatches it from my hand.

His fingers are wrapped tightly around my neck like I'm an insolent child as we march in terrifying silence back to his room. Wrath oozes from his every pore, and my stomach twists with mounting anxiety as I ready myself for battle. Once inside, he slams the door hard enough for it to bounce back open.

"Get in," he says, pointing to the cage in the corner of his room I had completely forgotten about. He shoves the bedroom door closed and this time, locks it from the inside with a key.

"No," I shout at him. "I'm not getting in that fucking dog cage. Do you want to tell me what the fuck happened in that room tonight? Did you have sex with that girl who went back there with you and those men in the demon masks?"

He stalks over to his desk, leaving my questions unanswered, and opens the top drawer.

"Kieren," I stammer, unable to find my breath when I see what he's holding. "What the fuck? Why do you have a gun? Stop, put it down!" Tears stream down my face as he takes two steps closer. I get down on my knees, unable to stop my body from trembling.

"In," he says, nudging my ass with his foot.

A sob shakes free as I crawl backwards inside the confines of the cage, wincing as the bottom wires dig painfully into my kneecaps and palms.

"Please, Kieren," I beg as he latches the cage door shut and then secures it with a combination lock. "Please, don't do this. I'm sorry. I'm so sorry. I just... I saw you go in there with her. I thought..."

"Shut the fuck up," he barks at me. "If you say one more fucking word, I'll duct tape your mouth shut and your hands behind your back."

I gasp for air through my sobs as I awkwardly try to lay down on my side, curling my knees into my chest. Kieren places the gun on top of his desk like a cruel reminder of my helplessness.

I watch him climb back into bed. Cold bites at my bare skin. My teeth chatter as I heave, squeezing my arms tighter around my legs as if they are scraps of a blanket.

A gun...

A fucking gun....

I have to get out. I can't be involved in whatever this is anymore. Pointing a gun at my head and making me sleep in a fucking dog cage is where I draw the line.

He's lost his mind, and I fear this time, it's for good.

———

At some point, between convulsing because I was so cold and losing sensation in my legs, I must have fallen asleep.

"Kieren," I call. My voice is hoarse from crying and spending the night sleeping nearly naked on the floor. "Kieren!" I call louder.

"Kieren!" I shout, banging against the door of the cage. "Let me out!"

He doesn't move.

"Kieren, let me out! I have to go to the bathroom!"

He rolls out of bed at a snail's pace, rubbing the sleep from his eyes before acknowledging my desperate pleas.

"Kieren, please," I beg.

"Alright!" he shouts with annoyance, standing. He crouches down in front of the cage, twisting the combination of the lock and jerking it down to pop the mechanism open. The curved bar snaps up, and Kieren flicks the latch of the cage to the side, allowing the door to swing open.

I glare at him as I crawl free. My legs are stiff from sleeping in a tight ball, and it takes more than one attempt to stand.

He flops back onto his bed, unashamed by his actions. The black Glock sits on his desk, untouched. I know it's a Glock because when your shitbag of a mom remarries a mobster who runs a racketeering ring out of your childhood home, you end up seeing more than your fair share of firearms.

My fingers curl into fists, but I resist the urge to slam the bathroom door in Kieren's face. I don't know what version of Kieren is out there this morning, and I don't want to take my chances. Plus, now that a weapon has entered the chat and been pointed at my head, the stakes have, needless to say, escalated. I must tread carefully, at least for the next few hours until I can get out here. To distract myself, I rage-brush my teeth until they have a pearlescent sheen and start a shower.

Hot water streams down the crown of my head as I slowly come back to life. Every memory from last night I suppressed so I could get a lick of sleep resurfaces with a vengeance.

He held me at fucking gunpoint.
Jace called me Kieren's trophy.
He put me in a fucking dog cage.
The hidden room within a room.
He threatened to duct tape my mouth shut.
The putrid smell of decay.
He made me sleep in a FUCKING DOG CAGE.

Just as I want to scream, metal shower curtain rings scrape across the rod. I startle but don't turn around. The loofa I keep here hangs around the shower knob. I unhook it and hold it under the container of body wash while I pump out enough soap to wash an elephant. I start rage-cleaning every inch of my skin, summoning the same vigor I found when brushing my teeth. Frothy, white foam slides down my shoulders, my back, my breasts. I scrub at my ass and vagina, not caring that Kieren is naked beside me, because I hope he's doing the same with his parts after whatever he did in that hidden room last night. After sleeping with his dried cum residue on my skin, I need it gone. My face is last to be cleansed, although I cried off all my makeup, and my eyes are still puffy and red.

The second I'm finished with my shower routine, I reach for the curtain, ready to towel dry and get the hell out of this place, when Kieren grabs my upper arm.

"Stop," he says with chilling firmness.

I stumble until I feel the cool tile of the shower wall against my back. Kieren's body presses into mine, shielding me from the cascading water. His forearms are on either side of my head; his groin is flush with my stomach. Droplets cling to his long, dark lashes. Rivulets stream down his tattooed chest, his defined abdomen, catching in the pubic hair around his cock.

My gaze flicks up to his. Hot tears sting my eyes, clouding my vision.

"You put me in a cage," I finally whimper. I can barely get the words out. My chest heaves in tight, rapid bursts as I try to clamp down my pain.

"You broke my trust," he grits.

"That's bullshit Kieren. You held a gun to my fucking head and made me sleep in there the entire night. What the fuck is wrong with you?"

"Wrong with *me*? I woke up and you were gone, Monroe. I thought you had been taken. You have no idea what these heathens are capable of, especially on a night like last. But to find you snooping around in the fucking basement? Are you kidding me? Don't ever let me catch you down there again, do you understand? You don't know the pressure I'm under. You don't know the sacrifices I have to make for my future."

"Then tell me," I plead. My fingertips skim the stubble on his cheek.

"I can't," he says with a heavy hang of his head.

"I'm losing you again," I cry. "Just like sophomore year. I'm losing you."

He shakes his head. Water runs down his face, but he makes no attempt to wipe it away. Steam envelopes us in stifling heat, and I start to feel like I'm suffocating.

"I'm right here, Monroe. But I need you to understand something." He lifts his head and his dark brown eyes stare directly into mine. "You are part of this now. You are Sigma. More than that, you're mine. As I've already told you, if you try to run, I'll catch you. If you hide, I'll find you. But most importantly, if you try to fuck up what I've worked so hard to achieve, if you get in the way, I will be forced to choose, and I fear it won't be you."

I suck in a ragged breath at his words. Suddenly, the shower feels too hot, my head too light. I push him off me and scramble over the tub ledge. I don't even bother with a towel.

My knuckles turn white as I grip the sink, struggling to breathe; struggling to make sense of what apparently is my new reality.

The tap squeals shut, and the water stops. Kieren steps out of the shower with ease. A soft terry cloth towel is wrapped around my torso, encasing my wet skin from my breasts to my thighs. Gooseflesh blankets my entire body, and my sopping wet hair has left a generous puddle at my feet.

"Don't you ever do that to me again," I growl, whirling around to see him true. "Whatever is going on with you, since these Ceremonies started, scares me. You're different."

"I'm not," he says insistently, kissing my damp forehead. "I'm the same person I've always been. The same person I thought you loved."

My face quivers with unleashed emotions.

"Why are you doing this to me?" I croak.

"Doing what? Protecting you? Loving you?"

I shake my head as crocodile tears fall. "You don't. You don't put someone you love in a fucking cage at gunpoint!"

"I'm sorry, Monroe, if you think I overacted, but try to see it from my point of view. It was four in the morning. I had barely slept and was hardly able to function. I roll over and find you missing. I panicked. Then when I found you snooping around behind my back, I snapped. You pushed me to my limit," he explains unapologetically. "If you don't want me to snap, don't do shit like that!"

"I can't do this," I say through ragged breaths. His arms wrap around my back as he pulls me into his chest.

"Yes, you can," he insists.

"Why do you have a gun, Kieren?"

"For safety, obviously."

"For your safety or mine, because I sure as fuck do not feel safe."

"Stop, Monroe," he soothes, kissing the top of my head as he strokes my wet hair. "You need to calm down. You should know by now not to push me like you did."

I try to steady my breath. "What happened last night in that room? Did you and the elders have sex with that woman who went back there? Please, don't lie to me."

"How do you know they're called elders?"

"Jace told me," I admit.

"Why does that not surprise me," Kieren scoffs. "No, Monroe. I swear on my life. On my grandfather's life. I did not have sex with that woman."

I swallow the lump in my throat, the fear that he had been unfaithful.

"Monroe, why would I cheat on you? Look how perfect you are," he says, spinning me around to face my reflection. Perfection is not the word I would use to describe my present appearance. My eyes are bloodshot and puffy. My face is marred with patches of irritated, flushed skin. Dark crescents rim my under-eyes, and I look pale and exhausted.

"Tell me what happened, then, if it wasn't sex."

"It's an old Sigma ritual. A bunch of chanting. But there are rich and powerful alumni who take it very seriously, and I need to appease these people because I need them to donate funds to Sigma. We're fucking broke, Monroe. This chapter is one delinquent payment away from foreclosure."

"Sigma is broke?" I ask with surprise.

"Not Sigma as a whole, but our chapter has struggled for years. Maintaining this massive house on top all the expenses associated with the parties we throw has drained our coffers. I shouldn't tell you this. No one is supposed to know about our financial situation nor that Sigma alumni are attending these Full Moon Ceremonies. Especially that, because if word got out, I would lose everything I've worked so hard to achieve. I'd probably get expelled."

"I won't say anything," I promise.

A moment of understanding passes between us as we silently take in our reflection. The tendons of Kieren's forearms flex as he holds me flush against his chest, and despite the way I felt when I woke up, it feels like we've managed a truce.

"Do you still love me?" he asks. His voice cracks in a way that is both desperate and endearing.

I tense, uncertain if I'm ready to forgive him.

"Please, Monroe. I need to hear you say it."

My stomach knots with inner conflict. He needs me, and in this moment, I cannot remember who I was before Kieren, but I also fear who I will become if we breakup.

"Yes," I concede, setting my unresolved emotions aside for another time. "I do."

He kisses my earlobe and down the side of my neck at my response.

My towel plops to the floor, and I stare back at my naked self in the mirror. My teardrop breasts, my shaved pussy, the indentation down the center of my abdomen that Kieren now traces with his fingers.

"Kieren," I stammer, halting the progression of his hand.

"Don't push me away, Monroe. Let me give you what I wasn't able to give you last night."

He holds my questioning stare in the mirror. "What? Did you think I didn't notice how badly you wanted me to fuck you like that woman on the table? I could smell how aroused you were as you watched. I knew you wanted me to bend you over the dais and fuck you senseless. You wanted it raw, like an animal, and it killed me that I couldn't give you the pleasure you deserved."

The hand on my abdomen skims the curve in my waist and runs down my ass. I gasp when Kieren shoves two thick fingers inside my pussy from behind, pumping them in and out.

I hinge forward, watching him finger fuck me in the mirror, his eyes never leaving mine. He removes his fingers and runs the soft tip of his penis up and down my slit, lubricating his erection with my arousal, then sinks himself inside me, pushing the entire length of his shaft into my tight pussy in one thrust.

A choked moan leaves my lips at the sudden increase in pressure. His first few strokes are languid and deliberate as he stretches my walls. I bend forward, resting my forehead on my arms now crossed in front of me, and stand on my tiptoes to give him better access. Each thrust lifts me off the ground just a little, and fuck, do I want this.

"Look at me, Monroe," Kieren barks as he picks up the pace.

"I said, look at me." My head is jerked up from its perch by my hair, and even though my head feels too heavy to keep upright, I force the muscles of my neck to hold it in place.

Satisfied I won't look away, Kieren lets my damp strands go. The wet clap of his groin against my ass elicits heated groans, and just like the woman last night, I start begging. I beg him to fuck me harder, to ruthlessly spear my pussy like a savage, to slam into me until I burst.

I feel my orgasm begin to build alongside the sensation of mounting pressure.

"Pull out when you come," I plead as his thrusts quicken.

"Fuck, baby, yes. Yes, I want you to soak me. Fucking squirt all over this floor. Fucking drench me, Monroe."

I scream his name over and over again as he slams into me. The same two fingers that were inside me minutes ago press firmly against my clit, stroking, coaxing me to my breaking point before administering the pinch of pain I need to topple over the edge.

I've stopped breathing. My body clenches, turning red, waiting to push out my release.

"Kieren please," are the last words I cry before he ruins me with one last thrust so deep, I can practically taste him. He pulls out, shooting hot ribbons of cum across my back, and I explode. My pussy pulses with my orgasm as I simultaneously bear down, squirting onto Kieren's thighs just as he demanded. The sensation of such an intense climax, of that much liquid leaving my body, is... dizzying.

Is...

Oh God...

A fleeting thought to yell, to give warning that I'm going to pass out, flickers in my mind, but not fast enough.

I hit the floor.

And the world goes black.

30
MONROE

Six Months Prior to Present Day,
Morning After the March Full Moon Ceremony,
Sigma

"I told you, it's not fucking happening."

Kieren's loud voice startles me awake, and judging by the bright light flooding the bedroom, I must have been out for several hours.

"No, that's bullshit. I'm not letting that freak touch her. She's mine, Father."

I strain to listen as the conversation pauses.

"No, it's not that serious."

Another pause, and I feel my palms start to sweat.

"Maybe I will offer her, but on my terms and my timeline... Yes, I do get to dictate this... Because it's not your neck on the line or his, it's mine... No. No, she's not... Because I care! I'm the one who should reap the blessings, not him or any of the other fuckers in the room... Yes, of course I meant our family, not just me. Listen, Father, I have to go. I'll speak to you when I'm home."

The key turns in the lock, and Kieren's eyes flick to mine when he enters. I do my best to subdue my confused expression and greet him with a neutral face.

"You're awake," he comments with surprise. "How are you feeling? I was worried I would need to take you to the hospital."

"Fine," I rasp. "My head is killing me."

"Here, drink water," he insists, sitting next to me on the bed as he unscrews the top of a bottle. "I brought us lunch. When is the last time you ate?"

I shrug. "Maybe lunch yesterday."

"Has this happened before?" he asks, concerned.

"Yeah, I have a low red blood cell count. I've been anemic my whole life."

"You're anemic?" he asks with shock. "And you didn't think to tell me this in the three years we've known each other?"

"Sorry. Sometimes I forget I have this issue."

"Jesus Christ, Monroe. For a second there, I literally thought I fucked you to death."

I snort, spitting water all over my lap. "It wouldn't be the worst way to die," I laugh.

Kieren scoffs. "You have a twisted sense of humor, Monroe. I caught you when you fell, by the way. Barely, but I caught you."

"Am I supposed to thank you?" I jest.

"Wouldn't hurt, seeing as I stopped you from falling on your face and breaking your nose."

"You like my face too much to let anything happen to it."

I take a sip of water; the room now strangely quiet.

"How's your dad?" I ask, changing the subject. "I heard you

say *'father'* and assumed you were speaking to him on the phone."

Kieren scowls. "Oh, you heard that? What else did you hear?"

"That was it," I lie.

He sighs, leaning back on his elbows. "Nothing. He's fine, but all up in my shit, which is annoying as fuck."

"Is he excited to see you?"

"I doubt it. You know we've never had a typical father-and-son relationship, and he's not a very warm and fuzzy guy, even after what happened last summer."

"Am I going home with you?"

I've known Kieren has planned to visit his parents in Connecticut over spring break for weeks, and yet he's not once mentioned bringing me with him. Maybe the state of his father's health remains too fragile to introduce someone new, but it feels odd given the amount of time we spend together, not to mention our years of history. The words he said to me in a drunken rage at his birthday dinner in New York City during winter break our freshman year continue to haunt me, and in the back of my mind, I suspect they still hold true.

"If you're a good girl," he says with a menacing smirk. "But you'll have to earn it, puppy."

I roll my eyes at him and slide off the bed to open the take-away bag. Breakfast bagels, thank god. I need real sustenance.

"I'll drive you to the sorority or your apartment to get clothes and anything else you need after we eat," Kieren comments.

"Why?" I ask before biting into the overstuffed egg and cheese sandwich.

"Because you don't have many things here."

"That's because I don't live here," I answer, covering my mouth with my hand as I chew.

"You're my girlfriend, you should stay here. Besides, the thought of you not being here at night makes me spiral. I need you here for your safety."

"For my safety?" I ask incredulously.

"Monroe, I don't think you understand. When I said you were mine, I meant it in every sense of the word. Why wouldn't you want to live with me? Is there someone else? Did you not mean it when you told me you loved me?"

"Don't be ridiculous," I retort through a mouthful of bagel sandwich.

"Then what's the problem? I'm getting sick of your fucking games, Monroe."

The bite I had taken sits partially chewed in my mouth as I furrow my brows at his capricious accusation.

"Do you remember what you said to me earlier this morning?" Kieren asks.

I give him a slight shake of my head because I barely remember the shower I took.

"You said you didn't think you could do this. You were sewing your seeds of doubt, like you always do right before you run, and there will be no more running, Monroe. You can't keep telling me you love me and then leave the second things don't go your way. After last night and that stunt you pulled, we're going to do things differently, starting with your security. Whenever you leave this room, it will be with me or with an escort."

I manage a painful swallow. "You can't keep me captive in your room, Kieren. That's absurd!"

"No, what's absurd," he snaps, sitting up to glare at me as I huddle on the floor at his feet, "is that you fail to comprehend the target you have on your back as my girlfriend. Do you think I don't hear the whispers? The envy of what we're doing here at Sigma? The jealousy wielded at the women who have been initiated as Sigma Little Sisters? Everyone is getting an escort, Monroe. Sigma protects their own, especially you. Above all else, you, so do not forget, Monroe, that you are not only a part of this now, but as my girlfriend, you are the face of Sigma Little Sisters. Every dick with a pulse is out to fuck you, and I'll be damned if I let anyone touch what's mine, because the only one who gets to make you scream is me."

"Kieren, this sounds incredibly paranoid, even for you. Escorts? Security? You sound like you truly have lost your mind."

He closes his eyes and laughs to himself. "Yeah," he agrees with a mocking sneer. "I lost my mind a long time ago, Monroe. My mind, my soul, my humanity. But you know the one thing I refuse to lose?" he asks, looking at me with determined zeal. "It's you."

31
MONROE

Five Months Prior to Present Day,
Thursday Before Spring Break,
Junior Year,
Dornell University

I glance out of the corner of my eye at my shadow. Harrison sits two seats down from me with his laptop out, pretending to be a student in this class. I don't know what he's doing; maybe he's working on one of the courses he's actually enrolled in, or maybe he's typing a minute-by-minute update for Kieren detailing what I ate for lunch, how many times I've taken a piss, and how many breaths I take per minute.

This is madness, and I'm convinced there is something deeply wrong with me.

When Kieren declared I would be monitored at all hours of the day for my own security, something inside of me started to shut down. At first, I found having a constant companion to be irritating, because most of the time, it wasn't Kieren, it was one of his henchmen. Barrett I cannot stand, although Harrison is not much better. At least he rarely speaks.

After nearly two weeks of my new normal, I no longer feel like I'm living. I'm just... existing. I'm living in a void, and I don't understand how I got here or how to get out. For days on end, I've done nothing but wake up, shower, wait for my escort, go to class, come back, and wait for Kieren. I'm physically present, but mentally and emotionally gone. My brain registers sounds and visuals, but everything is muffled, like I'm under water, listening, watching, drowning.

A pestering feeling lingers at the tip of my cortex, like I've been here before, but I can't remember when or how or why. It's a memory I cannot recall, and the nagging sense of déjà vu haunts me. I can tell my body recognizes this state of being because the numbness I feel is less like a shell and more like armor. I don't feel fear. I feel acceptance.

Unable to focus, I open a new tab in my browser and type in the address for Dornell's campus news website, *Dornell Daily*. My blood turns to ice as the page loads. On the homepage of the website is a picture of a smiling female student with the headline: *Rory Copeland, Freshman Student Missing*.

My breath grows choppy as I click on the article. A quick glance to the right tells me my shadow is engrossed in whatever he's reading on his laptop screen, but I don't want to take any chances, so I shrink the size of the browser window down to a small, barely legible box. I scan the news story, squinting as I read.

> *Rory Copeland, freshman architecture major and recent*
> *pledge of the sorority Delta Delta Delta, has been missing*
> *for over seventy-two hours. Friends and classmates reported*

seeing Rory this past Saturday at her sorority and with her study group at the library. If you have any information on Rory's whereabouts, please contact the local police immediately.

I study the picture of Rory, and an image of a woman with shoulder-length, chestnut brown hair, just like that on the webpage in front of me, pops into the forefront of my mind. I see her backside, her exposed buttocks, her red lace thong, her hair pressed flat against her head from the blindfold...

Cold sweat beads along my hairline and upper lip. My fingers quiver. A tightness in my chest makes it impossible to get a breath down.

Suddenly, the auditorium floods with noise. The professor must have delivered his closing remarks because students begin to pack up their belongings. With uncertainty, I do the same, realizing I didn't absorb a word said during the seventy-five-minute lecture. Harrison's prying eyes find mine, and I wonder if he can see the panic on my face.

"I need to stop by my sorority," I state, standing with purpose. I don't bother asking Harrison if he minds driving me across campus. The new pledge class is doing roommate and room selection tonight in anticipation of moving into the sorority house at the start of the next academic year. Kasey undoubtedly will be there, and I desperately need confirmation that I'm not crazy.

Grey clouds blanket the sky, threatening rain or possibly snow depending on how low the temperature drops tonight. After a teasing glimpse of spring weather, the cold has returned. Students are still bundled in their winter coats and boots to trudge through the dirty slush on the sidewalks. Everyone is eager for a sliver of sunshine, a signal that the relentless upstate New York winter is loosening its hold at last.

The tires of Harrison's Toyota Land Cruiser slosh through the half-melted, muddy snow, creating a soothing lull. I close my eyes and drift to the gentle rocking motion of the car as we drive the main street connecting the south-east campus quadrant to north campus, where many of the sorority houses reside.

Sunday night, after Kieren drove me to DG and waited for me outside in his car while I facilitated the weekly chapter meeting, neither of us spoke to each other. I stayed in his room, compliant, and finished my classwork due on Monday, alone. He said he had to oversee Sigma's weekly fraternity meeting and then preside over some hazing bullshit of the newly admitted brothers. He stumbled in around one a.m., drunk and smelling like weed.

When I was bored last week, I went through his medicine cabinet for answers, but it only resulted in more questions. Namely, the only medication present was a bottle of prescription-strength pain pills for his ongoing TMJ issue after a high school car accident rearranged his jaw structure. I've gone through his medicine cabinet before, when he first brought me to his house in Connecticut our freshman year, and I remember seeing several other medications for the treatment of anxiety and mood stabilizers.

I know Kieren has a lot on his plate, not to mention all that happened last summer with his father, and I wish he would consider therapy. I've mentioned it before, but my suggestion clearly triggered him. Apparently, I'm the one who needs therapy to work through my daddy abandonment issues and the tumultuous relationship I've always had with my mom. Frankly, I don't disagree. I know I need a fuck ton of therapy, but therapy is expensive and unfortunately for me, cost prohibitive.

Monday morning of this week, while I was getting ready in

Kieren's en suite bathroom wearing nothing but a towel, he woke up, stalked into the bathroom to pee, took one long, rakish look at me, then ravaged my body with a raw desire I hadn't felt since he returned at the top of the year. No chains, no nipple clamps, no e-stimulator machine like he normally enjoys using, just fucking and kissing on his bed until our lips were swollen and our need satiated. I missed my first two classes that day, and it took every modicum of strength I had left to leave his bedroom. If Harrison weren't my designated chauffeur, I probably would have skipped the entire day of lectures.

But when I got back to Sigma Monday evening, the earlier version of Kieren had vanished. He was cold and distant, hardly acknowledging my presence, gone again for hours. What I don't understand is which version of Kieren is the real him. Just when I think we've settled into a way of being with each other, things shift. This hardened version of him is the one I remember from our freshman year. Back then, I chalked it up to exhaustion and anger from the Sigma pledge process, but I'm not sure that conclusion holds. Sophomore year, I watched him lose himself, and when the alcohol wasn't enough, and the cocaine and ketamine weren't enough, he let the demons that plague his mind win.

I walked away at the end of my sophomore year. But these oscillating versions of Kieren, a detached, power-hungry monster one minute and possessive, love-starved boy the next, have stripped me to the bone. I worry the former version of Kieren is most aligned with his true self, and that the fleeting moments of insatiable desire and doting concern are nothing more than performative. Maybe Kieren isn't the only one who battles addiction issues, because somewhere along the way, I've become the addicted princess who willingly cohabitates with the devil, trapped in a castle of my own volition.

I know this, and yet I'm still here.

Why?

Why am I still here?

I'm living with my boyfriend, and yet why do I feel so empty and alone?

Why can't I find it within myself to leave him?

I have a phone, a car, and friends, even if my friends are currently living on the other side of the Atlantic.

Tears break free under my closed eyelids. I force every muscle in my face to tense, to freeze, as I collapse in silence. Only when I've held my breath to the point of fainting do I succumb and suck in a ragged breath.

"Are you okay?" Harrison asks in that lifeless, monotone voice of his that makes me want to throat punch him. I almost forgot he was here, which is stupid because he's always fucking here.

No Harrison, I'm not fucking okay.

But I don't say that because I know where his loyalties lie, so instead I say, "I'm getting my period." I don't explain further. There's no need, because what more does a simple man require than the thought of a bleeding vagina to get him to shut the fuck up.

———

"I just need twenty minutes," I say as I slam the car door. Honestly, I don't know how much time I need, but I also don't give a fuck.

I wipe the tears of my impending nervous breakdown away and march up the stairs of Delta Gamma. The padlock flashes with acceptance, and I swing open the front door only to be blasted by a panic-inducing ruckus of fifty-plus female voices talking simultaneously.

I stick to the perimeter of the large dining room. Every few steps, one of the members will look up from her conversation and offer me a friendly smile or wave. The mask I don as sorority president feels heavier with each wear, because underneath the mask, I'm cracking. Unravelling. Crumbling into a pile of ash.

Ten paces in front of me, I spot her.

"Hey Kasey," I say, bending down to tap her on the shoulder. She startles slightly at my touch, and I feel guilty for interrupting what seemed like a juicy gossip session. "Could I talk to you for a minute? It'll just take a second."

"Oh, sure."

She gives me a wary half-smile and pushes her chair back to stand. I motion with my index finger that we should head to a different room for this conversation and make my way to a quiet nook in the foyer.

"How are you doing?" I ask, turning to face her.

Kasey's eyes meet mine and then quickly look away. "Fine, you know. Excited for spring break."

Her clipped answers give me pause, and I can sense she's deeply uncomfortable in my presence. It's... heartbreaking. I'm supposed to be a confidant, a mentor, a mother figure to these young women, especially to Kasey, who is my Grand-Little. I was supposed to be a friendly face, accessible and caring, before Kieren gave me a different face, one that I didn't ask for and quite frankly, no longer want.

But apparently, this new face is permanent, and the reason why I've hardly been at my sorority this semester. I've cancelled just as many chapter meetings as I've held. I've let emails from sorority headquarters about our finances go unanswered. I've not even done the bare minimum, and it's painfully obvious to everyone. I have not been the leader I had hoped to be when I took this position. I knew it was a thankless role, but I'd intended to show up and try.

I push my failures as sorority president aside and compartmentalize them for a later date. "The other night," I begin, "you said someone had been running their mouth about... you know."

I don't want to say the words '*Sigma Little Sisters*' out loud, and I wonder if my extreme paranoia is out of fear, or if I've just been brainwashed by Kieren.

"Was the name of that someone Rory? The same Rory who is missing?"

Kasey's eyes flare with terror. "Please, Monroe. It wasn't me. I swear it wasn't me."

Tears roll down her cheeks before she can cover her face. A sob rips from her lips.

"Let's go upstairs," I say, and tenderly press my palm to her shoulder. She begins walking, and I follow, neither of us uttering a word as we ascend the creaky steps.

I pull my keys from my purse to unlock my bedroom. A stale, musty smell wafts into the hallway from days of disuse when I push open the door. Kasey takes a seat on my bed, wiping her nose on her sleeve.

"Please, Monroe. You have to believe me. You have to tell him that it wasn't me."

"Wait, Kasey, I have no idea what you're talking about," I admit as I sit down beside her. "Did something happen? Did someone say something?"

"Kieren thinks it was me," she sniffs.

"Thinks what was you?" I push, still completely in the dark.

"Some of the girls, Rory and these two other girls who are sophomores, Arden and Tessa, said they are writing this article for the *Dornell Daily*. They said they want to expose Sigma, and that Sigma Little Sisters is just a way to get women to have sex with guys in the fraternity. They think it's degrading, even if it's consensual, because of the power dynamic. Tessa tried to get me to contribute my story to the article because of what happened with Barrett."

I furrow my brow, unsure if I want to know, but I can't help my curiosity.

"What happened with Barret?"

"You didn't hear?" she asks.

She pulls down the collar of her sweater to expose the top of her shoulder, and I gasp. Brown and purple remnants of what must have been a nasty, circular bruise steal my breath away. It reminds me of... teeth marks.

Instantly, I'm transported to a vision of myself, looking at my own reflection in the mirror at Kieren's home in Connecticut. It was early fall, around October, my freshman year. Kieren and I had been dating for barely a month. It was the first time he revealed his primal side, and it was also the first time I felt my sexuality come alive. But seeing the same bite marks on someone else...

"Jesus, Kasey," I stammer. "Are you okay?" She quickly pulls up her sweater.

"It's not a big deal. Honestly, in the moment, I was into it, but the next day, when I ran into Tessa in the bathroom at Sigma, she saw my shoulder and flipped out. I was only wearing a bra and Barrett's boxer shorts and didn't realize the extent of the bruising."

"Barrett felt horrible. Truly, he did," she rationalizes. "We were both recklessly high that night. After Barrett helped Kieren with the Ritual, he came back to his room, and we did more molly, or... I'm not really sure what we did. I don't remember," she admits sheepishly.

My heart leaps into my throat, and I selfishly disregard

Kasey's ordeal. "What do you mean, '*Help Kieren with the ritual?*'"

The only knowledge I have about what happens in the hidden room is from Kieren, and I'm not convinced anymore that he told me the truth.

"I don't know," she says quietly. "He said he can't talk about it because it's a secret Sigma thing, but he confidentially told me it's just a bunch of chanting. That's why some of the brothers wear those different masks."

Annoyingly, that tracks with Kieren's retelling, but still, it doesn't sit right with me.

"I know I should be more careful," Kasey pivots. "Barrett said there is security footage of someone staggering on their front lawn at four a.m. that night, and they think it's Rory. She was wasted and must have wandered out of Sigma – like sleepwalking – but Tessa thinks foul play was involved. She said she didn't see Rory upstairs or at all after the Ceremony."

Without warning, Kasey launches into a hysterical sob. "Please tell him I would never betray Sigma. I would never do that to Barrett."

She swipes at her tears with the heel of her palm. "Saturday night, he kept calling me his girlfriend," she sniffs. "He wouldn't let anyone else touch me."

She shakes her head. "Barret is so fucking pissed at Tessa. I don't know what's wrong with her."

"What do Tessa and Arden look like?" I blurt out, realizing my abrupt need to know their appearances stems from that festering kernel of doubt in the back of my mind.

"Tessa has long black hair that's kind of wavy, about my height, I think. Arden has dark brown hair with caramel-colored, ombre highlights. She has it cut in a super cute bob. Every time I see her, I'm jealous of how stylish her hair looks. I could never pull it off. Sorry, I guess all I recall about either of them is their hairstyle."

I nod, trying to picture the two women. I'm sure if I saw their pictures, I would recognize them, because I generally know most of the sophomore women in the Greek system from rush. You practically have to memorize names and faces so you don't accidentally put down the wrong name on your bid card, thinking it was someone different. I'm also surprised there are sophomores in the ranks of Sigma Little Sisters, since I thought all the initiates were freshmen.

"For what it's worth, Kieren hasn't said anything about you betraying Sigma. He didn't say anything of the sort about the other women either. I wouldn't worry, but if he brings it up, I'll make sure he knows you weren't involved."

It's not an outright lie, but rather a withholding of the truth, and it sickens me. I should tell Kasey to run. I should tell her never to set foot in Sigma again. But what if I'm wrong? What if Rory did unintentionally stumble outside, and her disappearance is a horrible, tragic accident? What if I'm the paranoid one? What if Kieren lied, and the Ritual is a group sex thing? The woman walked into that hidden room without protest. Did she know and go willingly?

My mind spins and spins and spins until I'm on the verge of vomiting.

"You can come talk to me anytime, Kasey. I'm here for you, and I won't let anything happen."

She manages a pained smile. "Thank you," Kasey whispers. "I'm going to fix my makeup before going back downstairs, but I'll see you around? Maybe at Sigma?"

"Of course," I say as the pangs of regret tear at my chest.

I head downstairs and back to Harrison's vehicle.

"Can I ask you something?" I begin, pulling the door closed.

"Sure," he answers gruffly, annoyed I can tell to have to engage in conversation.

"Where did you and Barrett go with the elders after the Ritual was over? You two drove them somewhere, right?"

Color drains from Harrison's face. His eyelids twitch, but his gaze is locked straight ahead.

"I can't talk to you about this," he states.

"Why?" I push.

He refuses to answer or look at me.

"Why?" I ask again, loud and demanding.

His unflinching focus on the road ahead is a bit too forced. Pale hands grip the steering wheel a bit too hard. I don't ask again. He could have said anything, made up any lie. He could have said they drove the elders back to their hotel, or went to get food, or to do a late-night alcohol run. But he didn't. He panicked, and his silence gives away his complicity.

Because, what if I'm not paranoid?

What if that unsettling feeling in my gut is subconscious confirmation?

And the worst question of all: What the fuck do I do if I'm right?

32
MONROE

Five Months Prior to Present Day,
Thursday Before Spring Break,
Junior Year,
Sigma

My eyes have gone bleary with exhaustion. Again, I check the time. Nine minutes past midnight. One more question to go before I'm done with this problem set. I mutter silent words of encouragement in an attempt to hype myself up and flip to the next page in my textbook. My stomach gurgles another demand for food, and I curse myself for not stuffing bars and snacks into my purse while I was at DG. Sigma's chef must have taken cooking lessons at the same school as DG's chef, Colleen, because the food here is borderline inedible. I grabbed the only two appetizing items from the buffet – an apple and a bowl of plain rice – before Harrison escorted me upstairs and locked me inside

Kieren's room. Fuck, I'm so hungry. The logistics of ordering food to Sigma make it impossible since I can't even leave this fucking room to retrieve the delivery.

I debate the merits of eating my own shoe when labored footsteps enter the adjoining common room. The familiar sound of a key sliding into a lock tells me this is Kieren, and I brace myself.

We lock eyes when he opens the door. The pungent, sour smell of beer tickles my nose as he closes the distance between us. His biceps flank my shoulders as he leans into me, gripping the edge of his desk where I sit.

"Stop working," he rasps, nuzzling the side of my neck.

"I wish. I have one more question, and then I'm finished."

"Grades don't matter, Monroe," he growls as he pulls my hair back to kiss the sensitive area directly below my earlobe.

"They do if you're not a nepo baby and want a career."

His insincere chuckle puffs against my skin. "I'm your career, baby."

Kieren straightens and jerks my chair backward. He spins the seat around until my face is level with his groin. He tilts my chin upward and smirks down at me with hazy, dilated pupils.

"How high are you?" I scowl.

"Don't you worry about me, Monroe," he slurs. "The only drug I'm on is you."

He staggers over to the bed and plops down. I watch him yank off one boot and then another before succumbing to his stupor. His tight black T-shirt ripples across his pectoral muscles as he rests a forearm across his eyes. Convinced he's seconds from passing out, I swivel around and scoot myself toward the wooden desk to finish my work.

"Get over here and sit on my face," he barks. I give him a skeptical side eye even though his eyes are closed and I know he can't see me.

"It's not a fucking request," he snaps. "You have five seconds to take your pants off and sit your pussy on my fucking mouth."

Annoyed, I abandon my homework. He's clearly drunk and high, but I don't feel like dealing with his bullshit, so I choose the path of least resistance.

The pillow behind his head dips as I place a knee on either side of his face. His hands climb up my outer thighs, landing on my hips, but his eyes remain listlessly shut, and I don't know how I'm supposed to enjoy this when he's barely conscious.

His hands grip my skin, tugging me toward him until my center is flush with his lips. A hushed, broken moan escapes my throat as his hot, wet tongue spears my entrance. I lean forward and place my hand against the wall for support, a movement that apparently displeases Kieren because he growls an objection and pulls me closer.

Nails dig into my flesh as his tongue glides up my slit. I squirm at the sensation, unable to relax, unable to stop my mind from cycling through the myriad of information I learned today.

"Sit still," he rumbles. His words might be muffled by a mouthful of pussy, but his reprimand is clear. I force myself to breathe and let my weight settle on his face. Satisfied with my acquiescence, he envelops my clit with his mouth, working the sensitive nerves with even pressure from his broad tongue. The inner walls of my pussy throb with the steady force of his suction as my orgasm builds.

My breasts rise and fall with hitched pants as my release begins to coil. I'm infuriatingly close but not close enough. If only I could quiet my fucking thoughts. I pull one of his hands to my breast and with my hand on top of his, knead the soft flesh until my nipple hardens. I curl his fingers into a human version of a clamp. The ache inside me, the need to feel more than just his mouth, throbs.

"Please Kieren, I need more," I beg.

My lips unleash a guttural cry of gratitude when his where-withal returns, and his two fingers squeeze the hard bud of my nipple until it hurts. With my help, he holds them in place as I grind my clit against his mouth while administering my own pain play. Kieren's hands are practically inanimate props at this point, which I try not to think about as I work myself closer and closer to the edge.

"Kieren," I moan. His name spills from my tongue once, twice, and as I cry out to him for a third time, my quiver reaches a crescendo, and finally, my pussy pulses with release.

Time reenters my mind-space as I slow my breath, and a dirty, uncomfortable feeling steals my post-orgasm endor-phins. In careful, steady movements, I lift myself from his face, crawling down the length of his torso. His cheeks are coated with my arousal, slick and glistening in the dull light of the bedroom. His lips are slightly parted, eyes closed, unconscious like he's in a dream state. As if I needed more confirmation, I shimmy further away until my knees are between his legs. Unzipping his pants, the sight of his heartbreakingly limp dick makes my throat clench.

Tears flood my eyes, and my brain can't decide which part of this situation hurts the most. Is it that my presumed boyfriend is so drunk and high that he passed out while plea-suring me, or is it that I continued to take from him anyway, shamelessly grinding myself against him, using him like a toy to find my pleasure?

Or, is it that my boyfriend is so disgusted and bored with me that he has to get ripped out of his mind to stomach inti-macy? Because, of course. Of course, this would happen.

Because I'm not worth it, am I? Because girls like me don't get the prince. Girls like me will never be enough.

We aren't the ones who are picked to be loved.

This is my reality. It's the truth I've always known, regardless of how many lies I tell myself. I'm the one who never wins. I'm the trashy knockoff of the real thing.

I am the greedy little no one, deserver of nothing.

33
MONROE

Five Months Prior to Present Day,
Friday Before Spring Break,
Junior Year,
Sigma

pen the door, open the door, open the door, open the door...

Darkness surrounds the terror of my thoughts. A voice. My voice? Familiarity descends. I know this room. I sat in that desk chair last night until two a.m., finishing the problem set due today. The bookshelf, the small refrigerator, the metal dog cage in the corner...

I lie frozen and listen. Gentle breathing sounds. Kieren is in bed with me. The door of his bedroom is closed, locked, I'm sure.

Nothing has changed in the few hours I've been asleep, yet

a paralyzing terror has seized my body. I wait, unsure if it is safe to move, but also unsure why it wouldn't be.

I play a game with myself – the kind where I tell myself when I reach the number ten, I'm going to get up. I'm going to move. But it's a tortuous crawl. I get to ten and start over.

On my fifth attempt, I tell myself this time I will really commit. I won't chicken out. It's all in my head.

It's all... in... my... head.

Five.

Come on, come on, come on.

Six.

You can do this.

Seven.

Do it.

Eight.

DO IT.

Nine.

Fucking suck it the fuck up Monroe and GET UP.

Ten.

I press into my palm, rising, and silently swing my legs over the bed. Heat chokes my neck.

Now go, I tell myself.

I stand, my feet planted firmly on the floor, and look around.

Where am I going?

With feather-light footsteps, I tiptoe to the door, praying the floorboards don't creak this time, but then I look at the floor and remember it's not wood, it's concrete. Why did I think the floor was made of wood?

My hand lifts, extends, and encircles the metal knob. Twisting slowly...

Immediately, I drop my hand when I feel resistance, panicking that my attempt to test the lock was heard.

I swivel around without moving my feet.

Still asleep.

I pad with equal vigilance to the en suite bathroom and close the door, wincing as the old hinges squeal. The latch clicks into place once the door is fully shut, and I allow my lungs to fill to capacity.

Last night, after Kieren passed out underneath me, I formulated a semblance of a plan.

I'll ask Harrison to drive me to my apartment. My tampons are there, *which isn't a lie*, and I'm getting my period, *also not a lie*. I start the shower, hoping the ambient background noise will rouse Kieren so I don't have to do it myself.

Details crystallize as droplets of water pebble around my feet. My aunt Nikki lives in Queens. If I can make it to New York City by bus, I can take the metro to Forest Hills and take a taxi the rest of the way. I'll have to leave my laptop and belongings so as not to raise suspicion. It's fine. I can figure out the money to buy new things. Next week is spring break, so I'll have time to sort through loose ends. Kieren's driving home to Connecticut tonight, so he'll be preoccupied with family matters next week. He never confirmed whether I was going with him, which makes me think I'm not, so this plan might actually work. Soap suds swirl around the shower drain as I rinse them away, revealing pink patches of skin from where I've inadvertently scrubbed myself raw.

Hurriedly, I towel-dry my hair and apply a double layer of moisturizer to my face since this will be the last time I have access to my skincare and makeup products. I ration a travel-sized face wash, a tube of mascara, and concealer. The rest is too big. I debate whether or not I should take my phone charger but ultimately settle on leaving it behind. Two clean pairs of underwear will go unnoticed, I tell myself.

I inhale a prolonged breath of encouragement, and then

gently, convincingly, run my fingertips across the filmy skin of Kieren's forehead. His clothes from last night are now stale and wrinkled with a mix of sleep and sweat. In a parallel universe, the musky smell hanging in the air would be arousing, but now, it's depressingly pathetic.

"Kieren," I whisper, cupping the far side of his face. "Kieren, I have to go."

He huffs a strained exhale. Hot air puffs from his nostrils against my skin. I caress the side of his face like one would do to a lover, and a lump of remorse catches in my throat.

"Kieren, I need to leave. Can you let me out?"

His eyelids flutter partially open as if even the dim light in the room is too harsh. "Why? Where are you going? You don't have class."

"I started my period and need to get stuff from my apartment. Harrison can drive me. You don't need to get up."

He groans as he moves onto his side, reaching around me for his phone on the nightstand. He types what I hope is a text to Harrison to come fetch me, before rolling face down into the pillow.

I anxiously check my phone. Twenty minutes have passed since Kieren's text, and the success of my plan hinges on making it to the College Town bus that departs for the downtown Greyhound station at precisely ten a.m. I mentally start the process of summoning sufficient courage to wake Kieren again when three forceful knocks rattle the bedroom door.

"Kieren, it's me," announces a deep male voice. Kieren presses himself upright, faster this time, although that's not saying much, and lurches an unhurried procession to the door. I watch in dismay as he pulls out a keyring from his front pants pocket, sliding each key into its corresponding lock one by one.

This entire time.

In his fucking pocket.

I'm not sure I've ever felt this level of crushing devastation before. Why did I just accept my captivity? Why didn't I fucking try? How mentally fucked up does one have to be to just *sit there* and do nothing?

Kieren sways back to the bed. Immediately, I stand. I take two steps and hold my breath as we pass each other, half expecting this to be a trick. Half expecting him to grab my arm and hold me back. The soft thunk of his body on the comforter sounds like a gunshot in my mind. I force myself to walk at a pace I think is normal, falling into stride three steps behind Harrison.

Step one is complete.

———

"I'm so sorry you have to drive me, Harrison. I know it's early. I swear I don't mind walking."

"It's fine," he grumbles as we get into his car.

Like usual, we ride in silence. My fingers twitch as they rest on the top of my thigh. Students on the sidewalk pass by in a blur. As he pulls to the curb outside my apartment, it takes substantial concentration to speak.

"Do you want to come upstairs? I'll only be a few minutes, but up to you." I try to keep my voice even, but I worry he can sense I'm overcompensating.

"No," he answers without glancing up from his phone. Thank God. I hadn't planned for the curveball of him coming inside, and I curse myself for even offering the option.

I unlock the apartment door, out of breath from bounding up the stairs, and pray none of the foreign exchange students are milling about in the living room. The air is perfumed with the smell of coffee, but luckily, no bodies are present. I dart down the short hallway and unlock my room. The lock is sticky, and I'm out of practice. I start to panic, convinced I hear footsteps from one of the other occupants, and I can't get trapped in a conversation right now.

At last, the key turns. I slip inside, shutting the door behind me. A quick glance around my room tells me everything is as I left it the last time I was here – a time I can't even recall. The comforting gravity of my own space pulls me down. I allow myself three breaths. Three breaths of solitude. Three breaths of regret.

Blinking back to reality, I snatch a handful of tampons from a box in my closet and hope they will be enough to get me to my aunt's house in Queens before I bleed through my pants.

The window in the back of my bedroom is agonizingly uncooperative; the wooden slats require ample jostling to slide the frame up. I manage to get it halfway, which I decide is sufficient space to climb through. Lowering the window requires a similar ordeal, one that feels much more precarious from the fire escape. Descending the rickety, black metal stairs without falling off is a risk I must take, and I realize I have a sizable jump waiting for me one flight down unless I can figure out the ladder.

I can't.

It won't budge.

I climb onto the rungs, awkwardly lower myself until I can hang, and let go. My legs scream when I hit the pavement, launching me backward onto my butt and into the grime of the alleyway. Tiny, sharp fragments of stone and glass cling to my palms. I do my best to brush them off in the few spare seconds I have before I break into a sprint for the bus stop. The alley spits me out a block north of where I need to be, which is close enough to see the parked bus actively loading passengers. I weave through the many students walking on the sidewalk, scurry across the street as discreetly as possible, and make it to the end of the queue.

The bus doors swing closed. I'm one of the last people to board and sit in the first open seat I find. Momentum of the bus lurching into motion jostles me into the person sitting to my right. I plant my feet firmly on the floor as the bus tires roll over the uneven pavement of College Avenue. Looking out the windows on the opposite side of the aisle, I see Harrison's car still parked outside my apartment. The bus passes too quickly for me to see his face, and I hope he's still scrolling through his phone, oblivious.

Is this the end? I wonder. The end of my college experience? The end of my relationship Kieren? Will I come back? My sole focus was to escape, but I hadn't thought through the last two months of the academic year. Now I worry I've been too dramatic. Did I really need to go to such great lengths to get out of that bedroom?

I remind myself of all my reasons. He locks me inside his bedroom, he doesn't let me go anywhere on my own, he's spiraling into a version of himself I don't recognize and don't want to be around, he has forced me into a dog cage at gunpoint...

You made the right decision, I reassure myself.

But that stupid voice in the back of my mind asks, *Will you miss him?*

And... *I will.*

I will miss the man I thought he could be.

I choke on my heartbreak, coughing into my hands as the weight of where I am drags me under. Because it didn't have to be like this, but the Universe had a different plan for him, and for us.

The bus swings a wide turn into the Greyhound station. A line has already formed outside a bus idling in the parking lot.

The exterior flap for the lower luggage compartment is open. People wheel their suitcases to the driver as he loads them into the cavity, now halfway full. I make my way to the end of the line and take out my phone so I can pull up the digital copy of the ticket I purchased last night.

Fourteen missed calls from Kieren. *Shit. He must know.* I didn't feel my phone ring, but even if I had, I wouldn't have answered. Harrison must have complained that I was taking too long. I assumed this would happen eventually, but thank God, I'm already here, ten feet away from boarding the charter bus to Manhattan.

I watch in a daze as the line inches closer to the door with my ticket pulled up on my phone. Someone already on the bus is getting off. It registers, but it doesn't. Because this can't be happening. I'm seeing things.

His expression isn't one of anger or exaltation. He looks at me with grave concern, like he's been fraught with worry, searching for ages. Those in the line step aside as Kieren descends the charter bus steps. His clothes are different from last night. He looks human, albeit pale in the light of day.

Each stride toward me happens in slow motion. Sounds around me stop. His eyes don't deviate from mine as he closes the final few inches between us and wraps his arms around me in an embrace that feels unexpectedly tender.

"You're here," he sighs with relief against the crown of my head. "I thought I was too late."

I don't understand the emotions I feel. I don't understand why I, too, feel relieved. I feel so inexplicably relieved that he found me.

My body is flush with his, cocooned by his warmth, as he holds me tight.

And then I start to cry.

He cares.

He didn't want to lose me.

But I need to stay strong, I remind myself.

The war between my brain and heart rages like two beasts in battle.

"How did you find me?" I manage.

"You share your location with me, don't you remember?"

I... No, I don't remember. I don't recall ever sharing my location with him, but clearly, I must have done it at some point for him to find me so easily.

"Let's go home," he says, tilting my tear-streaked face up toward his. Kieren reaches for my hand, and I accept my fate, following him to his car.

I don't object or put up a fight.

I don't even try.

Because right now, the part of me who hates him can't remember why, and the part of me who loves him feels like my lost prince has come to rescue me at last.

———

Walking back into Kieren's bedroom, I sense a profound shift. At a glance, nothing has changed. My computer and the few things I keep here are as I've left them, but the air is different.

I am different.

I'm stepping back in time to a place where I no longer belong.

I sit down on the bed, lost in my emotional awakening.

I love him. I *have* loved him.

But this time, I need to let him go. Oh God, why didn't I feel like this at the Greyhound center, when we were in public and surrounded by other people?

Kieren lowers to his knees, pressing my thighs apart to slot himself between my legs.

"Why are you crying, Monroe?"

At first, I shake my head, knowing once I say the words aloud, I'll never be able to take them back.

His thumb gently grazes my cheek to wipe away the fallen tears.

"This is over for you, isn't it?" he asks. His question is laced with sadness, enough so that I force myself to look at him.

Years of longing for this man, of hoping, of wishing. Years of thinking how perfect he could be, *we could be*, if only a few things were different. If only he would accept me for who I am, and my lack of stature, maybe then, he would love me. If only he could figure out a way to control his demons and his drug use, maybe then, he would love me.

But *maybe then* has come and gone.

He'll never accept me, and he'll never change.

"I'm sorry," I whisper.

He nods, and an unbearable tightness clamps around my throat, one that is as freeing as it is devastating.

A long silence hovers between us, and I can't bear to look at him.

"See, the thing is Monroe, this isn't over for me."

I don't think I heard correctly.

"What?" I mumble, confusion halting my tears.

He stands, looking down at me with terrifying vitriol.

"You think," he begins, his nostrils flaring, "you can just end this? With me? You think you can just fucking walk away? From me? From this?!"

He spits out each rhetorical question like I am an ungrateful harlot who should be burned at the stake.

"No," he says with a deranged laugh. I gawk at him, blinking, convinced I'm dreaming. He's an apparition. This isn't real. This is not his true reaction; it can't be.

This is... This is...

He slides open the small top drawer of his desk.

"Get in the fucking cage," he commands.

My mouth twitches with unsaid words, but I can't find my voice. The barrel of the Glock is feet from my face.

"Get in the fucking cage!" he screams, shaking the gun at me.

I scramble off the bed, jumping up to the wall. "Kieren stop!" I cry. "Don't do this, please!"

He stalks over to the cage and kicks it with a force so violent that it causes the door to fly open.

"In!" he screams at me.

But I don't move. I recoil against the wall, frozen with terror.

"No, please!" I plead, holding my hands in front of my face as I brace myself.

Cold steel presses against my temple. "I said get the fuck in," he says in slow, deliberate snarls.

I start to hyperventilate as I cross the room and crouch in front of the metal door. The wires on the bottom of the cage bite into my palms as I crawl inside. The cage door slams shut, followed by the click-clack of the padlock.

"I'll be back in a few hours," Kieren announces as he places the gun back into the top drawer of his desk. "Don't bother screaming. No one can hear you anyway. And even if they could, no one here fucking cares."

———

I've been curled in the fetal position, sobbing, for hours. The sharp pain of the metal cage digging into each pressure point resting against it – my hip, my shoulder, the side of my head – somehow is dull compared to the unforgiving pain inside my mind. I haven't even gotten to the point of my own failure. I'm stuck in a loop of despair, wondering how another human being, someone who I thought cared for me, could treat me so horribly. What did I do to deserve treatment this vile? Why am I condemned to a life of suffering?

Keys jingle in the many locks, snapping me from my spiral. I push myself up to see Kieren clamor into his bedroom with at least half a dozen shopping bags from the local supermarket. He drops them to the floor without acknowledging me, heads into his bathroom, and slams the door.

I peer through the crisscrossed metal wires, my eyes swollen and puffy, but am unable to discern the contents inside the bags.

Kieren reemerges from the bathroom with a toiletries bag and tosses it onto his bed.

"What are you doing?" I squeak.

"Packing."

"Am I coming?" I ask timidly.

"What do you think?" he deadpans.

Cold terror races through my veins.

"Let me out of here," I demand.

Bile rises in my throat at Kieren's mocking laugh.

"You can't keep me in here!" I shout. "I'll die, Kieren!"

"Then maybe you should have thought of that before you tried to get on that fucking bus! You're lucky I'm a nice person, Monroe. I got you all this food," he shouts, motioning to the grocery bags.

"You can't keep me locked in your room all week!" I shout back, trying to mask my breakdown. "I'll call the police!"

"With what phone?" he asks with bitter sarcasm. "This phone?" he jeers as he holds my phone up for me to see before tossing it into his backpack. "Yeah, I don't think so. This phone is coming with me. Oh, and don't think I forgot about email. I've also disconnected the Internet router."

"You can't do this. You can't hold me prisoner. People will come looking for me, Kieren!"

"Who?!" he asks with a mocking laugh as he tosses clothes into a weekender duffle bag. "Who's going to come looking for you, Monroe? Your friends don't give a fuck about you. You've been here every night and not once have I heard you talk to any of them. None of your sorority friends. Not even Gabi. Your mom's fucking incarcerated, and your dad left your ass when you were three. So, guess what, Monroe? I'm all you've fucking got."

He zips the bag closed and unhooks his laptop from the charging cable running behind his desk.

"If you do this to me, consider me dead to you! We are done! And I promise, I will hate you for the rest of my life," I scream with shaky breath. Hot tears of panic stream down my face.

Kieren shakes his head, chuckling to himself as he stuffs his laptop into his backpack. "You're worth more to me dead than alive, you know?"

"What is wrong with you?" I cry. "You're a psychopath!"

"Yeah, well old habits die hard, I guess," he says, unbothered, as he squats in front of the cage to twist the combination of the padlock. The metal hook pops open, and Kieren rises to his feet, pocketing the lock.

"I don't care if you hate me," Kieren admits, sliding open the top drawer of his desk. I remain in the cage, motionless, as he unloads the magazine of bullets, including the remaining bullet in the chamber. "In fact, I always knew we would end up here. I guess we just arrived earlier than I predicted."

"If I'm worth more to you dead than alive, then why don't you just fucking kill me?" I grit out.

"Because, like I said, this isn't over for me. But I can't bring you to Connecticut, I think you know why, and you're too much of a liability to have running around. You've proven as much."

"We aren't over until I say we're over, and spoiler alert Monroe, that's never going to happen," Kieren says in a deranged sing-song voice. "The only way you get to leave me is in a fucking body bag, so I suggest you take some time this week to reflect on how you're going to be better. Hopefully, a week of solitude will help you remember how much I've fucking done for you, and how you would be nothing, have nothing, if it weren't for me. When I return, I better find you sitting naked on my bed, legs splayed wide, begging for my forgiveness. When I slide my dick into your tight cunt after nine days away, I want you to moan my name loud enough to raise the dead. I want you to tell me how sorry you are for trying to leave me, and how you'll never, *ever* try to run again."

I suck down jagged breaths amid tears of anguish.

"You may hate me, Monroe, but you'll never hate me enough to make me stop. I'm not going anywhere, and neither are you."

He bends down to nestle the unloaded Glock and magazine into his backpack, grabs the strap, and tosses it over his shoulder. In two strides, he picks up the weekender bag from his bed and looks down at me, his dark, soulless eyes are devoid of any remorse or humanity.

And it's in this moment when I truly know.

No one is coming to save me.

Just like before.

Just like Kieren said.

I'm all alone.

"Food should last you until next Sunday. The windows have been sealed shut by paint, kind of a fire hazard, they're bulletproof glass. So don't bother trying to break them or the door. I don't even think an axe could chop through this wood," he says, looking at the door to his bedroom with sick admiration.

"Remember what I said."

His last words to me ring hollow because all I hear is the deafening sound of three deadlocks sealing the bedroom, and me within, shut.

34
MONROE

Five Months Prior to Present Day,
Spring Break, Junior Year,
Sigma

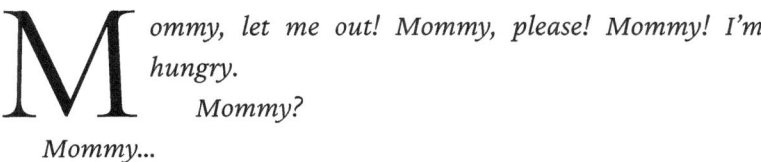ommy, let me out! Mommy, please! Mommy! I'm
hungry.
Mommy?

Mommy...

I gasp for air, unable to find oxygen. Cold sweat coats my skin.
The pillow under my head is damp and musty.

This is the third night I've had the same nightmare.
Trapped in a room I can't quite see, with dolls I can't quite
reach, starved. The room smells like urine and tears and
hunger. Sometimes, the dream is so vivid that it feels real.
Sometimes, I wonder if it was real.

I don't remember the first house I lived in with my mom before we moved in with my stepdad Kerry. I guess my dad lived there too, at some point, before he left. Now and then, an image of my grandmother standing over a stove in a small kitchen, cooking, will pop into my mind. I see mint-green tiled countertops and birch-wood cabinets, the same style of cabinets that were in my grandmother's house in Ohio. Maybe the image is a figment of my mind. I've never had this nightmare before, and I'm inclined to think it's my imagination subconsciously responding to my forced captivity.

After Kieren left on Friday afternoon, I crawled out of the cage and across the floor to sit against the bed. My brain was in shock, I know that now. I sat and stared at the door, in a trance, listening to water drip from the faucet in the bathroom. When the room became too dark to see my own hand, I started sobbing, silently at first. Tears ran down my face, catching under my chin, pooling around the collar of my sweatshirt.

I found my voice when silver light from the rising moon pierced through the darkness. With my knees curled into my chest, I drained every tear from my body. I cried until my eyes were nearly swollen shut, and the muscles in my face ached. I cried until my bones throbbed with exhaustion. Then came the rage.

I threw my body at the heavy wood door again and again and again. Each time, I ricocheted backward. Each time, I got up and kicked and screamed and pounded at the door.

I screamed until my throat became raw.

I screamed until it was clear that Kieren was right—either no one could hear me, or no one cared.

With no phone to check and no connection to the Internet, I had no idea what time it was at any given moment. My mind had so thoroughly detached from my physical body, that it didn't even occur to me I could turn on the lights.

Finally, I stumbled into bed and managed to pull the covers over my battered limbs. Small cuts and bruises pulsed with pain, but the discomfort paled in comparison to my fatigue. Despondency set in, and thankfully, deciding I had suffered enough, my mind shut down.

Saturday morning, or afternoon, I had no idea really, I woke with a renewed sense of determination and spent the next forty-eight hours in a productive frenzy. I rationed all the food Kieren had left, which was a fucking joke, because the only food I found in the grocery bags was loads of trail mix, granola bars, a few handfuls of protein bars, and a box of bland cereal. Water would have to be sourced from the tap since Kieren conveniently left his mini fridge empty, which was not the end of the world. To put a positive spin on things, it was like a nightmarish camping trip, unpleasant, but I would survive.

Later the same day, I felt the first trickles of blood, indicating my cycle was starting, which is when a new panic set in around the amount of bathroom supplies I would need over the course of the week. I had enough tampons to last one, maybe two, days. In addition to the half-used roll of toilet paper on the holder, I found three more under the sink. My first inclination was to sit on the toilet all day if worst came to worst, but then I decided Kieren's t-shirts would make perfectly suitable sanitary napkins.

This discovery sparked an idea, and I wondered why I hadn't thought to raid his drawers already. Every inch of his bedroom, closet, and en suite bathroom was scoured with a fine-toothed comb. Expired medications, old toiletries crusted over with product, random keys that unlocked nothing, multiple pairs of my underwear stashed in different drawers from three years of an on-again, off-again failed relationship, condoms we don't use, chains, whips, fully charged magic wands, nipple and clit clamps, restraints, gags, handcuffs, butt plugs, Kieren's abomination of a mask he wears to the Full Moon Ceremonies along with my own...

At least I'll be able to get myself off while I'm stuck in this prison.

After categorizing and organizing for two days, I had an improved sense of spirit. I had no Internet, but I had textbooks, which gave me purpose.

Sunday night, the nightmares started.

Claustrophobia set in on Monday. When I became convinced the room wasn't getting enough fresh oxygen and I was going to suffocate, I started stabbing the paint-sealed window frame that borders the fire escape with stray pens I found around the room until the pen would break and I'd have to source another.

Today, Wednesday, I ran out of pens.

I press the side of my face into the cold floor as I lie on my stomach. At this point, I don't think the difficulty I feel when breathing, the inability to take in a full breath, is in my head. The oxygen in this room is dwindling, rapidly, replaced by the carbon dioxide I exhale. Soon, my consciousness will become impaired. I'm already dizzy. The nauseous feeling I've had since yesterday might be from my lack of real food, but it also might be the beginnings of carbon dioxide poisoning. The sliver of space between the door's edge and the floor is the only ingress of fresh air. It's not enough. I'm going to die from suffocation. Maybe I should accept my fate now. I could end it. I could shatter the mirror, get into the bath...

A painful lump rises in my throat.

You're going to survive him, Monroe, I tell myself. *You've already survived so much worse.*

I manically inhale and exhale like a dog sniffing at the base of a door. What else can I use to get that window open?

Jesus Christ, Monroe! You have nail polish remover!

I spring to my feet, my will to live restored.

How did I not think of this? When Kieren made me effectively move in, I took more than what I thought I might need. Even though I hardly paint my nails, I did have a few bottles of red polish and one travel-sized bottle of remover in one of my toiletry bags. If I can soak the paint and find a new tool to scrape it, maybe I can free the window frame. As I rummage through my toiletry bag, I find a pair of metal nail clippers with a built-in nail file, the kind with a sharp curve on the end. It's a stretch, but I'm desperate.

———

Friday, I shovel the last handful of trail mix into my mouth and chew slowly, meticulously. My food rations are gone.

I think about all the ways I'm going to kill Kieren.

I wonder what he would taste like.

I salivate just thinking about his charred flesh covered with barbeque sauce.

But the window pane has shown signs of progress.

Hunched in position, my left buttock propped on the short ledge of the window, my right foot skimming the floor like a bicycle kickstand, I resume my plight.

The rhythm of my work is hypnotic.

Scrape, scrape, jiggle. Scrape, scrape, jiggle.

The travel-sized amount of nail polish remover wasn't enough to completely dissolve the paint, but it did soften it enough to scrape. My makeshift tool, the nail clippers, is my lifeline.

"You can imagine my disappointment when I didn't find a screwdriver," I say to the empty room. "Though, not unexpected. Kieren is a prissy, little bitch, after all. Never had to lift a finger in his life. Probably doesn't even know what a screwdriver is, or a hammer. The child doesn't even have scissors. Scissors! Why can't we have scissors?"

"Because you're too small to know how to use them," I answer myself.

"But what if I want to cut my doll's hair?" I ask.

"Stop cutting your doll's hair, Monroe. Do you have any idea how much those dolls cost? You should be grateful you have any dolls at all," I answer.

Blonde hair, blonde hair, blonde hair, blonde hair, I repeat to myself. I love my doll's blonde hair. It's so pretty.

"Mommy, I want blonde hair," I say, my voice high and innocent in pitch.

"Don't you want beautiful brown hair like mine, Monroe?" I answer in my best pretend-serious, adult voice. "If you dye it, you'll ruin your hair, and then you'll have ugly, frizzy hair and no man will ever want you."

Jiggle, jiggle, jiggle.

Crack.

I pause in disbelief, stunned by the noise. Half of the window frame has come loose.

I scamper from my perch and wrap both hands around the handle. With all my might, I pull up until my vision blurs and my head feels light. Nothing moves.

I pull a second time, stopping only when I feel like I am on the verge of blacking out.

Collecting myself, I take a deep breath of carbon dioxide and pull a third time.

A tiny, barely audible crack.

Keep going, I scream at myself.

I pull a fourth time.

A fifth time.

A tenth time.

A twentieth time.

It's not until somewhere around twenty-five that I feel my knees buckle right before my head hits the floor.

35
KIEREN

Five Months Prior to Present Day,
Spring Break, Junior Year,
Connecticut

"Father."

I begrudgingly acknowledge the man who cannot be bothered to look away from his computer monitor.

"Kieren," he responds without pausing his keyboard strokes. "When did you get in?"

This bastard knows I arrived home yesterday. How can you miss my fucking car in the driveway? But his behavior doesn't surprise me. My father's never been a warm individual. He sees the world as a series of gains and losses. Affection and praise are tools he uses to manipulate his desired outcome. Disdain and neglect are his weapons of choice when you fail to meet his expectations. The fact that my mother has stomached his behavior for almost twenty-five years is mystifying, but I'm sure she has her reasons – the kind of reasons that can afford a mansion in Connecticut, private tennis lessons, Birkin bags, and whatever the fuck else a black AMEX can buy.

I'd wager a Bentley that there's a voodoo doll under a floorboard somewhere in this house with a sewing pin shoved through the chest. She almost got lucky last summer, but the motherfucker pulled through. I will say, she put on a good show.

"Your mother's at the club having lunch with Clarissa Fitzroy and her daughter, Serenity. Do you know Serenity Fitzroy?"

Of course I know Serenity Fitzroy. Anyone who attended a private school on the East Coast is familiar with Serenity Fitzroy. Although she attended Brearley, which is an all-girls private school in Manhattan, we ran in the same circles. She's also fucking gorgeous. The epitome of an aristocratic, purebred beauty, rumored to be entangled with a member of the Luxembourg royal family, although I don't believe a direct heir. Pity.

"Yes. Why?"

He shrugs, cold, impassive. "The Fitzroys are a new client."

I raise an eyebrow in surprise. "Really?"

"Indeed they are, son. It seems the work you're doing has already begun yielding dividends."

I know I'm expected to take over Hunt Wealth Management when I'm of proper age and tenure at the firm, but I hope to fuck I never speak like my father, where every other word ties back to an investment reference.

"Good to hear," I say. It's the closest I will ever get to a compliment.

"We need to talk about your situation," my father says, pausing mid-keyboard stroke at this statement. He crosses his arms in front of his chest to face me head-on, readying for a fight, and even though I know his statement is about Monroe, I don't want to give him the satisfaction.

"Is this in reference to Mom's plans to convert my bedroom into a Pilates studio? Because I can assure you, I don't care."

"No," he sneers, taking the bait, "it's in reference to your *feelings,* which seem to be getting in the way of our plans."

"I have no *feelings,*" I say, straightening, because even though I know it's a lie, the bitter taste of Monroe's betrayal still lingers in my mouth, and I'm so angry and worked up that I can't sort out how I really feel about her right now. I cannot believe she fucking tried to escape like she's a goddamned hostage. A Greyhound bus? Really? That took planning. Was I going to bring her home with me to meet my parents? Absolutely not, but had I sorted through alternatives like staying with her at a nearby hotel? Of course.

But Monroe cannot help herself. She's obviously convinced I'm the bad guy and had the audacity to look me in the fucking eye and tell me she was done. She admitted she wanted to walk away, and I thought I had made myself perfectly clear that she is never, ever leaving me. Even *if* the feelings were mutual, you don't just *walk away* from your duties as a Sigma Little Sister, definitely not when you're a figurehead like Monroe. Now, she's made a mess of things, and this is yet another clusterfuck I'll have to clean up. The work of a martyr never fucking stops, does it?

"Bullshit," my father sneers. "If that were the case, you'd have no problem sharing her as all Sigma brothers are required to do with their Sinners. And now, thanks to your *feelings,* you've managed to piss off X."

"Fuck him," I snap. "Can't he be satisfied with the dozens of other Sinners waiting around to suck his demon dick?"

"Well, thanks to your stubbornness, his *demon dick* is now

focused on her, and he doesn't just want her body. He wants her blood."

"You've never been able to see the bigger picture, have you Kieren?" my father continues. "Too focused on yourself. If you were strategic, you would have immediately seen the chess pieces at play, but mental stamina has never been your strong suit. You continue to think like a child, always focusing on the moves right in front of you, never thinking ahead. I have half a mind to ensure you'll never inherit this firm, because your shortsightedness will drive it into the ground within the first year."

A manic laugh bursts from my lips. "Do you honestly think you're in a position to judge me when you're the reason I'm up to my knees in this shit?"

"I knew you didn't have it in you. Your grandfather would be disgraced to learn you've chosen pussy over power." The sneer on his face makes it clear that he's ignoring my valid point.

I bristle at the slight as my gaze instantly flicks down to the Sigma ring I forcefully inherited. Four years ago, my grandfather was a ruthless savage before the onset of dementia turned him into an innocuous vegetable, and while I've always known I possess similar traits, I'd like to think my barbarism is more refined. My grandfather was overt with his greed and callousness in a way I always found unbecoming. Even as a young child, I admired him, but I knew I could do better.

My father knows I have it in me, but he wouldn't be my father if he didn't find some way to belittle me. It's his way of keeping me hungry, but what dear old Dad doesn't realize is that someday, I'm going to fucking eat him.

"Let me be clear," I snap, jabbing my pointer finger on his polished oak desk. "*I'm* the one doing the heavy lifting. *I'm* the one cleaning up your mess. If you weren't so fucking dumb to..."

"Call me dumb again, son, and I'll rip out that repulsive nose ring of yours with my bare hands, you insolent child. It's bad enough you have those tattoos. You have no idea how the world works."

"Oh, I have a very astute understanding, Father. You forget I've worked at Hunt Wealth Management. You forget I spent the majority of last year helping *you* cover up the money *you* lost your clients because the Ponzi scheme *you* were using to pad returns and pay yourself a fat management fee went belly up. I've always been the fucking scapegoat for your mistakes. You weren't even man enough to own up to what you had done. You were going to take the easy way out, remember?"

My father's face goes pale at the mention of his botched, pathetic attempt to take his own life.

"And I *will* inherit this firm one day," I continue, "and I'll be damned if I inherit a steaming pile of shit. X has gotten everything he wanted. I'm under no obligation to share her or offer her, so he can take his extortion and fuck right off."

"Understand that X will get what he wants one way or another, Kieren, so your attempt to protect your little girlfriend is futile, and I'd rather you not drag our family name down in the fucking process!" my father shouts.

"Will that be all, Father?" I sneer, pivoting on my heels.

"Give X what he wants or kiss your trust fund goodbye," he states with cold-blooded finality.

I whip around to face him, having already turned to leave. My father cocks his head to the side, smirking like he's cornered his prey, as I glare at him with roiling indignation.

"You wouldn't fucking dare," I seethe, because Monroe was never part of the deal. Four months ago, when I was finally able to leave Connecticut after cleaning up my father's shit, bringing back the Ritual of Sacrifice for X and the rest of the sick fucks was all I had to do to *graduate to my father's satisfaction*.

But I knew this would happen. I knew as soon as that fucker X set his red, bloodthirsty demon eyes on Monroe that he would go running back to my dad like a little bitch when I didn't let him have her. And I knew once my weasel-dick dad found out I had been keeping my pet hidden, he would see this as the perfect opportunity to extricate me from my own fucking inheritance.

As expected, Monroe has become a pawn in his money-grabbing chess game. How fucking predictable, Father, but once again, you've underestimated the ruthless monster you raised. You don't think I have it in me, but you don't realize how far I'm willing to go to ensure I get what's rightfully mine.

"Let me remind you who receives the funds within your trust if I decide you haven't graduated Dornell to my *satisfaction*."

I grind my teeth because he knows I already know the answer, and I'm sick of rehashing this same goddamn conversation.

"Me," he smirks, delighted with himself. "Part of me hopes you'll try me, because there's an awful lot of cash sitting in your trust. So much so that you'd never have to work a day in your life if you choose that path. X might pull the plug on our deal. Hunt Wealth Management might fold, leaving you and your mom to fend for yourselves, but me, I'll be just fine. Your trust is stashed in an offshore account, one the Feds will never find. I'll be long gone by the time the news breaks, sitting on an island in the Caribbean with a beer in my hand and whores on my lap, living out my days on your tab."

My father shifts in his seat, grinning with pride at the

notion he was able to outwit his protege son at last. "Fuck with me, and I'll fuck you right back, boy. Now, be a good heir and go visit your mother at the Club. Serenity Fitzroy would be quite the perfect match for you. Perhaps you should swing by and say hello to your future wife."

36
KIEREN

Five Months Prior to Present Day,
Spring Break, Junior Year

Murder would be too kind of a death for my father, and as satisfying as it would be to watch him choke on his own blood after I slit his throat, pulling the rug out from under him when I take over Hunt Wealth Management after graduation will be lightyears better. I doubt my fool of a father bothered to read every legal clause of my trust fund, because if he had, he would have made sure he never woke up from his coma last summer.

That's the funny thing about details; they'll kill you if you aren't careful. Could I have reminded the daft egomaniac about said details earlier when he was waxing poetic threats? I sure as fuck wanted to, but then I would lose the element of surprise. *And I love a good surprise.*

It seems my fucktwat father has forgotten that after I graduate Dornell to his *satisfaction*, my trust is awarded to me with no further strings attached. Sure, the money is generous, but I'm delighted to see my father thinks money is all I'm after. If the asshole weren't high on his own narcissism, he would have noticed that my future position as CEO of Hunt Wealth Management is guaranteed, automatically bequeathed to me per the terms of my trust. Specifically:

> *My grandson, Kieren Arthur Hunt III, shall take over the position and title of CEO of Hunt Wealth Management on the earlier of: (1) completing a ten-year tenure at the firm; or, (2) if his father, Kieren Arthur Hunt Junior, should fall physically and/or mentally ill and/or be deemed unfit to continue to serve the firm in a CEO capacity.*

I'm sure any doctor and court would agree, certainly if persuaded with the right monetary incentives, that an attempt to take one's life would deem one mentally unfit to serve the firm in a CEO capacity. Who's the shortsighted one now, Father?

What was it you said? Oh. Right. *"Fuck me and I'll fuck you right back."* Unfortunately for you Father, I invented this game, and despite your opinion of me, I can play it better than you.

And as for this proverbial game of chicken we're playing with X and Monroe, I'm warming up to the idea. In some aspects, it's the perfect solution to my problem. I can't marry a dead girl, and neither can anyone else. I've also been stressed about what to do with Monroe over summer break. I'll be working at HWM, of course, and initially I thought about renting a house in Connecticut for us both, but with me gone all day, a house is too easy to jailbreak. She'll either run the first chance she gets or poison me in my sleep. And I might be a monster, but not the kind that would keep a woman locked up in my basement.

Actually, wait. I am literally that kind of monster. *Ah fuck*, I sigh to myself, *maybe I took her punishment too far*. At the onset, a week locked in my room with food and water didn't seem that big of a deal, but in retrospect... I waffle on whether or not I made the right decision, but it's too late now. Hopefully she's alive when I get back to Sigma and no worse for the wear.

I just...

Fuck.

My vision frustratingly grows compromised with moisture, and I have to swipe at my eyes to see the road clearly. It didn't have to be this way, but here we are, standing together on the edge of a cliff.

I need her.

I. Need. Her.

She's been the only consistent presence in my life that has truly and deeply loved me. Despite all I've put her through, she always comes back, and God do I love that about her. I've manipulated and molded her into my perfect girlfriend. For fuck's sake, she's been locked in my room at Sigma for the last week and there isn't a doubt in my mind that she'll apologize for her behavior the moment I walk through the door. She'll be pissed. She might even hate me. But she'll never fucking abandon me.

Except when she *did* try to abandon me two Fridays ago, and if I hadn't intercepted her when I did, she would be gone. She left all her belongings. Computer, clothes, makeup... She planned to *disappear*. But she made sure to take those fucking diamond earrings I bought her, because we both know they are worth more than all her other possessions combined. Fucking social climbing bitch.

Fuck!

I hate her.

I fucking hate her.

What kind of girlfriend abandons their boyfriend as if they never existed?

God, I have misjudged her. I always want to think the best of her, but time and time again, she never fails to remind me of exactly the type of person she is underneath her mask of innocence. She's not kind, nor caring. She's calculated.

Let X have her. Let her be an offering. This is the outcome she deserves, and for all the time and effort I've put into cultivating her, giving her everything I have, I'm rightfully owed the benefit of her sacrifice. *I deserve the blessings from her blood.*

But, how will I be able to face her? I'll have to keep her placated until May's Full Moon Ceremony, the last of this academic year. April is too soon. For me, and for the role she plays. I want her just once more. Maybe twice. Maybe as much as fucking possible. I want to breathe in her fucking scent, taste her on my tongue, and hear her scream my name just a bit longer. I'm not a sane person, but I am an opportunist.

After the May Ceremony, everyone will focus on final exams and be heads down until the end of the school year. No one will notice her absence, and when she doesn't return next year, no one will care.

Well.

No one but me.

37
MONROE

Five Months Prior to Present Day,
Spring Break, Junior Year,
Sigma

I'm pretty sure I have concussed myself.

I'm not sure if it's the same day or a different day. Muted sunlight shines through the dull, cloudy sky. Was it like this when I passed out?

It takes considerable effort to roll onto my side.

My head throbs.

I should drink water. Do pain pills count as food?

Standing is out of the question. Slowly, I crawl to the bathroom.

Wrapping my hands around the ledge of the porcelain countertop, I hoist myself up. My limbs shake with fatigue. Cupping my hands under the faucet, I bend down to slurp the pooled water.

When is the last time I showered? Maybe a bath tonight. Or today. Or, whenever. Does it even matter?

The putrid, metallic scent of bloody, used tampons and homemade pads fills my nose, which is fitting since I've transformed into a member of the walking dead.

Back to work.

I don't bother to look at my reflection. I don't want to know, nor do I care.

Sitting on the window ledge feels too precarious, so I wheel over Kieren's desk chair. With an elbow propped on the windowsill, I wearily rest my chin in my palm.

What was I even doing?

Right.

Scraping.

————

I'm past hungry.

I don't get out of bed on Saturday until what I assume is late afternoon.

I smell, or I think I smell, so I decide it's time to bathe.

Floral-scented body wash mixes with the foul odor of decaying blood. Little flies swirl around the full wastebasket, landing on the mirror as I finally work up the courage to look at my reflection.

I don't know this person.

Purple rings encircle my bloodshot eyes. My skin is ashen. My face gaunt.

I have no fight left in me.

I barely flinch at the scalding water as I carefully lower myself into the tub.

My head lolls to the side, and I sense myself drifting.

But that's okay.

The devil can take me.

I've had enough.

———

Try one more time. Try.

TRY!

My eyelids flutter open. The bedspread, the pillow...

I don't remember getting into bed. Pushing myself to a seated position is a momentous task.

I hobble over the window, teetering with each step.

One more time, I tell myself.

I wrap my fingers around the metal handle, squat slightly like a professional weightlifter, and yank...

A strained groan fills the room as I pull, and pull, and...

"FUCK!" I scream at the top of my lungs.

I stumble, the abrupt shift throws me off-balance.

"No," I laugh, hysterical in my delirium. "No, you can't. No, it's not possible!"

I wrap my hands around the handle once more, pulling, jimmying the frame, pulling more, until crisp, cold air floods into the room. Dropping to my knees, I inhale the glorious fresh atmosphere. Relief floods my system. Oxygen.

Moisture clusters along my lashes at my victory. I've done it...

Blinking my eyes open, I look outside and to the right of the open window. The fire escape is within reach. Granted, I'll have to carefully balance on the windowsill and swing a leg over the railing in a tricky maneuver that could result in falling to my death, but I've never been scared of heights. My grandmother used to tell me how I would climb anything remotely climbable, determined to see how high I could get, and then jump. She said I was convinced I had the ability to fly and would flap my arms like a deranged chicken with each leap. By some miracle, I never broke any bones.

Scaling this fire escape won't be a problem, although I do question the imbecile who designed a fire escape that didn't run directly under the window for easy access. But then again, this is a fraternity, likely built by men, for men, and only a man could have designed something so inferior.

Hastily, I start shoving critical belongings into my backpack. Computer, charger, wallet, purse, a few items of clothing, and my toothbrush. Gagging at the smell in the bathroom, I tie the trash bag closed in the small waste can. I know what I'm about to do is disgusting, wrong in every sense of the word, but as I watch the blood-filled trash bag drop three stories and land behind the bushes that ring the lower level of Sigma, I feel nothing but triumph at my purge. Hopefully, a wild animal finds it and decides to take up residence in the bushes. Hopefully, that animal is a fucking wolf.

I ready myself, leaning my hip onto the windowsill, but I pause and wonder if I should take Kieren's ceremonial mask as evidence. No, I decide. No one will take me seriously unless I have real proof that Sigma is behind the disappearance of Rory. I need those emails between Kieren and X, not to mention a body. They'll think the mask is nothing more than a costume and that I'm nothing more than a lunatic.

An idea sparks in my mind. Kieren's ring. If Rory's body is found, the brand on her ass cheek like mine, the Sigma symbol set in the middle of crossed lines, combined with Kieren's ring, might be enough to arouse suspicion. It wouldn't be enough for an indictment against Kieren himself but certainly shine a scrutinous spotlight on Sigma as an organization. And, if I can get this story in the right hands, perhaps it will be enough to open an investigation. I mean, I know nothing about the law, but the brand is practically a fucking monogram.

Later, I tell myself as I swing a leg over the ledge. I take a deep breath, and...

Tires.

Gravel.

Shit.

I scramble back inside the window, barely shutting it, when Kieren's black BMW pulls into the back parking lot. Jumping out of view, my heart pounds. Blood rushes to my head, and I brace myself against the wall until the dizzying blackness in my vision subsides.

Shit!

I toss my backpack onto the bed and frantically unpack, returning each item to its original spot so nothing looks out of place. Footsteps thunder down the hall like a death march. I hadn't gotten this far. I hadn't planned for this scenario.

Grabbing my textbook, I leap onto the bed.

A key turns in the lock.

Anxiety snakes up my throat like a vine as I pretend to read, and I don't know if it's instinct or learned behavior, but I know exactly what to do. I should spit in his face. I should hide behind the door and throw this book at him.

But I won't.

Because right now, I need food more than I need redemption.

The door creaks, announcing his presence. My eyes flick up to meet his. Dark, roiling, hostile.

He drops his duffle bag to the floor and wrinkles his nose. I can only imagine the stench in this room. If I were a braver person, I'd wear it with pride, but I'm not.

I'm hungry and I'm weak.

I'll get food, then I'll escape.

He saunters over to the bed, crossing his arms in disdain when he stops.

"Well?" he asks. "What do you have to say for yourself?"

"I'm sorry," I squeak, intentionally keeping my voice soft and meek. "You were right."

His lips quirk in satisfaction.

"Did you miss me?"

I nod, averting my eyes in submission. I know it's what he wants to see, and I know it's the part I need to play if I have any hope of getting the fuck away from him.

He kneels, leaning forward to run his hands up my thighs. This is the first time his touch has felt foreign and unwanted. I allow it, willing my mind to go numb, willing my heart not to feel.

"Is my puppy hungry?"

I nod again as my mind fights to hold back tears that desperately want to fall. I don't want him to know the depth of my hunger, or to understand food is a weapon he can wield.

"When is the last time you showered?" he sneers, curling his lip in disgust. "You look like shit."

"Yesterday," I mumble.

"Take a shower and put some fucking makeup on. I'm not taking you to get food until you look presentable. I've got things to unpack in my trunk. You've got..." He looks at his watch, contemplating how generous he wants to be with his time. "Twenty minutes. When I'm back, I expect you to be ready."

I hold my breath as Kieren leaves, locking me inside once more. My fingers shake as tears plop onto the open pages of my textbook, my eyes glaze over, and my mind short-circuits.

A monologue plays in my head like an involuntary reaction, repeating over and over to do what *she* wants. I can't make it stop, so I squeeze my eyes closed, hearing my own voice narrate as if it's a movie.

Play along. Play the good girl.

You know how to do this, Monroe.
Pretend everything is fine. Get the food.
If she thinks you are angry, she will punish you.
Do what she wants.
Be a good girl.
Get the food.

But is this a memory, or have I become clinically insane? I hear the textbook thump closed before I realize I had moved my hands. Crawling off the bed, I peer out the window. The trunk of Kieren's car is open as he leans inside, reaching for something. I squint in curiosity, but as he straightens, there is no mistaking the four-gallon jugs he wrestles free.

Bleach.

38
MONROE

"What are you doing?" I ask in horror as Kieren retrieves a chain from his closet. I've played the good girl all day. I've pretended not to hate him. I've stayed put, done everything he asked.

"What does it look like?"

"Stop, Kieren!"

"Hold still," he growls, yanking my ankle forward.

"You literally lock us in here at night! You don't need to chain me to the bed as well! What if I need to use the bathroom?"

"The chain is long enough. It'll reach."

I gawk at the hollow monster who now inhabits the deteriorating physique of the boy I foolishly fell back in love with at the beginning of the semester – the healthy-looking boy who convinced me he was in recovery and *trying* to be better. And while the dark circles under his eyes and haunted expression conjure memories of the addict he was one year ago, this is a different kind of evil. This is worse than addiction. This is madness. I'm convinced he's suffered a psychotic break, unable to discern reality from the insanity whirling inside his mind.

"You're sick, Kieren. You're sick and you need help!"

"Fight me and I'll remind you that there's a bullet in this room with your name on it."

"You're disgusting, and I hate you!" I seethe, forgetting myself, forgetting the unstable psychopath who sleeps next to me in this bed.

The cuff around my ankle clicks as Kieren tightens it closed.

"As I've already told you, I don't give a fuck, now lie down."

"If you think I'm spreading my legs for you, you're sorely mistaken."

Kieren's huffed laugh mocks my defiance. "I don't want your pussy, Monroe. I'll get it soon enough, anyway. Now lie down or I'll put you in the fucking cage. Is that what you want?"

My chest heaves with fury. "One day," I manage through gritted teeth, "you will regret this."

"And one day," Kieren adds apathetically, "you'll be dead."

39
MONROE

Five Months Prior to Present Day,
Night of the April Full Moon Ceremony,
Junior Year,
Sigma

"Open your mouth," Kieren tells me, holding my pills for the evening.

I open, extending my tongue.

"Water," I grimace, waiting to swallow. As Kieren turns to fetch a bottle from the small fridge in his room, I maneuver the pills under my tongue. He twists off the cap and hands it to me. I take a small sip, letting him see my throat bob.

"Show me."

I open again, displaying my bare tongue.

"Good."

Kieren grabs his ceremonial mask off the bed and walks into the bathroom. Carefully, I spit out the pills and silently place them inside my partially unzipped backpack. I wasn't sure which mirror Kieren would use to adjust his mask, the standing floor-to-ceiling one in his bedroom or the one over the sink in the bathroom. I got lucky. He picked the bathroom. If he hadn't, I had planned to say I needed to pee one final time before heading to the basement.

Since Kieren returned, I've barely been allowed one minute alone, although bathroom usage doesn't count, thank God. When I'm in his room, I'm chained to the bed. When I'm in class, Harrison is with me. My phone has been confiscated. The only device I have is my computer, and when Kieren does leave the bedroom for a few scant minutes, he unplugs the Internet router set up in his adjoining common area. Besides, the time to email Gabi and the other girls has come and gone. Months ago, I was too embarrassed to tell them I had taken Kieren back, and I don't have the heart to email them now. I don't want to drag them into this, not while they're abroad and having the time of their lives. But that leaves me with no one else.

Tonight is perhaps my one and only opportunity. Jace will walk me upstairs after the Ceremony, and maybe I'm wrong, but I refuse to believe Jace is cut from the same cloth as Kieren. He'll lock me inside the room, but I don't think he'll chain me to the bed. I'm not sure how aware Jace is of my situation, but I hope his ignorance is of the honest kind.

While Kieren is busy with his disgusting initiation duties, I'll make my escape. Darkness will be on my side. I'll run.

A loud knock raps against the door.

"What?" Kieren barks, striding from the bathroom. I can't believe there were moments when I found this masked version of him, exuding power and greed, to be desirable. I can't believe I let myself love him.

"One of the elders wants to speak with you," a voice outside the door says.

Kieren opens the door halfway, and I crane my neck to see a masked Jace standing in front of the man who wears the gold-horned demonic mask. *Is this X?*

Kieren looks back inside, and I quickly look away, though I fear not quickly enough. The door abruptly closes.

"What is it?" I overhear Kieren ask.

"Your father tells me you will not share your pet." The other voice rakes down my arm like steel knives. The same demonic, inhuman voice I remember from the last Full Moon Ceremony, and I can only assume by *'pet'*, he means me.

"No."

A small exhale of relief leaves my lips.

"Offer her tonight then."

Offer me? Offer me to who? I thought Kieren just said he wasn't going to share.

"I'm not done with her yet, and we have a more pressing offering to deal with."

Done with me? None of this makes sense.

A hollow laugh rings in my ears. "Moloch doesn't want dissenters. You displease him. Remember, boy, I can make your life disappear with the snap of my fingers. Your family will lose everything."

What do I have to do with Kieren's family losing everything?

"She will be offered next month – my grandfather's birthday, no less – but I get to spill her blood. Not you."

I've stopped breathing. *I must have misheard. Please tell me I misheard.* Thoughts of Rory, the girl who went missing last month, flood my mind. *Oh my God. They're killing us, aren't they? Picking us off one by one like fish in a barrel.*

"You don't want to play this game with me. You will lose," the man snarls.

"You forget something. You're in my house. My rules. Threaten me and I'll bring us all down. You think I give a fuck about my family? I don't even give a fuck about myself."

"Your father was right. He warned me about your... temperament."

"My temperament?" Kieren laughs. "By all means, *push me.* I'd love it if you did."

I cower, shaking, as I sit on Kieren's bed in my black lace panties and bra.

It all makes sense. *This... this is real, isn't it? But why? Why kill innocent women? For the fucking sport of it?* Fire rages under my skin with the heat of a thousand suns, and in this moment, I get why women cut off men's dicks.

But, Kieren... He's led me to this, duped me into believing we were in a relationship. Every move he has made, every grand gesture, every word said that made me think he cared. I played right into his carefully calculated plans until I didn't. And now, I'm his prisoner. I'm the prized cow, the one who fetched the first-place blue ribbon, waiting for slaughter.

"Fine. Next month," the voice agrees.

The door blasts open. A black ceremonial cape flows out of the adjoining common room. Kieren slams the door shut. His fury fills the room as he prowls to the bed, stopping inches from my feet. I gaze up at my captor, drinking in his unfiltered, true self for the last time. His unblinking dark eyes, the roiling swirls of gold on his mask, the tribal black tattoos down his torso that he has no ancestral right to bear, the bulbus Sigma ring on his pinky finger.

Kieren.

The boy I once loved.

The boy turned con man.

The boy who realized he would never be able to control his own demons, so he became one instead.

Standing to the right of the dais, I lower to my knees for the last time, because I'm getting the fuck out of this prison tonight. The basement, decorated in shades of sin, looks different without the veil of psychedelics. It looks basic, childish, like an oversized room was poorly decorated in the same shade of red cloth by boys who know no better. I search for the details of finesse I thought I had previously seen. My memories are of a plush, underground sex club, lavish and refined, and not of fraying curtains, carelessly constructed makeshift beds, stained chairs, and trays piled high with condoms.

In walks the procession of women, and my heart sinks. How naïve we had been to think we were part of an elite club, led to believe we were taking part in something akin to a mystical midsummer solstice ceremony.

This isn't a ceremonial room. It's a feeding pen where the women are led to slaughter like sheep in a pasture.

In the back of the room, hiding like cowards, I see the 'elders', the handful of men who I doubt hold any real power in the world, so they have to take it from young women. How disgusting it is to let these women believe these men wear different masks because they are seniors who take part in some harmless chanting at the end of the night.

A gold horn peeks in and out of view. X. The alpha controlling the pack, surrounded by his hyenas, waiting to feast on easy prey in their circus tent. I wonder their ages. Thirty? Forty? Fifty? All this because some sick old men want to cheat on their wives and fuck nineteen-year-old pussy?

My fingers instinctively curl into fists.

What have these old men promised in exchange? A guaranteed job upon graduation?

"But I get to spill her blood."

Kieren's words spear me like a pincushion. *They are killing us.* Why?

Why?! I scream to myself. Is the value of a life worth so little? But then I glance around the room, remembering those in my presence. Wealth, power, greed. A pyramid for the aristocratic rich, built atop the blood and bones of those like me, born without a cent to their name.

"Kneel," Kieren commands, as he takes his position. Words flow from his mouth like poisoned honey. Words that we swallow because we are told they are medicine, and we recite them because we do not realize the severity of the words we willingly repeat.

"The spilling of Sigma's secrets is punishable by death."

"A death which I will gladly accept should I prove disloyal."

"Should I be called upon in the name of Moloch, I offer my soul as sacrifice."

"Let the Ceremony begin," Kieren booms. Lights dim to the point of near darkness. Music thumps. Men and women move in a dreamlike state. Some couple right away. Some cluster together in groups. It's as I remember, but the glossy sheen of lust and abandoned inhibitions is missing.

I know I'll soon be called upon. I've mentally prepared for this moment. Even though I've shared a bed with Kieren for the last week, we haven't been intimate. If he's sober, he's cold and uninterested. If he's not, he's too high to care. I've come to know the type of mood he's in by the way his footsteps sound as he approaches the bedroom door. I can tell how high he is by the number of times his key scrapes the lock before making contact with the keyhole. I know the mask I need to wear, the role I need to play, to placate his temper.

As heartbreaking as it is to see him out of his mind, he usually passes out within five minutes. Once I hear the telltale sound of his soft snores, I'll resume whatever work I was doing before he returned. When he's awake, I'm too on edge to focus. I'll pretend to read my textbook, and eventually, he becomes indifferent.

I can sense the moment he decides to disengage. He'll go into the bathroom or lie down on his bed and scroll through his phone. Then, the charged energy in the room temporarily subdues. This has proven to be a good time to ask him to order food. It always takes me several minutes to work up the confidence to speak, to let him hear my voice. The first few seconds are the scariest, when my brain analyzes his shift in energy, and I'll know if the bear is annoyed but agreeable or irritated and now irate.

Minutes pass, and he hasn't called me to his lap. But I can sense the tension. I can sense he wants to, but knows I may refuse, and doesn't want others to see him rejected in public. I know if I initiate, it will please him, and I don't want to give him a reason to be angrier than usual tonight. I need him to let me go upstairs with Jace. I need him not to think twice about locking me in his room without chaining me to the bed. I need him to think I took the pills when, in fact, I didn't.

Swallowing my dignity, I reach out and skim the calf of his black pants. He looks down at me, and I give him my best attempt at innocence.

He leans forward and more tenderly than I would have expected, helps me to my feet. I climb onto his lap, straddling his groin. He stiffens underneath me, and I feel his length press against my panties.

I gaze into his hollow eyes as I run my palms up his bare chest, wishing that a shred of his humanity would shine through, because I don't know if I can go forward with this, and I don't know if he can, either.

Does he know it's over?

Does he sense deep down that this is the last time?

I avert my eyes in apology, and to my shock, he lifts his mask. Our stares lock, and it's the first time I've seen him, *really seen him*, in weeks. His gaze flicks between my eyes and lips. I feel my soul whimper with want, and I close my eyes, pulling his mouth to mine, and taste him.

I moan, craving him, needing him, thirsting for his touch. His forgiveness. His approval. His love and acceptance. I know with every swipe of my tongue against his that I may walk away from this man, but I will spend an eternity wishing I had his heart.

His fingers push aside my thong. Weeks without intimacy has me pulling back to study his face. He slides two fingers down my labia as he looks at me in question, silently asking if this is okay. I don't confirm, but I don't stop him, and despite the voice screaming in my head, I slowly rock into his touch. His eyelids flutter closed as he pushes his fingers inside my hot center, as if this act alone is enough to send him over the edge, and I want so badly to believe the expression painted across his face is one of regret. The threat of tears stings my eyes. I can't look at him. I can't watch him fall apart.

I fumble with his pants, unsteady and out of practice. His fingers slide from my center to help, and it takes several awkward attempts to line up the head of his penis with my entrance. I bounce slowly, grinding myself against the base of his shaft, savoring the moment when he tilts his head back in sweet relief like he forgot how good we feel together. Like he forgot me. I lean down to kiss him again, this time hungry. I wish we were upstairs. I wish we were experiencing this moment in private. Maybe it's an act, a performance on his part for the crowd. For the man in the back. But I'm going to tell myself that it's not.

"Make me come, Kieren. Make me come," I plead breathlessly against his lips. I pick up my pace, directing his fingers to my clit. He remembers what I need, doesn't he?

Without warning, hot cum floods my inner walls. I pant, out of breath, but slow myself as I realize what happened. Kieren's chest heaves from his release. His closed eyes open halfway, apologetically meeting mine, as he realizes it too. For some couples, this might be insignificant, but it's significant for us, because never has Kieren let this happen.

A tear falls from my right eye, then another from my left.

It's over.

We are over.

And we both know it.

This was our crestfallen goodbye. Our swan song. A half-hearted, lackluster fuck before I'm severed for good.

Kieren reaches up to brush away my tears when that god-awful metallic voice rasps behind me.

"It is time." The low, demonic voice rumbles at my back. I turn to look at the man with the gold-horned mask and then back at Kieren as he reaffixes his own.

"Five minutes," Kieren responds, holding up his hand with five fingers spread wide.

I wait until I'm sure the man has turned away to lift myself carefully off Kieren's lap. His release slides out of my pussy, coating his fingers as he tucks himself into his trousers.

"Jace will take you upstairs," he says, clearing his throat without making eye contact. The pain of being discarded smacks me in the face. I blink away more tears as my feet hit the raised platform, unsteady. In the back of the room, I see a slender woman with pale, milky skin and long, wavy black hair. Her back is to me, and I can tell by the knot of fabric at the back of her head that she's blindfolded. Jace pushes off a nearby wall and walks toward me, steps away from crossing paths with Kieren. Two men in black, demonic elder masks with black horns flank the woman, each holding an elbow, guiding the woman toward the hidden room.

Jace stands five feet in front of me, and I make the oversized step down from the dais to the floor. I begin to walk. Jace turns away.

My freedom.

My freedom. My freedom. My freedom.

But I can't.

I can't live with myself.

So, I run.

The room isn't large. It takes two breaths to get to the back.

"No!" I scream, grabbing the woman who I'm sure is Tessa. I grab her left arm from behind, freeing it from the masked elder before he can react.

"Tessa run!" My scream gurgles in my throat as I desperately pull her arm, trying to get her to run with me. "They're going to kill you!"

A body slams into me from the side. Thick arms are around my waist, hauling me backward as I scream.

"They're going to kill you! They're going to kill all of you! Run!"

"Run!" I scream, kicking, fighting, clawing at the arms around me as they lift me off the ground. "Run!"

"It's a trap!"

Kieren bursts from the hidden room. A half-masked man grabs my ankles, holding my legs closed so I can no longer kick. The room is a blur of blood red and tears.

"Run!" I sob. "Run!"

The basement door shuts behind me.

"Let me go!" I scream as I'm carried up the stairs. "Let me go!"

"Stop it, Monroe. Stop!" the man carrying me shouts. I know it's Jace, because even though he's manhandling me, he's not hurting me. If it were Harrison or Barrett holding my torso, I would have broken ribs.

"Get her upstairs," I hear Kieren shout from the base of the steps.

I stop fighting. I failed. I failed, and now he's going to kill me. I couldn't save Tessa.

"Please don't do this," I beg through sobs as Jace and Harrison carry me into Kieren's bedroom. "Please, Jace. Don't leave me in here. Don't leave me alone with him. He keeps me in here. He starves me. Please, if you have any ounce of humanity left inside you, please help me. Please!"

Only a handful of seconds pass before the bedroom door Jace had closed behind us flies open with so much force that it slams into the wall.

"What the fuck is wrong with you?" Kieren screams at me. "Do you have any idea what you've done? Any idea what you've cost me? What you've cost my family? And his family, and his?" he screams, his voice hysterical, as he points to Jace and Harrison.

Kieren grabs a pill bottle from his desk. He's shaking with rage, barely able to twist the cap open, continuing to scream every hateful thought he's ever had about me.

Something inside me snaps.

And I scream right back.

"You're a murder! You're all fucking murders! You're killing them! You're going to kill me! Do you think I'm stupid? Do you think I don't know what's going on? Do you think I don't hear you when you talk to that man about *offering* me? About spilling my blood? Who is making you do this? Is it him? Is it X?"

A hand collides with my cheek, and I taste the coppery tang of blood.

"Don't you ever fucking say that name again," Kieren

screams, and then before I can comprehend what he's doing, he shoves his palm flat against my mouth, forcing the pills inside.

"Hold her down," he growls. Harrison pins me in a bear hug. "Take the fucking pills," Kieren yells. He clamps my mouth shut but I refuse to swallow.

"Give me the ketamine," Kieren shouts. My eyes flare in horror as Harrison hands him a water bottle.

"Drink it," he grits, shoving the water bottle into my mouth until I have no choice but to swallow.

"Kieren, stop! She'll overdose," I hear Jace yell.

"I don't give a fuck, she's dead anyway. Put her in the cage. Put her in the fucking cage!" he shrieks.

Harrison shoves me down to the floor, stuffing me inside the metal door with his huge, rough hands.

"Out!" Kieren barks to Harrison and Jace, pointing to the door. I glare at Jace who now stands there stone-faced, unwilling to further provoke Kieren's unhinged madness, only to see him avert his eyes. My only two witnesses quickly vacate the room without a word, without so much as a flicker of objection or concern on their faces for what Kieren might do to me if left alone. Sobs catch in my throat, and suddenly, I can't breathe. I can't see... *His gun... His rage...* The room begins to spin, and I just know... I'm going to die.

"FUCK!" Kieren screams at the top of his lungs and then kicks the cage over and over. The metal rattles violently, shaking me within until I'm dizzy to the point of throwing up from both fear and motion sickness.

"I'm not a murder. I am a fucking God!" he spouts. He crouches down, slamming the door. The lock hanging from the metal wire is clicked closed.

"Make no mistake, Monroe. I'll do whatever it fucking takes to protect my name, my title, my legacy. Something you know nothing about because you've been a bottom feeder your entire miserable life. You're the dregs of society. You're a fucking parasite who just lost its host. I will destroy you," he rumbles, shaking the cage with his fury. "You're roadkill, and I'm going to relish these next thirty days. I'm going to drain you. I'm going to suck every drop of spirit from your worthless body, and by the time the next Full Moon Ceremony comes around, you'll be begging for death. And I'll be there, holding the knife, ready to slit your *fucking throat.*"

He stands, turning to leave, but then whirls around and slams his boot into the cage one last time.

The room is cold and silent. My hands tremble as I remove my ceremonial mask Kieren had custom-made for me.

This isn't a mask for the living. It's a mask for the dead.

40

KIEREN

Five Months Prior to Present Day,
Night of the April Full Moon Ceremony,
Junior Year,
Sigma

"What the fuck was that?" X seethes after the Ritual of Sacrifice is finished. Blood runs from three open slits – throat and both wrists – then pools onto the recently bleached clean floor.

"Bad combination of pills," I say dismissively.

"Go fucking get her and bring her down here now. We sacrifice her tonight," he spits, stepping into my space. I know I'm in no position to talk back, but if he advances one more fucking inch, I'm going to throttle him right into the still-burning statue of Moloch. The circular window on the ceiling of the Sacrifice Room has been tilted open to let the putrid smell of charred blood escape into the night sky. The moon is hidden behind the clouds of incoming weather, but it presides over us nonetheless.

"We've already discussed this matter. Next month," I state, trying my damnedest to rein in my emotions since my problematic *feelings* are what got me into this fucking mess with Monroe in the first place.

"She's unstable and unpredictable. She needs to be offered tonight. What difference does thirty days make to you?"

I can't answer his question because truthfully, I don't know. Logically, he's right. Tonight or thirty days from now makes no difference. The end result is the same. I've already made my peace with this outcome, but for some stupid, infuriating reason, I can't find it within myself to let her go. In the back of my mind is the knowledge that I hit her tonight. I hit her, drugged her, then had Harrison stuff her inside that cage while I screamed her damnation. Part of me can justify my actions, knowing that frankly, she deserved worse. Her betrayal gouged an irreparable hole in my heart and almost cost me everything. How could she do that to me? But part of me doesn't know who that person was upstairs. The more I wear this mask, the more I've become the mask, and I don't think I can switch it off anymore.

They've backed me into a corner with Monroe. Embracing my abhorrence like I did tonight, hating her to the point of wanting her dead, is the only way I can let her go. A sliver of my soul remains, but goddamn do I wish it didn't.

"Not *yet*," I say with finality.

"Hear me when I say this, I can break you. I can break your entire family. The deal I made for your insolent father can be gone by morning."

"Pull the fucking deal, I dare you," I snap back. "Trust me when I say that if I go down, I'll sink the entire fucking ship. You, me, my father... I don't give a shit. You think I give a fuck what happens to my family? I've already told you, I don't even give a fuck about myself. But just know, *X*, that if you pull our deal, that beautiful blonde girl upstairs in my room right now, waiting for me with her legs spread wide, will be gone by morning, too. I know what you want. I know you're pissed I didn't let you have her, but she's my... fucking... bitch. You got that? I'm the one who fucks her, and I'm the one who will spill her blood. She's my offering, and you should be licking my boots with gratitude that I let you even be in the same fucking room as me when I slit her throat. I know that shit gets you off, you sick fuck. So, if you want to stroke your cock to the image of my bitch getting sacrificed, then you'll back the fuck off. Next month. Not any sooner."

X glares at me, roiling with fury. I overstepped, and I know it, but I owe this man nothing. I owe my father nothing.

Thirty days from now, when I watch Monroe take her last breath, I'll owe Sigma nothing, too. I'll have given them everything. I've given this fucking fraternity my soul. I'll have nothing more to offer at that point, because there will be nothing left inside me save for an outline of my once beating heart.

41

MONROE

Five Months Prior to Present Day,
Night of the April Full Moon Ceremony,
Junior Year,
Sigma

I cower in the corner of a familiar home, hidden from sight.

"I'm done, Jeanine," a male voice shouts. "I can't take it anymore. I can't take your manipulation!"

"How convenient for you," my mom shouts back, "to decide you don't want to be a father anymore. So, what? You're just going to leave me? You're going to leave me with a kid? With nothing?"

The man's silhouette is hazy in the door and then gone.

I hear my mother's garbled sobs.

Angry footsteps get louder.

"This is all your fault!" my mom screams into my face, yanking me up by the arm. "If you had been better behaved, your dad wouldn't have left me!"

I'm dragged through a hallway and shoved inside a room.

"Go to your room, you ungrateful child. You don't come out until I say you can come out."

I see myself shouting for my mother to come back. I see myself trying to open the door, but it's locked. I see myself climb into bed, pull the covers up, and cry myself to sleep.

———

"Do a good job brushing your hair, Monroe. I need you to look perfect."

I watch myself standing in front of a mirror as if I'm watching a movie. I'm bouncing with excitement.

"Mommy, how much ice cream can I get? Two scoops?"

"One scoop," my mom corrects, her expression stern and focused. "I don't want him thinking I raised a greedy, ungrateful child who has no self-control."

I sit at a round, white table with my mom and a man I don't know. My mom smiles at the man, flirtatiously touching his arm with her hand. Under the table, I see her knee touching his.

I straighten my back like my mom taught me, and smile. I take small, lady-like bites of my ice cream, even though I know it will melt before I can eat it all.

My mom and the man look at me, talking to each other, and smile. I smile back in my best little girl way. My mom seems happy. I'm happy. I've done well.

I'm back in the familiar house, sitting on the gold carpet, playing with my dolls. I hear my mom on the phone. She's upset. Fear rises in my throat. The phone call ends. She screams, and I leap to my feet, but she's faster.

"This is all your fault, Monroe. Mark said he doesn't want to date someone with a kid, but it's because you were so embarrassing, eating your ice cream like you've never had food before."

I run to my room. She intercepts me just as I make it across the threshold, grabbing the doorknob.

"No dinner for you tonight or breakfast either. No more food until you learn not to eat like a pig!"

The door slams closed. I hear the lock turn.

———

I sit on the floor of my room. There is a painful feeling in my stomach. My underwear are wet from where I had an accident. I remember my mom telling me she was going out on a date last night, so she locked me in my room to keep me safe.

I think maybe she forgot about me.

And I tried to hold my pee, but I couldn't make it.

I start to cry, thinking about how mad she will be when she sees my accident.

I cry harder when I think about how hungry I feel.

———

I'm in the living room of my childhood home. Life is moving quickly, like I'm in fast-forward. My grandmother is in the kitchen while I play on the floor. I smell the food she is cooking. The front door opens, and it's my mother, dragging two suitcases and a large purse.

My grandmother comes out of the kitchen, wiping her hands on a towel.

"Well?" she asks. Her voice sounds hopeful.

My mother drops her things and starts crying.

"He doesn't want to come back. He said I'm an abuser. That I'm a narcissist and he never wants to see me again."

"But what about Monroe?" my grandmother asks.

I look at my mom, waiting, but she shakes her head.

My grandmother sighs. *"What are you going to do? Monroe can come stay with me."*

"No, I need her here. She's all I've got." My fleeting excitement is dashed.

"Well, you can't lock her in her room anymore. She's in kinder-garten now. They'll send Child Protective Services out here if she misses too much school."

"How am I supposed to meet anyone? I can't afford a babysitter."

"At least put a little potty in her room and leave her with some food."

Betrayal stabs me in the heart. My grandmother... She knew.

I watch myself sitting alone in my room with a large bag of potato chips. I take one at a time, eating slowly, making them last. My dolls are nearly bald from overuse. Braiding their hair, brushing their hair...

I watch myself braid and unbraid. Braid and unbraid.

Braid and unbraid...

I walk through my childhood house, this time as an adult. I walk into my mother's bedroom, where she sits in front of the vanity, smoking a cigarette while putting on makeup.

I stand behind her. Every painful memory, every hungry night, every time I was blamed, every time I was called ungrateful, down-loads into my consciousness, and I remember.

I remember what she put me through, and I see myself now and think about the times I've subconsciously thought myself unworthy. I understand now. I remember all that happened, my suffering, my heartbreak. I was just a little girl who wanted to be loved.

But she was never capable of loving me, and I blamed myself for her shortcomings.

My entire life, I've blamed myself.

My dad, piece of shit that he is, was right.

I breath in, deeply and profound, raising my arms above my head. I grab all the memories. I pull them down, wadding them up into a ball. I squeeze them between my fingers, crumpling them until it physically hurts.

You don't own me anymore.

You don't deserve me. You don't define me.

I look down, and at the base of my feet is a gaping hole. Metal teeth gnash together, churning, destroying.

I take one last look at my memories, and then I let go.

I don't need to watch them be shredded, because my body feels it, deep within my bones.

———

"One more thing Monroe," I hear my grandmother say. Her voice sounds so near; she could be kneeling next to me.

I look up and see I'm in a new place. There are other kids here. I don't know them, but I hear them playing. I sit crisscross applesauce. The linoleum wood floor is cold and clean. Before me is a coloring book, the cartoon outline half-colored, and crayons.

Standing, I go to find my mother, remembering that I've gone with her to a babysitting job.

"What are you doing?" I ask my mom when I find her in a bedroom.

She's in the closet, twisting a knob. My adult self recognizes the safe, although I know my child-self didn't comprehend what she was doing at the time.

"Shhh, Monroe. Be quiet," she hisses. *"I'm listening for the clicks."*

42
MONROE

Not three.

I spin the dial slowly.

Not four. The resistance didn't change.

I spin further and feel the resistance give ever so slightly.

Click. Barely perceptible.

It's five.

Zero is the first number. Five is the second. This must be a date.

My eyes and ears are keenly focused while my brain spins like a washing machine, processing. The parallels are unmistakably clear. How he had preyed on my deepest insecurities that my brain had buried, caged off from the rest of my day-to-day consciousness as a form of protection. Or survival. But he found them, and then he weaponized my vulnerabilities, turning me against myself.

The love bombing, the gaslighting, the belittling, the blame when he felt me pull away, the unhinged, desperate behavior when I threatened to leave. The isolation when he knew he had lost me. He ground me down to the bone, and I let him.

But I can't blame myself for persevering the only way I knew how, pulling tools from a rusty, forgotten but not gone toolkit. I can't blame myself for clinging to each breadcrumb of counterfeit kindness with the desperation of a starving child, because I was the starving child, and you can't fault a child for wanting to be unconditionally loved and not made to earn affection like a puppet on a string. It was give-and-take with my mom, I gave and she took. It's been give-and-take with Kieren. I see that now, and I can't chastise myself for losing a game I was never going to win.

If I weren't being held hostage in a dog cage by my psychopath ex-boyfriend, who plans to literally kill me, I would have the strength to get up and walk away. I'm sure it would hurt, like it always does when you rip off the Band-Aid. But a kind boy once told me that the devil doesn't deserve my tears, and he was right. Maybe one day, I'll find him again, if the Universe allows me to find peace.

Click.

The number one.

Whatever accidental trauma my brain expunged over the last few days while I was in and out of consciousness has been a gift. If I didn't wish him dead, I might thank Kieren for opening my eyes to what I otherwise may never have seen.

I feel lighter, validated now that the pathways to examine

the darkest areas of my past have been cleared. It wasn't easy to remember. In fact, it was excruciating, and I wonder if my screaming sobs were real or imagined. But in a way, it felt like closure. I can see how those buried memories were subconsciously plaguing me. My childhood needs were holding me back, allowing me to fall victim to old patterns. Never again.

For starters, I'm not letting my abusive, narcissist mom back into my life. Never will I answer another phone call, and even if she does get out of prison one day, I'll never let her see me. Calls, texts, emails... let her try. I am done. And if I can let my own mother go, I can let Kieren go, too.

I sit in the stillness of my newfound levity, feeling my body. Feeling the metal wires of the cage dig into my shoulder as I press against them, holding the lock taut. My legs have gone numb from the lack of space to stretch them fully. My throat is so dry, I can barely swallow, but I don't dare drink the water. I've already made that mistake, and it cost me another day of hallucination down memory lane. My hunger has returned. Small, circular disks of brown dog food spill from the bowl in the cage like a feeding trough. I'm not embarrassed to admit I've eaten them.

Under the surface of my skin, a sensation boils. At first, it was a simmer, bubbling alongside my initial feelings of revelation and repose. Now, it tingles with a heat so hot, I might explode. It demands release, like a volcano awoken after centuries of forced dormancy.

Rage.

Rage for being treated like I'm worthless. Rage for what my mom did to me and my grandmother's complicity. Rage for how my mom paraded me around like I was flypaper, a tool only good for one thing; a tool you trash once it has served its purpose.

Rage at Kieren for preying on my need to feel wanted. For years, he preyed on my wounds, exploiting them for his own wanton desires. I feel nothing but hate for this man. I loathe the air he breathes. I'm going to get out of this fucking cage, and then I'm going to kill him.

Fury simmers under my skin like a furnace. Once I get my hands on my little Icarus ex-boyfriend, I'll burn him and every monster in this hellhole to the motherfucking ground.

Click.

Two.

Zero-Five-One-Two.

May twelfth. It doesn't take a scholar's mind to know what this day signifies.

My death day.

How fucking original.

———

"Jesus fuck, Kieren. It reeks in here."

No shit, Jace. That's what happens when you keep a human in a cage for over three days, I think, wishing I could speak to Jace mind-to-mind.

"It's because she pissed herself. I've already had to change her once."

Right... I do vaguely remember Kieren pulling me from the cage, swearing at me. This explains the puppy pee pad crunching underneath me for the last two days.

"Was she lucid?"

"Barely. I take her out once a day for a walk around my room, don't worry."

Jace makes a disgusted, scoffing noise, and I make a mental note to remove him from my kill list. "It's not right, Kieren. We should take her to the hospital. She might have brain damage."

"You're so fucking weak, Jace."

"Dude, it's just… she's your girlfriend. Drop the act. Everyone knows you love her. You've been obsessed with her for the past three years!"

"*Was* my girlfriend, and no, I don't. Not anymore."

"Bullshit. We all watched you fuck her on Saturday night with your tongue down her throat like you couldn't get enough, like we've done at each one of these Full Moon Ceremonies."

"Does watching her ride my cock make your dick hard, Jace?"

"Give me a fucking break, you two put on a show, and you know it. The king and his trophy queen. You can't leave her in there. She's going to starve to death or die of dehydration."

"She has water."

"But it's laced."

"Are you such a bitch Jace, that you wouldn't do this to Gabi? If she had cost us what this bitch cost us? Are you telling me you're fine with human sacrifice but draw the line at physical imprisonment?"

"Leave that bitch out of this. You and I both know if it were Gabi, I'd do far worse than put her in a cage, but Monroe didn't fuck you over like Gabi did to me," he growls out before changing his tone to something softer. "The two are not the same. The opposite, actually. All I'm saying is you're taking this way too far."

"And you're about to take a bullet," Kieren quips at Jace in that cocky little bitch-boy voice of his, and I'm reminded of my first impression of Kieren when we met our freshman year, right here at Sigma, no less, for a return-to-campus barbecue: entitled, elitist brat.

I hate this man. I hate this man with every fiber of my being.

Threatening me with the gun is one thing, but threatening his right-hand man as well, like taking a life is a fucking joke to him?

"Fuck you, Kieren. Shoot me or shut the fuck up. I know you're mad, as I would be. I'm not saying what Monroe did was right. It was stupid and reckless. I'm sure you got an earful from that gold-horned motherfucker. I'm sure he threatened to end whatever scheme he's got you wrapped up in, just like he does with my father. That asshole extortionist must have all of Sigma wrapped around his pinky finger. I wish I knew this guy's identity, but then again, based on his fondness for ending human lives, he probably kills anyone who figures it out."

"He probably sacrifices them," Kieren chuckles, again, as if murder is funny. These rich pricks think they're so goddamn untouchable, don't they?

"I think we should cancel the Little Sisters mixer tonight."

"Why?" Kieren sneers.

"Because the girls are freaked out!"

"I thought we had this under control? She had a psychotic break because of the drugs. That's all."

"It's not just Monroe. People are going to start asking questions. It's been two now."

Kieren releases an exaggerated sigh of satisfaction. "And doesn't it feel good, Jacey? I'm sure your daddy is happy."

"Jesus Christ, you're unstable," Jace mutters.

Kieren scoffs. "I've been unstable my entire life; welcome to the fucking party. Listen, Sigma has been practicing the Ritual of Sacrifice for over a century. We have people on our side. Powerful people. People who can make problems go away. Besides, the administration and police have already been handsomely taken care of I'm told, so I need you to sort your shit out, Jace, and remember who the fuck is in charge here."

"Keep the mixer," Kieren states. "Tell the brothers to be on their best behavior to smooth over any disharmony, especially Barrett. He's getting too rough with his bitch. I saw the bruises on her neck at the Full Moon Ceremony."

I mentally move Barrett up on my list, right below Kieren and immediately preceding Harrison, the useless lackey who restrained me while Kieren shoved pills down my throat.

My heart breaks as I think of Kasey, and how I lied to her. I lied to her *for Kieren. Goddammit, I'm so fucking culpable.* If anything more happens to her, I'll never forgive myself. I hear my breath hitch as my rage builds, and I pray the monster in the room doesn't notice.

"Fine," Jace acquiesces.

I can sense Jace is staring down at me as I pretend to be asleep. He wants to do more. He wants to help. I don't understand this hold Kieren has over him, aside from the gun, which, when directed at Jace, is nothing more than an empty threat. Let's be honest, Jace is going nowhere, and both he and Kieren know it, so why is Jace subjugating himself to Kieren's will? I assume the gold-horned reference is to the elder I believe is X. What extortion scheme is Jace referring to? What control does this guy have over these families?

Does this have something to do with the comment about Jace's father being pleased about the murder of two women? Who *are* these people who take *pleasure* in the extinguishment of a life, *and why?* What sinister motive is behind these heinous crimes? I know the ultra-rich and powerful are all sorts of fucked up, but am I to believe this is done simply because they can?

The thought nauseates me. If I had food in my stomach, I would puke it up. But I can't unpack this mystery right now, and certainly not in my compromised circumstances.

Please God, I utter in silent prayer, *I know I'm not your favorite. I'm far from your chosen. But if you ever allow me freedom,*

I promise you, I will dedicate the rest of my life to eradicating this cancer that is Sigma, and especially X. I will bring justice to its victims, if it's the last thing I ever do, even if it costs me everything in return.

The mixer tonight is the perfect cover. I've made it this far. I can make it a few more hours.

43
MONROE

Five Months Prior to Present Day,
48 – 72 Hours After the April Full Moon Ceremony,
Junior Year,
Sigma

Kieren's fingers scratch my shoulder, petting me through the wires of the cage like the barking dog he thinks I am, the dog who will never bite.

He's wrong.

"I'll only be gone for a few minutes, puppy. Just to make sure everything is going to plan downstairs. Then I'll be back. You'll be a good girl, won't you?"

I lie motionless, controlling my inhales and exhales. Controlling my rage. If a speck of humanity ever once existed within Kieren, it's dead now. I can't blame his actions on psychosis; this is punishment for embarrassing him in front of

X and the rest of the fraternity. When you're rotten to the core, no amount of medication or therapy can purify your soul.

The three deadbolt locks on the bedroom door clunk into position in rhythmic succession. I force myself to count to sixty as I turn the numbers of the combination lock.

Fifty-eight. Fifty-nine. Sixty.

Pop.

The door of the cage gives a small squeak as I slowly push it open. The crossed metal wires dig into my kneecaps as I crawl out.

Standing takes considerable effort. My vision is blurry, and my muscles are weak. Several seconds pass before the black spots dissipate. The level of iron in my blood must be at rock bottom. Convincing my legs to move is another delay I didn't anticipate. I'm clumsy, and it takes more time than I can spare to pull open the bottom drawer of the wooden dresser. A pair of black leggings sits on top of a grey Dornell logo sweatshirt. I spend five seconds searching for socks I don't find. A pair of my sneakers, thankfully, are in his closet where I left them, coated with a thin film of dust. When did I wear them last? Is it possible that I've been trapped in that cage for almost a week?

I lost track of time. I meant to mark the days by the rise and set of the sun, but I was too out of it, too crippled by low blood sugar and dehydration to do anything but sleep. My body completely shut down to keep me alive.

I check the top drawer of Kieren's desk. Locked.

His wallet rests haphazardly next to his keyboard, and I take the one hundred and forty-three dollars inside, unlace my shoe, and stuff the cash under my foot. My black lace bra, the one I had on Saturday night and am still wearing God only knows how many days later, is too flimsy to hold the bills securely.

Dammit, I need to go, but the water and protein shake in

the mini-fridge claw at my hunger. I pull out a bottle, twisting the cap open, and chug. I do the same for the protein shake, putting both empty bottles back on the cold shelf. I don't know if this scant amount of hydration and calories will make a difference given my severe deficit of both, and seeing as I'm still dizzy, my guess is it didn't do jack shit, but I owe it to myself to try.

The heavy, wooden window frame resists as I wiggle it upward. Dammit, fucker, *move*! I clench my jaw and apply all the strength I can muster to heave the uncooperative, dinosaur of a window open. Damp, spring air floods the room, temporarily stealing my breath as I gasp through the rush of fresh oxygen. My lungs have acclimated to the bare minimum and are overwhelmed by the abundance of such a basic human right. Never again will I take fresh air for granted. The fire escape looks different in the dark, scarier and more treacherous, but I'd rather fall to my death than spend another minute held captive in that bedroom, caged and forgotten.

I swing a leg over the windowsill and into the night sky, with nothing to my name but hope and a prayer.

44
GABI

Present Day,
Early October, Senior Year,
Sigma

"It's me," I whisper in response to the scathing look I'm given from a girl I recognize as a sophomore in my sorority. "Gabi!" I say for assurances.

I'm met with a look of confusion and perhaps, intrigue.

"Don't tell anyone. I was told I need to make sure Sigma is on its best behavior," I lie, although it's not entirely untrue. When you have a closed mixer between one fraternity and one sorority, typically, all members of said houses are invited. Never has a fraternity closed off a mixer to the sorority's upperclassmen, but Sigma has gotten brazen with its predatory behavior. Clearly, they've lined the pockets of the university's administration. I'll go so far as to add local law enforcement to that list of beneficiaries. Hell, probably all law enforcement in general.

I fall somewhere in the middle of the queue of women entering Sigma. My heart pounds as I near the front door where two bouncers stand, surveying the procession. I don't recognize either of them, which gives me confidence. There is one person who would, without question, be able to pick me out of a crowd, disguised or not, and getting thrown on my ass in front of my entire sorority is not exactly my idea of a good time.

As I shuffle forward in the line, doing my best to act casual, I contemplate when exactly I lost my mind. I'm sneaking into my ex-boyfriend's fraternity with a switchblade in my bra and a wig on my head. Honestly, who do I think I am? Fucking MacGyver? My mom has always told me I'm too bold for my own good, and tonight, she might just prove herself right as I willingly walk inside the belly of the beast.

I step into the foyer, and the line stops.

"Drink or go home," the fraternity brother says to the woman in front of me. He hands her what looks like a shot of alcohol, *but is it?* Shit, I didn't anticipate getting drugged tonight. The woman throws back the shot without question, and as I step forward, I am given the same treatment. Not wanting to draw attention to my face, I toss the liquor back without hesitation. The burn of room-temperature vodka slides down my throat, and I choke on a gag. At best, I have thirty minutes until whatever illicit substance I just ingested kicks in, because I'm no fool and that shot was not just vodka.

Music thumps loudly overhead as I prowl the perimeter of the living-room-turned-dance-floor. Men and women mingle, clustered together. Some glance in my direction, curious as to the identity of the loner girl clinging to the corners of the room. I pretend to look at the photos of each Sigma pledge class hanging on the walls, biding my time until I can slip away unnoticed.

I've made it to the current decade of pledge class photos and start to feel fuzzy. I need to make a break for the basement now before the full effect of whatever substance is coursing through my veins kicks in, and I end up being Sigma's next sex cult recruit.

I do a quick scan of the room and still don't see any Sigma brothers I recognize.

It's now or never, Gabi.

Keeping up the charade, I meander around the room until I get to the hallway that leads to the first-floor bathrooms. Hopefully no one is the wiser as I slip around the corner, making a show of actually going inside the bathroom in case any eyes are watching.

I laugh aloud at my reflection, feeling more confident and cheerful than I should. I look fucking ridiculous, but in a funny way, and I wish my friends were here to laugh along with me at my absurdity.

Regrouping, I crack open the bathroom door and poke my head into the hall. No one on either side. I slither through the narrow opening and slink down the corridor toward the set of fire doors I know open into a stairwell. While there are other flights of stairs within Sigma, these stairs are the only set that dead-end at the basement. The metal bar clacks as I push into it with my body, even though I'm deliberatively moving at a snail's pace to minimize the sound. Slipping through the other side, I hold the handle as the spring hinges pull the heavy door shut. The click of the latch is relatively soft, and I don't hear any echo of voices or clamor of footsteps, so I assume I'm in the clear.

Quietly, I descend the stairs to the entrance of the basement. No lights guide my way other than the ambient light from the stairwell above, and it becomes darker and colder with each step. Shivering, I finally make it to the bottom and repeat the same set of precautions when opening the door, careful not to make a sound.

The door hisses to a close behind me as I step into total darkness. My skin crawls with an uncomfortable feeling as I stand frozen in the pitch-black basement beneath Sigma's fraternity house. You would think I would still be able to hear the thump of music from upstairs, but my ears ring with eerie silence. When my mom and I helped Monroe clean out her recently deceased grandmother's house during the summer between our freshman and sophomore years, I sensed an unnatural heaviness then, like our every move was being watched. I have that same paranormal feeling again, although this time, the sensation is overpowering, almost like someone, or something, is in the room with me.

The hairs on my arms stand straight up as I grasp for my sanity. I know the basement door is right behind me, but I feel untethered and out of control. My heart palpitates at a quickening pace as I start to convince myself that whatever spirit is lurking in this dungeon is inches from my face.

Remembering my phone, I fumble to find the zipper of my purse. My shaking hand makes searching in my bag near impossible. I can't feel anything. My fingertips have gone numb with fear. Right when I decide to abort my mission, I make contact with my phone case, and the blue hue of the illuminated screen glows from inside my bag. I pull it out, my lifeline. The glow gives me enough courage to navigate to the flashlight feature, and I tap it on.

Light spears through the blackness. I point the flashlight at each wall and exhale a sigh of relief when I don't see a demon in waiting.

But I do see three very large animal cages.

That's fucking odd. I wasn't aware Sigma had pets, but it wouldn't surprise me to learn they're also harboring exotic animals. Shit. I didn't contemplate the possibility that there might be a hungry snow leopard down here. Maybe that's why it's so fucking cold.

Cautiously, I pace the room. At what I presume is the front of the space sits a set of risers. This could be a stage? The elevated platform comes up to my knees, and my mind races through a host of scenarios.

I should take a video, I think, which is probably the only intelligent thought I've had so far. The entire point of my heist was to secure documentation, yet here I stand gawking at a makeshift stage, because I wonder if this is where fraternity members sit to get sucked and fucked by random women while everyone watches. My thoughts turn to the anonymous video I have on my phone of Jace in this exact same scenario; the video I should delete, but can't bring myself to do so. Was this the very spot where it happened? Disgusted, I back away.

I point the camera and flashlight toward the front of the room behind the platform. What appears to be a large amount of furniture is piled high and covered with black cloth. I suppose since I'm down here, I should look underneath, but I'll save that task for last.

I continue my circle of the room, disheartened by my underwhelming discoveries. As I approach the animal cages, something catches my eye. A patch of long, light-colored hair glows beneath my phone's flashlight. Mesmerized, I reach out to touch the strands. Silky and fine, like *human* hair. Like... Monroe's hair. Like... Kasey's...

A large hand clamps down hard across my mouth, and I scream.

"What the fuck are you doing here?" a male's voice snarls. My eyes flare in panic as I continue to scream against his palm, but his arm is wrapped around my torso, hauling me backward.

Wind knocks from my lungs when my back hits the wall, and in the same swift motion, my wig is pulled from my head.

"What the fuck is wrong with you, Gabi? Why are you down here? How did you even get in?"

The skin of Jace's hand smells salty and sour under my nose. My body shakes with adrenaline, but my mind is slow to catch up. I should feel terrified of Jace, but my brain is still stuck on the memory of him cheating, and I just feel so much fucking rage.

My phone flashlight creates a silhouette of his body, pressed firmly against mine, and I have no idea where I find the gall, but I roll my eyes and start laughing.

"Is this funny to you?" he spits, and I nod. I fucking nod, because yes, this is more than funny. This is ludicrous.

I squirm under him and drop my phone into my unzipped purse, masking us in darkness. Giving my eyes a chance to adjust, I slowly glide my fingers playfully up his arm until I reach his hand, pulling it down to free my mouth. To my dismay, he doesn't resist, and I'm not proud of what I'm about to do next, but fuck it.

"What's wrong, Jace? Aren't you happy to see me?" I rasp in my most seductive bedroom voice. I find the hem of his shirt and tuck my hand under the soft cotton, running my fingertips up the length of his abdomen until they find the heirloom gold chain necklace he keeps hidden under his clothes, which once belonged to his grandmother.

He shudders as I run the pad of my thumb over the necklace, a tenderness I often did when we were together, and the hand he once had over my mouth has now found its way to the curve of my hip. His other hand is pressed against the wall above my head, and I can sense he wants to lean onto his forearm and let his guard down but just needs a bit of encouragement.

"Are you going to throw me out again?" I tease, trailing my descending fingers over each protruding abdominal muscle.

"Or is it possible that maybe, you miss me?" I ask as I somewhat violently shove my hand under the waistband of his pants and underwear, landing on the soft flesh of his semi-hard cock.

Jace groans, unable to help himself, as I gently palm the velvety skin of his shaft.

"Do you miss this?" I whisper, coaxing out his erection with each stroke.

"Stop, Gabriella," he growls through clenched teeth, but makes no move to stop me.

"Do you miss us?" I ask, impressed by my manufactured longing. I'm giving quite the believable performance. He doesn't answer. The man can barely get a breath down. His cock is thick and hard underneath my palm, and in a moment of self-indulgence, I swipe my thumb over the tip, obnoxiously satisfied by the amount of slick precum I find. For how long would Jace let this continue? Part of me wonders what would happen if I kiss him, but that's a line I won't cross, not for his sake, but for mine.

"You know what I think about every day, Jace?" I ask, rubbing him harder as a distraction while I fish out the switchblade from my bra.

His pants are pathetic whimpers.

"I think it's too bad you're such a cheating piece of shit!"

My kneecap mercilessly rams into his groin, bludgeoning

his balls. He grunts, doubling over in pain, as I shove him back-ward. He stumbles but manages to grab my tank top, and I strike, slashing the blade of my knife across his upper arm. Never have I heard such a satisfying cry.

I bolt, sprinting across the basement, flinging the door open, and race up the stairs.

The metal bar of the fire door makes a deafening crack as I slam into it and burst through, running down the hall and away from the dance floor. I hear Jace's voice scream my name behind me, but I don't care to look back. Another male shouts at Jace, asking him what's going on, and again, I hear my name.

I run around a corner, and then another, praying that I'm following the same path I had several weeks ago when Jace carried me over his shoulder to an exit on the side of the building.

The next turn I take reveals a door, and if this isn't right, I've come to a dead end, and I'm fucked. Throwing the door open triggers an alarm. They'll be on me like bloodhounds in an instant if I don't move faster.

Fallen leaves crunch under my feet as I pump my arms. Male voices echo among the trees, and soon, I know I'll be surrounded.

Too late.

A body springs from behind a nearby tree trunk, but I don't stop. Fingers curl around the back of my tank top.

"Gabi, stop running!" a female voice hisses.

"This way," she tugs, and I don't know why the fuck I do this but I follow her.

"Climb down here," she orders. "Follow me."

"What?" I choke, certain she's asking me to leap to my death into the waters of the gorge below.

"Get down!" she snaps. I get down on all fours and gingerly

extend a foot behind me. She grabs it and yanks, causing me to yelp.

"Over here!" a male voice booms.

Her hands guide me as I scramble down the stone, and once it seems like I've made it to a landing point, she jerks me up by the arm, and together we shuffle into what feels like a nook. Our backs are pressed against damp, cold stone, and as my eyes readjust to the dark, my surroundings materialize under the silver light of the crescent moon.

"I swear I heard something," a male voice explains, labored from running. I stop breathing. The volume of his voice makes me think he is directly overhead.

"Keep looking," another voice barks.

Twigs crunch. The angry rush of water below drowns out the shouts of the search party, but I know they're still looking. If Jace finds me, he will kill me for what I've done. I'm going to have to transfer schools. I *should* transfer schools. I can't stay here. God only knows the number of men hunting for me right now. Wait, do they have *actual* bloodhound dogs? Is that what the cages are for?

A hand touches mine, and I jolt. I had completely forgotten that I'm standing under a ledge with another fucking person!

"It's okay," she says in a whisper that's barely audible. "They won't find us here, but we have to be silent. They will look for several hours."

I turn my head toward the voice of my savior, expecting to see the face of a woodland fairy, the kind I read about when I was a child.

The blue hue from the moon traces her prominent cheekbones, kissing the full curves of her lips, and I debate whether I actually did fall to my death.

"Are you real?" I silently mouth back.

A quivering smile spreads across her face, and I can almost

make out the ocean blue of her eyes, twinkling like the waves of the sea as they catch the moonlight.

Tears fall from her eyes as she nods, squeezing my hand.

I thread my fingers through hers, squeezing tighter, until I can feel the recurring thump of my friend's pulse.

The world has lost its mind. Nothing makes sense. Nothing but this. Staring out at the night's sky, hand in hand, with my best friend.

45
GABI

Present Day,
Dornell University

Monroe silently points at a silver Audi sedan parked along the side of the street. For all I know, it could be two a.m. or it could be five a.m. Each time I asked Monroe if it was safe to move, she shook her head. Even though Jace can't call or text me because I've blocked him, I was too paranoid to check my phone.

But the most difficult part of the last few hours, by far, has been not being able to ask my best friend, who has been missing for the last five months, where the fuck she's been.

"Put this hat on," Monroe instructs after we both shut our respective car doors. I secure the red Dornell baseball cap in place. My long, dark brown hair is already pulled into a tight bun at the nape of my neck, similar to how Monroe has her blonde tresses styled to look as incognito as possible.

"Okay, first of all, what the fuck?" I begin as she starts the car, glancing into each mirror to check for headlights, flashlights, really lights of any kind. "And why does your car smell like beef jerky?"

"Because I have twenty-some-odd bags of beef jerky in this car. Want some?" she responds, lifting a can of Diet Dr. Pepper to her mouth as if getting hunted by Sigma bloodhounds and having an obscene amount of dehydrated cow in your car is just a normal Wednesday for Monroe.

I rub my temples, listening to Monroe aggressively gulp down the drink.

"I don't even know where to start," I admit.

"So don't. Let's save it for later," she responds.

I gape at her. "Save it for *later*? Monroe. You've been MIA for months and months. The last message you sent to our group chat was in March, and it was only to like a photo. Are you even still enrolled as a student at Dornell? Fine, you know what? Let's start with an easy one. Where were you?"

"My Aunt Nikki's."

"In Queens?"

"Yes," she confirms.

"This entire time, you've been in *Queens*?"

"More or less," she shrugs. "I did help my step-cousins with a few odd jobs here and there around the tristate area, but for the most part, yes. I've been in Queens."

I let this knowledge settle, part of me furious to know she's only been a handful of hours away, chilling at her aunt's house, and not locked in a cage in Sigma's basement like I had thought.

"I would have visited, you know," I add. "Do you have any idea how fucking worried I've been?"

"I know, but I couldn't risk it," she responds.

"Why? What happened?"

"I don't think you're ready to hear the answer."

"Fuck that. I'm your best friend. I need answers. Why did you disappear?"

"Well," she begins, "long story short, Kieren held me captive in his bedroom for weeks on end, and when I tried to fight back, he lost his mind, trapped me in a dog cage, and drugged me with psychedelics."

I squeeze my eyes closed in concentration. "I can't even begin to comprehend what you just said."

"I know! That's why I said you aren't ready to hear what happened to me. And the captivity part is only the tip of the iceberg."

I lean back against the headrest, my brain in overdrive. "Did you go to the police?" I ask.

"No. They're in on it. Everyone at this fucking university is in on it," she states, taking another sip.

"Why were you in the woods?"

"Simple. I was going to break into Sigma, but then I heard the alarm go off and saw you running like a banshee. I figured some shit was going down, so I chased after you."

I abruptly pivot in my seat to glare at her in disbelief. "How long have you been here? Back on campus, I mean."

She huffs a long exhale in contemplation.

"Since you texted me that Kasey went missing."

"You fucking got my text messages and didn't respond?!" I shout.

"I had my text messages forwarded to my new number. Kieren still has my phone, Gabi. And my old school computer. I don't know what he's monitoring. I'm sorry. I wanted to respond, truly I did, but I didn't want to put you in danger."

"Why didn't you just text me from your new number, or email me from a new email address?" I demand, unable to control the harsh edge to my tone.

"You don't understand, Gabi."

"Then help me understand!"

"He was going to kill me, Gabi! Those other girls who went, quote-unquote, missing are dead. This bullshit Little Sisters operation is just a cover. A feeder operation! They pluck unsuspecting women out of the pool and kill them!"

"I fucking knew it," I say, grinding my teeth. "I knew it, but no one would believe me. When you say, '*they*,' do you mean Kieren and his sycophants?"

"Yeah, Kieren, Barrett, Harrison and Jace are all in on it. Others probably are as well. But they're just puppets for this guy X and the other Sigma alumni who get off on this shit."

"Are the alumni the ones who wear the black demon masks with horns?" I interject.

Shock fills her eyes. "How do you know that?"

"Because I saw them. I was hiding outside Sigma, trying to find a way to break in, when a bunch of guys in black robes and devil masks got out of an SUV and went in through the back door."

"Why were you trying to break in?" she asks.

"To find you! Obviously," I scoff. "I thought Kieren had you trapped in there, and I guess I wasn't that far off from the truth. Just five months too late."

"They're dangerous, Gabi. If they catch you snooping around, they'll kill you without hesitation."

I huff in exasperation. "Tell me something I haven't heard. Jace has practically threatened to kill me himself if I'm caught." I chew at my fingernail, wondering why Jace didn't drag me upstairs by the hair tonight and parade me in front of his high lord, Kieren the Great. "I don't understand why they are killing them. If this was a human trafficking situation, their motivations would be clear, but killing? What benefit does that have?"

"I don't know," Monroe admits. "That's part of the reason

why I'm back. I need to get proof and put the pieces together. I'm going to take them all down, Gabi, if it's the last thing I do, but no reputable journalist will take a risk on publishing this story if I don't come with receipts. I wish I had better connections."

"Who caught you tonight?" Monroe asks, pivoting course.

"Jace," I swallow.

She cocks her head in confusion. "And he didn't try to kill you?"

"Well, I mean, he caught me snooping around in the basement, and then I shoved my hand down his pants to distract him, and just when he got hard, I kicked him in the balls with my knee and ran. Oh, and I sliced his arm with this," I add, pulling the switchblade from my purse.

"Cute knife," Monroe compliments, but I hear the sarcasm in her tone. "But he's probably outside your apartment, waiting for you to return."

"You mean, *our* apartment," I correct.

Monroe shakes her head. "I don't live there anymore."

"That's not true. All your stuff is there!"

The conflicted pain contorting Monroe's face breaks my heart. "The person I was and the life I had before Kieren did what he did are over, and I've made my peace with that reality. I can never go back. Not to Dornell. Not back to the way things were. Kieren took that life from me. He took the worst parts of myself and turned my own fears and insecurities against me. I'll never forgive him, but I've got to move on, which I will do right after I kill him," she says in such a matter-of-fact way, that I almost think she's joking.

"So... you're just going to kill him and then what? Are you really throwing in the towel, and not going to graduate after you've worked so hard?"

"You don't understand, and that's okay. I hope you never understand, Gabi."

Tears slip past my lower lashes. "It's not right, Monroe. You can't let him do this to you."

"It's too late, Gabi. It's already been done. The best I can do is figure out a new path for myself, but not until I expose the truth. Those women deserve justice. Kasey deserves justice. Their families weren't even able to hold a proper funeral, because they're still *'missing'* in the eyes of law enforcement."

"They found a body, you know," I say, unsure if Monroe has the latest information.

"Oh, I know," Monroe confirms, and the look on her face makes part of me wonder if she had a hand in the appearance of the body found floating in the gorge several weeks ago.

"Okay, so, what now?" I ask. "What's the plan? How do we kill him?"

"The plan is to get you home safely," Monroe responds.

"You're not coming? Not even to see Ele and Viv?"

"The fewer people who know I'm back, the better. Besides, if all goes according to plan, I won't be here for long."

"You keep mentioning this plan of yours, yet you haven't told me any details."

"Why would I tell you the details? That would make you an accomplice," she deadpans like she's in the fucking mob. Who is this person, and what did she do with my friend?

"Fuck that, I want in on the plan," I say firmly.

Monroe laughs in a way that makes my skin crawl. "No, trust me Gabi. You don't."

"Jesus, Monroe! You just got back and now you're already pushing me away? You don't get to tell me what I can and can't do. Besides, you told me that fucking asshole Jace is in on what's happening at Sigma. Also, he clearly made no effort to help you last semester, even though he knew what you were going through. He let you be tortured, for fuck's sake! I'm not going to let him get away with it," I say, clenching my fists at the thought. If I didn't want to kill Jace before, I sure as fuck want to kill him now.

"You really do know how to hold a grudge," Monroe smirks. "I'll tell you what. Sleep on it, and if you feel the same way in the morning, you can meet me at my storage unit at ten a.m. tomorrow. Let me use your phone, and I can pull up the location. Take an Uber. Come alone."

"Spoken like true member of the mob," I snort.

"Let's just say I learned a thing or two over the summer," she says. "Oh, and one more thing. I have a set of spare car keys in the top right drawer of the desk in my bedroom. If you come, bring those. It will save me the trouble of having to break in and get them."

"You could just come through the front door like a normal person," I chide.

"I'm no longer a normal person, Gabi."

The traffic light changes from red to green, and thankfully, I don't see Jace's motorcycle or car parked anywhere along the empty street. I guess he's not waiting to ambush me after all.

"No sign of Jace's car. You got lucky," she comments, glancing around as she pulls up outside our apartment. The bars are long closed by now, and College Avenue is practically silent, content to sleep off its hangover until sunrise.

I slip out of Monroe's car, glancing over my shoulder to see she's waiting to make sure I get inside without issue. My head spins with unasked questions, but I suppose I'll have to wait until tomorrow. This is far from the reunion I had imagined, and the knowledge that Monroe doesn't plan to come back to Dornell makes my stomach knot with heartbreak. Whatever Kieren did to her must have been much worse than she shared to make her want to shed her prior self like a bodysuit that doesn't fit anymore. Anger doesn't begin to describe my mix of emotions.

He took everything from her. Why is it that the victims are always the ones who lose and are forced to restart? It's not fair. I want to make him pay for what he did to my best friend. Kieren, Barrett, Harrison and especially Jace. I hope Monroe's plan involves suffering of the worst kind, because if it doesn't, those four are dead men walking.

46
GABI

Present Day
Early October, Senior Year,
Dornell University

"Wake up Gabriella," a gentle voice whispers. A lucid dream. I scrunch my face, willing the noise away.

"Wake up," the voice nudges softly. Warm breath tickles my ear, and I release a clipped whimper. My eyes flutter as my brain fights with itself. Stay asleep, it's just a dream. Open your eyes, this is real.

A strange pressure pricks my neck. I breathe in an extended inhale, and...

"What the fuck?" I try to scream, except my words are trapped by the hand Jace rams against my mouth.

"If you try to fight me, I'll slit your throat," he growls.

I whine as the sharp edge of the knife nips at the fragile skin of my neck.

"Hmm, how does it feel, Gabriella?" His scratchy voice reminds me of our freshman year, tangled together under the sheets, talking and fucking until the sun came up. What a stark contrast to this morning. My freshman self could never have imagined there would be a day when I'd find Jace in my bed, holding a knife to my throat, hating me more than he's ever hated anyone in his life. Never could I have imagined the elite fraternity he was so eager to pledge, the revered Sigma, would corrupt him to the point of becoming unrecognizable.

"You were so bold last night when you sliced my fucking arm," Jace seethes. "It's only right if I return the favor."

I squirm, my pointless pleas muffled under his palm.

"But I think I'll start with your body first," he says, repositioning himself until his chest is flush with my lower abdomen and his face eye-level with my breasts. I don't dare move, convinced he's going to accidentally slice my artery. "You touched me last night, Gabriella, and you said things to me. Things you shouldn't have said."

I lie helplessly as I take in his words, my vulnerability on full display in my thin cotton thong and equally thin white T-shirt.

"You know what happens if you scream, right?"

I nod, and when Jace removes his hand from my mouth, I remain compliant.

Fingertips graze the side of my ribcage as he lifts the hem of my T-shirt with his free hand, exposing my bare breast. My breath hitches as he begins to knead, gently squeezing the tender flesh.

"Do you remember when you used to beg me to do this, Gabriella? Do you remember telling me how badly your tits would throb when you were aroused? Or how I would massage your aching, full tits like this while you straddled my lap and fucked me?"

I don't answer him, but the whimper I'm unable to contain gives me away.

"Maybe you remember how I would suck your sensitive nipples, like this," he rasps, encasing the painfully hardened peak with his warm mouth. I try not to react. I try not to writhe under him, not only because he's holding a blade to my throat, but because I'll be damned if I let this man have any power over me. But, fuck...

His hot, wet tongue swirls around my nipple, sucking and licking, leaving a trail of cooling saliva with each pass. I don't realize my death grip on the sheets until he starts nibbling at the swollen bud with his teeth.

"Jace," I plead. But he doesn't stop. Instead, he sucks my nipple with the fervor of a newborn baby, remembering exactly how my body responds to this type of stimulation. I can feel my flush bloom, and I start to short-circuit. Within the span of a few hours, we've had more physical contact than we've had over the last two years. My brain is frantically trying to quell my body's natural response, but it's losing control by the second.

Popping my nipple free, Jace cups his palm over my breast, teasing the now chaffed, delicate skin. I tense my muscles in a fruitless act to remain unresponsive, even though I can feel them quiver, dangerously close to coming undone.

"Do you remember any of that, Gabriella?" he smirks.

Pure evil. This man is pure fucking evil. "No," I croak.

"No? Then why are your panties wet?"

Embarrassment spears through my body like white hot lightning. My instinct is to look, to see if he's bluffing, but I remember my compromised position and decide I'd rather not slit my own throat by leaning forward.

He releases my breast and crawls on top of me like a bear. "I need you to know something," he growls against my ear. "Last night you called me a cheating piece of shit. Not once did I cheat on you, so if you're going to come into my house, and fondle my dick, then…"

"Then why is there a video?" I finish for him, although I know this was not what he intended to say.

Sincere confusion flashes across his face. "What the fuck are you talking about?"

"There is a video. I have it on my phone."

Dumbfounded, he sits back on his heels, and I exhale a sigh of relief when I no longer feel the blade against my skin.

"You're lying," he challenges.

"I'm not," I assure him.

"Show me."

I reach for my nightstand, inadvertently bending my knees so the soles of my feet can press into the mattress, giving me the boost I need to grab my phone. I lean back against my pillow, unlocking the device. I haven't looked at this video in months. There was a time when I would watch it every day, multiple times a day, torturing myself with the proof of his infidelity.

It takes a few minutes to scroll through two years of photo and video history, an undertaking made even more arduous by the soothing strokes of Jace's fingers on my upper thigh. I can hardly focus. I'm not even sure he's aware of his own hand movements, because at one point, touching me like this would have been second nature to him. Jace Carver is on my bed, kneeling between my spread open legs with a front-row view of the tiny, triangular scrap of fabric separating my pussy from open air, and even though he is fully clothed, the tent in his pants is uncomfortably obvious.

"Here," I say, handing him my phone as I try to avoid

looking at his groin. I pray the tent has deflated. Jesus, is watching this video going to make him even more aroused? The thought makes me ill. I can't look. I can't fucking look, or I'm going to need a trashcan.

He presses play on the video, and suddenly, I'm forced to relive one of the worst moments of my life. The catcall hollers of the Sigma fraternity members standing around him as a naked blonde pushes his legs apart. The euphoric look of pleasure on Jace's face when she unzips his pants and lowers her mouth onto his erect dick. The backward tilt of his neck as her head bobs. The way his hands guide her hips as she climbs on top of him, straddling his lap, and fucks him.

Jace hits pause, but I know the video keeps going. I've watched her bounce up and down on his dick until I've become nauseated. On several occasions, I've actually thrown up.

"But I'm the slut, right?" I ask through gritted teeth. "I'm the whore."

"Where did you get this?" he demands. His tense face is severe, almost stoic, as his eyes search mine.

"Why does it matter?" I push back, hoisting myself onto my elbows. "It doesn't change what you did."

"Who sent this to you?" His expression remains infuriatingly unreadable as he taps the screen.

"What are you doing?" I snip, growing more agitated by the second by his lack of reaction to this massive reveal.

"Texting it to myself," he explains. "Who fucking sent it?"

"I don't know. I didn't recognize the phone number, and when I responded, my text didn't go through."

The muscles in his jaw tick with tension.

"When?"

"The day before I broke up with you."

He freezes, and his fury-filled eyes flick to mine.

"Why... didn't you fucking say anything?" he asks. His

words are slow and deliberate, like an animal about to snap. I scoff at his unbelievable audacity.

"Why didn't I *say anything?*"

He glares at me, expectant, and the rope I've wound tight around my emotions unfurls at last.

"That video was from your Sigma initiation. A week before you fucked that woman, you were in my childhood bed, in my family's home over winter break, fucking me with tears in your eyes because, and I quote, you *'loved me so much that it hurt,'*" I snarl, annoyed that I ever let myself fall for such a cliché line.

"The day after this video was taken, you crawled into my bed and fucked me without protection, like I let you do for the rest of the goddamned semester because I *trusted you*. You never would have told me. You were content to let me stay oblivious, knowing the entire time that I had been faithful and you had not."

"You *destroyed* me," I continue, unable to stop myself at this point. "So why would I tell you the real reason when it was so much more satisfying to watch you fall apart like the cheating piece of shit you are? You didn't deserve the truth, Jace."

"Fuck you Gabriella," he has the nerve, *the fucking nerve*, to say.

"Retribution is a fucking bitch, isn't it Jace? Now get the fuck out of my bedroom!" I shout. If Ele and Viv didn't hear our conversation before, they surely have now. Tears threaten to spill from my eyes. I want to scream at him. I want to gouge his eyes out with that fucking knife in his hand.

The only leverage I've had over this man, the ruse that I've kept going for years, is gone, and I'm furious with myself. I'm furious because I stupidly thought he would feel *bad*. I expected him to show a semblance of remorse, but he didn't, and why would he when he knew the entire fucking time that he had cheated? He knew, and he didn't care. And now, he has the gall to be mad *at me.*

One leg at a time, he climbs off my bed, refusing to break eye contact. His chest heaves like he wants to say something, to retaliate. He certainly could. He's the one with the weapon in his hand. I glare at him, picturing myself leaping from the bed, grabbing the knife, and stabbing him over and over in the chest until the last bit of light drains from his eyes. God, it would feel so damn good.

"Gabriella," he says in finality.

"What?" I hiss.

"Lock your fucking window."

47

KIEREN

Present Day

"What the fuck is your problem?" I shout from my cushioned armchair at the sound of Jace slamming his bedroom door. Barrett and Harrison sit on the adjacent couch, the former meticulously rolling a joint, while I stare out into the hall as if she might walk through the doorway at any second.

"Fucking Christ," I grumble, standing.

"Jace, open up," I nag, pounding my fist against his door.

"Fuck off Kieren," he shouts from inside.

"You do realize I have the master key that opens every bedroom in this fraternity, right?"

His door flies open. Jace storms past, refusing to make eye contact. A gym bag is slung over his shoulder, and I've always admired that Jace chooses to sort out his demons by throwing weights around like a Neanderthal. Personally, that seems like a lot of wasted effort and time to me. Why opt to sweat like a pig with the rest of the general population when you could make all your troubles go away with one single pill?

I trail him down the hallway, already annoyed by his insubordination.

"I asked you a fucking question, Jace." My hand lands on his shoulder.

"Back the fuck off, Kieren," he yells, jerking his arm away.

"You find your bitch? Is that what this is about?"

He averts his eyes, and I know I'm right.

"Any sign of Monroe? That cunt probably put her up to it. She's back, I can feel it." My skin tingles at the mere thought of seeing my sweet puppy again.

Jace scoffs. "Let it go, Kieren."

"Excuse me?"

"Let Monroe fucking go," he snaps.

"You saw her, didn't you?"

"No, I didn't, but I'm sick and tired of hearing about her. Your paranoia is getting on my last fucking nerve."

"Why isn't Gabi here?" I demand.

"Why would she be?" he barks.

"Because I told you to bring her *here*. I'm done with her Scooby-Doo spying bullshit. I want her here, in a fucking cage, where she belongs, and if you aren't man enough to collect her, I'll do it myself."

"If you fucking touch her," he seethes, "I will break your goddamn neck."

Crossing my arms, I shift my weight as I scrutinize him. "You're getting fucking sentimental, aren't you? Let me remind you that I'm the one in charge here. You forget how quickly I can bring you down."

Jace laughs, and my wrath boils. "I'd like to see you try, you fucking pussy. And no, I'm not getting sentimental."

"Then what's this about, Jace? What happened?" I grumble.

"You happened," he grits accusatively, jabbing a finger into my sternum. "You sent that video to Gabi, didn't you?"

"What video?"

"Freshman year. The video of me from Sigma initiation; the video you told me *didn't exist*."

Ah, the video. The truth surfaces at long last. I pretend to think, but who am I kidding, of course I did. Jace was pulling away, and in no world was I going to let that happen.

"Jace," I say with cruel smugness, "you were distracted. You were going to throw all of this away, abandon your duty to Sigma, for some fucking pussy. We couldn't have that, now could we?"

His lips press together in a thin line, and I can't help but grin.

"Hear me when I say this, Kieren, if you fuck with my life again, it will be the death of you. Once we graduate, I am done with you, done with Sigma, done with this entire fucking nightmare. I never want to see you, or anyone else from this godforsaken place, again."

"Oh, Jace, you wound me," I tsk. "Don't worry, we won't run in the same circles. You'll be slumming it with the rest of the Wall Street finance grunts working for your daddy, battling it out for a paycheck. Unbearably mediocre, just like the rest of your family, feeding off my scraps."

The scathing look he gives me makes me want to laugh. He's trying so hard, but he knows I speak the truth.

"Off you go," I shoo. "And do try not to get another staph infection. I'd hate for something unfortunate to happen to you right before the next Full Moon Ceremony."

48
JACE

I crank up my music to a deafening volume in the hope that it will drown out my spiraling thoughts. Between Kieren and Gabi, I don't know who I hate more.

I *tolerated* Kieren in boarding school, mainly because we had the same group of friends and for whatever fucked-up reason, it made my dad happy to know Kieren was part of my circle. I knew we'd cross paths at Dornell, especially because we both intended to pledge Sigma, but then he ended up as my fucking roommate freshman year. To think, if I had been roommates with anyone else, none of this bullshit would have happened.

I never would have met Gabi. I never would have gotten roped into Kieren's Sigma atrocity, or at least not to the extent I am now. Maybe, I would have even been happy instead of fucking miserable day after day. What I wouldn't give to rewind time. Dornell was supposed to be the time of my life. Finally, I'd be away from my dad and not have to listen to him gloat about my older brother, Reid's, success. Growing up under the thumb of a power-hungry Wall Street baron who never wanted a second child to begin with was trial enough. Dornell was the finish line. Finally, I would be free, but then Kieren shackled my college experience to his, and because I fell into a deep depression when I was a sophomore, I've resigned myself to being nothing more than Kieren's subservient lackey, going through the motions, for years.

I want out.

I want this abominable nightmare to be over.

My trust fund doesn't become fully mine until I turn twenty-five. The money isn't even that significant, but it's enough to move to Costa Rica and start a new life. That means I'll have to bend to my father's will for three years. He wants me to follow in his footsteps, just like Reid, but finance has never interested me in the same way it has my father and brother. Working on Wall Street as an investment banking analyst at the same firm as my father might be worse than doing Kieren's dirty work. I'd be quite literally under his thumb, because he won't just be my father, he'll also be my corporate overlord. The man does not do favors, or at least, not for me.

If this scenario happens, I'll die. I won't make it. I'll shrivel up like a weed, trampled and forgotten.

My father seems open to the idea of me working overseas. I'd still be working at the same company as him, but with the buffer of time zones and absence of physical proximity, I'll survive. I can withstand three years of discomfort if it means finally getting the pot of gold at the end of the tainted rainbow.

Once upon a time, Gabi and I had talked about moving in together after graduation. The job opportunities she's interested in are all based in New York City. I'd find a way to stomach my father if I had her to come home to each night.

What kind of twisted, selfish fucking person breaks their boyfriend's heart and then repeatedly stomps on it for two years? I know I fucked up. I should have told her, but honestly, I hardly remember that night. The seniors hazed us into oblivion, which I know isn't an excuse, but if Kieren hadn't made a point to remind me of my infidelity the next day, I would have convinced myself it was a dream.

That fucker lied to me. I asked him if there was evidence, and he said no, but I should have known better than to trust Kieren. Life is a game to him, one where he takes sick pride in his ability to manipulate his desired outcome. I should have seen this coming. I knew he was jealous of my relationship with Gabi, not because Monroe didn't love him, but because time with Gabi meant time I wasn't spending with Kieren. He's so goddamn needy and paranoid, always convinced people are going to leave him. And guess what? He deserves to be left. He's a terrible fucking person. Monroe didn't deserve what he put her through, but at the same time, she was the one who kept coming back.

Not Gabi, though. That fucking bitch could care less about me. I wonder if she would even feel bad to know she was the reason why I hit rock bottom. She's lucky I didn't push her further this morning. Once the scent of her arousal filled the room, it was game over. I could have kept going, but as much as I wanted to hear her beg, I knew I'd just be hurting myself by ripping open old wounds. My wounds, not hers.

Maybe I should have slit her throat. Lord knows I've fantasized about it. Bringing her to Sigma as Kieren wants would be the ultimate form of payback. Gabi's not cut out for what happens in the basement. It would break her, and I would relish in watching her crumble.

49

GABI

Present Day

"Hold on. I don't think so," Ele reprimands as I try to leave the apartment without being noticed. "What happened last night?" she insists, stalking up to me.

"Is there any coffee left?" I inquire, intentionally deflecting her attitude when I notice the mug clutched between her hands.

"Only if you tell me why I heard a male's voice coming from your room this morning and why you were shouting."

I glance down at the phone in my hand to check the time. Nine fifteen. Deciding I can spare fifteen minutes, I drop my backpack to the floor and head to the coffee pot.

"It was Jace," I admit.

"What the... holy shit," she stammers. "Did you two..."

"No," I say firmly. "He's an asshole and broke in through my window to, shocker, threaten me again."

Ele looks visibly shaken, but I shrug as I pour vanilla coffee creamer into my mug. "What's new?" I scoff.

"Well, that's disturbing that he's stooped to breaking and entering. Did you find anything at Sigma?" Ele inquires.

I shake my head and blow on the steaming coffee. "Just, more of the same," I lie. "You and Viv are right. But of course, Jace managed to see me, hence the lovely visit."

"I'm sorry," Ele offers, looking down at her feet.

"It's fine. I'm over it," I say with a wave of my hand. "Anyway, I'm headed to the library."

"If you can wait forty-five minutes, I'll go with you," Ele says.

"Would you mind if I went ahead? I need to clear my mind, and walking helps."

She gives me a sad smile. "Of course. I'll meet you there later. Maybe I can even rouse Viv. I think she is back with Sophie," Ele whispers, jerking her head in the direction of Viv's room.

"That makes me happy," I say with genuine sincerity.

I rinse out the half-consumed cup of coffee and place the used mug in the dishwasher before discretely calling an Uber. "I'll see you later," I call to Ele who is halfway back to her bedroom.

Sometimes I feel I should be more concerned with my ability to lie with ease, but then again, I deserve a medal for maintaining a two-year lie. Even though fuckboy Jace didn't show it, I know it got under his skin. I let him think the reason why I broke up with him was because he just wasn't doing it for me anymore. Not feeling good enough is his Achilles Heel, and I hope, no I pray, Jace felt as heartbroken as I did. But I'll never know, and he'll never tell me, which I suppose now is for the best, because I plan to obliterate him along with the rest of Sigma's squad of villains. They'll be no mercy, motherfuckers. We're coming for you.

———

Well, this place is in the middle of nowhere, I think to myself as I exit my Uber. If Monroe needs to hide a few dead bodies, she picked the perfect spot. Down the road, I noticed an old church and several dilapidated houses, your typical rural structures.

Gravel crunches under my sneakers as I walk down the driveway toward the storage facility. It's unclear if there is an office, and Monroe didn't give me the number of her unit, so I keep walking until the silver Audi she was driving last night comes into view. It's parked in front of a blue garage door that is halfway up, which I take as an indication that I'm in the right spot.

"Monroe?" I call as I approach.

A head of blonde hair appears in the gap of space. "In here," she motions with urgency, and I trot over to the partially opened storage unit. Getting under the door requires more crouching than I initially thought, but once I'm fully inside, the reason for the partially closed door becomes clear.

"What *is* all this?" I gape, taking in my surroundings. Monroe closes the garage-like door the rest of the way before walking to my side.

"Impressive, right?" she asks with earnest pride.

Apprehension and perhaps a slight bit of concern ripples across my mind. Monroe looks physically the same as I remember, but there is a hardened edge to her face and a crazed hunger in her eyes. Her irises are the same shade of deep blue, but now that I see them in the light of day, they have a terrifying twinkle, churning like an unhinged ocean tempest ready to swallow the ship whole.

"I guess. Did you buy these guns?" I gawk.

"No, my step-cousins gave them to me. Same with all the other stuff," she says as we both take in the arsenal of weapons Monroe has displayed across two rectangular folding card tables.

"What do your step-cousins do again?" I ask, turning to look at her.

"It's best you don't know," she responds. Based on what Monroe has shared about her step-family and the fact that her mom and stepfather are imprisoned for racketeering, I assume involvement with organized crime runs in the family.

I scratch my head, wondering what the fuck Monroe has planned. In addition to the four handguns, there are two axes, multiple rolls of duct tape, zip ties, knives of various sizes, small blow torches, and the most peculiar of all, a wetsuit, oxygen tank, and scuba gear.

"Are you planning to actually kill people?" I ask cautiously. I half assumed her comment about killing Kieren was a joke.

"No. Just maim them beyond repair," she grins. "Should I tell you the plan and you can decide if you want to be involved or run away as fast as possible?"

"Sure," I respond slowly.

Monroe drags a large black suitcase into view. "Feel free to make yourself at home. Need a soda or snacks?" she asks.

"Monroe, where have you been staying?" I pry. My back-pack hits the ground with a thud, and I sit down beside it on the cold concrete floor. "I brought a few bars," I say, unzipping my bag.

"Umm, around," is all she offers.

"Around?" I question as I tear open a protein bar.

"An inn outside of town. It's cheap and clean enough. Plus, they take cash."

She sidles down next to me and pulls out a bag of trail mix followed by an unopened bag of beef jerky from the suitcase. "More beef jerky?" I poke.

"It's affordable and I'm iron deficient," she shrugs, shoving a handful of trail mix in her mouth. "Okay, so the plan," she begins, dusting off her hands as she reaches inside the suit-case. Out comes a legal pad of paper affixed with a pen. I can see Monroe has written a list on the top page and as I hinge forward to read her notes, all I can think is that my friend has lost her fucking mind and I'm awestruck.

This is not the placating, compassionate, and privately insecure Monroe of the past. She's... different, like she's been supercharged into a leveled-up, possibly deranged, version of her original self, who I can't help but admire. Given how severely Kieren took advantage of her, I'm inclined to think this new side of Monroe is a good thing.

"There are things I, or we, depending on your appetite for brutality, have to collect, starting with the location of Kasey's body. I have my suspicions, but I only have so much oxygen left in that tank. Barrett and Harrison probably know. I saw them put an oddly-shaped object in the trunk of an SUV one night after a Full Moon Ceremony and leave with the elders. When they came back, it was just the two of them."

"I'm sorry, the *Full Moon Ceremony*?" I ask.

"Oh, right. I forgot you don't know the backstory. Okay, rewind," Monroe says, swiveling her hands in a circle. "Once a month, on a night when there is a full moon, Sigma holds what they call a Full Moon Ceremony. The guys all wear these black, demon goat masks that cover half their face, but other than that, they are shirtless. Kieren has this gold Ceremony mask. Honestly, it looks like a demon cow. He's also shirtless, but he wears a black cape. Then the elders, the alumni that attend, the same ones who you saw walking in the back door of Sigma when you were looking for a way to break in, are decked out like it's Halloween. Some are in head-to-toe black, so black shirt, black pants, black cape, black satanic demon mask with horns. I've seen a few go shirtless, but those aren't the ones who go into the hidden room. Then there are the women, the *'Little Sisters'* who attend these Full Moon Ceremonies. They're in lingerie and lace masks. Everyone is on drugs, and it's one giant orgy."

I cough, trying and failing to swallow a bite of my protein bar. "I'm barely following along, but continue," I say.

"It's a lot, I know," Monroe agrees.

"Did you participate in these orgies?" I inquire, trying to neutralize any judgement in my voice.

Monroe picks at her shoelace. "Yeah," she says, and I can sense her guilt. "Not in the orgy part. Well, kind of in the orgy part. I only had sex with Kieren, but he has this throne that sits on an elevated platform, so I didn't participate in group sex, but I watched it happen."

"Did Kieren have sex with other women in front of you?"

"No, he didn't seem interested. He would just sit on his throne, and I was in his lap... I'm sure you can put the pieces together. Can we move on from that part?" she asks. The topic has her completely folded in on herself, and I can't help but reach out and place a hand on her knee.

"Of course. I'm sorry. I'm not judging you if that's what you're thinking," I offer.

"It's okay," she scoffs. "I judge myself enough for the both of us." She looks up to the grey, metal ceiling and sighs. "Anyway, they do these Full Moon Ceremonies. The first one was just an orgy and initiation for the Little Sisters, but toward the end of the second one, some of the men wearing demon masks along with Kieren and Barrett, took one of the girls into the hidden room."

"There's a hidden room?"

She nods. "In the back of the basement. I managed to get in there once, and I'm pretty sure there's a hidden room within the hidden room. Kieren caught me, so I was never able to find out."

"What made you think there was a second hidden room?"

"Because it felt oddly drafty, and I felt a difference in the wood paneling. Oh, and then I saw a symbol carved into the wood that matched my brand."

"You were branded?!" I gasp. "We kind of heard about this from Kasey's roommate, who said she accidentally saw Kasey's brand when she was changing one day, but it's just so hard to believe!"

"Trust me, it gets worse," Monroe laments. "But I understand what you mean. We're in college. C-o-l-l-e-g-e," she says, drawing out the word *'college'* with slow emphasis. "How the fuck does a secret society like this exist at an Ivy League school like Dornell and no one is the wiser? How do three fucking girls go missing and authorities write off their disappearances as suicides? How are spoiled, rich private school boys who've never had to get their hands dirty a day in their prissy, privileged lives pulling off the murder heist of a century? And why? These are the answers I don't have but intend to find out."

"Okay, so getting back on track," I say, "we need to know where Kasey's body was buried, or dumped, I guess."

"Right," Monroe confirms. "And we need to connect Sigma to Kasey's death."

"How do we do that?" I ask.

"The brand. We have to get the brand, which is going to be

the most difficult part of this plan, because the brand is Kieren's ring."

"That hideous black and gold ring I saw on his pinky finger is a brand?"

Monroe nods. "I don't know how it works, but I'm sure we can figure it out when we get our hands on the ring. The top of the ring is not the same design as the brand, but Jace told me Kieren's ring is the brand, so I have to imagine it comes apart in some way."

"Jace told you that?" I ask curiously.

"I don't know if he was supposed to, but he let it slip one night when walking me back to Kieren's room after the Ceremony."

"I fucking hate him," I seethe. "He broke into my room this morning through the window over the fire escape," I huff, managing another bite of my protein bar.

"Holy shit!" Monroe gasps, eyes wide with shock. "I was certain after he wasn't waiting for you last night that you were in the clear. What happened?"

"Just the usual. He threatened me, like he's been doing this entire semester, telling me to stay away from Sigma or else. I was so mad, I told him about the video, so... he knows now. Yay," I feign, still upset with myself.

"Wow," Monroe says as she slowly nods. "Actually, this is good for us, because there's only one person who could have recorded that video and sent it to you."

"I know you think it's Kieren," I say.

"Gabi! Kieren is a snake. He's a narcissist. He obviously sent that video to you so you would break up with Jace, and Kieren could get his number one lackey back. That man is calculated, and we've all played right into his plans for *years*. Jace will know it was Kieren, and maybe it's the catalyst we need to create a rift between them."

"Maybe," I say halfheartedly. "How are we going to get the ring, and get Barrett or Harrison to tell us Kasey's location?"

"Torture them," Monroe deadpans, and I can't help but laugh.

"No, seriously," I say.

"I'm serious," Monroe confirms. "Why do you think I have guns and knives and shit? Because I'm a collector? Gabi, this is where things get serious. I am going to hunt them down when they are isolated and least expecting it. I've been studying their schedules. And as for the ring? Break into Sigma, or better yet, walk in through the front door. Kieren is the only person with a gun, as far as I know."

"Kieren has a gun?" I gape.

"I didn't tell you? Thought I did. Well, in any manner. Yes. Kieren has a gun, and he held me at gunpoint multiple times, which is how he forced me into a dog cage."

"Oh my God," I sigh, feeling my stomach twist with nerves.

"If you're not up for this, it's totally fine. I don't expect you to help. You'd be crazy to get involved, and this is my mess, not yours. But unfortunately, we don't have much time. The next Full Moon Ceremony is in nine days – two Saturdays from now. This is the time to strike. I won't let another woman be killed on my watch by these sick fucks."

"But do you think a body and Kieren's ring are enough for an indictment against Sigma? You said yourself that the police are in on it, and even if we get outside resources involved, these agencies move at a snail's pace."

"I know," Monroe admits. "I need to steal Kieren's computer. I know he has emails between him and the elders because I accidentally saw them once. But you're right. None of it will happen fast enough, which is why I plan to burn Sigma to the fucking ground."

50
MONROE

Present Day

Gabi gives me a slight nod as she exits the back seat of the car my step-cousins let me keep for helping them out this summer. I return the nod and pull away like a nameless, faceless Uber driver dropping off another passenger. Unless she changes her mind, I'll see her again tomorrow morning.

Guilt eats away at my mind for roping my best friend into this bullshit. She has no idea how suicidal this mission is because she thankfully has not had to experience the horrors happening inside Sigma. Kieren is lawless and out for blood. My blood. I'm sure he looked for me this summer. My step-cousins were convinced they saw him in his black BMW driving around Jackson Heights, but this alleged sighting happened at three p.m. on a Tuesday and I had assumed he would spend the summer in Connecticut working for his father's firm. They begged me to let them take care of Kieren, but he's my mess to clean up. To paraphrase the words that my dear, piece of shit ex-boyfriend said to the freak show they call X, if he's going to die, *I get to spill his blood.*

Not that I actually plan on killing him, but lord knows I've thought about it. I'll admit, breaking into his room through the same window I used to escape and slitting his throat in the middle of the night is tempting, but then I would be the villain, and I refuse to become the bad guy in this story. Besides, I have bigger plans for Kieren, and I think it's time he has a taste of his own medicine.

I should be more forthcoming with Gabi about said plans. I should tell her the full scope of the revenge scheme I've been plotting for months, especially since I suspect her true underlying motives have nothing to do with making Kieren pay and everything to do with making Jace suffer. She didn't ask if I saw Jace participating in the orgy part of the Full Moon Ceremonies, but I know it was at the forefront of her mind. Truthfully, I don't remember seeing Jace indulge. He was always standing against a wall, observing and monitoring the night to make sure nothing got out of hand, like breath play gone wrong for example. Maybe I should have told her as much. But my hardened heart is a more selfish, vengeful version of who I once was, and I don't think I'll ever make my way back to the girl I was before Kieren trapped me in his literal and figurative cage.

It hurts to dwell on the past, so I don't. I need to maintain my laser-like focus on the tasks ahead. Today's setting sun will mark nine days until the next Full Moon Ceremony, and I can't risk my emotions getting the best of me. The taking of innocent lives ends now – innocent being the key differentiator. Perhaps I'm just as soulless as Kieren, which I hate to admit at this juncture in my life is fine by me. I always knew we'd end up in hell together.

Gabi is one of the strongest people I know, but even the strongest can be broken. The success of my plan requires a woman on the inside, something that can only happen if Gabi is captured. Kieren won't harm Gabi himself, but he'll take sick satisfaction in making Jace do it. If Jace is still the man I think he is, he'll crack, which Gabi knows she can wield to her advantage. I was foolish to think maybe I could scrap my grand plans and infiltrate Sigma myself. The target on my back is too large, which, as initially suspected, is why I need to remove myself from the equation.

This is the part I can't share with Gabi. She might never speak to me again after all this is over, but maybe one day she'll understand why I needed her to believe I was gone. It's the fucked up fuel she'll need to survive when they try to make her break.

We have nine days. Nine days for Gabi to overcome all odds and confiscate the evidence we need. Nine days as a phantom to become the final nail in Kieren's coffin. Nine days to stop Sigma, at least on this campus.

Nine days to enact justice, assuming neither of us gets killed in the process.

51
GABI

Present Day

I open the front door to our apartment as quietly as the old hinges will allow, hoping my friends are out and therefore not home to grill me with questions. But alas, Ele is perched on the couch like a judge presiding over her court of textbooks and notepads when I shut the door behind me.

"Hey," she calls from the living room area. "I texted you, but you didn't respond. I was at the library but couldn't find you."

"Oh, sorry," I offer. "I didn't realize I had zero reception until I left."

"It's okay. Everything alright? You look troubled."

Troubled would be an understatement.

I double down on my anxious, stress-riddled expression and avert my eyes, chewing on my bottom lip for good measure. "I got a call from my mom when I was walking home.

She took my dad to the hospital this afternoon because he was complaining about chest pain, and we decided I should come home for a few days to be there for support."

Seriously, how the fuck do I come up with these lies? I'm starting to scare myself at how second-nature my storytelling abilities have become.

"Oh my God, Gabi, I'm so sorry!" Ele says, standing from her spot on the couch. "I'm really sorry," she says again, now embracing me with a hug. I hug her back, squeezing her into me like I might never see her again because it seems that is a likely scenario.

As Monroe explained her plan today, the nervous knot in my stomach grew until it had the weight of a brick. Despite claiming otherwise, I know she's going to kill Kieren and destroy everything in her path. I'm not a fool. This revenge plan doesn't end with the two of us riding off into the sunset with Kieren's ring and computer, ready to air Sigma's dirty laundry to the world. I'm not even convinced that Kieren is the head of the snake. Because while I'm certain Kieren would have no qualms about bringing back the tradition of Sigma Little Sisters, he's not mastermind or evil enough to toss murder into the mix for his own sick pleasure. No, it has something to do with the alumni who wear the black-horned satanic masks; I'm sure of it.

My gut tells me there is more to Monroe's story, and I aim to make her tell me over the next few days. I figure once the blood starts flowing, literally, she'll be more inclined to open up. Something tells me Monroe knows where the answers are hidden, and access to Kieren's Sigma ring and emails are only the first of many steps to uncovering something much bigger and more sinister than we can even imagine.

"Thanks Ele," I say, releasing her from my grip. "I'm

headed out tomorrow morning, so if I don't see you or Viv before I leave, I'll be in touch over text."

"Okay, please do," Ele insists. "If there is anything we can do to help, don't hesitate to let us know. We want to be there for you."

I give her a weary smile and head back to my room to pack an overnight bag. Once the revenge shenanigans begin, I don't think it will be safe to stay at my apartment, so I'll stay in whatever rundown hotel Monroe has picked as home base.

I still can't decide if I'm okay with the inevitable carnage that's about to happen. Barrett and Harrison are justifiable collateral damage. Both are horrible humans and deserve the worst – Barrett for what he put Kasey through and Harrison for holding Monroe down while Kieren shoved pills down her throat. Goddamn, the guilt I feel for leaving Monroe to fend for herself last semester eats me alive. Of course, Jace deserves to go down with the rest of them for having no balls whatsoever and for being the worst fucking person in the history of this planet.

Kieren deserves to die, and I don't know why Monroe won't just kill him. Fucking kill him! Fuck all this plotting and hoping the system works in your favor to expose the bad guys. Spoiler alert, it won't! Climb in through his window and slit the fucker's throat. That would make taking his ring and computer a thousand times easier. *Ugh,* I hope I can convince Monroe to see the error in her ways.

My stomach growls from lack of real food, maybe I can persuade Ele to walk with me to get a sandwich from the corner bagel store before they close. Fucking up men who have at least a hundred pounds on me will take strength. Now that I think of it, I should get a bunch of bagels to-go. Monroe can keep her diet of beef jerky and trail mix, I need real sustenance, because if I'm going to stab someone tomorrow, each strike needs to count.

52
MONROE

Present Day

I signal to Gabi to start running. The morning is brisk with the onset of fall. If Dornell is lucky, snow won't start falling in earnest until after Thanksgiving. Autumnal mustard and crimson leaves blanket the trail, filling the crisp air with an earthy sweet smell.

Barrett breezes past the row of trees we've hidden behind lost in his music and completely unaware that he's no longer the apex predator ruling these woods.

It's me, motherfucker. I'm the predator now.

I sprint to fall in line behind Barrett's long strides with Gabi at my rear, syringe at the ready. I picked this stretch of the trail specifically for its secluded bend, far enough from the trailhead to be empty of any hikers. Most stop once they get to the waterfalls, since that is the main attraction of this hike and venturing beyond becomes risky the further you get into the woods. Well, those hikers would be right. Not Barrett, though. I've clocked him running this trail every morning for the last two weeks. Same time, same place. Predictably dumb and perfectly primed for a bear attack.

I pick up my pace, now close enough to show up in Barrett's peripheral vision. He glances sideways, suddenly realizing he has company, but I'm faster. I spear the needle into his upper shoulder and push.

"What the fuck," he shouts, but the sedative works instantly, and Barrett tumbles to his knees before falling face-first into the dirt. I hear Gabi's sneakers skid to a halt behind me as I remove the syringe and turn Barrett onto his back. His eyes are glassy but he's still conscious.

I wish I was inside his head right now, taking in the sight of two people dressed in all black, wearing black balaclavas and Purge masks that say "GOD" across the forehead. Terror shines through the whites of his eyes, and even though he can't see my face, I grin.

I crouch down next to him as Gabi rips off a piece of duct tape as I instructed her to do and hands it to me.

"Barrett," I tease, sounding like the devil reincarnated with the use of the voice changer. "How brave of you to go running here. There are bears around these woods, you know?" I tsk as I duct tape his mouth closed. Gabi makes quick work of his legs and wrists, binding each set of appendages together with zip ties.

"Guess what?" I ask, leaning down next to his ear. "I'm the bear." I pull back, wishing his face could make an expression. He can't move of course, but the fear in his eyes gives him away.

"Oh, and what do we have here? Bear traps!" I exclaim with a manic sort of joy. Gabi hands me one of the circular metal teeth traps. "How fitting, because I hear you like to bite."

I get to work setting the bear traps and tag Gabi in, because I don't want to monopolize the fun. Barrett begins to moan his discomfort, and we've got sixty seconds before the sedative completely wears off.

"Where's Kasey?" Gabi growls. Barrett gives a slight shake of his head, pretending that he doesn't know. "Hard way, then?"

Barrett squeals like a pig, his face turns beet red and veins bulge from his neck. The first bear trap snaps into place around Barrett's calf and shin. I can't imagine the pain, or can I?

"Let's try again," Gabi coaxes as she rips the duct tape off his mouth like she was born to do this. "Where's Kasey's body?"

"I don't... know... what," Barrett grins out through the pain.

"Next trap," Gabi instructs without hesitation, and I grin like a fiend under my mask, because *damn!* Color me impressed because Gabi's a fucking natural. My step-cousins would love her. This time, I snap one around his bicep. The trees ring with the sound of his strangled screams.

"You know where this last one goes, right?" Gabi taunts. Barrett lifts his neck, a clear indication that the sedative has almost entirely worn off, and we're out of time. It's too bad he can't see the unhinged smile on my face as I crouch near his groin, pointing down at his dick, but alas.

"No, no, please, please, I don't know anything!" he begs.

"But you do, Barrett. We saw you leave with her body," I say. It's an educated guess, but I'm confident I'm right.

"Fine, fine," he pants. Blood seeps out from the appendages where the teeth of the metal traps have sunk into his skin.

"The footbridge," Barrett grunts.

"Which one?" I push, pulling down his running shorts, and gross, as expected, his shriveled cock is barely of average size. Yet another small-dicked, mediocre man who couldn't stomach the truth of his inadequacy in the real world, so he joined Sigma. *Say goodbye to your pencil dick, Barrett.*

"Please no, please no," he pants, looking down at me again.

"The Sackett footbridge over the lake," he relinquishes.

"You helped them?" Gabi interjects, going off script, but it's fine.

"She was already dea..."

A scream so loud it makes the birds take flight rips from Barrett's lungs as the last of the three bear traps snaps around his dick and balls. Gabi quickly replaces the duct tape, muffling his cries. Tears stream from Barrett's eyes as the metal-toothed vice ensnares his now purple and bleeding organs. We should add another piece of duct tape to his mouth, but I'd taken the time to write "Kasey's Killer" with my left hand earlier this morning, and it'd be such a shame to cover up that truth.

53
KIEREN

Present Day

"Fuck off," I shout again at the insufferable asswipe banging at my bedroom door.

"Kieren, it's a fucking emergency!"

I roll onto my back, uncertain of the time. My morning wood threatens to burst through my black cotton boxer briefs, even though I suspect it's no longer morning. I unlock my door to find Jace looking anxious as fuck.

"What time is it?" I mumble, rubbing sleep from my eyes.

"Have you not checked your phone today?" Jace quips.

"Buddy, I'm in no fucking mood, just tell me what's going on." A searing pain throbs at my temples, no doubt the result of last night's alcohol and cocaine cocktail.

"Barrett's in the fucking hospital getting a blood transfusion."

"Shit," I stumble, physically and mentally taken aback. "Why? What happened?"

"I don't know. Some hikers found him in the woods bleeding out. You know how he runs every morning."

"Bleeding out?" I interject. "Was that fucking idiot running off the trail? I swear to fuck, I always knew that guy was missing a few brain cells."

"Kieren," Jace hisses in a low and serious tone. "I have a bad feeling about this. I think someone knows."

Immediately I think of Monroe, but how could this be her if she's not here?

My fingers tingle like they're charged with electricity.

She's back.

She must be back.

"It's Monroe," I say, certain I'm right. *Needing* to be right.

"How could it be fucking Monroe?" Jace wails. "No one has seen or heard from her since April. She's not here! Besides, Barrett is a big guy. To overtake him would require size and speed. Enough with your paranoia about Monroe, Kieren. We need to think through other options."

"Maybe we should cancel next week's Full Moon Ceremony," Jace states, clearly trying his best to sound neutral to the outcome, but I know his bitch ass is secretly begging I'll agree. *No fucking chance, Jacey.*

"Or, maybe it's a jealous ex-boyfriend," I offer to spite him. "Is Barrett conscious?"

"I don't know, he's in the hospital. Get your fucking clothes on so we can go talk to him," Jace barks, irked I didn't take the bait.

"Maybe it's Gabi," I jeer, annoyed Jace has yet to deal with his problem. "She's been poking around. I told you to bring her to Sigma so we can cage her, yet you continue to disobey my orders."

"There is no way that was Gabi. She hates nature. She's never been hiking a day in her life."

"There you go again, defending her."

"I'm not defending her, I'm using common fucking sense! I told you, I don't give a fuck about that girl. If you want me to bring her here to appease this theory of yours, then fine, I will. The only reason I haven't is because I fucking *hate her* and I don't think I can stomach that degree of physical proximity."

Jace can lie to himself all he wants, but I'm getting really fucking sick of hearing him lie to my face.

"Give me ten minutes. I'll meet you downstairs," I huff. My brain is going to explode if I don't take some pain medication immediately.

Jace shuts my door and I glance longingly at the space where her dog cage once sat. *You've come home to me, haven't you puppy?* My cock twitches at the thought of seeing Monroe again in the flesh, pinning her under me while she fruitlessly squirms to get away. Would I have to tell anyone that she's back? X wouldn't need to know. Maybe, I don't have to kill her after all.

That's a joke.

Of course I do.

After what she cost me last semester? After X almost pulled the plug on our deal?

After she ran?

No. She's fucking dead.

54
MONROE

Present Day

"Jesus Christ Monroe," Gabi calls once we're out of earshot. We rip off our respective Purge masks and balaclavas, stuffing them into the backpack we left at the rendezvous point. "I didn't think you were going to do that!"

"Hurry," I scold her. "We need to get back to the car. We'll talk about this then."

We pull on the red Dornell sweatshirts and baseball hats we had brought to mask our all-black outfits. If we pass anyone on the way out, they will assume we're hikers like everyone else, none the wiser. Besides, neither of us look particularly brawny. How could two itty bitty girls take down such a big bad wolf on their own?

The rest of our jog back to my car is done in painful silence, and I know the second the car doors shut, Gabi is going to give me an earful.

"Monroe, what the fuck is wrong with you?!" Gabi launches into me right on cue. "He's going to lose his penis and maybe testicles too! He'll be a eunuch for the rest of his life!"

"So? Let him," I snap back, starting the car.

"What did you say?" she presses.

"I said, *let him*. Let him fucking suffer for what he did to Kasey. He abused her, and he was probably the reason why she was chosen to be killed. I hope he loses his dick. I pray he spends the rest of his life dick-less and pissing from a goddamn stub. I hope each time he looks down at his mangled dick, he remembers her name, and I hope his shame plagues him until his dying day."

"What in God's name happened to you last semester, Monroe? Since I'm out here putting my neck on the line, at least have the decency to tell me what Kieren did."

"I told you. He drugged me and put me in a dog cage."

"What else?" Gabi screams. Her shrill voice is a second away from piercing my eardrums. "Don't fucking lie to me, Monroe. I'm your best friend!"

"And where exactly were you, *best friend*, when I was being treated like a prisoner? When Kieren wouldn't let me leave his room without Harrison as a handler, following me around from class to class and even to the fucking bathroom? Where were you when Kieren locked me in his fucking room for nine days over spring break with nothing but a few bags of trail mix and no phone or Internet? Where was my best friend when I was trapped and spiraling in an abusive relationship that I couldn't escape?" My vision bounces between Gabi and the road, and I barely make it around the curve without running into oncoming traffic. The pain I've buried deep in my soul starts to crack open, and I know I'm on the verge of a nervous breakdown.

I swerve abruptly to the side to pull over. "And I know," I continue, "I'm guilty of taking Kieren back. But he manipulated me! He's a fucking psychopath narcissist! He locked me in a dog cage *for days,* Gabi, while I hallucinated my worst fucking nightmares. He laced my water. He starved me. I had nothing to eat but fucking dog food, and guess what? I ate it! Have you ever been so hungry that you've eaten dog food, Gabi?"

My chest heaves as I try to get my breathing under control. Gabi stares at me with horror-filled eyes, on the verge of tears. "I'm going to ask you one more time," I say with as much steadiness as I can muster. "Do you want out? You don't need to go on this plight with me, because believe me when I say what I'm going to do to Harrison will be worse than Barrett. If you don't have the stomach, get out now."

"I have the fucking stomach," she sniffs as tears fall. "Why didn't you say anything, Monroe?"

"Because I was embarrassed! What was I supposed to do, Gabi? Send you a message while you were in Spain, having the time of your life, to tell you I'm a fucking idiot and got back together with Kieren, only for him to pull the rug out from under me yet again? I knew what you would say. So I said nothing, hoping you would reach out or send me a fucking email or some shred of a lifeline, but you didn't. Then by the time things got really bad, it was too late. He took my phone, Gabi. He would unplug the Internet router so I couldn't get online."

"He cut me off from the rest of the world," I shoot back as my voice cracks under the pressure of my bottled trauma. "And I had no one," I sob.

She reaches across the car for my hand, squeezing it in solidarity. "I'm so sorry, Monroe. You're right, I abandoned you, and I'll never forgive myself because what he did to you is unspeakable. I should have noticed the signs. When you went quiet in our group chat, I should have reached out to make sure you were okay. You're my best friend and I should have been there. I should have done better, but I didn't. I don't know how to make it right other than to say I'm here now."

Gabi wipes at her tears with the heel of her palm. "I'm here now," she repeats, "so don't you fucking threaten to eject me. I'm not going anywhere. I'm not leaving you to do this alone. In fact, give me one of those fucking guns. If Harrison gives us any trouble, I'll shoot that motherfucker myself."

———

"What the fuck?" Harrison mutters when he starts his car and the tire pressure icon flashes for all four tires. Of course, the corpulent prick didn't notice his tires were slashed before getting in the vehicle, but his absentmindedness worked in our favor.

Harrison prides himself on being above the rules of campus parking, often parking in reserved faculty spots. The great thing about faculty parking lots is that they're rather detached from the main campus buildings and therefore, get less foot traffic, which is perfect when you plan to smash a windshield and graffiti a car.

The cock of my pistol gets his attention. His body tenses as I press the barrel to his temple. I can see his eyes looking at me in the rearview mirror, but both Gabi and I are wearing our disguises from earlier.

"Harrison," I rasp as the snap of duct tape being unrolled fills the cabin of his SUV. Within seconds, Gabi covers his eyes with duct tape and begins wrapping circles around Harrison's head and the headrest.

Crawling from the backseat and up through the center console, I keep the gun pressed against his forehead, making sure he knows that I could fill this car with chunks of his brain matter at any given moment. The unwinding of duct tape is louder now as Gabi secures his torso and arms to the seat.

"Who are you? What do you want?" Harrison demands. Still some fight in him, I see, but that will be gone soon. Sweat leaks from his oily pores as I straddle his lap.

"Where did you dump Kasey's body?" I ask, my tone hollow and metallic from the voice changer. It's possible Barrett lied to us, so I figured it's best to get a second opinion.

"I don't know what you're talking about," he snaps, trying to maintain his insipid disposition, but if the profuse beads of sweat streaming down his temples could speak, they'd be squealing just like his buddy Barrett had squealed when I snapped that bear trap around his dick.

"No?" I coo mockingly. "Well, if you're not going to talk, I guess you'll have no use for your tongue."

I jam my hand into his mouth, snatching his tongue before he has a chance to react.

"Blade," I request, trading my gun for a carving knife. Gabi obliges and takes up the task of holding the gun to Harrison's temple now that she's finished with the duct tape.

"You like staying silent, don't you Harrison? Pity."

"Wait," he squeals like the little bitch he is, but I don't let go of his tongue. "Beebe Lake," he manages, and I'm thankful I have on surgical gloves. His rank breath is hot against my face as he pants, and I know if I look down, I'll see that he's pissed himself. The smell makes it obvious. What a fucking pussy. How quickly these men fall once outside of their protective Sigma bubble.

"Beebe Lake is a large body of water," I respond. "Where, specifically, did you dump her body?"

I yank his tongue further, ready to slice.

"Sackett footbridge," he lisps.

"Hmmm," I growl. "Three women are dead and yet you stay silent. Consider this a blessing, then," I say as I slice through the thick tendon of his tongue, severing the front half.

Blood sprays, then gushes from his mouth as Harrison screams. Such a sweet sound, but the sound of him choking on his own blood is sweeter.

I lean over and pull on the door handle. Gabi does the same from the backseat, careful to collect all our accessories. We each pull a can of spray paint from our war bag. Gabi runs to the other side, while I work on the driver's side. Finished, we toss our things into the car, and Gabi gets behind the wheel while I fish out my coup de grâce.

"Bye bye you piece of shit," I mutter to myself and revel in the satisfying crunch of my baseball bat shattering his windshield to pieces.

55
KIEREN

Present Day

"Where the fuck are all these sirens going?" I ask Jace, not expecting an answer. He shrugs as we pull to the side of the road to let another police car pass.

"Follow it," I say curiously.

"I thought we wanted to get to the hospital?"

"Humor me," I grunt. Instinctively I take out my phone to scroll through social media to see if any students have posted about the commotion, but everyone seems to be in the dark and speculating.

Multiple flashing emergency vehicle lights barricade a parking lot on the east side of campus. "Something must have happened in there," Jace notes. "I can't get past."

"Park the car here, let's go on foot," I order.

"Here?" Jace asks skeptically. "This isn't a parking spot."

"Park on the side of the road and put your hazards on. Who cares?" I shout as I slam the car door shut. Jogging across the street toward the parking lot, I snake past first responders unrolling caution tape until I reach what appears to be the natural border of the scene. Students stand shoulder to shoulder, and even though I'm a head taller than most of them, I shove my way through.

"Holy fuck," I stammer, coming to a halt. An SUV I recognize as Harrison's is fifty feet in front of me, surrounded by police officers and firemen. An ambulance has pulled as close as it can get given there are still other cars in the parking lot. Four men work together to pull an unresponsive body from the driver's seat and onto a gurney. Blood coats Harrison's mouth and chin. His shirt and top of his pants are stained red.

"Is that Harrison?" Jace gasps behind me, finally catching up. I nod, barely able to process what my eyes see. The windshield of his car is smashed inward. Splinters jut out like spiderwebs from the point of contact, and if I had to guess, I'd say the person who did this used a baseball bat.

"Say their names," Jace reads aloud, and then whispers a stunned, "Jesus Christ."

Gawking, I look over at him. In minutes, I know images of Harrison's spray-painted SUV will be plastered across social media.

"Come on," I say, turning around. "We need to get out of here."

Jace and I waste no time getting back to his car, and when I climb inside to the passenger's seat, I feel my phone start to buzz relentlessly. I make the mistake of taking it out of my pocket, only to see notifications of texts, calls and direct messages on social media flash across the screen in rapid succession.

"This is fucking bad," Jace shouts as he changes gears and merges onto the road.

"Don't go to the hospital," I instruct.

"Yeah, no shit. That place will be teeming with police."

"I'm not worried about the police," I say.

"Maybe you should be," Jace growls as he makes an illegal U-turn.

"Fuck," I spit as an image of the other side of Harrison's car hits my social media feed.

"What?" Jace demands. I show him the image of the words "*Sigma = Murderers*" spray painted on the passenger side of Harrison's car.

"Goddammit, Kieren," Jace yells. "This is your fucking fault. You're the reason we're knee-deep in this shitstorm. Goddammit!" Jace curses again, banging his fist against the steering wheel.

"You fucking know I had no choice, Jace," I yell back. "But it doesn't matter now, does it? We're all fucking guilty. Me, you, and the entire goddamn frat. If one of us goes down, we all go down."

The temperature of my blood skyrockets under my skin, and I fist my hair in frustration. "This is fucking Monroe!" I shriek, bending over until my head is between my legs. "She did this! You know she did this!"

"Fuck, this can't be happening. How is this possible? And now we're all fucked because you couldn't get your shit together and figure out how to control yourself around her!" Jace shouts. "Why did you have to treat her like a fucking dog, Kieren? And then your dumb ass let her get away? You're a fucking moron!"

For once, I'm stunned. Jace has never spoken to me with such loathing. I'm sure he's thought it plenty of times, probably all the time, but to say it out loud and to my face, no less? He's getting bold, and I don't appreciate bold.

"A moron?" I argue back. "Smooth, Jace. Is that the best your Ivy League brain could come up with?"

The tingling in my fingers starts to subside as an idea formulates in my mind. "Listen, we don't need to stress. This was just some scorned ex-girlfriend or unstable student who has an axe to grind with Sigma because we didn't let his loser ass in. Besides, *'Sigma = Murderers'*?" I huff a laugh. "Murders of whom? Where are the fucking bodies? That body that floated up a few weeks ago was ruled a suicide, remember? They've got no fucking proof. They don't have shit!"

I lick my lips, barely able to contain the giddy excitement I feel for my own brilliance. Jace is so fucking dumb sometimes. "Further, I doubt we get so much as a second glance from the cops, but if we do, as I see it, this is a Harrison and Barrett problem. They were the ones targeted, not us, and not anyone else. We'll say we have no idea why anyone would accuse Sigma of something so vile and deflect any scrutiny back onto Harrison and Barrett. Maybe they are murderous heathens after all, but we had no idea."

"You are a sick fucking monster, you know that?" Jace says with disgust.

I clench my jaw, triggered by his judgment. "Jace Carver with the observation of the century, ladies and gentlemen. How about you take a look in the goddamn mirror because I'm not the only monster around here with blood on my hands."

"I need to go for a ride and clear my head," Jace says as we pull into the parking lot behind Sigma.

"By all means," I wave dismissively.

"I don't need your fucking permission, Kieren."

I throw Jace one final glare as he speeds out of the Sigma

parking lot on his death trap. Although I'm not sure she's the type to partake in criminal behavior, I hope to God that Monroe is the one behind these attacks, because that would mean she's back. And if she's back, she's coming for me, and if she's coming for me, I'm going to fucking catch her.

56
GABI

Present Day

"It's all over the news and social media," I say to Monroe who continues to pace the length of the motel room.

"Maybe we went too far with the spray paint," she contemplates.

"I mean, Sigma will be on high alert. We practically sent them a public invitation to their own funerals. I wonder if they will cancel the Ceremony?"

"No," she answers, shaking her head. "Knowing Kieren, he won't take any precaution. In fact, he'll double down on his recklessness, daring whoever is behind these incidents to do something brash."

"I'm positive he thinks it's me," she states. "If it were just Barrett, he'd speculate, but after Harrison, the crime scene alone would be enough to be conclusive in his mind. This is good, though. This is what we want," she says with conviction. "It will work in our favor."

"How?" I stammer.

"Because we'll be able to walk right in, through the front door no less," she insists as if it's obvious.

"Again, how?" I ask. I see the wheels turning, but I'm worried wheels are the only thing taking up space in Monroe's brain at the moment.

"He'll throw a party as bait. He *wants* me to come get him, and he knows an open party gives us easy access. Watch. I bet it will be tomorrow. He'll think it's the perfect response to the accusations against Barrett and Harrison, playing them off like they're a hoax from a deranged fanboy. Sigma as a whole will need to appear unbothered."

"You do know him well." I have to give her that much. "But do you really think he'd be so chauvinistic?"

"Do I think the man who put me in a dog cage to starve while killing women for fun believes he's invincible and would be stupid enough to let us walk right in? Yes! This is a *game* to him! He might as well pull out a megaphone and start begging."

"I still don't understand why you don't just kill him. You clearly don't have an aversion to blood or torture. End him and get this nightmare over with!"

"I didn't kill Barret or Harrison. Maybe I left them inches away from death, but they'll pull through. I'm not a murderer. I'm not like them, even if these guys do deserve to die, I don't have it in me to take a life. I'm not God. Besides, death is the easy way out for people like Kieren. He stole my life, Gabi! If I manage to make it through, I'll never be able to go back to being who I was. Monroe as you knew her is dead and buried, she died in that fucking dog cage."

She pauses, then admits, "I had my step-cousins help me establish a new identity."

"What do you mean *'establish a new identity'*? Like steal someone's identity?"

"Same thing."

"Monroe! Who are you and when did you become okay with being a criminal? If you're caught, you'll go to prison!"

"Umm, news flash Gabi, we just tortured two men and defaced personal property. We're fucking criminals!"

"I guess you're right," I lament, flopping back onto the oversized, stiff chair.

"Let's go over the order of operations again," Monroe states. "If things go south tomorrow, I plan to take the fall."

"Absolutely not," I protest.

"Gabi! I've got nothing to live for! You do!"

"What happens if we're caught and they put us in one of those dog cages?" I ask, terrified by the high probability of this outcome.

"Survive," Monroe deadpans. "Survive and play off their insecurities. If Kieren catches me, I'm dead, and I've accepted that outcome. If you're caught, I'd bet Jace will insist on being the one to inflict your punishment, and if that scenario happens, you know what you have to do, right?"

I nod with trepidation I hope Monroe doesn't see. In theory, one could argue I've been conducting psychological warfare on Jace Carver for over two years, toying with his emotions for my own satisfaction. But if I'm on his turf and subjected to torture like Monroe, I don't know if I'll be able to withstand his wrath. Trapped in his bedroom, forced into a dog cage and starved?

I can't let myself think of that outcome. It won't happen. Our plan tomorrow will work, and then I'll never have to see Jace Carver's face again.

57
JACE

Present Day

Forty-five minutes on this fucking bike, and I'm still just as angry as I was when I dropped Kieren off at Sigma. He's out of his mind and in over his head. He knows it too, but Kieren Hunt will never admit defeat. I'm not sure he's even still human underneath his shell of narcissism. It would do him good to lay off the pain pills and drugs. I know he has chronic jaw issues from when he wrapped his car around a tree in high school, but he's well past the point of using prescription medication for its intended purpose.

Monroe destroyed him when she left, but in fairness, they destroyed each other. Kieren has always been controlling, but the extent of cruelty he put Monroe through was hard to bear witness. The black eye he got from Knox this past summer was more than deserved. I still can't believe Kieren had the balls to publicly brag about his inhumane treatment of her. He'll never conceded his true feelings, and certainly not now. He's too far gone at this point. Maybe at first he acted out of desperation because his inheritance was on the line, but now he wears his psychopathy with pride. The Hunts are a fucked-up bunch of people, more so than my family, and I thought no one could top the cold brutality of my father.

I suspected one day Monroe would come back, but never did I see her returning as a bloodthirsty vigilante. How the fuck do you even pull off something of that severity?

Kieren, like a fucking dog with a bone, is convinced it's Monroe because he wants it to be her. But, I'm not completely convinced. I saw the fear and horror in her eyes when she was locked up. He's going to do something stupid, I can feel it, in the name of luring her to Sigma, where he'll have the home turf advantage.

My bike idles to a stop at the red light on College Avenue. I hadn't intended to come this way, but now that I'm here, the need for peace of mind overrides all other thoughts. Hopefully, she locked her window like I fucking told her to, which means I'll have to use the front door.

The downstairs door of her apartment building is ajar. Not surprising. Apartments in College Town aren't exactly known for their world-class security, even if hers is on the nicer side. A mix of my own musk and sweat fills the narrow space of the stairwell as I trudge up to the second floor.

I bang loudly on the door and wait. She might not be home, but it's Friday and typically seniors have this day free. When no one answers, I bang again, my frustration growing with each collision of my fist against the heavy red door.

"Open up," I shout, and finally, someone on the other side turns the deadbolt lock.

"Can I help y... What are you doing here?" Gabi's roommate asks, glaring at me from inside their apartment.

"Where is she?" I demand, but I don't bother waiting for an answer. I push past the woman blocking the doorway, practically body-checking her on my way through.

"Where are you going? You can't go back there! She's not here!" the woman calls after me as I stalk down the hallway. I've technically never entered this apartment from the front door, but I have a guess as to which room is Gabi's based on the fact that I know her room borders the alley.

Maybe I should be embarrassed to admit the amount of time I've spent standing in the grime behind this apartment. At first, I didn't know which room was hers, but when I happened to be walking through the alley at the start of my junior year, I saw her changing through the window. That's how I knew which window was hers when I paid her a visit a few days ago.

I can't recall why I was in the alley in the first place, but for a period of time, voyeurism became my favorite late-night hobby. There's nothing like leaning against a filthy brick wall with a bottle of cheap whiskey in your hand, waiting to see if your ex-girlfriend has another man in her room to satiate your relentless spiral of depression. Thank God that time of my life is behind me. Say what you will about Kieren, but when he came back, he gave me purpose. Obligation to Kieren pulled me out of the well, even if he was the reason I fell in the first place. Maybe, though, things would have always ended as they did. Now that I've seen Gabi's true colors, video or no video, our breakup might have been inevitable.

I can practically feel the burn of whiskey in my throat as I stop in front of the bedroom door I assume belongs to her.

"She's not here!" her roommate wails, who unknowingly just confirmed I'm standing outside the right room. "You need to leave, Jace. You're not welcome in this apartment."

The look I give this woman when she tells me I'm not

welcome could burn down a house. To her credit, she holds her ground. I contemplate knocking but quite frankly, I'm sick and tired of fucking waiting.

"Jace!" her roommate screams when I kick down Gabi's bedroom door. The door bounces off the adjoining wall with a crash. I march inside to find the room eerily empty. I know I was just here, but it feels different – like I didn't notice any of the personal details before that make this room uniquely hers.

Looking down at my boots, it feels wrong to trek in dirt from the outside into such a pristine space. I scan the small area. Feminine but not girly with a faint hint of her floral perfume. Seeing her room when she's not here feels wrongly intimate. The heathered violet comforter is neatly tucked under the matching decorative pillows at the top of the bed, a bed that I was on twenty-four hours ago, kneeling between her legs with a knife to her throat like a fucking lunatic.

I'm so... *lost.*

A hard lump rises in my throat, pressing painfully at my esophagus.

"Where is she?" I grumble, turning around to face the menacing stare of her roommate, the one who I believe is named Ele.

"Not here," she says through clenched teeth as she crosses her arms in front of her chest. "Her dad is ill. She went home."

My eyebrows raise in disbelief. "When?" I demand.

"This morning," Ele hisses.

"You saw her leave?" I press, still unable to process the truth I've uncovered.

"No. She left at the crack of dawn, but I saw her packing a bag last night. What's this about, Jace?"

"Nothing," I say curtly as I sidestep her clearly pissed off roommate. I don't even make it out of the apartment before I break into a run.

58

KIEREN

Present Day,
Sigma

"What?" I ask lazily as I answer the phone.

"You want to tell me what the fuck is going on up there?" my father barks.

"You saw the news?" I ask, stalling while I collect myself. I shouldn't have gotten high, but I needed to take the edge off.

"The news? Hell, every Sigma alumni in the tristate area who is part of our client roster has called me. My phone's been ringing nonstop for the past two hours."

"It's fine, Father. I have it under control. It's just a jealous ex-girlfriend or some slighted loser we didn't let pledge," I slur.

"An ex-girlfriend?" my father scoffs, latching onto that singular part of my explanation. "You expect me to believe an ex-girlfriend severed the Rothchild boy's penis with a bear trap?"

I sit up abruptly, causing a rush of blood to drain from my head. "What did you say?" I ask, lightheaded. God, I'm like fucking Monroe and her anemia.

"And cut out the other boy's tongue!"

"A bear trap?" I stammer.

"Do you not know what's going on at your own fraternity, Kieren? You have an enemy who's out for blood."

Oh, I know she's out for blood.

"This is not some jealous girl with an axe to grind, unless she's the one who hired a hitman. A woman doesn't have the stomach for violence of this nature."

I rub my forehead, and frankly, I don't know if I should be petrified or in awe of my sweet puppy. Did she really have it in her to inflict this level of bodily harm? Cut out Harrison's tongue? Slice off Barrett's penis? Could she really be so full of vengeful acrimony, that she's become a tornado of blood-thirsty viciousness headed straight for me?

Goddamn. Come get me, you fucking psychopath queen.

My cock stiffens under my pants, and this bullshit conversation with my feckless father needs to end.

"It's under control, Father. I need to go."

"Listen here, boy. Both of us know the absolute mess you caused this family back in April with that mentally unstable girlfriend of yours. X was ready to pull the fucking plug. Do you recall how much damage control I had to do to smooth over your fuck-up? You and your pathetically weak emotions. X and the others will be there next weekend, and I need you to get your shit together or kiss that little trust fund of yours good-bye. I will not have this conversation with you again. Next time, it's over for you, Kieren."

The line goes quiet, *finally*. What I wouldn't give to stab an icepick through that man's eye or sever *his* balls with a bear trap. I grin at the thought.

Fuck, I hope it's Monroe. A low rumble reverberates in my throat as I unzip my pants and fist my cock. I want it to be Monroe so fucking bad. I scramble to my knees and reposition myself at the top of the bed so I can brace my forearm against the wall as I lean forward. *Get this fucking pillow out of the way*, I think to myself as I begin thrusting my hips, fucking the hand squeezed around my cock like its Monroe's tight, hot pussy.

I want to kill her. I want to fuck her so goddamn much that I can't think straight. Can't she just come back to me? Can't she just be mine? I bear down, finding friction in the mattress, as I fuck my own hand with my eyes pinched closed, fantasizing about her slick, pink cunt. How good it would feel to slam into her, to hear the slap of our groins, to dig my nails into her thighs, to hear her scream my name... I'll break her apart. I'll shatter her to fucking pieces and lick her wounds right before I slit her fucking throat.

And then I'll drink her blood like it's holy water, ready to cleanse my blackened soul. I'll lick the rivulets of crimson off her perfect, pert breasts. I'll spread open her thighs and feast on her clit, lubricating her cunt with her own blood, and then I'll fuck her again. And again. And again. I'll fuck her as blood spirts from her neck, coating me in her very essence as I fill her with mine. A cry rips from my lips as ribbons of cum shoot onto my wall, catching the edge of the mattress. Beads of sweat run down the tattoos covering my chest. Monroe loved my tattoos. She fucking loved...

A silent sob chokes my thoughts.

She was mine.

Mine until I ruined her.

She fucking loved me.

And after I kill her, I know just what I'll do, because since the day she left, it's all I can think of.

When they toss her lifeless body into the icy depths of the lake, our tragic love story will finally come full circle.

Because I'll go with her.

59
MONROE

"What did I tell you?" I ask smugly as I park the car I inherited from my deceased grandmother on the side of the road at the edge of Sigma's property. Gabi gave me grief about taking this car instead of the Audi, but this car is registered in my name and the Audi is not. If tonight goes as I hope it will, leaving behind a car that belongs to me at the crime scene is a critical part of my plan.

Sigma is swarming with life. A short queue of women dressed in super hero costumes are gathered outside the front door. Granted, it's a bit early to call this a Halloween celebration, but who doesn't love an excuse to dress up like an unhinged slut capable of destroying the world?

An email went out late yesterday to sorority presidents and social chairs. Since I'm technically still president of Delta

Gamma through the end of the semester, I've not yet been removed from the email lists. Actually, I'd wager it has nothing to do with technicalities and everything to do with sheer laziness. Sigma announced they would be throwing a theme party on Saturday night, but only freshmen and sophomores were invited. God, Kieren is so fucking predictable. I bet he's sitting in his room right now waiting for me.

I flip down the sun visor to take one last look at my deranged, fallen superhero makeup. Both of us wear red lipstick that is smeared and chaotic, with excessive eyeliner that somewhat masks our identities, should we find ourselves in a situation where we need to remove our Purge masks. Neither of us had any costume apparel appropriate for the theme, but black spandex shorts and nondescript black tank tops will work just fine. All one needs to do is make sure your cleavage is on full display, and men forget to look at your face.

We do, however, have on these fun black leather thigh holsters for our weapons. They look more decorative than tactical, and when worn high up on the thigh, it draws attention to that coveted space between our legs. Men love the fantasy of fucking a kinky dominatrix, and we love a man who's distracted.

The only questionable props are our axes, but we need them to smash in the fire alarm. If I manage to get inside Kieren's bedroom, I can also use the axe to chop open his desk, or chop off his dick, whatever I need to do really to get the job done.

"Get in, get the ring, get out," Gabi repeats as we begin the trek across Sigma's front lawn. The hulking stone structure thumps with music and flashing colorful strobe lights. We step into the orb of one of the large LED spotlights beaming a massive circle of white against the grey stone structure.

"Look at us," I smile, pointing down to the silhouette in the grass of our axe-wielding selves.

"We look like bad asses," Gabi notes.

"We *are* bad asses," I correct her. "Listen, whatever happens in there," I begin.

"Don't say it," Gabi interjects, cutting me off. "We're here for one job, and one job only. Now let's make these mother-fuckers pay."

"Pull down the masks," I instruct. "Trust me."

There's no time to disagree. We're at the entrance. I swallow the fear eating away at my confidence and hold my head high as I saunter up the front steps, past the waiting line.

"Stop," one of the guards at the door bellows, stepping into my path.

"Don't you know who we are?" I ask snidely, lifting up my mask to give him a disgusted look. Confusion passes over his face, and I can smell his uncertainty.

"We're Little Sisters," I say in a low, chiding voice. "And I'm pretty sure I've sucked your dick. Now move aside."

His eyes flare with embarrassment as he stumbles out of the way.

"Good boy," I say, bopping him on the nose for emphasis as I stride past. Pulling my mask back down, I don't bother to look around. The scene never changes. Kieren's not down here. I can feel the tug of his presence like a magnet. He's upstairs.

I turn back to Gabi and point once to the hallway and again up toward the ceiling. She gives me a nod. Let the fucking games begin.

―――――

We take our time meandering up the multiple flights of stairs until we can no longer go any further. No need to rush this part and ruin the fun. The stairwell spits us out at the opposite end of the fraternity from Kieren's room. I drag my axe on the floor behind me, as if contact with the ground is how the weapon gets its charge.

Here kitty, kitty, I think to myself, although I might be saying it out loud. Adrenaline clouds my senses, making me feel laser-focused yet manic at the same time. I round the corner and see the beginning of my end.

Encased in a small glass box is the fire alarm, that, once triggered means there's no going back. From the moment we set foot in Sigma and up until now, we've been cosplaying. Two women dressed as murderous, axe-carrying, weapon-bearing superheroes who could turn around at any moment, go home, and order a pizza.

Five steps and it's over.

Four steps and it's over.

Three.

Two.

One.

The shrill bleat of the alarm screams to life as I swing the blade of my axe at the glass box like an unhinged psychopath. Here we fucking go.

I shift my axe into my non-dominant hand and sling it over my shoulder as I unsheathe my knife from the holster. The entrance to Kieren's common room is less than ten feet away. Scantily clad women and half-naked men stream into the hall as we approach, bewildered. I pause my swagger and cock my head to the side, aware that my Purge mask reads 'GOD', and raise my hand with the knife to point at the first doe-eyed frat boy I see.

Pop. Pop. Pop.

Gabi fires off three rounds at the ceiling and the boy in my direct line of sight looks like he's about to shit himself.

Screams shake the walls as we near. Those already in the hallway crouch against the wall, covering themselves with their hands, like that will do any fucking good.

As the chaos within Kieren's common room comes into view, I can't help but smile. Women and men alike scramble over padded leather couches and chairs in an attempt to hide. From the corner of my eye, I see someone try the handle of Kieren's bedroom only to find it won't budge. Locked. Good to know. Won't waste my time there.

Kieren sits poised and calm in an armchair at the center of the room, grinning at me like a Cheshire cat on crack. *Found you kitty.*

The three steps I've taken inside the common room happen in slow motion. Swirling around me are cries, shrieks, bodies slinking past me in an attempt to exit unnoticed, and the thunder of heavy footsteps as people try to run. Not Kieren. He doesn't move an inch. I see Jace out of the corner of my eye duck behind a chair, and I pray to God that Gabi sticks to the plan and stays in the hallway.

With one more stride, I close the distance between us, now face to face with my once-captor. I lift up my mask. A strange numbness has cocooned my mind. My body continues to move, but of its own accord. We lock eyes, and his dark brown irises, filled with pure desire, feel like they bear the weight of my soul. His chin tilts upward as I get closer, so close that I now stand between his casually spread legs. Without thinking, without breathing, I let the handle of my axe fall from my hand and climb onto his lap, straddling him as I yank his head backward by the scruff of his hair.

My lips, smeared with blood-red lipstick, crash against his. His tongue spears my mouth and I taste what once was the most raw and carnal love I've ever known. I rock my hips into his groin as his hands trail along the curves of my body, hungry yet surprisingly tender. I expected a fight. I assumed we both would have weapons drawn, but he doesn't launch a counter-attack as I expected he would. He doesn't even try.

Pulling back until my lips barely graze his, I find his left hand and wrap my fingers around his ring.

"Give it to me," I say, my voice sounding more like a plea than a demand. I press the sharp edge of my knife to his neck as I try to pull it over the first joint of his finger, leaning forward to kiss him while I work. It begins to slide, now almost halfway off, but my angle is awkward.

"Never," he rasps against my lips, trying to yank his hand away, but I planned for this, faster and stronger than I was five months ago. The tension from our opposing forces, like a finger trap gag toy, creates the perfect opportunity.

In one rapid motion, I slam his pinky finger down on the armrest of the chair. My thick carving knife is through his flesh and bone in an instant, chopping the part with the Sigma ring cleanly off.

I can't believe that worked...

I'm stunned, but I don't have time to be stunned. I only have time to run.

It happens so fast that Kieren doesn't initially register the pain, but in the seconds it takes me to scramble off his lap, he unleashes a scream I've only heard him make once before - *the night I escaped*. Kieren's scream echoes down the hall as Gabi and I sprint for the stairwell. Unfortunately, the only way out is to go back the way we came. I toss the knife to the ground and pull the gun from my holster as I clutch Kieren's bloody half-finger and Sigma ring for dear life.

Gabi still has her gun and axe as threats to clear the way, but the large living room is empty due to the continuous blare of the fire alarm.

"Drop the axe," I shout at Gabi as we dash out the front

door, hurling ourselves down the steps like gazelles, and weave through the mingling party-goers now clustered on the lawn.

"Ditch the masks," I yell in reminder as we race across the grass. We make it to the car I left unlocked, because why would anyone try to steal this ancient piece of shit? The ignition turns over with agonizing delay.

"Go! Go!" Gabi screams as the car finally jolts to life. I shift the gear into drive and slam the gas pedal all the way to the floor. Wheels churn atop the pavement before the car lurches forward. *Do not fucking die on me,* I curse.

"Monroe!" Gabi shrieks, looking behind us, as headlights careen down Sigma's driveway.

There is absolutely no way this car can outperform a BMW, the kind of car both Kieren and Jace drive. I just hope I've given us enough of a lead to make it to my final destination.

60

GABI

Present Day

"Monroe, where are you going?" I scream as she drives like a maniac down the twisted road.

Headlights close in on our car, and panic consumes my mind. I can't think straight. I have no idea how Monroe is driving a car right now, because I can't find words to speak.

"Take off the ring and give the finger back to me," Monroe shouts, handing me the bloody finger. "In the glovebox!" she instructs over the roar of the engine. "Open the condom."

"Monroe, you've fucking lost your mind!"

"Do it!" she screams at the top of her lungs.

My fingers shake so badly, I've lost all dexterity. I free the bloody ring and hand the appendage back to Monroe. The car jerks violently from side-to-side, and papers spill from the glovebox but I manage to catch the condom. The ring is going in the condom, I've figured out that much on my own, but why?

"Hurry!" Monroe shouts, which only makes my fingers shake more. Using my teeth, I tear the condom wrapper open and free the slimy, translucent latex.

"Tie it and shove it up your vagina!" she yells, daring a glance over at my lap, which almost costs us the next turn.

The headlights have caught up to us and now honk violently. They keep trying to pass, but Monroe cuts them off. As terrified as I am of whomever is in the car, I'm certain we're going to crash.

"I can't!" I wail, reaching inside my panties. My vagina is a steel trap of fear right now and there's no way I can fit this bulbus ring inside.

"Fucking do it!" Monroe screams, and tears slip from my eyes as I press the uncomfortable, gargantuan piece of jewelry up into my vaginal canal like a dry tampon. Our surroundings have gone pitch-black, we're out of the city, and Monroe's headlights barely provide enough visibility to drive.

The car jerks violently to the right as Monroe takes a turn fast enough to flip us over. I swear to God I feel the tires lift from the road. Somehow, we don't flip, but the car behind us is relentless, and suddenly, we're thrown forward as the car chasing us slams into our bumper.

"Hold on," Monroe cautions, but it's too late. The car behind us slams into our rear again, and this time, sends us spinning off the road. Monroe tries to course correct as she slams on the brakes, but it's no use. The car flies, airborne, headfirst into a thicket of trees. Airbags deploy on impact, and I know instantly it's over. Life is over. We're fucking dead.

The driver's side door is flung open, and I look over to see my friend struggling to regain consciousness.

"Get out," a male voice demands. I'm ninety-nine percent

certain it's Kieren, but my ears ring with the sound of airbags detonating. Before I have time to register what's happening to Monroe, my door is also flung open.

A large body shoves its way across my chest to unbuckle my seatbelt.

"No!" I scream when I realize what's happening. "No!" I begin to kick and thrash my arms, anything to get away from Jace's hold, but he's too overpowering and drags me from the car by my waist despite my best efforts to cling to any scrap of seatbelt or doorframe.

In my haste to get back in the car as we escaped Sigma, I forgot to replace the gun in my holster, and now I realize I'm weaponless. As Jace pulls me to the road, my screams die in my throat when I see the horror unfolding in front of me, illuminated by the headlights of the black BMW.

"Shit," I hear Jace curse under his breath as he sees it too. Monroe stands on the ledge of the bridge at gunpoint.

Jace's firm hand wraps around my forearm and both of us start running.

"Kieren, stop!" Jace pleads as he skids to a halt ten feet from the madman. "Don't do this!"

Kieren's right arm is fully extended, the barrel of his gun pointed directly at Monroe's forehead, as he presses his wrapped, bloody left hand against his chest. Blood covers his white T-shirt and skin. It's smeared across his face and down the side of his neck. I don't know how he's even standing given the blood loss.

"Give me back my ring," Kieren demands. His outstretched arm shakes like he barely has the strength to hold it up.

"Come get it," Monroe taunts.

"How about I kill your fucking friend?" Kieren snaps, whirling around to face me. I scream, thinking this second is my last, when Jace shoves me behind his body.

"Move, Jace!" Kieren barks.

"Kieren, we need to get you to a hospital," Jace states in a shockingly measured and calm tone. "Put the gun down."

"No!" Kieren wails like a deranged animal. "She deserves to die. They both deserve to die!"

"And we'll kill them," Jace offers in placation. Despite knowing this would likely be my fate, I'm still dismayed and pissed to hear Jace say it out loud. To offer up my life so easily...

"But not like this," Jace continues. "Come on, Kieren. Not like this. We caught them, okay? It's over. Let's take them back to Sigma, put them in their cages. You can fuck Monroe until she begs for mercy. We can kill them when the time is right. No one is going to come looking for Monroe, you said so yourself. It's the perfect way to lessen the scrutiny, and we both know Sigma can't afford any more scrutiny right now."

Seconds tick by in silence, and I hold my breath thinking Kieren will agree to this outcome, even though I can't believe the options on the table are life in a dog cage or death.

"No Kieren!" Jace shouts, and I shove him aside just in time to see Kieren stalk up to Monroe, holding the gun inches from her heart.

61

KIEREN

Present Day

"You fucking bitch," I growl in her face. The chill of death permeates my limbs, and I shake uncontrollably. I estimate I have an hour tops before I'm unconscious.

"Is this what you want, baby?" Monroe coos, squeezing my bloody finger in the hand she holds over the water. "If you're going to kill me, then go ahead."

The demented smile on her face is one that could bring me to my knees. *Fuck, my beautiful puppy. So goddamn perfect.*

So goddamn dead.

"You don't look so good, Kieren. Better listen to your friend and go to the hospital."

"Give me...my... ring," I stammer, words now becoming difficult to form.

"Did you like it when I kissed you earlier?" the bitch

continues to taunt. "I felt your stiff cock between my legs. It's a shame you'll never get to fuck me with it again."

"Fuck you, Monroe," I spit. This is *not* how we were supposed to end. I was supposed to fucking *catch her.* I was supposed to have her again, fuck her again, call her mine again. And *then* kill her.

Failure sluices through my veins like ice, and *I don't fail.*

"Shut... up," I shake. "Shut up, you worthless cunt."

"Worthless? Now there's the Kieren I *once loved,*" she insincerely pouts. Her glinting, deep blue eyes mock me with sick delight, and at the intentional flaunt of her bygone love, I snap. Because she was always supposed to love me, no matter what I fucking did. *Mine until the bitter end.*

Pushed to the edge of my sanity, my vision begins to blur. My hand grabs her throat, my physical movements now disconnected from my brain, and I squeeze with as much strength as I have left. "Do it," she begs, barely able to get a breath down. "Do it, you fucking pussy."

Rage. My entire body floods with rage. I can't see. I can't stop myself from shaking. I'm losing control.

"Come find me in hell, Kieren, and when you do, I'll give you a big fucking kiss."

I don't know if I did it. I don't know if I pushed her, or if she slipped off the ledge of the footbridge, but in the blink of an eye, she's gone.

Then I hear it, and the sickening crack of her body colliding with the still water of the lake swallows me, and all I had planned for my sweet puppy, whole.

EPILOGUE
MONROE

Two Months Prior to Present Day
Queens, New York

"That's a strange mix of things you've got in your trunk," my aunt Nikki comments as she circles the silver Audi A4 gifted to me by my step-cousins. It was the least they could do given all the work I did for them over the summer. To their credit, they gave me a decent amount of cash and a fuck ton of firearms, so I guess we'll call it even.

"Guns, axes, knives of all shapes and sizes and a scuba suit with a full tank of oxygen. I didn't know you knew how to scuba dive, Monroe?"

"You can learn how to do anything by watching a handful of YouTube videos," I answer with a shrug as I rearrange the items in my trunk so the weapons are concealed under the false flap.

"Thanks for not telling my mom I was here all summer," I say earnestly. I was certain the first phone call my aunt Nikki would make when I showed up on her doorstep would be to Otisville, but true to her word, she didn't.

"Not my place. Not my business," my aunt responds. "For what it's worth, Monroe, I always found your mother to be rather hard on you, placing blame where blame wasn't deserved."

"That's the understatement of the century," I scoff. "She's a raging narcissist who used me as bait to lure in new boyfriends."

Aunt Nikki takes in my words as she studies her shoes. "She cares about you though, in her own way."

"I doubt she knows how to care for anything or anyone other than her own needs," I say, slamming the trunk shut as I walk around to the driver's side door.

"Your cousins told me what you asked for, by the way. You planning to make a run for the border after whatever it is you're doing with all that weaponry is done?"

"Something like that," I say. The regret and sorrow in my voice gives my true feelings away. I always did wear my heart on my sleeve.

My aunt nods. "A clean slate. I understand. You did well this summer, you know? You'll always have a place with us, if you want to continue exploring your talents. Your cousins were quite impressed. They said you're a natural."

I huff a laugh, unsure if I should take that as a compliment or if I should be seriously concerned about my ability to switch off my morality when the situation requires a bit of finesse.

"Will you come back and visit, or at least find a way to let me know you're alive?" she asks.

I nod. I owe her that much for the kindness she showed me

these last three months. My belly was always full, and I had a bed to call my own. Most importantly, I had freedom.

"You know my new name, right?" I ask.

"I do," she says with a sorrowful nod.

Closing the distance between us, I wrap my arms around the woman who let me stay with her rent-free as I pieced myself back together.

"Thank you," I say, "for all that you've done for me."

Tears fall from her amber-brown eyes. "I wish you luck, Monroe, for whatever it is you have planned and wherever it is you're going."

I offer her a grim smile as I open the car door.

"Monroe," my aunt calls, turning around. "Forgiveness can be a powerful thing."

I chew on her departing words as I debate how to respond. She means well, so I don't want to hurt her feelings with a flippant response, but sometimes forgiveness is not the magic healing potion people believe it to be. Sometimes, forgiveness is a goddamn farce.

"It is," I agree as I climb into the car. "But so is death."

TO BE CONTINUED

A MEANINGFUL PLAYLIST

Against my better judgment, I have included a playlist. Music is very personal, but if you're like me and scenes you read in books play in your head like a movie, having a soundtrack to accompany your imagination enhances the experience. Below are the songs that played in the background of my mind as I wrote Sins of the Sigma, CAGED and COLLARED (Books 1 and 2).

These songs are listed in an order that is meant to accompany the emotional and action arc of the book from beginning to end. I've also included sneak peek songs for Book 2, Collared. Are the Book 2 songs meant to be Easter eggs? I don't know (* she says with a devious smile *).
You'll have to find out.

CAGED, Book 1
Wish You Were Here, Incubus

Right Here, Staind

What It Takes, Aerosmith
(this song is for our boy Jace)

Way Down We Go (Stripped version), KALEO

You Don't Own Me (feat. G-Eazy), SAYGRACE, G-Eazy

The Offering, Sleep Token

Zombie, Bad Wolves
(specifically, the Bad Wolves cover of the original song by The Cranberries)

How Could You, Jessie Murph

One Step Closer, Linkin Park

Living Dead Girl, Rob Zombie

COLLARED, Book 2 Sneak Peek
My Own Prison, Creed

Praying, Kesha

The Apparition, Sleep Token

Crawling, Linkin Park

We're In This Together, Nine Inch Nails

Meet You At The Graveyard, Cleffy

Listen on Spotify

AUTHOR'S NOTE

If you have made it to the end of CAGED and have now arrived at this Author's Note, please know you have my utmost gratitude. Truthfully, I was nervous readers wouldn't enjoy book 1 of this series, and therefore write off the series entirely, because there was no happily ever after for the bad guy and the good girl in book 1. And listen, I love this archetype, which, as a dark romance author and fangirl of the genre, I have both written and read. But I knew going into this book in particular that I would not write a typical dark romance, and as I hit publish, I hoped readers would enjoy a story about an FMC who, at the end of the day, chooses herself.

In the following paragraphs, I'm going to talk about my own experience with alternative therapies as well as difficult memories and traumas from my childhood. I felt it important to share, because it is my own healing journey that inspired parts of Monroe's character, as well as certain experiences that happen to her in book 1 (for example, if you're thinking about the chapter where she recalls buried childhood trauma while under the use of psychedelics, you would be correct).

Please do not read beyond this point if reading about parental abuse, growing up with a parent who is a narcissist, or the death of a parent from cancer may be triggering or uncomfortable. I understand that reading about others' experiences can be difficult, so I ask that you please prioritize your mental health. (Also, please note I write under a pen name, and below is part of the reason why.) Lastly, if you're going to read the rest of this Author's Note, please do so with an open mind and compassion.

My backstory (This is where shit gets real. Proceed with caution.):

I was diagnosed with severe depression in my late twenties. At the time, I believed I had become depressed after the death of my mother, who passed away from breast cancer. And while this is partially true, as I've gotten older and spent more time reflecting on the events of my childhood, I can say with confidence that a large part of my depression is the result of prolonged and frequent mental, emotional, and physical abuse (both threatened and witnessed) against my mother, my younger sibling, and myself by my alcoholic and narcissist father. There's a term out there called Complex PTSD, or CPTSD, which, if you're curious, I encourage you to look up.

This abuse was never seen outside the walls of my childhood home. To everyone else, family, friends, and the community, my father was a model citizen. He always came to my sporting and school events. He was respected and even revered. No one saw the monster he was behind closed doors.

I have a handful of excruciating memories from childhood that I think about constantly. The rest of my childhood, by and large, I don't remember, or didn't until I underwent alternative therapies. The most difficult part of my journey has been the inability to speak to my mother. Why did she stay despite his abuse? In their early years together, did she know he was a narcissist? And the worst question, one which will never get answered: How did she survive him?

When my mom was diagnosed with breast cancer, she was diagnosed at stage 4. Words cannot describe the utter horror I experienced when my mother finally let me see her bare chest. I could literally see the large masses under her skin, right above her heart, with my naked eye. For a period of time, I harbored intense resentment toward her for being too stubborn to go to the doctor sooner. How did she let it get *this* bad before seeking medical attention?

Looking back, I think she knew. I think she knew she was dying, and while many might disagree, I think she was ready. I think she was exhausted. I think she had given all she could to me and my sibling, pushing her mind and body to the brink for our sake. But, our bodies and minds can only suffer so much abuse. The body keeps score, as they say, and in the end, she didn't survive him, and that truth breaks me.

There came a point in my adult life where the pain became too much. I would think about my past and my father and feel hopeless. Why did these things have to happen to me? And why do I have to continue to feel so much pain?

So, in my somewhat recent adult life, I decided to try alternative therapy in addition to the talk therapy and medica-

AUTHOR'S NOTE

tion I was already doing. I underwent guided journeys where psychedelics were administered with the intent of helping my mind remember and reexamine childhood memories, to thank my younger selves for being so strong, for persevering despite unimaginable circumstances, and above all, for protecting me. During this experience, I was able to let my younger selves know that I'm strong enough now. That I've got it from here. And that I no longer need to hold on to the past. My memories don't define me, and I'm ready to let them go. The administer called it *'composting'*, which is a term I quite like, and in my own experience, felt akin to *'shredding'* or a profound sense of release.

After doing this work, I've come to realize pain is not always meant to be bad.

Let this sink in:

Pain is passed down from generation to generation until someone comes along who is strong enough to carry it.

I understand now that the pain I carry is not a burden. It's a gift, and I carry this pain with the hope that doing so will break generational trauma. I carry it not for myself, but for all the different versions of me, both younger and older, in the hopes that for the next generation and those that follow, there is no more pain to carry.

Lastly, I've found that treating my depression is an ongoing journey. Some years I've felt better. Some years I've felt worse. I never expect to be completely "healed" or "fixed", nor do I believe that's possible. I do, however, want to find and feel my own version of peace. I'm a huge proponent of therapy and medication in general, both of which I do, but everyone's mental health journey is different. Please don't interpret my experience as something you should do as well. Please consult your personal team of medical and mental health professionals prior to pursuing any form of treatments or therapies. If you don't have a team or doctor, please find one. Please only take medications as prescribed by a licensed medical professional whom you trust. Also, please know that not all therapists and therapies are created equal, and a negative experience with one doesn't mean a negative experience with the next.

If you've made it this far, thank you. Thank you for supporting me. And for anyone who identifies with what I've written above, please know you are not alone.

So, I say to you: Choose yourself. Choose your peace. Life is too short, and you are worth it.

And when you think of the monsters who hurt you, in the words of the great Kesha:

I hope you wish them farewell.

In gratitude,
    Summer

ABOUT THE AUTHOR

Summer Robert is a recovering corporate girlie turned weaver of angsty, dark romance stories that are as suspenseful as they are salacious. After leaving the corporate world behind, Summer published her debut dark romance series, GOOD HURT, and hopes she can continue to delight and captivate the reader community with her twisted and often emotionally devastating love stories, unhinged spice, and gut-wrenching cliffhangers. Summer loves a good Easter egg written between the pages as much as she loves surviving off of caffeine and vibes. And if you're looking for Easter eggs, given Summer is a hoarder and self-proclaimed connoisseur of perfume, the fragrance worn by the main characters might be a good place to start.

Most importantly, she's a mom of two small humans and one small, vicious, and spiteful yorkipoo. Summer currently resides in Los Angeles, and although she is originally a native Ohioan from a shockingly small farm town, she will forever call LA her home.

Follow Summer on social media for unhinged and entertaining posts about her books and characters, as well as book news and announcements. For behind-the-scenes goodies, lost chapters, and to dive deeper into Summer's books, join her newsletter.

TT: https://www.tiktok.com/@summerrobertwrites

IG: https://www.instagram.com/summerrobertwrites/

Website (Buy Signed Copies & Merch):
www.summerrobert.com

Follow Summer on Amazon

Join Summer's Newsletter